Brides & Bargains

KRISTI GOLD
MAUREEN CHILD
YVONNE LINDSAY

MILLS & BOON

First Published in Great Britain 2019
by Mills & Boon, an imprint of HarperCollins*Publishers*
1 London Bridge Street, London, SE1 9GF

BRIDES & BARGAINS © 2019 Harlequin Books S. A.

In Pursuit of His Wife © 2016 Harlequin Books S.A.
A Bride for the Boss © 2016 Harlequin Books S.A.
The Wife He Couldn't Forget © 2015 Dolce Vita Trust

Special thanks and acknowledgement are given to
Kristi Gold and Maureen Child for their contribution
to the Texas Cattleman's Club: Lies and Lullabies series.

ISBN: 978-0-263-27485-1

0419

MIX
Paper from
responsible sources
FSC® C007454

This book is produced from independently certified FSC™ paper to ensure responsible forest management.

For more information visit: www.harpercollins.co.uk/green

Printed and bound in Spain
by CPI, Barcelona

Kristi Gold has a fondness for beaches, baseball and bridal reality shows. She firmly believes that love has remarkable healing powers, and she feels very fortunate to be able to weave stories of love and commitment. As a bestselling author, a National Readers' Choice Award winner and a three-time Romance Writers of America RITA® Award finalist, Kristi has learned that although accolades are wonderful, the most cherished rewards come from networking with readers. She can be reached through her website at www.kristigold.com or through Facebook.

Maureen Child writes for the Mills & Boon Desire line and can't imagine a better job.

A seven-time finalist for a prestigious Romance Writers of America RITA® Award, Maureen is an author of more than one hundred romance novels. Her books regularly appear on bestseller lists and have won several awards, including a Prism Award, a National Readers' Choice Award, a Colorado Romance Writers Award of Excellence and a Golden Quill Award. She is a native Californian but has recently moved to the mountains of Utah.

A typical Piscean, *USA TODAY* bestselling author **Yvonne Lindsay** has always preferred her imagination to the real world. Married to her blind date hero and with two adult children, she spends her days crafting the stories of her heart, and in her spare time she can be found with her nose in a book reliving the power of love, or knitting socks and daydreaming. Contact her via her website: www.yvonnelindsay.com.

IN PURSUIT
OF HIS WIFE

KRISTI GOLD

All rights reserved including the right of reproduction in whole or in part in any form. This edition is published by arrangement with Harlequin Books S.A.

This is a work of fiction. Names, characters, places, locations and incidents are purely fictional and bear no relationship to any real life individuals, living or dead, or to any actual places, business establishments, locations, events or incidents. Any resemblance is entirely coincidental.

First Published 2013
Large Print edition 2019

Mills & Boon, an imprint of HarperCollins Publishers
1 London Bridge Street, London, SE1 9GF

© 2013 Kristi Goldberg

ISBN: 978-0-263-27485-1

Printed and bound in Spain
by CPI, Barcelona

IN PURSUIT OF HIS WIFE

KRISTI GOLD

One

Seated in a wicker glider on the mansion's stately porch, Nasira Edwards admired the beauty of the Wild Aces, the ranch her brother, Rafiq, had bought his beloved bride-to-be, Violet. Nasira appreciated the way landscaped lawns gave way to green pastureland. She relished the warm May breeze, the climate so different from London this time of year. When she had originally traveled to Royal, Texas—home to the legendary Texas Cattleman's Club—she had done so to prevent Rafe from exacting revenge on his friend, Mac, for a mistake she had made over a decade ago. She had come to clear the air, right past wrongs, and fortunately she had succeeded. Yet that had not been the only reason behind the journey. She yearned for the peace this place could provide, yet peace had not come. The lingering pain of loss was simply too overwhelming.

In response to the memories, she withdrew the brace-let from the pocket of her dress and studied the tiny sil-ver rattle charm she had received upon confirming her pregnancy. A surprising gift from a husband who had not embraced fatherhood. Still, she had viewed the wel-come gesture as a symbol of hope for a bright future, until the day all hope had been splintered like shards of fragile glass.

Her palm automatically came to rest on her abdomen, now as barren as her life had been for a while. The baby she had so desperately wanted, and tragically miscar-ried, had changed her completely. Odd how she could miss someone she had known for such a brief time. And strange how badly she missed Sebastian, though he had been emotionally absent for the past six months. She had had no choice but to continue to put physical dis-tance between them in an effort to reassess their future.

When the door opened to her left, Nasira expected to find her brother, Rafiq, checking on her welfare. In-stead, Rafe's friend, Mac McCallum, stepped outside and gave her a pleasant smile. "Are you doing okay?"

She did not deserve his good humor or respect after what she had done to him in the distant past. "I've been enjoying the Texas sunset."

"Looks to me like that old sun has been gone a while," he said. "My sister sent me out here to tell you dinner will be ready in a few."

Food held little appeal in recent days. "I appreciate Violet's hospitality, but I am not very hungry."

"Suit yourself, but if you keep going this way, you'll be blown to New Mexico if the wind picks up steam."

She smiled reluctantly and stood. "I suppose if that is a possibility, I should attempt to eat something. Are you staying for dinner?"

"Not tonight. I'm meeting up with Andrea."

Nasira suspected Mac had feelings for his personal assistant that went beyond the boardroom, even if he could not admit it to himself, according to her future sister-in-law, Violet. "Is this business or pleasure?"

He frowned. "Business, of course."

"It's rather late in the day for that, is it not?"

"Unfortunately it comes with the territory of McCallum Enterprises."

When the discussion lulled, Nasira saw her chance to verbally make amends for past mistakes. She studied the wooden planks beneath her feet for a moment before regarding him again. "I wanted to extend another apology for what I did to you all those years ago. The guilt has been unbearable."

Mac lifted his shoulders in a shrug. "Hey, you were young. We were both young. You were just trying to get out of an arranged marriage to a man twice your age."

That ill-fated visit to the university to stay with her brother had set a horrible course that had led to Rafe's need for revenge. "Yet I was wrong to use you to achieve that goal, especially when I climbed into your bed for the sole purpose of having my father discover us. And because our father blamed Rafe for not looking after me, that led to his determination to seek revenge on you. I shudder to think what might have happened had I not come here to intervene."

"It all turned out okay," Mac said. "He's no longer trying to buy up the town to get back at me, he's going to marry my sister, and we're going to be one big happy family."

Nasira was happy for them all, but still… "Even after Rafe's torture and confinement for years due to my errors in judgment, he has forgiven me. I suppose I need to know if you will forgive me as well, though I would understand if you would not."

"Consider it done, Nasira. That's old water under the bridge now that Rafe knows I didn't really sleep with you. And since he's marrying my sister, I consider us all one big happy family."

Relief washed over her, though she couldn't claim to be happy over the state of her own marriage. "I so appreciate your understanding."

"No problem. Mind if I ask you something?"

"Not at all."

He raked a hand through his dark blond hair. "Don't take this wrong, but I'm wondering what the hell your husband was thinking when he let you get away?"

The course of the conversation made her somewhat uncomfortable. "It is rather complicated. Sebastian is complicated. After ten years of marriage, at times I wonder if I know him at all."

"One thing I do know. When a man doesn't realize the value of his wife, that's borrowing trouble. I just hope he comes around soon and realizes what he'd be giving up."

If only she could believe Sebastian had the capacity to be transformed into someone who would fight for their relationship. "I truly appreciate your concern and understanding, Mac."

"You're welcome. Guess I'll be heading home to the Double M now." He started toward the steps but paused and faced her again. "Before I leave, I'd just like to say it's fairly clear you don't need another big brother, but if you ever want a sounding board, you know where to find me."

How nice to come upon such a benevolent man. She certainly had not received so much compassion from her own husband in quite some time. "Thank you."

Mac returned to her and rested his palms on her shoulders. "Keep your chin up and keep standing your ground. You deserve the best."

Until six months ago, she had believed she had been blessed with the best of everything. Almost. "For the sake of clarification, Sebastian is not mean or cruel. He is simply too controlled and at times, distant. I have often wished he would lower his guard and demonstrate some sort of emotion, but I've accepted that it will most likely never happen—"

"Unhand my wife, you bloody bastard!"

Nasira barely had time to comprehend what she had heard before her estranged husband rushed onto the porch, drew back his fist and hit Mac in the chin, knocking the rancher backward against the brick wall.

When Mac gave Sebastian a menacing look, Nasira returned to reality in time to step between the men. "What are you doing, Sebastian?"

He pointed at Mac and sent him a menacing glare. "I'll not allow another man to grope my wife."

Never had she'd seen Sebastian act this way, and as much as she deplored violence, and despite her shock over his sudden appearance, she was pleasantly surprised, albeit somewhat mortified. "Oh, for goodness' sake. He is only a friend and he was not groping me."

Mac pushed away from the wall, rubbed his chin and glared at Sebastian. "If I didn't think so highly of your wife and her brother, I'd invite you to take this out into the yard and finish it, you jackass."

Sebastian balled his fists at his sides. "I would be glad to finish this."

Nasira spun on her husband. "Stop this right now, Sebastian. No one will be fighting if I have any say in the matter, and I do." She turned back to her friend and sent him an apologetic look. "Mac, I am so very sorry for my husband's behavior. I assure you he's not normally so impulsive with total strangers. And if you would not mind, I would like a few moments alone with him."

"No problem," Mac said before turning an acrid look on Sebastian. "I'm going to give you a pass, Edwards, and only because you're Nasira's husband. But don't push your luck by trying something like that again."

Sebastian straightened his tie and smirked. "If I find you touching Nasira again, I cannot promise there won't be a repeat performance."

"Just take better care of your wife and you won't have to worry about me."

After Mac disappeared into the darkness, Nasira prepared for a confrontation. "What were you thinking, and why on earth are you here?"

Sebastian opened and closed his fist. "I wasn't thinking, only reacting to a man with his hands on my wife. A man from her past, no less. And I have come to escort that wife back to London."

Her fury began to escalate. "First of all, nothing ever existed between myself and Mac, other than he was attempting to assist me in fooling my father into believing I'd been compromised."

"He looked as if he would like to compromise you in earnest a few moments ago."

She refused to give credence to his suspicions. "Your imagination is evidently running wild. And most important, I am not your property, Sebastian. I will return when I decide to return. *If* I decide to return."

"You're my wife. You belong with me."

At least he hadn't said she belonged *to* him, as if that were any consolation. "I came here to gain some perspective and I am going to stay until that is accomplished. You might as well climb back on the jet and wait at home for word from me."

"I refuse to go until this issue is resolved."

Despite his stubborn attitude, Nasira began to notice how handsome he looked and knew immediately she would lose her determination if he stayed. Too much time had passed since they had made love—the one thing that had always been right with their convenient marriage. Yet that had been his decision, not hers. "At the very least I will be here until Rafe and Violet's wedding at the end of the month."

"I'll wait as long as it takes."

She brought out the best argument to convince him to go—the shipping business he owned and ran. "I cannot believe you would ignore your duties and abandon the company for any length of time."

"I own the company. I can do what I please."

Such a frustrating man. "Do you have an answer for everything?"

He sent her a slow, easy smile. The smile he had given her all those years ago from across a very crowded ballroom, as if they had been thrust into a storybook scene. The smile that had convinced her to enter into an arrangement to escape her father's clutches. "Have you had dinner?"

No, and she had begun to feel the effects. "I have not, although Violet has prepared a meal."

"I'm certain she will understand if you would rather dine with your husband. We could continue our discussion then."

While Nasira took a moment to consider her options, the door swung open again and out walked Rafe, her tall, dark, handsome overly-protective brother.

He immediately eyed Sebastian with disapproval. "I see you did not follow my advice and remain in London, brother-in-law."

Sebastian looked equally miffed. "And when we spoke by phone two days ago, I made it quite clear I would make that decision without your interference."

Nasira stared at her husband before returning her attention to her sibling. "Rafiq bin Saleed, why did you not tell me you spoke with Sebastian?"

Rafe did not appear the least bit contrite. "You mentioned on numerous occasions you did not want to be disturbed by him."

"And he refused to allow me to speak with you when you ignored my calls to your cell," Sebastian added.

She despised it when men insisted she could not look after herself. "You had no right to take the choice out of my hands, Rafe."

"It makes little difference now," Sebastian said. "I'm here and I intend to make the best of the situation."

She only wished she knew what else he intended. That information would only be gained if she accepted his invitation to dine with him tonight. "I'm going to accompany Sebastian to dinner. I will be gone an hour or so."

"Do you believe that is wise, Nasira?" Rafe asked.

"We bloody believe that is none—"

"I can speak for myself, Sebastian. I am no longer your charge, Rafe. I can take care of myself. Tell Violet I truly appreciate her hospitality. We should go now, Sebastian, before I change my mind."

With that, Nasira followed Sebastian down the porch steps and when she didn't immediately spot a sedan, she paused on the pavement. "How did you arrive here?"

He nodded toward a shiny black truck at the end of the drive. "This is all they had available to rent at the airport."

Nasira covered her mouth to keep from laughing. "Oh, my. Can you handle that?"

He looked somewhat incensed over what he apparently considered an insult to his masculinity. "Of course I can handle it. I made it here, did I not?"

"All right," she said, and then continued toward the monstrosity.

Once there, Sebastian opened the passenger door and held out his hand. "Your cowboy chariot, madam. Let me assist you."

"I am almost six feet tall, Sebastian. I can manage climbing into a truck by myself."

"Only trying to be a gentleman, Sira."

The sound of his pet name for her stopped Nasira in her tracks. "Do you know how long it has been since you called me that?"

He winked. "Perhaps too long."

She had no clue where all the charm and machismo had been hiding. Following the miscarriage, he had spent long hours at work and little time with her. Perhaps he had turned a corner that would lead to change. Only time would tell. In the interim, Nasira would remain cautiously optimistic.

As they sat in the red booth in the Royal Diner, Sebastian found his wife to be predictably cool. And as always, very beautiful. The white cotton dress fit her to perfection, contrasting with her long, dark hair draped over her slender shoulders. Since her departure, he'd spent many a night in their bed, longing for her company. Since the loss of their child, he'd spent most of his time avoiding her out of fear. Not fear of her. Fear of losing her. Yet that was exactly what he had done by pushing her away. A bloody self-fulfilling prophecy that he couldn't explain without baring raw emotions.

Pushing the thoughts away, he turned his attention to the plastic-covered menu and scanned the unpalatable selections. "What do you recommend, Sira? The double cheeseburger or the fried catfish plate?"

That earned him her smile. "I realize this place isn't exactly your cup of tea, but I find it charming."

"I find it overly quaint and a heart attack waiting to happen."

"They do have salads and I hear the grilled chicken is very good."

He closed the menu and set it aside. "I will make do with the limited choices."

"What are you having?"

A tremendous urge to kiss her. "I'm going to sample the steak. And you?"

She laid the red-checkered napkin in her lap. "Definitely a salad."

"You should eat something a bit heartier. You're too thin."

"I am the same weight as I was before I left London."

"I'm only concerned about you, Sira."

She sent him a skeptical look. "Oh really? Where was all this concern over the past six months?"

He didn't feel this was the time or the place to get into such a serious subject, and thankfully a waitress arrived to interrupt their conversation.

She patted her rather large blond hair, pulled a pencil from behind her ear and a notepad from the pocket of the red apron. "Howdy. I'm Darla. What can I get the two of you darlin's to drink? Maybe some sweet tea?"

He couldn't quite fathom these strange Texas customs. "I prefer to sweeten my tea myself. With sugar and milk."

"She means cold tea," Nasira said. "I will take a glass with lemon."

He needed something much stronger to make it through this evening. "Bring me ale."

The woman raised a painted eyebrow. "Ginger ale?"

Bloody hell. "Beer."

"Sebastian, I cannot drive that truck," Nasira said. "For that reason, I suggest you forego the ale."

She did have a point and in accordance with his plan, he needed to prove himself worthy of her company. "Water will be fine."

"With lemon?" Darla asked.

"Why not? If that is fine with my wife."

Nasira frowned. "Of course it is. And I would like a salad with the dressing on the side."

"She would also like the grilled chicken," Sebastian added despite Nasira's disapproving look. "I'll have the rib eye. Make certain it's cooked through."

Darla looked somewhat appalled. "You mean well done?"

"Precisely."

The waitress jotted down the order then gathered the menus. "You two aren't from around here, are you?"

Sebastian sent her a mock grin. "What gave us away?"

"The men around here order their meat rare." With that, Darla waddled away, muttering under her breath.

Nasira immediately turned a sharp gaze on him. "Why do you insist on doing that?"

He opted to play ignorant. "Doing what?"

"Ordering my meals for me. I am quite capable of deciding what and how much I eat."

"I've always ordered for you, Sira."

"I know and I do not care for it."

"And you waited ten years to tell me?"

"It seemed simpler not to make waves and avoid conflict."

Did she think so little of him? "I'm not your father, Nasira. If you want something from me, you need only ask."

She stared at him a few moments. "I want another baby."

The one thing he felt he could not give her. "Impossible."

"Why, Sebastian?"

He could only offer her a partial truth. "You had a devil of a time when you miscarried. The doctor said—"

"That I am quite capable of conceiving again and carrying to full term. The risk is not any greater than any woman who has lost a child in the first trimester."

He imagined his own mother had believed that very thing. "Look, this is not the time or the place to discuss this."

She lifted her chin and leveled a determined glare on him. "Unless we discuss it, I will not be returning to London with you in the foreseeable future."

Sebastian swallowed around his shock. Not once during their time together had she issued threats. "We will talk about this some other time."

The waitress returned with their drinks, and they waited in silence for their order to arrive. All conversation ceased as they ate food that was surprisingly palatable. He spent a good deal of time watching the patrons, when he wasn't watching his wife pick at her meal.

Unfortunately, she only afforded him a glance when he asked, "How do you find the fare?"

"Adequate," she said and then took another bite.

He wondered if he would spend the next few days dealing with one-word answers while attempting to convince her to come home. Would she rebuff his advances, or eventually return to what they once had? He longed for the latter. He longed for her. All of her. First, he had to regain her trust and respect, if at this juncture, and in light of his mistakes, that were even possible.

By the time he had paid the bill, Sebastian worried he had ruined his chances at reconciliation.

Not yet. Not until he convinced her they belonged together, with or without children. How exactly he would achieve that goal remained to be seen. He knew only one way to do this—by using a tried and true technique that had never failed to turn her into clay in his hands.

"Sebastian, what are you doing?"

"Finding a private place to talk."

He had definitely found it, Nasira realized when he continued past the Wild Aces and took a dirt road that forked to the right. Once he reached the fence line, he backed the truck up beneath some low-hanging tree branches.

Before Nasira could voice a protest, Sebastian slid out of the seat, rounded the hood and opened her door. "Now if you will come with me please."

Clearly he had taken leave of his senses. "I refuse to traipse around in the dark, Sebastian."

"We're not going to traipse. We're going to sit in the back of this truck."

She felt certain that might not be in her best interests. "Why can we not remain in the front seat?"

"Because it's a beautiful night that should be spent beneath the stars and the moon."

She started to say they could barely see the stars but the opportunity to respond was lost when he reached in, took her by the waist, and lifted her out and onto her feet. "First that dreadful fight with Mac, and now you are manhandling me like some Neanderthal. What has come over you?"

"My behavior isn't necessarily so out-of-character for me, though it's been quite a few years since I've engaged in it."

Nasira released a cynical laugh. "You will have a difficult time convincing me that you ever behaved in that manner. In all the years I've known you, I have never seen you raise your voice, much less your hand."

He smiled. "Oh, you would be surprised what a scrapper I was in my formative years. I managed to get tossed out of three boarding schools before I finally settled down in my final year before university."

She could barely make out his smile, but she could

hear the pride in his voice. "That is definitely news to me and frankly somewhat appalling."

He leaned over and brushed a kiss across her cheek. "Are you certain you're appalled, or did it perhaps impress you?"

It had both surprised and in some ways set her senses on fire, not that she would dare make that admission. "It served to remind me what ridiculously volatile creatures men can be."

"Let's find a place to sit before we continue this conversation."

As long as they remained upright, she should be safe from giving in to his sensual charms. Then again, he had not attempted to touch her in so long, she could not even imagine that would be his goal. "Fine. But I only wish to stay for a while. I am fatigued from all the drama tonight."

"No more drama," he said as he took her by the hand and led her to the rear of the vehicle. "Now to ascertain how this bloody thing opens."

Before Sebastian could make a move to investigate, Nasira pulled the latch and lowered the tailgate. "It is really quite simple."

"How did you learn to do that?" he asked, sheer awe in his tone.

She shrugged. "I've seen Rafiq open one."

Sebastian reached out and brushed her hair away from her shoulder. "You are truly an amazing woman."

"Why? Because I can trip a release on a truck?"

"Because you are so observant and incredibly beautiful."

As much as she appreciated the compliment, she also recognized he had never paid her many, except about her physical attributes. "Thank you. I suppose we should get this over with so I can get a good night's sleep."

Without warning, he hoisted her up on the edge of the gate, causing her dress's hem to ride up her thighs. And while she made the appropriate adjustments, he climbed into the truck bed and had the nerve to position himself behind her, his long legs dangling on either side of hers. "Are you comfortable?" he asked as he circled his arms around her middle.

Uncomfortable would be more accurate; she didn't—or shouldn't—welcome the close contact. "No, I am not. I cannot have a decent conversation when I cannot see your face."

"You only have to listen to my voice."

Oh, that voice. That low, grainy bedroom voice that had enticed her on so many nights. And days. No matter how deep their conflicts had run, he had always been able to seduce her into submission. Granted, she had done her share of seducing as well, including the night she had conceived their child—without telling him she had stopped taking her birth control pills, which was information she had concealed until she had confirmed the pregnancy. Somehow he had forgiven the deception, or so he had said, yet she believed he had never forgotten it.

Nasira found herself leaning back against him, and turning her thoughts to the danger of succumbing to his power when he moved her hair aside and feathered kisses on her neck. "This is wrong, Sebastian," she said with little conviction.

"Remember that night in the carriage?" he said, proving he was bent on ignoring her concerns.

"Yes, I remember." How could she forget? On their honeymoon, he had arranged for a horse-drawn tour of Bath, which had led to taboo touching beneath the blanket, all leading up to a night she would never forget. The night she had lost her virginity and in some ways, her heart.

He slid one palm down her throat and traveled beneath the bodice where he cupped her breast through the lace bra. "I recall you were trembling, as you are now."

She hadn't noticed that at all. Her attention remained drawn to his fingertip circling her nipple now bound in a tight knot. "I was somewhat nervous."

"You were hot," he whispered. "I imagine you're hot now."

Before Nasira could prepare, Sebastian parted her legs with his free hand while sliding his other underneath the bra. "Pull your dress up to your waist."

The request was both startling and highly erotic. "Why?"

"So you might see what I'm doing to you."

As badly as she wanted his attention, she did not wish to make another grave mistake by giving in too soon. "This behavior will solve nothing, Sebastian."

He continued to fondle her breast without missing a beat. "I disagree. It will solve our need for each other. It will serve to remind us how we've always needed each other."

So caught up in his seduction, she clung to the last thread of sanity, relying on bitter memories to maintain her composure. "You haven't been concerned about my needs for months."

He kissed her cheek. "I know, and I'm bent on making up for my neglect. Can we for once stop thinking and allow ourselves only pleasure for a while?"

"But—"

He brought her head around and kissed her soundly. "Let me make love to you, Sira. Please."

She should issue a protest, she should be more resistant, yet she had become too caught up in the anticipation of how she knew he could—and would—make her feel. Too sexually charged over witnessing a side of him she had never seen before this evening—the jealous side, willing to defend her honor.

After she complied, he whispered, "Take off your panties."

This time she didn't hesitate to follow his directive, and after she lifted her hips and slid the lace down to her thighs, she no longer questioned the wisdom in allowing this to happen. After all, he was not a stranger. He was her husband, and she had been without intimacy for much too long.

While Nasira watched, Sebastian moved to the apex of her thighs and began to stroke her. A flood of heat and dampness caused her breath to catch in her chest. He knew how much pressure to apply. How to tease her into oblivion. The moments seemed so surreal—both of them in the back of a truck out in the wide open spaces of Texas, a warm breeze blowing across her face, her husband's hand between her legs bringing her closer and closer to the threshold of orgasm. She wanted badly to keep it at bay, to keep her eyes open, but all to no avail. When Sebastian slid a finger inside her, whispered a few words some might find crude, the climax crashed into her, bringing with it a series of strong spasms.

Nasira was barely aware that Sebastian had taken his hand away, but very aware when he moved beside her. When she heard the rasp of a zipper, she opened her eyes to see that he had shoved his slacks down his hips, revealing what the spontaneous foreplay had physically done to him.

"I need you, sweetheart," he whispered. "Come here."

She needed him as well. Much more than she should. "You want us to lie down in the back of this truck? I question the comfort in that." She also questioned her own sanity.

He grinned. "Who said anything about lying down? I am relinquishing control to you and hoping for a memorable ride."

Awareness over what he had intimated sent Nasira's pulse on a sprint. Every word he uttered seemed to be a jolt to her libido. Every suggestion added fuel to the building fire. Realizing the fit of the dress might not allow for enough room, she hopped to her feet to face her husband. She boldly unzipped the dress, pulled it over her head, tossed it and the bra into the bed of the truck and then pushed the panties down where they fell to the ground. She was totally, unabashedly naked and remarkably ready to finish this interlude immediately.

With that in mind, she climbed back into the truck on her knees to straddle Sebastian's thighs. Yet he thwarted that immediate plan when he said, "Wait."

She didn't want to delay another moment. "Why?"

"Birth control," he grated out.

Of course that would be his primary focus, and it should be hers as well. She lowered from her knees and sat on the gate, hugging her arms to her breasts. "I have not resumed taking the pills. I had no reason to do that."

She saw dismay in his expression before he stood and pulled up his slacks. "And you should have informed me immediately."

She suddenly felt very exposed, both physically and emotionally. She also sensed a hint of accusation in his tone. "If you are intimating I planned this so you could impregnate me, I was not the one who drove here for the purposes of seduction."

He released a rough sigh. "You're right, and my apologies for doubting your motives. However, if you consider our past, you certainly shouldn't blame me for my concerns."

Furious, Nasira came to her feet and grabbed her discarded clothing. "Obviously allowing this interlude under the circumstances has been a colossal mistake."

She glimpsed anger in his expression before she pulled the dress over her head, heard it in his voice when he said, "The sounds you made alone indicated you certainly enjoyed it."

"Evidently I am not immune to your charms," she said. "But mark my words, this will not happen again until we come to terms with our issues. And we have several, including your lack of trust in me and your resistance to having another child."

He slid out of the truck to tuck in his shirt. "We have a month to work out our differences and reach a compromise."

If they could work anything out. Nasira was not certain they could. "Presently I need to return to the house and you need to return to wherever you are staying for the duration."

He streaked a palm over his nape. "Actually, I haven't a place to stay at this point in time. It appears there are no rooms in the inns due to some rodeo event in the area."

Of all the irresponsible, ridiculous excuses. "You did not make arrangements before you decided to travel here?"

"It was a spontaneous plan."

An illogical plan in her opinion. "I can't very well have you in my room under my brother's roof. He is well aware we're having problems, and I prefer we not sleep in the same bed until we've had more time to work on our issues."

"I will take whatever room they have available if you don't wish me in your bed."

"There isn't another room, Sebastian. The house is still undergoing renovations and I have the only accommodations left."

"Then I suppose I shall sleep in the truck until other arrangements can be made."

Oh, for heaven's sake. "All right. You may stay in my room as long as you have no expectations and you leave before first light. I truly do not wish to explain your presence to Rafiq or to have him assume we've been…you know."

"I'm certain Rafe has engaged in…you know, since his intended is living with him."

"She is also pregnant," she added, curious to see how he might react.

"Really?" he said with little enthusiasm. "I didn't know the old boy had it in him."

"He does, and he is very protective of Violet, as well as me. On the other hand, he is not particularly fond of you at the moment. He assumes you have done something to wound me."

"And clearly you have allowed him to have those assumptions."

"Like it or not, Sebastian, your behavior for the past few months has been very hurtful to me."

He sighed. "And that is why I'm here now, to atone for my transgressions. Regardless, I promise to remain on my side of the bed until you are ready for me to fully atone."

When he suggestively winked, Nasira realized having Sebastian in her bed would not be wise for many reasons. "I will make a place for you on the floor."

He had the nerve to kiss her hand. "Whatever you wish, fair lady."

She wanted not to be so attracted him. She wanted not to want him, yet sadly she still did. "It is late," she said as she wrenched from his grasp. "And one more thing. When we arrive, be quiet. I prefer not to wake the household."

Two

"What is he doing here?"

Sebastian had barely entered the two-story foyer before being verbally accosted by his brother-in-law. "I'm accompanying my wife to the bedroom."

With her hand on the banister, Nasira sent a sheepish glance in Rafe's direction. "He does not have a hotel room for the night. However, he has promised to leave first thing tomorrow morning."

Rafe gestured toward a formal floral settee. "The sofa is available."

Angry over the suggestion, Sebastian dropped his bags on the ground. "I won't fit on the bloody sofa. And if you recall, I'm still married to your sister and I have every right to sleep with her. Once you're married, you'll soon learn that problems can and will arise in every union."

Rafiq took a step toward the stairs. "She does not want you here."

"I invited him, Rafe," Nasira said. "But only for the night. Now if you will excuse us, we are both exhausted from the evening's events."

"Quite memorable events," Sebastian added knowing he would probably incur his wife's wrath.

Rafe pointed at him. "I do not wish to see you here when I awaken."

Sebastian saluted. "Yes, sir, commander sheikh."

Without looking back, Nasira hurried up the stairs and paused at the landing before regarding Sebastian again. "Are you coming?"

He suddenly realized he should attempt to turn Rafe into an ally, not an enemy. "In a moment. I'd like to have a word with your brother."

He saw a fleeting look of panic in her eyes. "All right, if you two promise to remain civil."

A promise Sebastian hoped he could keep. "I have no problem with that."

She glanced past him toward her brother. "Rafiq?"

"I will maintain my calm," Rafe said.

"I am counting on that," Nasira said before she climbed the remaining stairs and disappeared.

Sebastian decided he could use a bit of a pick-me-up and with that in mind, he grabbed up the smaller bag, set it on the sofa, unzipped it and withdrew a bottle of mediocre scotch, the only thing he had been able to find at the lone liquor store in town. "Would you care to join me in a drink?"

"No, I would not," Rafe said.

"Then would you mind providing a glass. I find it somewhat uncouth to drink from the bottle."

Without speaking, Rafe left through a door at the back of the parlor. He returned a few moments later with a crystal tumbler he set on the white coffee table before taking a seat in a club chair across from the sofa. Sebastian poured himself a glass of the amber liquid. Though he preferred ice, he thought it best not to press his luck.

After taking a long drink, Sebastian settled in on the settee as the low-quality scotch burned down his throat. At this rate, the combination of booze and jet lag could very well land him on his arse. Of course, he could rest assured he would sleep well…on the bedroom floor.

"Where is your lovely fiancée?" he began when Rafe failed to speak.

"She is sleeping," he replied. "The pregnancy has fatigued her greatly."

Sebastian remembered that all too well from the time when Sira was carrying their child. He also remembered the sound of her mournful cries when she had lost that child. "I'm sure the wedding plans have also contributed to that fatigue. How are you faring with that, by the way?"

Rafe crossed one leg over the other. "I have left the preparation up to the women. I only require knowing where I need to be and when I should be there."

Sebastian doubted he would escape that easily. "I suppose that is probably best."

Rafe inclined his head and studied him. "I suspect you did not detain me so you could speak about wedding plans."

Sebastian finished off the scotch with a grimace and poured another glass. "No. I felt it necessary to outline my intentions toward your sister. Has she mentioned me at all?"

"She only intimated your marriage is in shambles and hinted the breakdown is due to your inattentiveness."

As hard as it was to hear, he couldn't debate that assessment. "I've only had her welfare in mind since the miscarriage. I wanted to give her as much space as she needed. I realize now that was probably a bloody bad idea to show up, unannounced."

"Yes, and it has created a problem that will not be easy to rectify."

It occurred to Sebastian that he could possibly elevate Rafe's opinion of him if he appealed to his ego by asking for advice. "You seem to be a man who knows the workings of a woman's mind. Do you have a suggestion on how I could get back in Nasira's good graces?"

Rafe didn't seem to be flattered, though. "Perhaps you should return to London and allow her to decide if she wants to resume the marriage."

Not the answer he'd hoped for. "Look, Rafe, we've invested ten years in this union—"

"Convenient union, not a love match," Rafe added.

Point reluctantly taken. "Nevertheless, I care greatly for your sister and I'm not willing to give up what we've had for a decade without a fight. But I need assistance in order to win her back. Who better to help me than her brother, who knows her better than most?"

When Rafe remained silent, Sebastian almost gave up until his brother-in-law said, "Shower her with small tokens of your affection."

"You mean flowers and jewelry?"

Rafe looked at him as if he were a total dimwit. "Not only material gifts. And do not concentrate solely on sexual matters."

No sex or hearts and flowers. What was left? "I'm afraid I am still at a loss."

"I have learned women appreciate gestures that might seem insignificant to most men," Rafe said. "They greatly enjoy breakfast in bed. Massages. Having their hair washed."

Sebastian could handle any and all of those things, as long as he had some privacy to do them. "I now understand what you're saying, but I do have another problem. If I am going to woo her, I bloody can't do it in a hotel."

"And I do not wish to witness this wooing." Rafe came to his feet. "I have a possible solution to your lodging issues."

Sebastian finished his second drink and stood, realizing all too well that he should have stopped with the first scotch. He'd always been able to hold his liquor but at the moment he felt as if he could fly without the benefit of his corporate jet. "What do you have in mind?"

"A private residence where you could reside during the duration of your stay. The owners are friends of a friend and they will be leaving for a trip out of the country for two months. I will call tomorrow and let you know if they are amenable to the request. It will be up to you to convince Nasira, without coercion, to join you."

Sebastian had no intention of coercing her. Not when he had other ways to convince her. "I'll try to persuade her."

"If you are unsuccessful, will you agree to return to London?"

Only if and when he had exhausted every option. "That seems fair enough."

"Good. I am going to retire now. I will inform you in the morning if I have secured the accommodations."

"Thank you, Rafe. I certainly value your opinions and your willingness to assist me."

The man seemed unimpressed with Sebastian's gratitude. "I am doing this for Nasira. Her happiness is paramount. I will not tolerate anyone who does not respect her wishes. Keep that in mind as you move forward with your goal."

Before Sebastian could respond, Rafe turned and started up the stairs without looking back. Sebastian dropped down on the settee and rubbed both hands over his face. If he didn't get up soon, he could end up sleeping on the sardine-can sofa.

On that thought, he trudged up the stairs and made his way to his reluctant bride's boudoir. He rapped on the door and when he didn't get a response, entered the room to the sounds of running water.

He had one of two options—leave and let her have her privacy, or shower her with affection in the shower. Option two earned his vote. As long as he proceeded with caution.

He stripped off his shirt, inadvertently popping a button, then sat on the edge of the mattress to toe out of his shoes. He carelessly kicked them off, barely missing the French doors leading to a balcony. In an effort to compose himself, he removed his slacks and underwear with more patience, then tossed them aside on the window seat to his right. When he rose from the bed, he realized he would have to keep a tight hold on his libido. He also realized he wasn't the only one standing.

"Down, old chap," he muttered when he walked to the door, then paused to take a deep breath to regain some semblance of control.

If he played his cards correctly, this could be the first step in demonstrating that he could be the kind husband his wife needed.

Nasira needed a shower and a good night's sleep. She also needed to know exactly what Sebastian was saying to her brother, but that could wait until morning.

Standing beneath the spray, she closed her eyes, bent on washing away the memories of those intimate moments under the stars in the rear—of all things—a Texas truck. Still, her mind whirled back to the interlude and the way Sebastian had so easily unearthed sensations she had greatly missed. Sensations she still experienced with a succession of tremors and tingling. Her husband had so masterfully manipulated her into oblivion with only a few strokes, and once more the heat began to make itself known....

Nasira shook off the images, stepped to the side of the spray and opened her eyes, determined to regain some perspective without undue influence from her spouse until she was forced to face him again.

The plan went awry the moment the glass door opened, Sebastian walked into the shower and moved behind her, as if he had a standing invitation.

His audacity momentarily stunned her into silence. Yet when he reached around her and grasped the bottle of shampoo from the mosaic tile shelf, she spun on him, putting herself in close proximity to a very naked, very virile, very *stimulated* man. "Do you mind?"

He took a quick sniff before placing some of the liquid in his palm. "I do not mind at all. In fact, I like the lavender. Now turn around."

She gathered all the reasons to resist him. Reasons that had ironically kept him from her over the past few months. "You may turn around and leave."

"Not until I wash your hair."

That would qualify as an unusual request. "Why?"

"Could you humor me, please?"

She caught the faint scent of alcohol. "Are you intoxicated?"

"Only with your beauty."

Clearly the liquor was speaking for him. "I smell scotch."

"I might have had a drink. Or two."

"I consider that inadvisable in light of your fatigue."

"I'm not too exhausted or too mashed to wash your hair. In fact, it would be an honor to do it. And I promise you will enjoy it."

Granted, she would, though she wondered who had kidnapped her stoic husband and replaced him with this considerate clone. She mulled the offer over a few minutes and surrendered to the prospect of pleasure—with one concession. "Oh, all right. But only if you will leave after you are finished."

"Agreed."

Nasira faced the tiled wall again and attempted to feign indifference. Yet when Sebastian slid his hands into her hair and began to massage her scalp, she practically melted against him. "That feels exquisite," she murmured.

Sebastian brushed a kiss across her cheek. "You deserve to feel that way. I recognize I've neglected my duties and haven't exactly been a doting husband."

She had never expected him to be doting, yet she did approve of this version of Sebastian. Then suddenly his hands drifted from her hair to her shoulders and came to rest on her breasts. Odd how he had not touched her in six months and now, as if someone had snapped on a sexual light switch, the former version of her husband had returned.

"You are exquisite," he murmured as he pressed against her bottom.

"You are a cad."

"Henry is the cad. I have no control over him."

Nasira stifled a laugh. "I have always wondered what would possess a man to name a cherished part of his anatomy after his prized horse."

He winked. "It's quite logical because that horse is a premiere stallion."

She elbowed him in the ribs. "Since you are finished

washing my hair, I need to rinse out the shampoo and you need to vacate the premises."

Against her better judgment, she turned her back to him, stepped beneath the flowing water and soaked her hair, giving Sebastian complete access to her body. He took supreme advantage of her vulnerable position by running his palms down her torso, over the bend of her waist and on to her hips.

Regardless of her nagging need for him, Nasira sidestepped Sebastian and sent him a frustrated look. "You agreed that when you were finished, you would leave."

He took the blue washcloth folded on the shelf and added a small dollop of gel. "I'm not finished yet."

Unable to move, Nasira watched as Sebastian washed her body, beginning with her shoulders and arms before he moved down to her breasts, and then her belly. He knelt and bathed each of her legs gently, all the while smiling up at her until he straightened. His crystal blue eyes seemed to darken as he shifted his attention to between her thighs. He lingered there for a time, teasing slightly, setting her on edge before he stepped back and draped the washcloth over the chrome rack to his left.

"There you go," he said. "Clean as a whistle."

"Why are you doing this, Sebastian?"

His eyes looked a bit hazy now. "Because I want you to relax. I'm certain you will sleep much better now."

Not very likely. Not when she still wanted him in every way. "I am onto you, Sebastian."

He attempted an innocent expression. "I'm sure I do not know what you mean."

"Yes, you do. However, you can attempt to seduce

me from dawn to dusk but we will still remain at an impasse."

"I was simply trying to be considerate." He grabbed the bottle of gel and began lathering his body. "Granted, a dawn-to-dusk seduction sounds interesting. Perhaps we shall try that in the near future."

"I'm going to bed now," she said as she quickly rinsed off without looking at him.

"I will join you shortly."

"I'll make you a nice place on the rug."

"I so cherish being treated like the family hound."

She sent him a quelling look as she opened the glass door. "We agreed on that arrangement."

He gave her a half smile. "Spoilsport."

As usual, he glossed over the seriousness of their situation with wit and sarcasm. Angry with him, and herself, Nasira left the shower, dried off, wrapped the towel around her and tucked it closed between her breasts. She then twisted her hair into a braid, brushed her teeth and returned to the bedroom, leaving Sebastian alone to finish his shower.

In the past, she would have crawled into bed without clothes but decided with her husband in the house, it would be best to dress in a short blue gown, as if donning silk armor. Of course, if Sebastian sneaked beneath the sheets in the middle of the night, the negligee wouldn't provide any real protection.

Protection. He would not attempt consummation without any form of birth control. He had made that quite clear earlier. In that case, she supposed she could be benevolent and allow him into the bed.

She questioned the wisdom of that reasoning when Sebastian entered the room, a thick white towel slung low on his hips. Even after all their years together, even after seeing him completely nude in the shower a few minutes ago, the sight of his lean swimmer's physique still took her breath away. Many nights she had explored all the masculine planes and valleys, at first under his tutelage, until she had learned exactly how to touch him and kiss him. She had possessed a certain power over him during those times. She dearly wanted to experience that now...

"Sira, are you all right?"

Startled into reality, Nasira averted her eyes and shook off the recollections, though she could not shake the heat. "I am tired."

"As am I," he said as he approached the bed. "So exhausted I could sleep on the floor. Oh, that's right. I'm supposed to do that very thing."

Nasira pulled back the comforter and pointed to the opposite side of the mattress. "I am willing to take pity on you as long as you maintain a wide berth between us."

He grinned. "You are most generous, my lady. And I promise I will be the perfect gentleman."

If only she could believe that. "I will hold you to that promise."

As Nasira slid beneath the covers, her husband returned to the bathroom then came back without the towel or any clothes whatsoever. "Could you possibly put something on, Sebastian?"

He frowned as he climbed into bed beside her.

"Sweetheart, you know I prefer to have nothing on when I sleep. So do you."

"We are guests in this house."

He rolled onto his back and stacked his hands behind his head. "I highly doubt Rafe or Violet will do a bed check to make certain we're appropriately dressed."

That led Nasira to another question. "What did you and my brother discuss tonight?"

He continued to stare at the ceiling. "The strange ways of women and the complete ignorance of men."

"Be serious."

"I am."

"Then please explain."

"At times women say one thing, then do another, while most men are painfully honest. You'd rather spend a day shopping and men would rather engage in sports. Women want to discuss their feelings. Men would rather discuss something as dull as the weather to avoid that at all costs."

"The last part is definitely accurate," she muttered.

"Perhaps that's because we don't necessarily have deep feelings."

"Or at least those you care to share."

Too weary to continue the conversation, Nasira turned off the lamp and turned her back to her spouse. "Good night, Sebastian."

"Sleep well, Sira."

If only she could. For at least an hour, maybe more, Nasira tossed and turned, well aware that her naked husband was very near…and deep in throes of slumber, as evidenced by his steady breathing.

Little by little Nasira began to drift off and soon found herself immersed in an erotic state when Sebastian's hand drifted to her breast. She reveled in the intimate stroking between her thighs. Once more she was captive to his skill and to her own sexuality. Another orgasm—the second one tonight—claimed her with remarkable force. Before the climax had completely calmed, Sebastian moved atop her then eased inside her. Steady thrusts, ragged breaths, undeniable mutual desire...

He whispered her name and she stroked his hair, as if nothing bad had ever transpired between them.

Then suddenly awareness dawned of what they were doing, and what they hadn't done. "Sebastian," she said in a harsh whisper. "We have to stop."

When Sebastian tensed and shuddered, she recognized she had been too late with the warning.

After he finally rolled away, Nasira waited for his reaction and wondered if he was even aware of what had transpired. She received her answer when he sighed, sat up and muttered, "Bloody hell, what have we done?"

She snapped the light on and studied his profile. "Apparently we had unprotected sex."

He shot her a borderline distressed look. "Apparently."

"This is not all my fault, Sebastian. I told you to sleep on the rug."

"You offered me the bed."

"You did not have to accept."

"You shouldn't be so sexy."

"You should have foregone the liquor."

He raked a hand through his tousled hair. "It's clearly futile to blame each other or concern ourselves with the consequences. What's done is done."

"If you are concerned about pregnancy, I was off the pill for almost a year before I conceived the last time. It is highly unlikely that would happen again after only one time."

He appeared skeptical. "Unlikely but not impossible."

Normally Nasira would be happy to know she might finally have a baby, but not with such serious problems still looming over them. "Would it be so horrible if I happened to be pregnant?"

After punching his pillow twice, Sebastian shifted onto his side, keeping his back to her. "That's a discussion for another day."

"A discussion we need to have very soon, Sebastian."

"Would you prefer I move to the floor?" he asked after a few seconds of silence, reverting back to the man who refused to have any semblance of a meaningful conversation.

She preferred he stop clamming up. "It's too late to concern ourselves about that now."

"Then good night, Sira."

"Good night, Sebastian."

As she stared at the ceiling, Nasira wondered how she could feel so bereft after making love with her husband. It was as if they'd returned to the days before she had left London—she was suspended in a state of emotional gridlock with a spouse who constantly erected emotional walls. Could they get past the standoff? In the morning she would decide once and for all if finding out would be worth the potential heartache.

Three

Nasira awoke to an empty space beside her and a strong sense of regret. She could only imagine what Sebastian was thinking. She wouldn't be surprised if he had already summoned the pilot of his posh corporate jet and flown back to London.

After showering and seeing to her morning routine, she dressed in white slacks and a sleeveless blue blouse, slid her feet into silver sandals and started downstairs to see if he had indeed left. When she heard the sound of two familiar male voices, she acknowledged she had been wrong in her assumptions, at least for the moment.

She reached the bottom landing, crossed the parlor and headed into the kitchen to find her husband and brother seated at the built-in banquette, having coffee together. They both quickly stood, looking as if they were errant schoolboys caught in a prank.

"Good morning, darling," Sebastian said, taking her aback with his friendly tone. "Sleep well?"

She didn't know if he was playing at being clueless or he didn't remember what had happened between them. "I slept well enough."

"Good because we have a busy day planned, thanks to Rafe."

Nasira leveled her gaze on her brother. "What does that mean?"

"I will let Sebastian explain," Rafe said as he started toward the parlor. "At the moment, I have to accompany Violet to speak with the caterer."

With that, he rushed away, leaving Nasira alone with her husband. "I find it difficult to believe my brother would involve you in the wedding plans, so I assume we're not expected to meet with the caterer."

"You would be correct. I asked Rafe to find us suitable lodging and he has the perfect place."

"Us?"

"Yes."

"I never agreed to that."

He gestured toward the chair Rafe had vacated. "Please sit so we can discuss this."

"Yes, let's." She settled in to the seat and waited for him to continue.

"Would you like coffee? Or perhaps tea?" he asked.

"I would like orange juice." And an explanation for why he clearly believed she would want to cohabitate with him, especially after his attitude last night.

He rose from the chair and walked to the refrigerator to retrieve the orange juice, poured her a glass and set it on the wooden table. He then took the chair opposite her and folded his hands before him. "I realize you left London to escape me, or perhaps our problems, but I am not willing to toss in the towel until we have explored all alternatives to remaining apart indefinitely."

Neither was she, though she understood they might never be able to compromise on the issue of having children. They never would unless he decided to actually discuss it. "You believe the only way we can do that would be to live under the same roof?"

"Yes, I do."

She had her doubts. "I know you, Sebastian. You will not tolerate a simple hotel room, and I do not believe you'll find a penthouse suite anywhere near Royal. If I decide to do this, I refuse to reside too far away from Rafiq and Violet."

"You're right, but there are houses available."

She suffered the second shock of the morning. "You purchased a house?"

He shook his head. "No. Rafe knows a man who is willing to open his home to us while he and the family travel abroad."

Living in a stranger's house did not seem like a favorable option. "What man?"

"His name is Sheikh Darin Shakir. I believe he hails from a country close to your homeland."

She had heard the name bandied about by Mac. "I know of him. In fact, his reputation precedes him."

Sebastian frowned. "In what way?"

"He killed a man several years ago."

"He's a bloody murderer?"

She gained some satisfaction from shocking her husband this time. "Actually, it is my understanding his love interest was being held captive by this criminal, forcing him to shoot the evildoer to save her life. Although I despise violence, I find the concept of coming to a woman's rescue somewhat romantic."

"I find resorting to murder somewhat disturbing." Sebastian sat back and sighed. "Perhaps we should explore other avenues."

"It's past history, Sebastian. He is very well respected and in fact married to the woman he saved. They have several children."

"Are you absolutely certain the man is safe? I refuse to put you in harm's way."

"As I've said, he is a hero in the town's eyes. I also know my brother would never send me into a dangerous situation."

Sebastian slapped his palms on the table and stood. "Then it's settled. We shall go meet this knight in tainted armor and see if the house passes muster. We need to hurry since they will be leaving shortly after lunch for the trip."

She refused to rush into the decision to join him. "I still have qualms about living together at this point in time."

"What qualms?"

"First of all, although I came here to confront Rafe, I also intended to have time away from you to think."

"On the contrary, last night you wanted to talk."

He did present a valid point. "Yes, but I'm not certain you would be willing to do that."

He rested his hand on the back of her chair. "If we decide the accommodations are suitable, I will strike a bargain with you."

Always the negotiator. "Go on."

"If you will give me one week and the arrangement doesn't suit you, or if I don't meet your expectations, then you are free to leave and I will return to the UK."

She mulled the proposition over a moment and decided that it did seem fair. After all, she truly wanted to attempt to mend the relationship if at all possible. "All right. I will agree to your terms."

"Great. Our chariot awaits."

She pushed back from the table and came to her feet. "I wouldn't consider that truck a chariot."

"I had another vehicle delivered this morning from Dallas. One that is more suitable. You'll see when I bring it around."

"Believe it or not, I find that somewhat disappointing."

He pushed a lock of hair behind her ear, a habit he had established from the first night they had met. "Why is that?"

"Sedans do not have beds."

Noting the look of sheer surprise on Sebastian's handsome face, she turned to retrieve her purse and sunglasses, smiling all the way upstairs and back down again. Perhaps she should not be encouraging her husband in a sexual sense, yet she could not seem to resist the desire his presence had resurrected. The ever present need.

If they had to exist in close quarters, she should make the best of their time together for however long it might last. If they jointly decided their marriage was over, she would make more memories to carry with her to override the bad.

If luck prevailed, the Shakirs' family home would be a happy place perfect for new beginnings.

"This isn't a house, it's a fortress."

Nasira tore her gaze away from the massive white stone structure to glance at Sebastian. "And this veritable limousine you've leased goes quite well with it."

He sent her a half smile. "It's a Jaguar, Sira. Only the best for my bride."

She didn't bother to ask how he had acquired it simply because she did not care. She only cared about meeting the mysterious man who resided in the residence. And of course, the woman who had been worthy of his rescue.

As soon as Sebastian pulled to a stop beneath the portico, a dark-haired, dark-skinned man dressed in black shirt and slacks emerged from the double iron doors. Nasira recognized him from the photograph she had seen at the Texas Cattleman's Club—Darin Shakir, sheikh extraordinaire.

He opened her door and greeted her with an intense look and a guarded smile. "Mrs. Edwards."

"Sheikh Shakir," she said as she slid out of the luxury sedan. "It is a pleasure to finally meet you."

"The pleasure is mine," he said with a nod.

Sebastian rounded the hood and offered his hand to Darin. "I truly appreciate your offer, Sheikh Shakir."

"You may call me Darin," he replied. "I have never embraced my royal status."

Nasira had also learned that about him, which could explain how he had settled in a place like Texas. Then again, so had her brother.

Darin showed them into the house where they were met by an attractive woman with red spiraling curls and bright green eyes. "Welcome to our home, you two. I'm Fiona Shakir."

"I am Nasira Edwards, and this is my husband, Sebastian," she said, beating her spouse to the punch.

At that moment, three dark-haired little boys entered the room and stood between the Shakirs like miniature soldiers. "These are our sons," Darin said. "Halim, Kalib and Samir."

Fiona rested her palm on the youngest one's head. "Otherwise known as Hal, who's ten, Kal, eight, and Sam, five."

The pitter-patter of footsteps echoed in the marble entryway, drawing everyone's attention to the little girl dashing into the foyer, her auburn-tinted curls bouncing in time with her gait. She immediately threw her arms around Darin's legs, leading him to sweep her up. "And this is Liana, our youngest," Darin said. "She will be three years old in three months."

When the little girl touched her father's face, and the stoic sheikh gave his daughter the softest look, Nasira's heart melted. "You have a beautiful family."

Fiona patted her belly. "Thank you, and in about five months, we'll be expanding it with another boy."

Nasira experienced a sense of awe and a slight sting of envy. "Four boys should be interesting."

"Very interesting," Sebastian said. "How do you manage caring for so many children?"

Fiona slid her arm around Darin's waist. "With a lot of love and sharing."

"And our nanny, Amelia," Darin added.

"A part-time nanny," Fiona amended. "When Amelia isn't here, I've learned to be extremely organized out of self-defense. Otherwise the house will be utter chaos and I'll be a raving maniac."

Darin pointed behind him. "Boys, return to the playroom." No sooner than he commanded it, the Shakir sons departed.

Fiona gestured toward the hall beyond the foyer. "Come inside and I'll show you around."

"I would enjoy seeing the livestock," Sebastian said to Darin. "We can leave the wives to tour the house and talk about us when we're out of earshot."

Darin finally smiled. "I would be glad to show you the stables."

"Take Liana with you," Fiona said. "She'll throw a fit if you walk outside without her."

Sebastian looked somewhat alarmed. "Is it wise to take a child around the horses?"

Fiona smiled. "She's fine as long as she's supervised."

Darin shifted Liana from one hip to the other. "We

have several Arabians if you and your wife would like to ride."

"It would be a pleasure," Sebastian began, "yet I'm afraid my wife would probably balk at the idea."

But Sebastian was wrong. "I would love nothing more than to go for a ride. I spent much of my youth on the back of a horse."

Sebastian frowned. "You've never told me that in our ten years together."

"You never asked."

"Ten years?" Fiona interjected as if she sensed the tension. "Darin and I have been married that long. Do you two have children?"

Nasira swallowed around the nagging lump in her throat. "Not yet."

"We have a very busy life in London," Sebastian added. "And we both enjoy traveling. Nasira is involved in charity work and my shipping business requires quite a bit of time."

Fiona shrugged. "Children are definitely time-consuming."

"And wonderful," Nasira said, determined to get her point across to her husband. "I definitely want at least one or perhaps two."

Sebastian regarded Darin. "Shall we begin the tour of the stables? We wouldn't want to detain you in light of your upcoming vacation."

Leave it to her husband to avoid the topic of children. And that gave Nasira pause. "I am very much looking forward to seeing the rest of the house."

"Right this way," Fiona said as she gestured Nasira forward.

They made their way through a large formal lounge with gleaming dark wood floors and several seating areas containing multicolored leather furniture and assorted club chairs.

She already felt at home surrounded by such opulence. "This is very grand but comfortable."

"Thank you, Nasira." Fiona nodded toward the sweeping staircase. "We have five bedrooms upstairs and our other family room, which is always a mess. So I'll concentrate on the downstairs for now. But feel free to explore when you're here."

Provided they decided to stay there, though she had to admit she would love it. "We so appreciate your hospitality."

"You are so welcome," Fiona said as she took off at a fast clip. "The two guest bedrooms are down here."

Nasira admired the luxury of the first bedroom Fiona showed her. It was accented in whites and grays with a plush king bed and gorgeous en suite bath. The second was equally remarkable though the color palette featured differing shades of blue. Nasira welcomed the fact that if serious conflicts arose during their time her, she could have one room and Sebastian could have the other.

"Amelia usually stays in one these rooms when she spends the night," Fiona began, "but we're taking her with us. Darin and I could use a little alone time, if you catch my drift."

Nasira was not familiar with the term, yet she did understand the meaning behind it. "I have no doubt enjoying private moments with your husband must be difficult in light of the children's needs."

The redhead grinned and winked. "We women have needs too."

Something Nasira had realized all too well last night. "Yes, we do."

Fiona led her out into the corridor and waved her forward. "The housekeeper, Annie, will be in every day if you decide to stay with us. And she prepares wonderful meals."

"That would not be necessary."

"I insist," Fiona said as she stopped in the great room. "Besides, Annie would be lost if she didn't have something to do. I promise she won't be in the way. In fact, you won't even know she's here most of the time."

A phantom maid was quite a novel idea. "Well I would not want her to feel unwanted."

"I can show you our bedroom if you'd like," Fiona began, "or we can take a look at the kitchen."

"I would love to see the nursery," Nasira blurted without thought.

"Then follow me."

They crossed to the opposite end of the house and walked down another long hall until Fiona paused at a door with a keypad. "This is the elevator to the upper floor. I'll leave the code in case you need it."

She could not imagine why they would. "Did I not see a staircase?"

"Yes, you did." Fiona smiled as they continued on side by side at a much slower pace. "We use it to get to the second floor fast if one of the kids needs us during the night. Darin is usually the one who hops out of bed first. He's a very light sleeper."

"How did the two of you meet?" Nasira asked, overcome with curiosity.

"In a Vegas lounge," Fiona said. "I happened to be bartending when he walked in and he thought I was someone else."

"Someone else?"

"Yes. An FBI agent. It's a long story but let's just say that particular night started a harrowing adventure that led to this wonderful life full of love and chaos and beautiful children. And speaking of children, this is where the babies stay."

Fiona opened the double doors to a large nursery that Nasira could only describe as a children's wonderland. A majestic white canopy crib draped in sheer pale green netting to complement the gender-neutral decor had been positioned between two windows. Stuffed animals of all shapes and sizes dotted built-in shelves that also held trinkets and framed photos of the Shakir children at various points of their life. It was a remarkable place that indicated a very happy family lived here.

Fiona pointed to a small bed to their right. "Liana still sleeps there for the time being. We'll move her upstairs to the big girl room right before the baby comes. At least that's the plan. I'm not sure how well her daddy is going to take not having her nearby."

Nasira could see where that might be an issue. "They seem to be very close."

"She's definitely a daddy's girl. You'll figure that one out if you and Sebastian have a daughter."

Regret and memories washed over Nasira as she walked to the crib and ran her hand over the soft coral blanket folded at the end of the mattress. How many times had she imagined her own baby in such a precious bed? How many times had she cried over the end of that dream? Her hand automatically came to rest on her abdomen, and then the familiar tears arrived as sudden as a summer rain. Unwelcome tears that she could not seem to control.

She felt a hand on her shoulder. "Nasira, are you okay?"

Not in the least. She turned around and sniffed. "I had a miscarriage six months ago. It was early in the pregnancy but still no less devastating."

Fiona snapped a tissue from the box on the changing table and handed it to her. "I'm so sorry, Nasira, and I can relate."

She dabbed at her eyes. "You can?"

"Like you, I had a first trimester miscarriage between Kal and Sam. It broke my heart."

Finally, someone who could understand and perhaps provide insight. "How did Darin react to the loss?"

Fiona shrugged. "He was extremely supportive even though he didn't touch me for a couple of months. I think he worried I might break."

"Sebastian avoided me for six months."

Fiona's green eyes went wide. "You haven't made love since you lost the baby?"

Nasira felt the urge to confess, yet thought it best not to reveal too much. "That was the case until last night, although I am still in a quandary over how it happened. In fact, the whole evening was rather odd."

"I'd think you would be relieved," Fiona said. "Six months is a long time without making whoopee."

"True, but Sebastian's behavior was completely out of character. First of all, he arrived at Rafiq's house uninvited and punched Mac McCallum because he believed we were having some sort of tryst, which is absolutely absurd."

Fiona gasped. "He did not!"

"He did. I was completely shocked by his behavior yet admittedly somewhat attracted to his sudden show of machismo. Sebastian is usually so controlled."

Fiona chuckled. "I know exactly what you mean because Darin is like that, too. But there's no shame in wanting to jump his bones after he defended your honor, even if he mistakenly thought you were fooling around."

Nasira had definitely wanted him, yet she had never been the aggressor in the relationship. "For the sake of accuracy, I was not exactly looking to rekindle our love life at that moment. Yet he convinced me to have dinner with him and then he virtually seduced me in the ridiculously large pickup truck he rented."

"Welcome to Texas, girlfriend. Sex in a pickup truck is practically a sport."

Nasira couldn't contain her smile. "That actually came later, in the middle of the night, after Sebastian had two toddies on top of his jet lag." She sighed. "You must think I am a complete dolt, telling you all the sordid details."

Fiona folded her arms across her middle. "Hey, I'm

a good listener, and it's sure not stupid to want to make love to your husband."

Then why did she feel so foolish? "I should not want him after what he has done. Or what he has not done. Not only did he avoid lovemaking, any serious communication between us has been at a complete standstill. He refuses to talk about our loss or how he feels about it."

"Darin isn't a great communicator, either," Fiona said. "But I can't imagine him completely shutting down and if he does try that, I have ways to make him talk."

"Sebastian has not only shut down, he acts as if he no longer wants children. Maybe he never has. In fact, I had to stop taking…" She had already revealed too much. Said too much. "Again, I do apologize for burdening you with my problems."

"Burden away, Nasira. We're members of the miscarriage club and it's not a good club to join."

"No, it is not."

Fiona's face took on a serious expression. "If you don't mind me asking, do you know why your husband suddenly changed his mind about being a father?"

This would be the most difficult part to explain. "Actually, we met and married very quickly and we never actually discussed it at length. I did know that his father and stepmother were adamant that he produce an heir because he is an only child, so I mistakenly assumed we would eventually have children. Yet it took years before we finally conceived." With some regrettable deception on her part.

"If he doesn't change his mind, what are you going to do?"

"I have no clue at this point in time." And she really didn't.

Fiona patted her cheek. "Stick to your guns, Nasira. It's one thing if both parties don't want a baby, but it's another thing if one does and one doesn't. Regardless, I hope you both work it out."

So did Nasira. "That's why we are here. I initially came to Royal to check up my brother and gain some space, yet Sebastian insisted on following me. We have both agreed to try to compromise. Hopefully, opening your home to us will aid in that goal."

"It's a magical place," Fiona said with a grin. "But just another bit of friendly advice. If he has sex on his mind, don't make it easy for him until you know you're both on the same page when it comes to the future. If he doesn't want to talk, then give him a little nudge."

If only she had mastered that tack. "What do you suggest?"

"Be a seductress, but play hard to get to get what you need. Eventually you'll have him eating out of your hand."

"Would that not make me a tease?"

"Sometimes we have to resort to desperate measures, Nasira. Playing cat and mouse always drives Darin insane, and I guess that's why we have so many kids."

They shared in a laugh and a surprising embrace before Fiona said, "Let's go see if the men have come in from the stables."

Nasira felt she should express her gratitude again.

"Let's. And please know how much I appreciate your candor and comradeship. You have bolstered my optimism."

"No problem, Nasira. We girls have just got to stick together."

The sound of feminine laughter filtered into the chef's kitchen, leading Sebastian to believe the two wives must be getting along famously. He couldn't exactly say the same when it came to his connection to Darin Shakir. The man spoke in brief sentences and appeared to be incapable of smiling, unless it was directed at his daughter. However, he had been a polite host during their tour of the stables, right down to pointing out where Sebastian should step to prevent ruining his Italian loafers.

As Nasira moved into the room, chatter went on around him but he tuned it out and focused on watching his wife. Even after all the years they'd spent together, Sebastian still found her grace and beauty breathtaking. He liked the way she kept her slender hands in motion when she spoke. He liked the way her dark eyes lit up when she laughed. He truly relished her breasts that were unfortunately concealed by her black hair falling in soft waves, crimped from the braid she'd worn to bed last night. He imagined those silken locks on his chest, along with her soft lips, moving down his belly and lower....

"Can I get you anything, Sebastian?"

He brought his attention to Fiona to find her sporting an odd look. "I could use a glass of water." Mainly to pour down his shorts to preserve his dignity.

"Would you like one too, Nasira?" she asked.

His wife frowned at him as if she had channeled his dirty thoughts. "No, thank you. I suppose Sebastian and I should take our leave so we can discuss your wonderful offer for us to stay in your home."

Darin stepped forward, the toddler still on his hip. "We will give you your privacy while we return to our packing. If you decide to stay, we will provide you with the key and the gate code so you may return at your leisure."

Fiona set a glass of water on the marble island next to Sebastian. "Liana, tell Mr. and Mrs. Edwards goodbye."

After Darin set the little girl on her feet, she immediately rushed to Sebastian and wrapped her arms around his legs. "Bye, bye, Mr. Man."

Seeing the grin on the child's face sent a spear of regret through Sebastian. He ruffled her dark hair and returned her smile. "Goodbye, Princess Liana. I am grateful to have met you and your noble steed, Puddles."

Her grin widened as she moved to Nasira and took her hand. "Bye, bye, pretty lady."

Nasira knelt at her level and touched the girl's face. "Goodbye, little princess. Have a wonderful time on your trip."

Fiona stepped forward and took Liana's hand. "Take your time, you two. When you're ready, just press the button that says *family room* on the wall by the stove and we'll come running."

After the couple disappeared around the corner, Sebastian faced Sira again. "Well, what do you think of the place?"

"I think it is very lovely."

"Not too shabby, I suppose."

"I also think your reaction to Liana was lovely as well."

He should have seen that coming. "She's a very interesting child though somewhat chatty. She is quite enamored of her pony."

"She seemed somewhat enamored of you."

"She is simply friendly." And he simply needed to divert Nasira's attention from the topic before she forced him to revisit his decision not to have a child. "By the way, there's a spa on the deck next to the pool. That alone would persuade me to stay."

"I cannot recall if Elsa packed my swimsuit."

"Elsa never forgets a thing. And on the off chance she did, we will swim in the nude."

She averted her eyes. "Keep your voice down, Sebastian."

Her innocence had come out of hiding. "Why? I assume this couple knows about all things sexual considering they are well on their way to creating an entire rugby team."

That earned him her smile and a wistful look. "You are so amusing. They have a wonderful family. They are quite lucky to have each other."

He realized how strongly his wife had been affected by the children. Children he could not offer her at the moment. Nevertheless, he hoped to come up with a plan that he would present later. Much later. "Are you still willing to reside here with me until the end of the week?"

"Yes, with a few conditions," she said.

He should have seen that coming. "And what would those be?"

"First, we stay in separate suites."

Bloody hell. "Why?"

"Because we need to concentrate on our relationship without any complications that will cloud our judgment."

Double bloody hell. "If you are referring to sex, you must admit that has always worked well between us. Why would we want to exclude that from our time together?"

She barked out a cynical laugh. "I find that somewhat ironic considering that until last night, you refused to sleep with me in every sense of the word for the past six months."

He couldn't provide an explanation without baring his soul completely. He had been taught by his father early in life that men did not give in to emotions. "I was simply allowing you to recover completely."

"Have you forgotten what happened last night when you were in my bed?"

"Actually, I barely remember it." Unfortunately.

"You do remember the birth control issue, correct?"

He had attempted to forget that, yet the possible consequences still haunted him. "Yes, I remember."

"Well, nothing has changed in that regard. We still do not have any protection against pregnancy."

Not yet, but he intended to rectify that with a trip

to the market. And perhaps he would pick up a box of chocolates along with the condoms. "I see your point, and I agree to your terms." For the time being.

"Second condition," she continued. "You must promise you will engage in meaningful conversations and answer my questions with candor without any comedy."

That would be somewhat difficult. "I promise I will try, as long as you promise to be patient."

"I will agree to those terms."

Simple enough. "Then I suppose we should tell the Shakirs we will be accepting their hospitable invitation."

Sebastian could only hope that agreeing to her terms would not prove to be his downfall.

Four

Later that afternoon, when they returned to the Shakirs' house, luggage in hand, they found a note on the door from the owners inviting them to enjoy their home, and lunch awaiting them.

After Sebastian keyed in the code to allow them entry, Nasira started for the guest wing with her husband trailing behind her. She paused in the hallway to turn and almost ran into a wall of masculine chest. "Which room do you prefer?"

"The one where you'll be staying."

She sighed and stepped back. "We've already discussed this, Sebastian. Until we have our issues settled, I insist we adhere to our initial plan."

"I am only being honest at your request."

And infuriating. "I will take the suite on the right

and you can take the one across the hall. I assure you, they are both very nice. I will meet you in the kitchen after I have settled in."

"Yes, dear."

Relieved her husband had not put up much of a fight, Nasira entered the blue suite and set her suitcase and garment bag on the bench at the end of the bed. She quickly hung her dresses in the huge closet and put away her other clothes in the bureau, then returned to the corridor to find it deserted. Without waiting for Sebastian, she immediately left for the great room, all the while reflecting on his interaction with little Liana. He seemed quite charmed by the toddler, and perhaps that meant there could still be hope for their marriage yet. Or perhaps it had only been a show for the proud parents.

When she reached the kitchen, Nasira found a spread of luscious salads, cheeses, breads and cold cuts laid out on the informal dinette set against a large picture window that revealed a remarkable view of the countryside.

"It certainly looks appetizing."

She turned to find her husband standing close by, hands in pockets. "It looks wonderful. All of it. The food. The pastureland. The pool and the spa. We might as well be staying at a resort."

He raked back a chair, sat and then rubbed his hands together. "Personally I could consume most of this."

She claimed the seat across from him. "Please let me have a bit before you take it all."

He winked. "Sweetheart, although I would like it all, I will take what you will give me."

She could so easily walk into his lair but remembered

Fiona's advice. She would play along for now before she would play hard to get. "I promise I will give you enough to keep you sated."

He appeared pleasantly surprised by her response. "I look forward to it."

As they dined, a heavy fog of tension hung over them. A palpable tension long absent from their lives. Nasira held tight to her goal to persuade him to talk about issues he had always suppressed. During this time together, she vowed to learn as much as she could about the man she had lived with for a decade, and she would do whatever that required.

"I found Fiona Shakir to be quite friendly," she said, breaking the silence.

"And clearly quite fertile."

"Would you please stop deriding her for choosing to have children?"

He pushed aside his empty plate. "I'm not deriding her. I'm simply stating the obvious."

Nasira opted for a change of subject. "What should we do this afternoon?"

His smile arrived as slowly as the sunrise. "I know what I would like to do for the remainder of the day."

Stay strong, Nasira. "I would like to hear your plans, as long as they involve remaining vertical."

"I'd say that's altogether possible and in my opinion, preferable during a lengthy ride."

Images of being taken against a wall plagued her. "Need I remind you of our agreement?"

He rubbed his chin. "I do not readily recall any clause prohibiting horseback riding."

She tossed her napkin at him and he caught it in one hand. "You cad."

"Cad? What did you think I meant?"

She pushed back from the table and stood. "Do not play ignorant, Sebastian. Since you've arrived, every time you open your mouth, innuendo spills out."

He had the gall to grin. "Perhaps you only assume that because you're having naughty sex thoughts."

That only heightened her irritation. "If that were the case, could you blame me?"

He released a rough sigh. "No, I suppose I couldn't. You have been greatly deprived, with the exception of last night. However, I would like to make up for that now if you will allow it."

She refused to give in so easily. "I appreciate the gesture, but you will have to make up for my deprivation without any expectations in regard to lovemaking."

He pushed the chair back, came to his feet and executed a bow. "My lady, I would be honored if you would join me for an equestrian adventure, and I promise no clothes will be shed."

She could not help but smile. "Yes, I will join you. And speaking of clothes, I will need to change into something more suitable."

He slapped his forehead with his palm. "I didn't bring anything but slacks and loafers."

"Then perhaps we should find something else to do."

"No, I'll travel into town to purchase appropriate clothing. Or perhaps I should say I'll mosey into town."

"Is it worth that much effort?"

He walked up to her and kissed her cheek. "*You* are

worth the effort. And I need to pick up a few more items that will benefit us both."

Before Nasira could respond, Sebastian strode out of the kitchen, leaving her standing there, pondering what he had up his sleeve. She would simply have to wait and see.

Nasira waited for what seemed to be infinity for Sebastian to return, until her patience began to wane. Dressed in designer jeans and fashionable boots, she located the path that led to the pasture and made her way to the stable. She soon came upon a large white rock structure surrounded by paddocks that held grazing mares and a few precious foals. It appeared everything about the ranch fostered new life and that only fed her melancholy.

When she entered the barn, Nasira found a lengthy aisle lined with stalls, mostly empty until she reached the end of the line where a beautiful bay stuck its head out of the top of the door.

She cautiously approached to measure the horse's reaction to her appearance. When she held out her hand and began stroking the thin white blaze between its eyes, she immediately received a soft nicker.

"Can I help you, ma'am?"

In response the unfamiliar voice, she turned her head to the right and spotted an older man with white-streaked hair peeking out from beneath his black baseball cap, whiskers scattered about his careworn face. She offered a smile and her hand. "I am Nasira Edwards, the Shakirs' houseguest."

His face relaxed as he gave her hand a hearty shake. "Oh, yeah. I met your husband earlier. He told me the two of you might be wantin' to take a ride today."

"And you are?"

He raked off his cap and grinned. "I forgot my manners. I'm Hadley Monroe but most people call me Cappy. I prefer that."

An odd name but a very cheerful man. "It is a pleasure to meet you, Cappy. I assume you work for the Shakirs."

He settled the cap back on his head. "Yes, ma'am. I take care of the livestock and my missus, Annie, keeps the house. That gelding you're scratchin' is Gus, or that's what I call him. He has some fancy name that's about a mile long."

She glanced at the mesmerized horse and smiled. "Do you live nearby?"

Cappy hooked a thumb over his shoulder. "If you go up those stairs back there, that leads to our place."

"Over the barn?"

He chuckled. "It's nicer than most people's houses. The nicest place I've ever lived in. Mr. Darin and Mrs. Fiona are good people."

"Yes they are."

The sound of footsteps drew Nasira's attention to the stable's entry to see a tall man striding down the aisle. She recognized the confident gait, the lean, toned body, the charming smile and handsome face. She did not recognize the chambray shirt rolled up at the sleeves, the jeans encasing those long legs or the cowboy boots covering his feet.

"Well, well," she said as he stopped before her. "Has there been a British invasion in the western store?"

Her husband's smile expanded. "As they say, when in Rome."

"Or Royal."

"I'm attempting to blend in. Do you not approve?"

She took a visual journey down his body and back up again. "Actually, I approve very much."

"I would think so since you seem to have an affinity for cowboys of late."

"Excuse me?"

"Your *friend*, Mac, the manhandling rancher."

The jealousy apparently had not abated, and that somewhat shocked Nasira, as well as aggravated her. "Oh, nonsense, Sebastian. Please get over that."

Without offering a rejoinder, Sebastian reached around her and stuck out his hand for a shake. "Nice to see you again, Cappy."

"Good to see you, too, Buck."

That turned Nasira around to face the grinning graying ranch hand. "Buck?"

"Cappy gives everyone a nickname," Sebastian said. "Isn't that right, Cappy?"

The older man touched the bill of his cap. "Yesiree, Buck. I call 'em like I see 'em."

Sebastian slid his arm around Nasira's waist. "What would you suggest for my wife?"

Cappy rubbed his chin for a few moments. "I can only think of one thing that fits. Beauty."

Sebastian laughed. "That would definitely fit."

Nasira felt heat rise from her throat to her face.

"Surely you can come up with something a bit more creative, Cappy."

The man grinned again. "Like I said, I call 'em like I see 'em. If you folks will excuse me, I'll go get Studly and bring him in so I can get back to work."

After Cappy left, Nasira faced her husband again. "Who is Studly?"

"Darin's stallion," Sebastian said. "His proper name is Knight something."

She had entered the land of strange names. "I would definitely prefer that to Studly."

"I'd prefer Studly to Buck."

Nasira could not help but smile. "Studly Edwards. It has a nice ring to it. Perhaps if we have a son we could use it."

Sebastian looked as if she had told him he had to sell the shipping business. "Darin told me to explore the path outside the back paddock. It leads to a nice creek," he said, changing the subject.

Of course he would avoid the topic of children. But as far as Nasira was concerned, they would be broaching that subject soon enough, and the discussion could determine their future.

Cappy returned leading a beautiful black Arabian with a large tooled saddle dotted with elaborate silver on his back. "Here ya go, Buck. He's ready to ride."

Sebastian frowned. "No English tack, I see."

"Nope," Cappy said. "But those prissy saddles aren't much different. This is just a bigger seat with a horn to hang on to. There's no need to bounce up and down unless you wanna do that."

The larger seat did not appear to be able to accommodate two people, which led Nasira to ask a question. "Will I have my own horse?"

"That fellow you've been scratchin' is all yours," Cappy said. "Gus will take good care of you. I'll get him tacked up and then you all can take off."

Nasira stood by as the ranch hand led Gus out of the stall and toward the rear of the barn. While she and Sebastian remained in the aisle, the stallion began to grow restless. "He appears to be rather spirited," she said. "Are you certain you can handle him?"

Sebastian scratched the horse's neck and that seemed to calm him somewhat. "If I can handle chasing a three-inch ball with mallet in hand on the back of a racing beast during a game of polo, I can manage one spirited stallion."

She had clearly dealt a blow to his ego. "Of course. How foolish of me to question your manhood."

"My manhood is never in question, sweetheart. You should know that after ten years."

"It is understandable I would have forgotten since I have had very limited exposure to your *manhood* for the past six months."

"Touché. Yet I do recall your manhood drought ending last night."

"Unfortunately I do not recall much about that at all, and neither do you, considering we were both half-asleep."

Cappy returned with the gelding, interrupting the banter and greatly embarrassing Nasira when she considered that he might have overheard. "They're all yours," he said. "Just go out the front, take a right and follow the trail past the back of the barn. Once you reach water, you're all out of path."

"Would we be allowed to explore the rest of the acreage, Cappy?" Sebastian asked.

The man chuckled. "Well, that would be close to two thousand acres, but if you want adventure, be my guest. Just take care not to get lost."

Nasira could imagine wandering around for days and days. "I believe we will stay on the path. My husband does not have the best sense of direction."

Sebastian sent her a quelling look. "Might I remind you that you have been known to become lost looking for the tube?"

"I have not."

"Yes, you have."

She suddenly remembered one incident from long ago. "For heaven's sake, Sebastian, that happened once right after we married and I barely knew my way around London."

Cappy cleared his throat. "I hate to interrupt, but I need to muck these stalls while you're gone. I'd like be done before midnight."

"Of course," Sebastian said. "Do you need assistance mounting your steed, Sira?"

She answered by putting her boot in the stirrup and hoisting herself onto the saddle. "No, I do not."

Sebastian laid a dramatic hand over his heart. "You wound me by not allowing me to make any show of chivalry."

She clasped the reins in one hand. "Knowing you

as well as I do, you only wanted an excuse to put your hand on my bum."

He frowned and mounted the stallion with ease. "Darling, you are going to lead our friend here to believe that I'm a scoundrel."

"If the moniker fits, *darling*."

Cappy narrowed his eyes and studied them both. "How long have the two of you been hitched?"

"Ten years," they responded simultaneously.

"Well, that explains it," Cappy said. "Just some friendly advice. The missus and me have been married nearly forty years. In that time we figured out when you find yourself bickering a lot, the best way to cool down is taking a nekkid swim together in the crick. You should try it."

"Crick?" Sebastian asked.

Cappy scowled. "That's Texan for creek. See y'all when you get back."

With that, the man disappeared, leaving Nasira and Sebastian sitting atop the horses, staring at each other. And when her husband presented her with a slow, knowing grin, Nasira pointed at him despite the seductive images flashing in her mind. "Do not even think we will be engaging in that behavior."

He shrugged. "I can see some merit in the man's suggestion."

So could she. Bent on ignoring him and her own questionable thoughts, Nasira nudged the gelding forward with her heels, not bothering to look back.

When she guided Gus through the stable doors into the bright sunshine, Sebastian rode up to her side. "Perhaps you should lead the way since I have such a *terrible* sense of direction."

She turned right on the path without giving him a passing glance. "Could we call a truce and concentrate on having a pleasant ride?"

"I suppose I could do that. Will I be allowed to speak?"

She sent him a sideways glance. "I highly doubt I could prevent that if I tried."

"Your request is my command."

Whether he could be quiet for any real length of time remained to be seen, Nasira thought as they rode down the path at an easy pace.

As they traveled on, she relished the feel of the sun on her shoulders, the scent of freshly cut grass, the wide expanse of open land before them where livestock grazed nearby. "Oh, look," she said, breaking the silence. "A baby cow."

"I believe the proper term would be calf," Sebastian began," although that does conjure images of a disjointed leg frolicking in the field."

It took great effort to contain her laughter. "Always the witty one."

Another span of silence passed before Sebastian addressed her again. "When did you last communicate with your mother?"

The question came as a surprise to Nasira. "When I became pregnant."

She could feel his gaze boring into her. "Are you saying she doesn't know—"

"About the miscarriage? No."

"Why haven't you told her?"

"She did not share in my excitement over the pregnancy. She has never been concerned about my life."

He released a rough sigh. "I've never understood your hesitancy to reconnect with her."

"She does not welcome that, Sebastian. I remind her of my father."

"You are still her child."

"Perhaps, but I was raised by the palace staff. She only gave birth to me out of obligation."

"In a manner of speaking, I can relate. I'm certain that was the reasoning behind my birth. And that insistence on producing heirs is no bloody reason to bring a baby into this world. Nothing good can come of it."

"We are both good people, Sebastian."

"Good people whose mothers were forced to bring us into being."

Nasira saw an opportunity to encourage him to expand on his feelings. "Yet your mother loved you, did she not?"

"Yes, she did, until her untimely death."

A death that he had never discussed in detail in Nasira's presence, despite the fact she had asked numerous times during the beginning of her marriage. Eventually she had given up. "What exactly happened to her, Sebastian?"

His jaw tightened, a positive sign of anxiety. "She became ill."

That much she knew. "What did that illness involve?"

Sebastian shaded his eyes and focused on the horizon. "I believe I see the creek ahead."

Sebastian's behavior was a certain sign of emotional avoidance as far as Nasira was concerned. "I assume it must be painful to discuss the particulars, but I would like to know."

"It doesn't matter how or why. It only matters that she left her only son orphaned."

The comment gave Nasira pause. "Is that why you've avoided having a child of your own? Do you fear you will somehow desert them?"

"No. I've spent a lifetime having the importance of an heir crammed down my bloody throat."

Denial or not, Nasira sensed she had touched on the crux of his reluctance. "Have you ever considered the absolute joy fatherhood brings?"

He continued to stare straight ahead. "Most people I know pawn their children off on the nanny for the sake of their sanity."

Her husband was either terribly misguided or overly cynical. "Not the Shakirs. You would have realized that if you noticed the way Darin looked at his daughter."

"I noticed." Sebastian's tone was oddly laced with sadness.

Nasira wanted so badly to reach him. To uncover the secrets he harbored in his soul. "And you have no desire to experience that love?"

He attempted a smile that did not quite reach his eyes. "I desire to find out if Studly can fly."

When Sebastian and the stallion took off, Nasira remained behind for a few moments, pondering his need to escape. The behavior was so unlike Sebastian the businessman. As long as she had known him, he had always been a take-charge man. A man who had never avoided any challenges. A man who had been inclined to run from all things emotional.

Before her husband put too much physical distance between them, Nasira spurred the gelding into a gallop. She did not catch up to Sebastian until she reached the tree-lined ribbon of water where he had dismounted. She found him standing on the bank, the stallion's reins secured to a low-hanging limb. She climbed off Gus, tied him to the tree opposite Studly and went to Sebastian's side.

"Why do you always do that?" she asked when he didn't acknowledge her.

He picked up a stone and tossed it into the muddy green water. "I find speed exhilarating."

Her frustration over his evasion began to escalate. "That is not what I meant, Sebastian."

"I know."

The acknowledgment surprised her. "You promised me you would make an effort to be open about your feelings."

He finally faced her. "I would prefer to have a nice, relaxing afternoon with my wife, not to dredge up past history and events that cannot be changed. Could we possibly do that and leave the serious talk for a later time in a place that is not quite so serene?"

She recognized that her husband responded better with gentle persuasion. "All right. We shall postpone the conversation for the time being."

"I'm glad you see it my way."

When Sebastian took a seat on a large stump and

began to remove his boots and socks, Nasira worried he had other activities in mind. "Surely you are not going to take Cappy's suggestion about going swimming naked in the creek."

He glanced at her and winked. "I will if you will."

"I will not." Though admittedly she would under better circumstances.

"I thought as much," he said as he rolled up his pants legs. "Never fear, my dear. I'm only going to put my feet in the water. Would you care to join me?"

Nasira eyed the muddy green stream and wondered what lurked beneath. "Should we be afraid of reptiles and man-eating fish?"

Sebastian stood and shed his shirt, revealing all the wonderful planes and angles of his chest that Nasira had always appreciated. "Reptiles and fish would be more afraid of us."

"I thought you were only removing your boots."

He hung the shirt on a tree limb and swiped a palm over his nape. "It's rather warm out. Feel free to take yours off, too."

She claimed the spot on the stump Sebastian had vacated but only bared her feet. "You are so amusing."

"You are so gorgeous."

She rolled up her pants legs and stood to find the grassy earth remarkably soothing beneath her soles. "You are such a flatterer."

"I'm sincere in my compliments." He held out his hand. "Let me assist you as we explore the murky depths of an uncharted Texas *crick*."

As much as she wanted to assert her independence,

Nasira thought it best to hold on to her husband for support in the event something unknown attacked her toes. She clasped his hand and allowed him to guide her down the sloping bank and into the water. "It is much cooler than I expected," she said, her words followed by a slight shiver.

"I think it's rather nice," he replied without releasing her. "And not a sea creature in sight."

"Not any we can see. We have no idea what might be lurking beneath the surface."

"I shall protect you, fair maiden."

No sooner than he had said it, Nasira lost her footing and began to fall backward, inadvertently wrenching her hand from Sebastian's grasp. She landed on her bottom in the shallow water, sending a spray of moisture into her face.

She sputtered and wiped her eyes then looked up to find her husband standing over her. When he offered his hand, she swatted it away. "What were you saying about protecting me?"

He executed a bow. "My sincerest apologies, but you took me by surprise. You are normally very coordinated."

She came to her feet and slicked back her hair. "The bottom is as slippery as glass. And heavens, the smell."

"How can I make this up to you?"

She glared at him. "Help me out of this awful creek."

"I have a much better idea." Apparently, it included Sebastian immersing himself in the water and surfacing with a smile. "Now we are both wet and smelly."

"Lovely."

He surveyed the area a moment. "Do you know what this reminds me of?"

"I haven't a clue."

"Our trip to Tahiti."

Her mind whirled back to that grand adventure during a time when they could not get enough of each other. "If I recall, that involved a secluded cove with a waterfall, not a narrow cesspool."

"The scent isn't that foul. It's the moss."

"It has to be the cod."

"I could be mistaken, but I believe cod is a saltwater fish."

"You and your trivial facts."

When she playfully pushed at his shoulder, he swept his hand through the water and splashed her again. The battle then commenced, each trying to best the other with liquid bombs until they were both winded with laughter.

Nasira could not recall how much time had passed since they had acted with such wild abandon. How long it had been since they had shared so much laughter. She felt so connected with him, yet somewhat cautious. They still had quite a bit to resolve.

"I believe it is time to retreat," she said, but before she could evade Sebastian, he reached out and pulled her to him.

"Isn't this much better than arguing?" he asked as he guided them farther into the creek until the water lapped at her waistline.

Unable to resist her sexy, damp, shirtless husband,

she draped her arms around his neck. "I suppose it is somewhat better." And welcome. And wonderful.

He feathered a kiss across her cheek. "This is the part I remember about Tahiti."

"Only we were not fully dressed, although at least you had the foresight to remove your shirt today. I highly doubt I will ever be able to get the swampy scent out of my blouse."

"We could simply remove your blouse now."

When he reached for the buttons, she wagged a finger at him. "Now, now. We have an agreement. Conversation first."

He managed to slip open the first button and parted the placket. "What would you like to discuss?" he asked as he traced the top of her bra with a fingertip.

A topic that would ruin the mood. "Nothing at the moment. We should return to the stable with the horses since your mount seems rather restless."

He glanced at the stallion now pawing the ground. "Could I at least kiss you before we leave?"

"You usually do not ask permission."

"I'm only following the rules, per your request."

That alone should earn him a reward. "I suppose a small kiss would be all right."

Clearly her husband did not know the meaning of *small,* as if she expected him to give her anything less than a thorough kiss. Yet when he lowered his lips to hers, she found the gesture to be more tender than deep. Soft and somewhat restrained…in the beginning. And then the passion took hold. A passion she could not fight. Yet if she did not stop him now, she might not be able to stop at all.

As unwise as it seemed, at that moment she simply did not care to resist him.

Five

Before Nasira could prepare, Sebastian opened her blouse completely, unfastened her bra and lowered it enough to pay attention to her breasts. He knew precisely how to use his tongue to bring her to the point of no return. He used the pull of his mouth to great effect, causing her to tremble slightly. She clasped his head to follow his movements as he shifted from one breast to the other and closed her eyes to immerse herself in the feelings. In spite of the voice telling her to resist, she felt needy and powerless and completely under his control as he worked the clasp on her jeans, slid the zipper down and slipped his hand into her panties. And suddenly her no-sex vow went the way of the prairie wind.

Somewhere in the recesses of her mind, she knew she should tell him to stop and regain control. "Sebastian," was all she could manage in a winded voice that she barely recognized.

He raised his head and whispered in her ear, "Remember Tahiti."

She could barely remember her name in light of Sebastian's intemperate strokes between her thighs. Yet Sebastian seemed bent on teasing her into oblivion, slowing his sensual caressing as if he wanted to prolong the process. She wanted to hold off the release, and oh how she tried, but her body would no longer allow it.

In a matter of moments, she feared her legs would no longer support her as she bordered on a climax. As if her husband could sense her predicament, he tightened his grasp on her, yet he did not let up until the orgasm began to build and build. He simply told her in a low, sensual tone how she felt, what he wished to do to her. What he *would* do to her when the time was right.

Nasira stopped thinking, practically stopped breathing as she let the heady sensations take over. She rode the release wave after wave until it had subsided. And then came the regret and remorse.

"You promised me," she said as soon as she recovered her voice.

He redid her jeans and bra then buttoned her blouse. "I apologize but I could not help myself. You're very alluring when you're wet. In every sense of the word. And you have to take into account that I presently require nothing in return, therefore it's not exactly sex."

"Good grief, Sebastian, that is semantics. We were not playing tiddlywinks."

"Definitely not. No squidgers were involved."

A litany of choice words ran through her brain, yet she could only think of one ridiculous provincial phrase. "Bite me, Buck."

He had the gall to grin. "We will explore that after dinner, Beauty."

"You are…you are…such a—"

"Skilled lover?"

"Plank," she said, repeating the slang she had learned in London.

"I've been called worse than a jackass," he said as he took her by the shoulders, turned her around and patted her bottom. "Let's go, old girl, before Cappy labels us horse thieves and sends out the guard."

She trudged out of the creek, squeezed the water from the bottom of her blouse and twisted her hair into a braid. After they had donned their boots and Sebastian had put on his shirt, they mounted the horses and started back to the stable in silence.

"Are you angry with me, Sira?"

Was she? "I am not happy that I've been so weak."

"You're not weak, sweetheart. You're a woman and you have needs."

She thought back to Fiona's declaration earlier. "You are correct. I do have needs. I simply do not care for you using that as a distraction from our real problems."

"First, you're miffed because I haven't paid enough attention to you, as you pointed out so succinctly before you left London. Now that I am attempting to make up for lost time, you no longer want my consideration. Which is it, Sira? Hands on or hands off?"

She wanted to scream from frustration. "Ignoring me isn't only about withholding lovemaking, Sebastian."

"Forgive me for facilitating your orgasm. All three of them, if my memory serves me correctly. Should you require another, you'll have to ask."

Nasira glanced at Sebastian to see if he appeared as angry as he sounded. "I will not be asking until I am assured we are on the right path to mending our marriage."

"That is your call."

Without warning, Sebastian took off again and this time, she immediately followed. Yet the gelding was not as fast as the stallion and her husband arrived a few paces ahead of her. After Sebastian dismounted and headed into the barn, she soon followed suit and led the Gus inside.

When Sebastian did not afford her a glance, Nasira tied the gelding to the stall's railing and faced him. "I know you are upset with me, but—"

"Upset?" He loosened the girth strap, pulled the saddled off and turned toward her. "Why would I be upset when my wife seems bent on rejecting my attempts to recapture some intimacy?"

She bristled at his hypocrisy. "Now you understand how I have felt the past six months."

He set the saddle on the nearby stand a bit harder than necessary. "I see. Your actions and words are based on retribution."

Something about his observation rang true. "As I have said several times, I refuse to have my libido cloud my judgment."

He released a cynical laugh. "I do not recall any refusal when I had my hand down your pants earlier."

The comment brought about a searing heat between her thighs, causing her to shift from one leg to the other. Before she could retort, Cappy came down the stairs and when he reached the aisle, gave them both a long once-over. "Did you two not understand the nekkid swimming part?"

The heat shifted to Nasira's face. "Actually, we were wading in the water and I slipped."

"I had to rescue her from the creek's clutches," Sebastian added. "My wife can be quite clumsy at times."

Cappy sported a skeptical look as he loosened the girth strap on Gus's saddle. "In case you're hungry, the missus put a roast in the oven for the two of you. She said it should be ready in about an hour and she'll be back later to clean up."

"I can do the dishes," Nasira began, "although I would like to meet her and tell her thank you."

"Annie's a stickler for giving people their privacy, and I'm thinkin' that's exactly what you two need, so I'll tell her you'll handle the cleanup."

Nasira didn't want the man getting the wrong idea. "We truly do not require privacy, Cappy. She is welcome anytime."

"If you say so." He pulled the saddle off Gus's back and grinned. "By the way, ma'am, you missed a couple of buttons."

Too mortified to offer an explanation, Nasira turned to retreat to the house without looking back, the sound of the men's laughter following her for the next few meters.

She was so angry, she practically stomped up the path. If her husband thought he would escape her ire, he was sorely mistaken. As soon as she took a shower, she planned to confront Sebastian over his amusement at her expense. Until that point, she would simply avoid him.

"Sira, wait up."

Nasira quickened her gait in response to the directive. "I am not speaking to you."

"Actually, darling, you just did."

Infuriating man. "Go away, Sebastian."

"Not until you give me the opportunity to apologize."

"I am not in a benevolent mood."

The comment seemed to encourage Sebastian's silence, or that was what she thought until she heard, "Damn my leg."

Only then did she turn around to discover her husband bent at the waist, both palms resting on his thighs. She could leave him standing on the path in pain, or she could see about his injury.

Nasira turned around, strode to him and hovered above him. "Did you suffer a wound?"

"Only to my pride."

Then he raised his gaze to her, grinned, grabbed her around the waist and tossed her over his shoulder caveman-style. "Let me down, you brute!" she said, to no avail.

"Not until we arrive at our destination."

"I cannot believe you lied to me about your leg."

"Actually, I did have a slight twitch of momentary pain."

"I have trouble believing that. Granted, you will have several pains if you continue to carry me like a bag of grain."

"Sira, you are many things. Weighty is not one of them."

She supposed she should consider that a compliment.

Once they reached the deck, Sebastian climbed the stairs and put Nasira down, yet kept her hand clasped in his. "I beg your forgiveness for my inconsiderate laughter in the stable. However, I did defend your honor after your departure."

She folded her arms around her middle. "Was that before or after you morphed into a Neanderthal?"

"I believe that was after I beat my chest and declared you my woman."

"You are such a comedian, Sebastian."

"I am a man quite enamored of his gorgeous wife, and I do hope she will forgive me."

She wanted so badly to remain angry at him, but he possessed the power of persuasion usually reserved for practiced barristers. "You are forgiven. Can I please bathe now?"

He winked. "Do you require assistance?"

"No, I do not."

Without awaiting a reply, Nasira turned and entered the house to wash away the remnants of murky river water—and the mistake she had made by believing she could distance herself from her husband, physically and emotionally. The more she was with him, the more she realized how good the majority of their marriage had been. Worse still, she recognized how much she truly loved him.

And as she walked into the bedroom and spotted the bracelet on the bureau, the reminder of their loss, she questioned whether he would be willing to give her the one thing she wanted most from him.

Only time would tell.

Sebastian sat alone at the dining room table, staring at the familiar number splashed across his cell phone screen. He needed to answer the call but dreaded it all the same.

After one more ring, Sebastian swiped the screen and said, "Hello, Stella."

"For pity's sake, Sebastian, where are you?"

His stepmother was nothing if not direct. "Texas."

"You went after her even after I advised against it."

"Yes, but before you go off on the virtue of patience, she is my wife and I have every right to seek her out."

"Yes, you do, yet it could make matters much worse."

"We're getting along famously."

"I hope that is the case," she said skeptically.

"It is. How is Father?"

The slight hesitation had him bracing for bad news. "Actually, he's had a cheery day. He played chess with the butler this morning."

Odd that his patriarch could remember how to play a board game yet at times forgot his own son's name. "That's good. He's a tough old guy."

"Yes, but might I remind you, the last time you spoke

to the physician, he told you he's going to continue to fade away, little by little, until we won't recognize the man he used to be, and he quite possibly will not recognize us."

Sebastian didn't need to be reminded of that. "I know, Stella. That's why it's imperative I work out my problems with Nasira and return to London as soon as feasible."

"And that is why you must consider having a child as soon as possible. I would like your father to go to the hereafter knowing he has an heir."

As if Sebastian needed more pressure in the procreation department. After all, his father had been partially responsible for his reluctance to try again with Nasira and wholly responsible for Sebastian's mother's death. "There is no guarantee that will happen before his demise."

"The doctor believes he still has a few years left in him."

But would they be good years?

Sebastian looked up to see Nasira standing in the open doorway, giving him a good excuse to cut the conversation short. "I will take your request under advisement. In the meantime, I'm going to have dinner with my wife. Tell Father hello from both of us."

Stella barely had time to say goodbye before Sebastian ended the call. He pushed the phone aside and studied Nasira. Her long, silky black hair cascaded over her shoulders. She wore a pink sleeveless blouse that complemented her golden skin and white loose-fitting slacks that hid her best attributes. Not an issue. He knew exactly what the cotton fabric concealed.

"You look very pretty tonight."

She pulled back the chair across from him and sat. "Thank you. I see you've gone from cowboy to corporate billionaire. If I had known you were going to wear a suit and tie I would have donned an evening gown."

"Force of habit," he said as he shrugged out of his jacket and laid it on the seat next to him. "Better?"

"A bit more casual." She bent her elbow on the table and supported her cheek with her palm. "Did you do all this?"

"Will I score a few points if I said yes?"

"You will score points if you tell me the truth."

"Actually, the table was already set. I did remove the food from the oven."

"It smells wonderful," she said as she unfolded the white napkin and laid it in her lap, prompting Sebastian to follow suit.

"That it does."

When he reached for her plate, she waved him away. "I am quite capable of helping myself."

"Far be it for me to tread on your independence."

She took a less-than-generous helping of the roast beef and vegetables. "You have a habit of doing that."

"I do?"

"Yes, you do. I suppose I cannot fault you considering I was rather helpless when we married."

She had been the picture of innocence. "You've grown quite a bit, Sira."

"I would hope so after ten years." She took a bite

then a drink of water from the cut-crystal glass. "Evidently Annie is fond of salt."

Sebastian took a much bigger bite of the fare and found it to his liking. But he thought it best to be as agreeable as possible. "Perhaps a bit. I just spoke with Stella. She told me to give you her regards."

"How is James?"

"She said he had a good day, right after she lectured me on leaving without giving her notice."

Nasira's brown eyes widened. "You didn't tell her you were coming here?"

"I left word through the servants. It was very much a spontaneous decision."

"I am certain she was worried."

"Possibly, but she was more concerned about other issues."

"What issues?"

He was hoping she wouldn't ask. "You know Stella. She is a broken record when it comes to producing an heir."

"That is understandable, Sebastian. She knows how badly your father would like to see that happen."

He had suddenly lost his appetite. "My father has no right to dictate my future after what he did…" He refused to go there for if he did, he would have to offer an explanation.

"What did he do, Sebastian?"

He took another bite that now tasted bitter as brine. "I'd prefer not to discuss it."

Nasira wadded the napkin and tossed it on the table.

"This is exactly the reason we are having problems. Your inability to communicate drives me batty."

"It's complicated, Sira. I see no point in dredging up the past."

"Perhaps you should since it's apparently affecting our future."

He shoved back from the table and began to pace. "You are asking too much of me."

"I am only asking for honesty, Sebastian. My intent is not to cause you pain. Does this have something to do with your mother?"

He turned midstride and faced her. "It has everything do with her."

"Please, come sit and tell me about her. Surely you have good memories."

More than she would ever know, unless he finally told her. Then he could gradually move into the bad, if he dared.

He reclaimed his seat and stared at the food now growing cold on his plate. "I have no idea how to begin to tell you about Martha Ella Edwards."

Nasira set her plate aside and folded her arms atop the table. "I know you were ten when she passed, so I suppose you can begin by telling me what you do remember."

He smiled at the recollections, the special moments that he had never shared. The painful times he couldn't share, at least not now. "She was extremely devoted to my father and to me. She used to call me her little drummer boy because I had a penchant for stealing wooden spoons from the kitchen and banging them on anything stationary."

"Clearly you were destined to be in a rock band."

"I thought that too after Mother bought me a real set of drums on my eighth birthday. But of course James could not endure the noise and had the servants toss them two days later."

Nasira laid her palm on his hand, which was now resting on the tabletop. "I am so sorry, Sebastian. I know you and your father have always seemed to be at odds, but I assumed that had to do with the two of you butting horns over business like two battering rams."

If she only knew the reason behind Sebastian's well-hidden resentment. If he let down his guard, she would. "I never approved of the way he treated my mother, as if she were no more than a concubine put on this earth for his pleasure."

"How could you believe that at such a young age? Was he inappropriate in your presence?"

"No. I only learned some facts later and drew my own conclusions."

"You are going to have to be less vague in order for me to help you move past this."

"I don't need your help, Sira, or your pity."

"I would never pity you, Sebastian, but I do believe you need to have someone as a sounding board. And I would hope after ten years together you could trust me enough to fill that role."

He pondered her words a moment and realized she was probably right. He also knew that by being totally transparent, he would be inviting a measure of pain. Yet he couldn't think of one soul he trusted more than his wife, and he had done her a disservice by not revealing his secrets. Only after doing so would she understand why he could not in good conscience go forward with their plans to have a child.

"I will tell you what you believe you want to know, but I assure you it's not pretty."

"I am stronger than you think, Sebastian."

He would not debate that. At times he wondered if she possessed more strength than him. "This secret, the one no one speaks of, has to do with my mother's demise."

Nasira leaned forward and sent him a concerned look. "Please tell me and end this suspense."

He drew in a deep breath and prepared to lower the boom. "My father killed her."

Six

Nasira placed a hand over her mouth to stifle a gasp. Myriad questions whirled through her mind like a crazed carousel. "Why? How?"

Sebastian disappeared into the kitchen and returned with a tumbler half full of his favorite scotch. "Why? Because he's a selfish bastard who only cares about his desires. *How* involves… "

When he hesitated, Nasira's anxiety escalated. "Go on."

Sebastian streaked a hand over his shadowed jaw. "He knew she was ill and didn't lift a finger to help her."

She sat back, her shoulders sagging from mild relief. "I truly thought you were going to mention knives or guns or perhaps poison."

He settled back into the chair and took a sip of the

drink. "He might as well have put a gun to her head by not seeking medical attention when she clearly needed it. I knew something was wrong that morning."

Nasira realized he was perched on the precipice of deep emotional pain. "The morning she passed away?"

He shook his head. "No. The last morning I saw her alive." He stared at some unknown focal point, as if he had mentally returned to that day, before he spoke again. "I had been on summer break from boarding school and it was time for me to return. Of course, I happened to be running late when Mother summoned me into her quarters. She was propped up in bed and she looked very pale. She told me she loved me and hugged me as if she didn't want to let me go. As if she knew it would be the final time. And I wrenched out of her grasp because I knew if I didn't leave at that moment, I would earn my father's wrath for making the driver wait. I never expressed my love for her, and I have lived with that regret for almost three decades."

Her heart ached for him. "You were only a child, Sebastian. You could not have foreseen the future."

He released a weary sigh. "Perhaps, and I would not have predicted what I would learn when I was called into the headmaster's office two days later. My father did not bother to personally retrieve me. He sent one of the bloody staff members to tell me my mother was dead. He did not shed one tear at the wake. Worse still, he admonished me for crying."

Nasira had always been fond of her father-in-law, who seemed nothing at all like the tyrant Sebastian had described. "I am stunned at his behavior. James has always treated me with kindness and affection."

Sebastian leveled his gaze on her. "You've never disappointed him, and I have never lived up to his standards."

"You are a brilliant businessman. I cannot imagine he would hand over the company to you if he did not truly believe that."

"He did so because he had no choice since I failed to produce an heir. I refuse to relinquish that control to him."

Had this been the reason behind his reluctance to have another child? A vendetta against an unfeeling patriarch?

She would not know the reason behind his resistance unless she asked, yet she sensed this might not be the time or place to do so. She did have another important question. "I understand James treated you poorly, but do you truly believe he neglected your mother's health issues? I've heard the staff speaking highly of their relationship."

Sebastian tightened his grip on the glass in his hand. "I heard the servants discussing a few details when they didn't realize I was eavesdropping. As we both know, they are the eyes and ears of the household."

"And did you confront your father over this idle chit-chat?"

He pushed the scotch aside as if it held no appeal. "At ten years old, I didn't dare try. Since that time, he has never been one to discuss personal affairs. Had I inquired, he would have dismissed me, as he did whenever I asked anything about my mother."

Her husband had based his conclusions on rumors, not fact, and that bothered Nasira. "Have you considered talking to Stella to verify what you heard all those years ago?"

"Yes, and she stated she wasn't at liberty to provide the details. Then she advised me to stop living in the past."

Stella's reluctance to clear the air was unacceptable as far as Nasira was concerned, albeit an indication of her devotion to James. But she did not feel she had the right to intervene…yet. Right now, she was thankful Sebastian had begun to open up for the first time during their union. She did not want to push her luck by applying too much pressure. "I am really very sorry about what you've endured, Sebastian. I wish there was more I could do or say to ease your distress."

"I'm not distressed," he said as he pushed back from the table and stood. "But there is something you could do."

She could only imagine what he had in mind. "Yes?"

"Accompany me to the festival downtown."

The request totally took her by surprise. "What festival?"

"I'm not certain. I believe it involves street vendors and a carnival. I thought it might be a good way to soak in the culture."

Quite possibly a good way to temporarily erase the past, Nasira thought. Understandable he would want to do that, and this time she would allow it. Still, she certainly would not refuse the opportunity to spend some quality time with her husband. She came to her feet and attempted a smile. "That sounds wonderful. I suppose I should change."

He stood, rounded the table and then touched her face. "You're a beautiful, remarkable woman, Sira. Never think you should change for me."

The sheer emotion in his eyes, the absolute sincerity in his voice, sent Nasira's spirits soaring. Perhaps they had reached a turning point, the prospect of a new beginning. Yet she acknowledged they would not obtain that goal until her husband was willing to tell her the unabridged truth.

Sebastian had avoided the whole truth like a practiced coward. He hadn't told his wife that rejecting parenthood had more to do with his fear for her safety and not his determination to avoid his father's interference. Someday he would reveal the bitter details behind his mother's death, but right now he wanted to leave the past behind and concentrate on the present.

With that in mind, he took Nasira's hand into his as they strolled the streets of Royal crowded with cowboys and kids, two of whom sprinted past them on the sidewalk.

"This place is certainly full of children," he said. "I'd expect to see the Pied Piper coming around the corner at any moment."

Nasira sent him a frown. "This is a festival, Sebastian. What else would you expect?"

Better manners. "True. The town appears to treat

procreation as a sport as revered as their Friday night Texas football."

As they continued on, one particular display caught his curiosity and caused him to pause. "What in the bloody hell is cow patty bingo?"

Nasira's gaze traveled to the group gathered around the exhibition. "Well, it clearly involves a cow and some sort of game board and… I believe it is best we keep walking."

He couldn't contain his laughter. "I could not agree more."

They continued on past several artisans with tables full of their wares. As they approached one fresh-faced young woman with baskets of multicolored flowers, Sebastian halted, released his wife's hand and selected a single red rose. "How much is this?"

"Two dollars," the blonde replied. "Or six for ten dollars."

"One will do." He withdrew his wallet from his rear pocket and pulled out a twenty-dollar bill. "Here you go. Keep the proceeds."

The teen appeared awestruck. "Thanks bunches. It's for a good cause."

"What cause would that be?"

"A new football stadium."

He started to argue that an orphanage would constitute a better cause, but thought better of it. "Best of luck on your venture," he said, then turned to Nasira. "For my lovely bride."

She took the rose and smiled as if he had offered the

moon and stars, not a simple posy. "To what do I owe this wonderful gift?"

He kissed her cheek. "For agreeing to wed the likes of me."

"Most of the time, I happen to like being wed to the likes of you."

She might rescind her half compliment if she knew of the lies he still harbored. "Shall we take our chances on the games up ahead?"

"As long as they do not involve cow patties."

"I believe they are games of skill involving tossing rings."

She hooked her arm through his. "Then by all means, let us test your skills."

Unable to help himself, Sebastian leaned over and whispered, "I'm definitely up for testing all my skills when we return to the ranch."

He expected his spouse to deliver a derisive glare over the innuendo. Instead, he received a surprisingly sultry look. "That is altogether possible if you are a good boy tonight."

Perhaps Rafe had been correct—simple gestures could pay off in spades.

When they traveled on toward the brightly-lit gaming booths, Sebastian spotted a young boy dressed in jeans and miniature cowboy boots, turning in circles in the middle of the sidewalk, swiping the tears furiously from his face. A group of boisterous teens approached him, seemingly oblivious to the distressed child.

Sensing disaster, Sebastian immediately removed Nasira's hand from his arm, swept the boy up and away from the danger of getting run over by unconcerned ad-olescents, then set him down near a street light, away from the crowd. "Are you lost, young man?"

He turned his misty brown eyes on him and sniffed. "My dad told me not to talk to strangers."

Sebastian took a step back so the boy wouldn't feel threatened. "That is banner advice under normal cir-cumstances. I only want to help you locate your parents and return you safely to them."

The child seemed to mull that over a minute before he spoke again. "A girl was chasing me and I lost my dad."

"What does your father look like?" Nasira asked from behind Sebastian.

When the boy turned his gaze on Nasira, he seemed to relax and smiled as if he were quite smitten. "He's got on a cowboy hat and boots and jeans and I think a blue shirt. Where'd you get it?" he asked, looking at the rose.

"Sebastian gave it to me." She pointed behind her. "We bought it at a booth not far from here."

"I might want to get one of those for my..." He lowered his eyes and kicked a pebble into the street. "Mom."

After exchanging a knowing look with Sebastian, Nasira offered him the flower. "I am certain my hus-band would not mind if you give her this one."

"Not at all." He did mind that the description of the missing parent didn't provide much hope of immedi-ately finding him. "Is your father tall like me?"

He nodded. "Uh huh. But he doesn't talk funny like you. Are you from Dallas?"

Nasira laughed. "We are from London, far across the ocean."

The child's expression brightened. "We learned about that place in school. I'm in the second grade and I like to ride horses and... Dad!"

Clutching the rose, the boy ran straight into the arms of a man sporting a suspicious look as he headed toward them. As soon as he arrived, Sebastian thought it best to offer an explanation before the presumed father jumped to the wrong conclusion. "We found your son quite distressed and lost. It seems you've arrived just in the nick of time."

"Looks that way," the cowboy said as he eyed the flower before regarding his child. "You know better than to run off without me, Brady. Your mother's going to skin my hide for not watching you better."

"I didn't mean to do it," Brady said. "Angie was chasing me and I ran too far, I guess. And then this man picked me up before I got run over by kids and the lady gave me her flower so I could give it to Mom."

"Mom, huh?" the father asked.

Brady shrugged and muttered, "Maybe Angie," then turned his attention back to Nasira and Sebastian. "They're from London. Do you know about London, Dad?"

"Yep, I do," he replied. "I also know that I told you to stay away from people you don't know."

Sebastian offered his hand for a shake in an effort to reassure the man. "I'm Sebastian Edwards."

The cowboy hesitantly accepted the gesture. "I'm Gavin McNeal, former sheriff."

No wonder he had looked at Sebastian as if he were a deviant. "You're no longer in law enforcement?"

His features went from rock hard to only slightly stony. "I gave that up to spend more time with this kiddo, and the one we have on the way. I'm a full-time rancher now, although I do pull deputy duty now and again if the department's shorthanded."

A clear message to Sebastian the cowboy could still hold his own around unwelcome strangers. "I'm certain your service to the community is very much appreciated. And to put your mind at ease, Brady did mention he wasn't allowed to talk to strangers. Of course, I assure you our intentions were perfectly honorable."

"Yes, they were." Nasira moved to Sebastian's side. "However, my husband has forgotten his manners as he has failed to introduce me."

That could be a rather large strike against him. "My apologies. This is my wife, Nasira."

"I am Rafiq bin Saleed's sister," Nasira added. "You might know him."

"Only by reputation," Gavin said. "I did hear something about some folks from England staying at the Shakirs' place, so I assume that's you. My ranch isn't too far from there and my wife, Valerie, and Fiona are fairly good friends."

Apparently news traveled at warp speed in this dusty Texas town. "We're only going to be here for a few weeks. Do you have any suggestions on sights we should see while we're here?"

"You should have dinner at the Texas Cattleman's Club," he said. "And when you do, be sure to check out the statue of Jessamine Golden. That's my wife's great-great-grandmother."

"I have seen the statue," Nasira said. "But I am sure my husband will find it quite interesting."

Brady began tugging on his father's hand to garner his attention. "Can we go ride the roller coaster now?"

"Sure thing, bud, as soon as I find your mama, who was hanging out near the arts and crafts last time I looked." Gavin regarded them again. "Nice to meet you folks, and thanks for corralling the kid. What do you say to Mr. and Mrs. Edwards, Brady?"

"Thank you for getting me not lost and for giving me the flower."

"You are quite welcome," Sebastian said.

"Goodbye, Brady," Nasira added. "I hope you have a wonderful time this evening, and I am certain Angie will appreciate the rose."

Gavin took Brady's hand and touched the brim of his hat. "Have a good night, folks."

Watching father and son walked away, Sebastian experienced a good deal of regret as he remembered a time in the distant past when he'd had the same relationship with his own father. The relationship that at one time he'd hoped to have with his own son, until he realized the lack of wisdom in that. He was amused as Brady started chattering about the funny-talking man being a superhero, and did they have those in London?

The comment caused Sebastian to chuckle. "From shipping magnate to superhero. Quite a leap."

Nasira tucked her arm into his again as they started

down the sidewalk. "I would thoroughly disagree. You are a natural-born rescuer."

He frowned. "I wouldn't go that far."

She tipped her head against his shoulder. "I would. In a sense you rescued me."

He had never looked at his marriage offer in that way, but he understood why she might. "Perhaps I saved you from a life of misery with a forced marriage to a man chosen for you, but you would have found a way out of the predicament without my assistance."

"I suppose that is possible," she said. "But I am glad that I met you that night at the gala."

"I'm grateful you gave me a second glance considering all those potential suitors surrounding you."

"Yes, but not one offered to whisk me away in their Bentley."

They exchanged a smile and walked on in silence, but one question nagged at Sebastian. "Have you enjoyed our life together, Sira?"

She paused a moment before answering. "We have had wonderful adventures and amazing travel. You have introduced me to many new experiences."

"No regrets?"

"Only one."

"What would that be?" he asked though he already knew the answer.

"We have no children."

He had strolled right into that one. "I understand you're still mourning the loss, yet I can't understand why you would want to risk your health after you had such a difficult pregnancy."

She stopped and faced him. "Life is not without risk, Sebastian. And at times risk comes with precious rewards."

He didn't know how to answer to satisfy her needs. He didn't know if he would ever want to enter that territory again. "Speaking of risks, would you care to climb on that giant Ferris wheel and take it for a spin?"

Nasira glanced over her shoulder then regarded him with a frown. "You know I am afraid of heights."

"You have no need to be afraid while in the presence of a superhero."

She smiled. "This is true. If I agree, will you promise to hold on to me?"

"You may count on my undivided attention."

"Then yes, I will join you on that contraption, and hope I do live long enough to regret it."

Sebastian led Nasira to the line of people awaiting their turn on the ride. When their time came, he approached the elderly gentleman in charge of the ride and withdrew his wallet. "How much, kind sir?"

"Three tickets."

Tickets? "I wasn't aware we needed those." He pulled a twenty out of his pocket. "Will this do?"

"I don't make change, mister."

"No change necessary."

The attendant grinned, displaying a remarkable lack of teeth. "I guess it'll do at that."

"Amazing how money opens doors," Sebastian said as they climbed into the car.

Nasira grabbed the railing and sat, looking somewhat fearful. "Amazing how rickety this ride seems."

He lowered next to her and wrapped his arm around her shoulder. "Just hold tight to your knight."

She surprised him with a soft kiss. "Happily, kind sir."

When the wheel began to move, sending them up toward the night sky, Nasira closed her eyes and tensed against him. He held her tighter, stroked her arm and rested his lips against her temple. He experienced such a fierce need to keep her sheltered from harm, and a secret fear that he could not be the man she would want in the future if he couldn't give her the child she desired.

But tonight, he could give her all his consideration and forget the chasm that still existed between them.

When they reached the top, the ride jolted to a stop, causing the car to slightly sway and his wife to clutch his thigh in a death grip. Stifling a wince, Sebastian lifted her hand and kissed her palm. "Open your eyes, sweetheart."

"Must I?"

"No, but you're missing an extraordinary view."

After a few seconds ticked off, she finally lifted her lids and looked around. "I must admit, all the lights are beautiful. They remind me of our holiday together two years ago."

While she must have been struck by sentimentality, he was hit by some rather sexual memories. "Ah, yes. Rome. We barely left the room."

"That is not true. We had several meals on the veranda."

He brushed a kiss across her lips. "That's not all we did on that veranda."

Her smile arrived slowly. "True. You have always been quite devilish when we travel."

"And you are always quite willing to dance with the devil."

"Evidently I cannot resist your charms."

He pushed her hair away from her shoulder. "Would you be willing to dance with me later tonight?"

Without giving him a verbal response, Nasira wrapped her hand around his nape and pulled his mouth to hers, taking Sebastian by surprise. As the ride began to move again, picking up speed, they continued to kiss as if they were youngsters in the throes of first love. But they weren't youngsters. They were husband and wife in the midst of a troubled marriage, yet he felt as if this could be the path to healing.

When the ride bumped to a stop, they finally ended the kiss only to be met by applause, whistles and cat-calls. Sebastian helped Nasira out of the car and they rushed away, then paused and shared in a few laughs.

Nasira wrapped her arms around his waist. "I do believe you have ruined my reputation."

He pressed a kiss on her forehead. "If you agree to return to the ranch now, I will endeavor to ruin it more."

She studied his eyes for a few moments, as if searching for something unknown there. "Sebastian, I...."

"What, sweetheart?"

"I think that is a marvelous idea."

Saying what she had wanted to say would have been a horrible idea.

Still, Nasira had come very close to voicing an emotion she had never admitted to him, or to herself, during their decade together. She loved him, and most likely had for many years. Love had not been a goal in their marriage. A marriage based on convenience and mutual need. Yet somehow she had introduced the emotion into the union when she had allowed Sebastian into her life, and into her heart.

That did not change the fact that her husband might not feel more than fondness for her. That did not negate that they wanted to journey down different paths and if he had his way, their future would not include having a child.

Yet as she rode back to the ranch, her hand resting lightly in Sebastian's, she did not care about compromise or doubts. She only wanted to enjoy this night with her husband in the event these memorable moments might be their last.

She leaned back against the headrest and sighed. "I realized something tonight that I have never considered before."

"You are not so afraid of heights?"

"No. I enjoy country living."

"That's why we have the country home in Bath to escape the hectic pace in London proper."

"I know, yet I feel a certain freedom here. It does sound odd, I suppose."

He pulled beneath the portico and shut off the ignition. "This place does afford quite a bit of privacy, which reminds me." He reached into the back of the car, retrieved a silver bag full of pink tissue and handed it to her.

"What is this?"

"Open it and you'll see."

She rummaged around and withdrew a bathing suit that was little more than a labyrinth of turquoise strings. "I have never flown a kite in the dark."

"Very amusing. We both need to relax, and what better way to do that than to swim."

"Isn't it too cool to swim?"

"The spa and pool are both heated."

She could imagine they would generate their own heat, yet she worried about the privacy issue. "I would still have to get out of the spa or pool." She shook the swimsuit at him. "This barely covers anything at all. What if someone happens upon us?"

"You have a robe, do you not?"

"Yes."

"Besides, you have a remarkable body. Why not show it off?"

"I do not think it is wise to show off my body this much when two other people reside on the property."

"Two people who've been instructed to give us complete solitude."

He had supported his arguments much too well, drat him. "All right. I will join you in a swim." She pointed at him. "But only for a swim. Heaven knows I wouldn't want to be caught doing anything else."

He gave her a winning grin, the one that had always won her over. Patently sensual, and slightly wicked. "Yes, dear. Only a swim."

As much as she would like to trust him, Nasira was not sure she should. Trouble was, could she trust herself?

Seven

The moment Nasira stepped onto the deck and slipped off the robe, swimming was the last thing on Sebastian's mind. The suit fit her to perfection, from the low cut of the bodice to the bottoms secured by two ribbons at her rounded hips that accentuated her long torso. Her hair flowed freely, straight and sleek, begging for his touch. When he honed in on the diamond hoop at her navel, her attempt at rebellion during her brief university days, he had fond memories of playing with the bauble with his tongue…as well as other more intimate places now covered by a small fabric triangle. That alone caused him to move down one stair to conceal the result of his sinful thoughts.

He had to remember to take it slowly, let the evening progress with no expectations in terms of lovemaking.

He needed to concentrate on making his wife feel appreciated and respected, even if it meant using his tongue solely to talk for the time being.

Unfortunately his randy libido seemed to be speaking much louder than his honor. He would simply have to quiet the urges and not appear as impatient as a lustful schoolboy.

Down, Henry.

When Nasira stuck her toe in the deep end of the pool to test the water, even that seemed overtly sexy to Sebastian. And when she executed a perfect dive, surfaced not far from him and slicked her hair back from her gorgeous face, he gritted his teeth to keep from going after her like a lion and a gazelle.

"Bravo," he said as she waded toward him. "You're a regular little mermaid."

She lifted her hair to secure the tie at her neck. "I almost had equipment failure when I dove in. Could you have not found something a bit more modest?"

At the moment he realized that might have worked better in light of his burgeoning erection. But then again, probably not. She could be wearing a heavy trench coat and he would still want her, especially if she were nude beneath it. He would like very much for her to be nude beneath him. Or perhaps on top of him. Standing up against the deck would also work to his satisfaction…

"Have you been rendered mute, Sebastian?"

For the most part, yes. "I'm sorry. Did you ask me something?"

"Never mind." She joined him on the step, keeping

a relatively safe distance between them. "The house-keeper turned down my bed. Did you notice if she is still here?"

No, but he did notice that if the bikini were a bit lower, he could possibly see her nipples. "I'm almost certain she performed those tasks while we were away."

Sira leaned forward, causing the top to gape and allowing him the view again. "It would probably behoove us to check."

"That might be breast." *Dammit.* "I mean *best.*"

She sent him a mock scolding look. "I have barely been in here five minutes and you are already misbehaving."

Guilty. "It was only a verbal faux pas, Sira."

"Then take care to mind your mouth."

And he did…by planting it on her mouth, disregarding his earlier cautions about going slowly. He expected she might shove him away, or perhaps push him into the water, yet she joined in as if she needed this as badly as he did.

After they parted, she tipped her head against his forehead. "I hate that I am so helpless around you."

He lifted her chin and forced her to look at him. "You are not helpless in the least, and you are not an innocent. You are as drawn to the devil in me as I am the vixen in you."

"So you think."

"So I know."

He loosened the ties at her neck but paused before he went further. "Tell me you do not want me and I'll stop."

"I…cannot."

Which was all the encouragement Sebastian needed to continue. He removed her top, tossed it aside and then toyed with the band riding low on her hips. "Stop now?"

She released a ragged sigh. "No."

After he slid her bottoms away and draped them on the chrome railing, he led her into waist-deep water and kissed her, his hands roving over her breasts. She soon pulled away, moved back and smiled. "The vixen says take off your bathing suit."

"Far be it for me to argue with her," he said as he shoved down his trunks, stepped out of them with effort, and hurled them onto the deck.

She crooked her finger at him. "Come here, devil."

They came together in another blast of heat, of that passion they'd known from the beginning. She scraped her nails down his back, while he attacked her neck with kisses and brought her legs up around his waist. It would be so easy to take her here, take her now, yet the nagging concerns over pregnancy prevented him from doing so. He should have brought the blasted condoms with him.

"Do it," she whispered with desperation as she reached beneath the water, took his erection in hand, and guided it inside her.

Driven by pure lust and need, he thrust into her, twice, before he gathered every ounce of strength and pulled out. "The bedroom," he managed around his labored respiration.

She looked at him and blinked twice. "Why?"

"More privacy." A lame excuse but the only one he could provide without completely destroying the mood.

"All right," she said as she lowered to her feet. "But hurry."

That request he could categorically fulfill, and he did as he took her by the hand and led her to the chaise on the pool deck. They wrapped up in the towels he'd brought, periodically kissing and intimately touching as they headed into the house. Once they reached the corridor leading to the guest suite, he paused and backed her against the wall immediately outside the door to his quarters.

He wanted her to remember this, to know how badly he wanted her, to make her want him as much. He parted the towel and suckled her breasts, first one, then the other, before sliding his lips down her torso.

Then he went to his knees, nudged her legs apart and sent his mouth on a mission between her thighs. He used his tongue to divide her warm flesh, tracing circles around and around that intimate spot, intent on driving her wild.

She bowed over him, running her hands over his scalp, her breaths coming in short pants. She dug her nails into his back so deeply, he thought she might have drawn blood. He didn't care. Giving her pleasure was well worth the pain.

"Sebastian." His name came out of her mouth in a harsh whisper as he stroked her with his tongue softly, then harder as he covered her completely with his mouth and suckled that sweet spot.

Her legs began to tremble and a low, sexual sound filtered out of her as she began to orgasm. He didn't let up until he had ridden out every pulse of the climax, then he kissed his way back up her beautiful body.

She reached for him again and demanded, "Now."

"Not yet," he said as he clasped her wrist to still her hand. Otherwise the act would be over in short order.

Without protesting, Nasira followed him into his bedroom. While she turned down the comforter, he opened the nightstand drawer and retrieved the silver packets. He turned and found her stretched out on her back on the bed, her damp hair a sexy, tangled mess, her knees bent in preparation for him. Yet when she spied the condoms in his grasp, she suddenly sat up on the edge of the mattress and lowered her eyes.

After laying the packets on the side table, he claimed the space beside her and rested a hand on her bare leg. "I realize this isn't what you want, but under the circumstance, it's a necessity."

Her gaze snapped to his, the haze of desire completely gone. "Is it?"

"We still have much to discuss in regard to that issue, by your own admission."

She pushed her hair back from her face. "Yes, you're right, but the reminder of our impasse took me aback for a moment. I suppose I simply wanted to forget our dilemma this evening. I wish you could have held off with the condoms a bit longer."

Frustration brought him to his feet to face her. "This wouldn't have been a bloody issue if you'd started taking the pill again."

"As I've said, I had no reason to do that when you were so bent on ignoring me." She pinched the bridge of her nose and momentarily closed her eyes. "I am so angry."

"At me?"

"At myself. I have walked into the same trap, succumbing to your charisma and allowing you to lead me away from our problems."

Now he was angry. "I did nothing of the sort. We are husband and wife and we should thank our lucky stars we still want each other so fiercely after ten years of marriage."

She let loose with a cynical laugh. "Of course you would see it that way. But sex is not a cure-all for serious marital problems."

If she only realized that was the only way he knew how to communicate his true feelings for her. The right words had never come easily for him. Neither had acknowledging his emotions. "Why can you not be happy with what we have? Why do you see the need to change everything?"

She pulled the sheet up to cover herself. "Because we cannot be truly happy unless we fix what is broken. Only until you open up to me completely can we move past our problems."

He knew where she was going, and he didn't want to bloody go there. "I've told you more about my mother's death than I've ever told another soul."

"Yet you have not told me everything, Sebastian. Aside from your father's careless disregard and your guilt over your last moments with your mother, there is something else keeping you from committing to fatherhood."

He clenched his jaw against the litany of curses threatening to spill out. "You have no idea what I went through."

She stood and leveled her gaze on him. "Then tell me all of it. Make me understand."

He didn't dare. "I am going to take a shower."

He turned to retire to the bath, only to have her call him back. "When will you stop running away, Sebastian?" she asked. "When it is too late for us?"

The words impaled him like a knife to his heart. "You're asking too much of me tonight, Sira. If it's too difficult for you to be intimate with me, then by all means, retire to your blessed bed and I'll stay in mine alone. If you happen to change your mind, then it will be up to you to come to me. In the meantime, I'll not bother you again."

And this time, he vowed to stay true to his word.

He had not spoken to her for two days. In fact, Nasira had barely seen her husband except in passing. He had spent much of his time in his quarters, sequestered away with his laptop.

Today that would come to an end, if she had any say in the matter. She had given him a wide berth to think about what she had said, but they had come to a crossroads. His time was up.

She opened the door to his bedroom without knocking, only to find him packing. A blinding fear overcame her, then resignation that perhaps she had pushed him too hard.

He afforded her only a glance while he placed a suit in the garment bag without speaking.

"Are you returning to London?" she asked, expecting an affirmative answer.

"No. I'm going to Dallas," he said, shattering her expectations, and filling her with relief.

She moved closer to the bed, but not too close. "Why Dallas?"

He dropped a few toiletries into a small carry-on bag. "I've managed to secure an invitation to an importers conference."

She folded her arms around her middle. "How long do you intend to be gone?"

He zipped the case and placed it on a bench at the end of the footboard. "I'll return tomorrow afternoon."

"Did it occur to you to invite me along?"

He sent her a sideways glance. "You'd be bored."

"I have attended these functions with you before."

He zipped the garment bag and turned. "Yes, you have, but that was before I knew you considered me a closed-off bastard who runs at the first sign of trouble."

"You ran from me the other night. You ran after I lost the baby."

He dropped onto the edge of the mattress and forked his hands through his hair. "Perhaps you're right."

It was an admission she thought she would never hear. She sat down beside him on the bed. "I am not willing to give up on us yet, Sebastian. I would like to accompany you on this trip and we will go from there."

"Well, I've always enjoyed having a beautiful wife at my side."

That ruffled her feminine feathers. "I do not want to go as your arm ornament. I want to be there as your equal. You have never viewed me as that."

He appeared extremely confused. "Where is this coming from?"

"Well, if we want to sincerely work on our marriage, then I think it's best to be honest. Many times I have asked about the company, and you brushed me off."

"I never thought you were interested in that part of my life."

"It should be part of my life as well. After all, my father was just as immersed in the shipping world. I might not have finished my degree, but I observed all aspects of the operation. I possibly know as much about it as you do."

Now Sebastian looked skeptical. "You mean that riveting world of routes, imports and exports, and shipping containers?"

"Yes, and the importance of making connections. I am quite capable of doing that. In fact, I'll wager I will make at least two this evening if I go with you."

"I've always enjoyed a good wager. And if you succeed, I will give you whatever you desire."

"Anything?"

"Within reason."

That probably eliminated her request for a child. "And if I do not succeed?"

"I will only ask that you be patient with me. I'm not good at all this sharing-my-feelings rubbish."

An odd facet of their relationship suddenly struck

Nasira. "Do you realize that up until six months ago, we rarely ever argued?"

He seemed to mull that over for a minute. "You are absolutely right. Perhaps that is because you are perfect."

He sounded strangely sincere. "Of course that is a fallacy."

"Not to me."

"Sebastian, I know I have some habits that must drive you batty."

He rubbed his chin. "It is rather disconcerting when you rearrange my bureau drawers."

"Guilty as charged. Can you not do better than that?"

"You laugh at all my randy jokes."

"How is that an imperfection?"

"Because no one else bothers. That possibly indicates a severe lack of judgment, or perhaps bad taste."

That made her smile. "What else?"

"You bring me a drink when I'm harried after a long day."

"Again, I do not see the problem with that."

"Perhaps I prefer to fetch my own drink."

"Do you?"

He grinned. "No. The truth of the matter is, Sira, nothing you do drives me to complete distraction. Actually, that's not the truth. I'm very distracted when you walk into the room, wearing nothing but a smile, and when you wake up beside me with your hair tousled and a sleepy look on that gorgeous face. You distracted me the other night from my goal."

"Yes, I realized I ruined that goal, yet you have to

know that was not my intent. I feel horrible we did not make love."

He took her hand in his. "I meant my goal to convince you I care beyond making love to you. I want another opportunity to prove that."

"I want that as well." And she did. "And I truly want to go with you to Dallas."

"All right, as long as you understand I only have a one-bedroom suite with a king-size bed. Of course, I suppose I could see if they have another room for you."

She shook her head. "That isn't necessary."

Looking extremely pleased, he patted her thigh and stood. "The jet is waiting so you should pack. Do you have a cocktail dress for the reception?"

She came to her feet and frowned. "Do birds fly?"

He softly touched her face. "Yes, they do, and I look forward to watching you fly tonight."

But Nasira feared that by hanging on to the marriage, she might eventually fall.

Sebastian spotted her standing across the crowded room. She wore a formfitting sleeveless black silk gown with matching heels, her wrists bedecked with diamond bracelets and her sleek hair flowing down her back. Her slender hands moved gracefully as she spoke with an older gentleman who appeared completely enthralled by the conversation, and her.

Sebastian couldn't recall the last time Nasira looked so very beautiful. Correction. He could. The first night he'd seen her at an event much like the one tonight. Also on their wedding day when she had been dressed in white satin and looked like the exotic princess she was, albeit a somewhat wary princess due to their spontaneous decision to marry. Perhaps he had rescued her that day from the clutches of her father's idea of a suitable spouse, but she had saved him from a life of loneliness.

"That's one looker right there."

Sebastian turned to his right to find a portly man with thinning hair clutching a martini and staring at Nasira with lust. "That happens to be my wife."

"I know," the miscreant said. "I just spent the last thirty minutes listening to her singing your praises. By the way, I'm Milt Appleton with M.A. Imports."

Sebastian downed the rest of his scotch then eyed the man's offered hand and reluctantly shook it. "Pleasure, I'm sure." Or not.

"Anyway," Milt said. "I'm looking for a shipping company that can handle my European routes. Your girl convinced me I should consider going with you." He pulled a business card from the inside of his coat pocket. "Here's my information. Give me a shout in the next day or two."

Sebastian took the card and pocketed it. "I will be in touch soon."

Milt pointed at Nasira and narrowed his eyes. "And take care of that one. She's one in a million."

Sebastian had begun to realize the absolute accuracy of that statement. She was graceful, intelligent, resolute and reliable to a fault. She had always been there when he needed her, and he had repaid her by not being there when she had needed him. Now that he finally got it, he had to figure out what to do about it. One idea came to mind, a simple gesture that would demonstrate how much she meant to him, even if he felt he could not give her the child she still desired.

On that thought, he crossed the massive room and came to her side. "I lost track of you for a moment, darling."

She presented a smile. "I have been conversing with this lovely gentleman. Sebastian, this is Mr. Walker. Mr. Walker, my husband, Sebastian Edwards, owner and CEO of the shipping company I mentioned. Darling, Mr. Walker is quite interested in the services you have to offer."

At least this one didn't seem to be interested in the services his wife could provide. "A pleasure to meet you, Mr. Walker," he said as he stuck out his hand.

"The pleasure is all mine," the man replied. "I've given my information to your wife and we'll discuss the particulars later. Speaking of wives, I should find mine. Have a good evening, you two."

After the aged businessman hobbled away, Sebastian slid his arm around Nasira's waist. "Clearly I have lost our two-contacts wager since I was recently confronted by your first contact, the lecherous Milt."

"He's harmless," Nasira said.

"And flirtatious, I gather."

"Slightly, yet nothing I could not handle."

Sebastian glanced to his right. "Would you care to dance?"

She looked at him as if he had lost all reason. "This is not a cotillion, Sebastian. It's a cocktail party."

"I hear music coming through the speakers and I believe I spy a dance floor."

She followed his gaze toward the bar before bringing her attention back to him. "Yes, that seems to be a dance floor. With no one using it."

He clasped her hand. "Then perhaps it's time to get this dance party started." When she began to protest, he pressed her lips with a fingertip. "Let's be bold for a change. Let's show them the portrait of two people who do not give a tinker's damn what anyone thinks."

Her grin came out of hiding. "Let's."

After Sebastian guided her onto the modest wooden dance floor, Nasira walked into his arms. Yet when she noticed several people staring, she immediately went rigid.

"Relax," Sebastian whispered.

"How can I when we are making a spectacle of ourselves?"

"If anyone takes exception, it's only because they're jealous."

She reared back and leveled her gaze on him. "Jealous of two people who are clearly wacko?"

"Jealous of me for having such a remarkable wife. Jealous of you because you are the most beautiful woman in the room. In the world, in my opinion."

"If you put it that way…"

Deciding to ignore the attention, Nasira rested her cheek against Sebastian's shoulder and swayed in time to the soft sounds of a bluesy instrumental. She relished the feel of his strong arms holding her close, the aromatic scent of his cologne, his skill. She had learned that he was a great dancer the first night they had met, when he had asked her to dance at the gala, much to her father's chagrin, whose cautions had gone unheeded. When she took inventory of her life and the decision she had made, only one regret remained. A dream she might have to disregard to keep her marriage intact.

Sebastian suddenly stopped moving and only then did she realize the music had stopped, and they were now surrounded by several other couples who had taken to the floor.

Her husband presented a proud smile. "See? We have started a trend."

She laughed with pure joy. "Yes, we have."

"Shall we dance again, fair lady?"

She had something else in mind. "Actually, unless you care to stay, I would rather return to our room."

He made a show of checking his watch. "It's still early. We could have a late dinner."

Obviously he did not approve of her plan for some unknown reason. "I have had enough appetizers to last for several days."

"I have not."

"Room service is still available."

"True. I will gladly accompany you to our quarters, as long as this does not entail heavy conversation."

That would come later. Much later. "Agreed."

Reclaiming her hand, Sebastian led her through the lobby to the glass elevator that would take them to the executive floor. They entered the deserted car and took in the plethora of city lights dotting the Dallas skyline as they ascended. Unfortunately the view left Nasira breathless, and not in a welcome way.

As if he sensed her trepidation, Sebastian wrapped his arms around her from behind and held her close. "I'm right here, sweetheart."

She leaned back against him. "I know, and admittedly it is a nice panorama."

He brushed her hair aside and kissed her cheek. "At least this time you're keeping your eyes open to enjoy it."

"You take good care of me, Sebastian."

"You deserve it, Sira. You deserve everything your heart desires."

If only he could agree to give her the most important of her heart's desires. Nevertheless, she wanted to spend the evening in a lighthearted mood with no old recriminations to intrude on their time together. She also intended to bask in the glory of winning the wager about making connections at tonight's party, and if good fortune prevailed, convince him to allow her to take an active role in the business. If she could not immediately become a mother, she could certainly establish a career beyond charity work.

Those plans began to fully form as they entered the penthouse suite a few moments later. She immediately crossed the suite and walked into the bedroom with Sebastian trailing behind her. Once there, she removed her jewelry then fished through her pocket and withdrew the best part of her plan.

She turned to find her husband seated in the club chair next to the sliding glass doors leading to the veranda, his hands draped on the chair arms as if he were the king of the castle.

She approached and offered him a handful of business cards. "Here are a few more contacts."

He took the stack and looked through them before regarding her again. "You are amazing."

She smiled. "Yes. Yes I am."

He set the cards aside and returned her smile. "I'm glad you have finally come to that conclusion."

She perched on the edge of the mattress opposite him. "I am teasing. I simply struck up a few conversations and that led to mentioning the company and what we have to offer."

"We?"

She prepared to plead her case. "Yes. I assume that since I made the effort, I should be rewarded with a measure of involvement. Also, three of the contacts are women and it would only be natural that I would be the best candidate to communicate with them. Of course, I would have to be allowed access to the contracts and the shipping routes…"

He effectively cut off her thoughts when he reached over, clasped her arms, pulled her up and brought her into his lap. "You have done a superb job," he began. "And you definitely deserve to be rewarded."

She could not resist rolling her eyes. "Exactly what do you have in mind?"

He pressed a kiss on her cheek and suddenly looked very serious. "I want to give you what you want most."

She clung to hope and prepared to be disappointed.

"You know what I want most, yet you have been adamant about not giving it to me."

"I've had a change of heart."

Did she dare utter the word? No. She had learned not to assume. "Please end the suspense and say it."

"I want to give you a child."

This almost seemed too good to be true. "Are you certain?"

"Yes. As long as we adopt."

Eight

In a matter of moments, Nasira went from euphoric to disappointed. "Why is that necessary when we know we can conceive?"

"Because there are many children out there who need homes. We have that home, two in fact, and enough money to provide a solid future."

She pushed out of his lap and turned to look at him. "I truly want a baby who is a part of both of us."

Frustration clouded his expression. "You're a humanitarian, Sira. I thought the idea of giving an orphan a home would appeal to you. There are plenty in Eastern Europe."

"It does appeal to me in the future, yet I want to know how it feels to carry our child to term. As a man, perhaps you find that difficult to understand."

"I do understand, but I'm only considering your health. Why put you through the risks of another pregnancy if it's not necessary?"

She worried he would never understand. "The doctor said—"

"I know what the doctor said." Sebastian shot to his feet and began to pace. "I'm certain they said the same thing to my mother, and we know how that turned out."

Now she was completely confused. "I do not understand."

He paused to face her again. "No, you don't, because I didn't tell you the entire set of circumstances behind her death. She was pregnant because my father insisted she go against medical advice and have another child."

Shock rendered Nasira momentarily silent. "When did you learn this?"

"At the same time I learned how he was neglecting her health issues right before she died."

"More hearsay from the staff?"

He glanced away. "Yes, but I'm sure they spoke the truth."

"How can you be sure, Sebastian? You were a child yourself. Perhaps you misunderstood."

"I didn't misunderstand," he said, his tone full of anger. "I heard a reliable source say she'd had several miscarriages and each one took its toll on her. My father apparently ignored the danger and impregnated her once again. I will not put you through that."

At some point in time in the near future, Nasira vowed to find out all the details, no matter what it took. "I am not your mother, Sebastian. I have had one miscarriage and only one. I have no reason to believe I could not see the next pregnancy to term. I am willing to take that chance, and I hope you are as well."

He walked to her and clasped both her hands. "Please don't ask that of me, Sira. The thought of something happening to you is unbearable. And to know I would be responsible is inexcusable."

When she saw the vulnerability in his eyes, Nasira realized she might never break through his fear. A fear she had never witnessed in him before. She still hung on to a shred of hope that maybe with time, and more medical intervention, he would come to realize that childbirth wouldn't detrimental to her health.

She felt compelled to hold him, to tell him all would be well, yet she felt as though he had erected an invisible wall around himself. "All right. We will stray from this topic for now and attempt to enjoy the rest of our evening."

He released a rough sigh. "I'm not certain that is possible."

"It can be. Perhaps we should take a walk."

"I would prefer to stay in for the remainder of the evening."

Normally she would expect an invitation into bed. But this was not a normal situation, as evidenced by the fatigue in his tone. "If that is what you wish."

"It is."

She struggled to come up with a plan that might buoy his spirits. She returned to their mutual past and better days for inspiration. "I have a proposition."

His smile arrived slowly. "I've always enjoyed a good proposition."

The bad boy billionaire had come back to life. "This involves dessert."

"Interesting you should use that term."

The real Sebastian had arrived, and she felt a modicum of relief. "I meant dessert as in cake, on the veranda. We have not done that in a very long time."

He turned her hands over and kissed both her wrists. "Perhaps it's time we begin to recapture what we've lost."

Nasira chose to interpret Sebastian's statement as reclaiming the routines that had once given them pleasure, aside from lovemaking. She gently wrested her hands away and walked into the living area to retrieve the menu.

While she flipped through the selections, Sebastian came up behind her and peered over her shoulder. "The raspberry truffle cheesecake looks good," he said. "Shall I order that for us?"

She closed the menu, laid it aside on the desk and then turned, which placed her in extremely close proximity to him. So close she could barely catch her breath. "Actually, I would prefer to order for myself."

"My apologies. I've already forgotten one important lesson—let Sira make her own culinary decisions."

In light of the sexy gleam in his eye, she would forgive him this slight slipup. "Apology accepted. And I would like the sampler that includes several choices."

He frowned. "Are you certain you can handle that much food?"

"I can because I am suddenly starving."

Oddly, her appetite had increased over the past two days. In fact, the last time she had been this hungry…

That was not possible, not after only one time. Not so soon. She was being silly. Optimism over resolving their issues was simply driving her cravings. That had to be the case.

Seated at the small table on the hotel's veranda, Sebastian watched his wife eat with total abandon and couldn't quite believe his eyes. "In all our years together, I have never seen you entirely clean your plate."

Nasira dabbed at her mouth with the napkin and set it aside. "It was very tasty."

"Apparently. Should I order you more?"

That earned him a frown. "I could not eat another bite. I believe the country air is making me very hungry."

"Sira, we're in the city."

"True." She shifted in the chair and studied the horizon. "I had no idea Dallas would be so metropolitan."

"Did you believe you'd find people riding around the city streets on horseback?"

"Of course not. However, I did see a horse-drawn carriage downstairs."

"Perhaps we should make use of one."

She brought her attention back to him. "It is rather late."

"Not too late to enjoy the sights."

"I thought you wanted to stay in."

Sebastian was so restless, he wasn't certain what

he wanted, except to be close to his wife. "It will be a nice diversion," he said as he pushed back from the table and stood.

"All right." Nasira came to her feet and pointed at him. "No funny business."

Damn. "I only wish to have the honor of your company." And that was a colossal lie, though he vowed to respect her wishes.

By the time they reached the hotel lobby and walked out the revolving doors, the sidewalks weren't as crowded as Sebastian had expected. Fortunately he spotted a carriage stopped near the curb only a few meters away. He approached the gentleman dressed in Western garb positioned in the driver's seat. "Good evening, sir. Are you currently for hire?"

The man stared down at him. "Actually, I was just about to head to the house."

Sebastian withdrew his wallet and offered the man two hundred-dollar bills. "Will this make it worth your while?"

The driver eyed the money for a moment. "My wife's got dinner waiting."

He pulled out another hundred. "Now you can buy your wife dinner."

"I s'pose I could take you a few blocks."

Greedy scoundrel. "I would think that amount would buy us a few kilometers."

Nasira elbowed him in the side. "*Darling*, the poor man wants to go home to his wife."

Her compassion had him looking like a pitiless cad.

"Of course. My apologies. I only want to show my brand-new bride a memorable evening."

The driver grabbed the reins and sneered. "Then let's get this show on the road so you can get on with the honeymoon. Just don't get it on in my carriage."

"For three hundred dollars, I should be allowed to prance naked in a parade," Sebastian muttered as he helped Nasira up into the seat.

After they settled in, he draped an arm around her shoulder. "Was that jab to my ribs necessary?"

"Were your derisive comments necessary?"

"The reprobate seemed determined to stiff me."

"He clearly holds his wife above work. And what compelled you to claim we've recently married?"

His faults had been laid bare. "Well, in a way I feel as if we are newlyweds. We've discovered quite a bit about each other over the past few weeks."

She mulled that over for a moment. "It is odd to think that two people who have spent so many years together would still have the capacity to learn more about each other."

He had told her things he had never uttered to another soul. Details he had planned to take to his grave. Yet he did feel less burdened knowing she now understood why he did not want her risking carrying his child after her previous miscarriage. "Let's promise that we'll continue this unusual pattern in the upcoming weeks."

She laid her head on his shoulder. "A stellar plan."

As they rode through the streets of Dallas, serenaded by the clip-clop of horse hooves, Sebastian tugged Nasira closer to him. Without a blanket to conceal them, she was not in danger of any funny business, as she had so aptly put it. That did little to quash his desire for her. That did not stop him from rubbing her shoulder with one hand and tracing slow circles on her thigh. She responded by making small sounds that served to heighten his need for her, and drove him to kiss her thoroughly. And she kissed him back with enough passion to make him want to say to hell with propriety, pull her panties down and take right there in front of the entire town…

The sound of applause forced them apart. There was a crowd gathered at the corner where they had stopped for a traffic light. Sebastian did what any good Brit would do—stood, executed a bow and gave them a royal wave.

When he settled back in the seat, Nasira began to laugh and he followed suit. Once they recovered, he leaned and nuzzled her neck. "You smell like lavender. Is it a new perfume?"

"You gave it to me for my birthday."

Unfortunately that purchase had been made three months ago by Stella when he had forgotten. "Ah yes. Now I remember."

She swatted his arm. "You do not, but you are forgiven."

"For everything?"

"For now."

He refused to ruin the mood by asking her to elaborate. Instead, he decided to put all his cards on the table at the risk of rejection. "Would you mind if I take you back to the room and ravish you?"

"Not in the least."

That had been much too easy, in his opinion. "Really?"

"Yes."

"Should I perhaps define ravish?"

"I assume you mean you wish to remove my clothes, take me to bed and have your wicked way with me."

"Precisely."

"My answer is still yes."

Shifting against the building pressure in his groin, Sebastian tapped the driver on the shoulder to garner his attention. "Kind sir, please return us to the hotel as quickly as possible and you will earn a sizeable tip."

The man glanced over his shoulder. "We've barely been three blocks."

Sebastian had no desire to argue the point. "Unless you want your bloody carriage serving as a boudoir, you will do as I say."

The jerk had the gall to grin. "You got it."

Sebastian settled back against the seat and smiled. "Let the faux honeymoon commence."

Nasira worried they might not make it past the elevator before clothes began to come off. Her resolute husband somehow maintained enough control to refrain from disrobing until they reached the suite. On the way to the bedroom, they began shedding attire and shoes and by the time they fell back on the mattress, they were entirely naked and completely entangled.

Sebastian suddenly stilled and rose up. "I want to slow this down. I want this to last and if we keep going, it will be over in a matter of minutes."

She pushed a wayward lock of hair from his forehead. "You will receive no objections from me."

He rolled her onto her side so that she was facing the glass doors and moved against her back.

"Do you recall our first night?" he asked as he ran his palm over the curve of her hip.

"How could I forget? I was so very nervous, and you were so gentle."

"You were also a virgin, something you didn't tell me until right before that pivotal moment."

"I wanted to seem worldly. I did not want you to know I was so inexperienced."

"You also didn't want me to know you'd never had an orgasm. You told me the morning after. I've always been curious why you had never pleasured yourself."

"That would have been considered forbidden."

"And have you experimented since we've been married?"

"Never."

"Not even over the past few months?"

She sensed his sudden bout of guilt. "No. I only wanted you."

He slid his hand to the inside of her thigh. "And I made you wait for months."

"Having you touch me was worth the wait."

As they lay there in silence, Sebastian plying her with gentle strokes, the lights of the city illuminated the darkened room, making the atmosphere seem highly sensual and romantic. Nasira closed her eyes, taking in the ambience and willing the climax to remain at bay. Yet her efforts proved futile, and she again gave in to nature's course and her husband's skill as she experienced blessed relief.

So deep was the blissful aftermath that Nasira wasn't aware Sebastian had left her until she heard the sound of him tearing a condom wrapper, a reminder that he still was not willing to conceive a child. She shifted to her back and wrenched the negative thoughts from her mind. And when he returned, she welcomed him into her arms and her body. Feeling the play of his muscles beneath her palms, she held on tightly as he moved inside her, deeper and deeper, faster and faster. She listened to the sound of his ragged breaths and knew the exact moment when his own orgasm took over. Then he whispered her name.

After a time, he rolled to his back and took her with him, their bodies fitting together like a perfect human puzzle. During the next span of silence, she expected to hear his steady breathing, indicating he had fallen asleep. Instead, he played with her hair and showered her face with gentle kisses.

She was beginning to give in to the lull of sleep herself when he sighed and rested his lips against her ear. "I love you, Sira."

Never in her wildest dreams had she ever believed she would hear those words, though she had secretly hoped that someday she would. Even now she believed she might be dreaming. She said the only thing she could manage to say. The words she had kept harbored in her heart for fear that if she voiced them, she would be lost to this enigmatic man forever.

"I love you, too."

While Sebastian continued to hold her close, Nasira felt as if all her wishes had come true. All but one. Yet now that she knew her husband truly loved her, would she be foolish to believe she might be granted the child she had always wanted? Perhaps that would be too much to ask, yet as she recalled both Violet's and Fiona's claim that Royal, Texas, was a place bestowed with magic, she desperately wanted to believe she could have some magic of her own.

Time had passed quickly since their return to the Shakirs' ranch. Sebastian and Nasira had shared three wonderful and blissful weeks full of meaningful conversation and memorable moments. She had never felt so cherished, or so loved, by her husband.

Sebastian had showered her with small gifts, had made love to her often and had barely tended to business. Following Violet and Rafe's wedding in two days, she planned to return to London with her husband and continue their marriage with an eye toward a bright future, even though he had given her no indication he wanted to work on having a baby. Yet she believed that with a bit more gentle persuasion, he would eventually come around, and hopefully she was not giving way to false optimism. If not, she would have to decide if she would be willing to adopt and give up the dream of feeling her own child growing inside her.

After finishing her morning tea in the kitchen, Nasira took the cup to the sink, and immediately felt two strong arms encircling her from behind. "How dare you leave me alone in bed?" Sebastian asked in a teasing tone.

She turned and kissed his unshaven chin. "If you recall, I am meeting Violet for breakfast."

He slid his hand beneath her blue tailored blouse and cupped her breast through her lace bra. "Do you need a ride?"

"I thought I would drive myself."

He rimmed the shell of her ear with his tongue. "That wasn't the ride I had in mind."

Of course not. "I do not want to keep Violet waiting. She is anxious enough with all the wedding chaos."

Sebastian slid his hands over Nasira's hips and pressed against her. "What time do you expect to return?"

She saw afternoon delight in her near future. "I assume in few hours. We have to go over the final details and that could take some time."

He scowled. "The blasted wedding is spoiling my fun."

She patted his pajama-covered bottom and stepped aside. "You have had more than your share of fun of late."

He leaned back against the counter, bringing his bare torso into full view and sparking Nasira's imagination. "If I can interest you in more fun, let me know. In the meantime, while you ladies are discussing catering and flowers, I shall be making a few calls to prospective American clients."

Before she forgot her duties and caved in to her own cravings, Nasira grabbed her bag from the counter and kissed her husband squarely on the mouth. "I should be back before lunch. Be naked and waiting in the bed."

He grinned and winked. "If you give me advance warning, I'll be waiting naked in the foyer. Or if you allow me to drive you, we could have a quick roll in the car."

"Definitely a cad," she said as she headed to the entry, plagued with visions of Sebastian taking her down on the plush rug or in the sedan. Or both.

Nasira fished the keys from the pocket of her dress and slid into the driver's seat, thankful Sebastian had encouraged her to learn to drive on the correct side of the road for when they returned for visits. She liked the thought of coming back to Texas to see her brother's baby and perhaps by then she would be carrying one of her own. Or perhaps it was much too soon to hope for that blessing.

Setting those nagging concerns aside, she navigated the country road with relative ease and arrived at the Royal Diner to find Violet's new Jaguar—a wedding gift from Rafe—parked in the lot near the street. Nasira selected the empty space beside the sedan, turned off the ignition and regarded her watch. The fact she was fifteen minutes late flew in the face of her usual punctual self.

After she entered the restaurant, Nasira caught sight of Violet and Mac's assistant, Andrea Beaumont, seated at a small table in the corner. She strode across the room at a fast clip, until a bout of dizziness caused her to slow her pace. Clearly she was in need of sustenance, yet the scents emanating from the kitchen served to make her a bit queasy.

"I am so sorry for my tardiness," she said as she settled into the chair across from Violet and set her purse at her feet. "I awoke a bit later than planned."

"I hope you had a good reason," Violet said with a teasing smile.

"I do too," Andrea chimed in. "Did your handsome husband detain you?"

Nasira felt heat rise to her face. "Actually no, but that is only because I climbed out of bed before he roused."

"In that case, you should have hung around a little longer," Violet said. "I take it you and Sebastian are mending fences and maybe making a baby in the process?"

If only the last part were true. "We are making very good progress. Now what have I missed in regard to the wedding plans?"

Violet studied the notepad before her. "Actually, I'm fairly sure everything is in place. The menu has been finalized and the flowers have arrived from Hawaii. The cake is going to be gorgeous and the tent should be set up by two. Andrea arranged for a quartet to play during the ceremony and she's confirmed Rafe and Mac's tuxedos are ready to go."

"Now we only have to make sure the groom arrives on time," Andrea added.

With the arrangements already taken care of, Nasira wondered why she had been invited to the lunch today. "What can I do?" she asked.

Violet grinned. "Make sure the groom arrives on time."

Nasira returned her smile. "I can certainly do that, although I believe my brother will be there early, anxiously waiting to claim his bride. What time would you like us to arrive?"

"I'll be getting dressed at the house around noon," Violet said. "I could definitely use your help zipping my dress, if I can get it zipped."

Andrea laid a hand on Violet's arm. "Stop it. You're barely showing."

Violet patted her slightly distended belly. "My baby bump is much bigger, and I'm sure the breakfast I'm planning to eat isn't going to help." She slid a menu in front of Nasira. "I highly recommend the buttermilk pancakes with a side of bacon."

Nasira's stomach lurched at the thought. "I believe I will have toast and tea."

Andrea pushed away from the table and stood. "You girls enjoy your meal. Unfortunately Mac has a full schedule today so I'm going to have to settle for coffee and a granola bar I have stashed in my desk."

Violet frowned. "Tell my brother to stop being such a slave driver."

Andrea released a cynical laugh. "That would be like telling a cowboy to give up his spurs," she said as she headed out.

As soon as Andrea left, Violet shook her head and sighed. "I'll be so glad when those two finally admit they want a relationship beyond business. Mac is so stubborn he can't see the forest for the trees. I really want to shake some sense into him."

"Most men are stubborn," Nasira said. "My husband included."

"But he's coming around, right?" Violet asked.

"Yes, he is." Nasira wanted to delve into more detail but decided not to burden her brother's bride with her problems. "How have you been feeling with all the wedding stress?"

Violet took a sip of water and leaned back in the chair. "Better than I expected. The morning, noon and night sickness has subsided for the most part. I could still fall asleep on my feet at times, which I've learned is typical."

Nasira recalled the fatigue, along with the overwhelming sadness after her loss. "It is normal."

"I'm so sorry for being insensitive, Nasira," Violet said, her tone laced with sympathy. "I know how difficult it's been since your miscarriage."

"It's all right, Violet. Enough time has passed where I no longer fall apart around pregnant women."

"Are you sure?"

"I am sure. I would never want you to feel you have to be guarded around me when it comes to your pregnancy. In fact, I am thrilled to have a new niece or nephew. And I would enjoy living vicariously through you until I have my own child. After all, you can give me advice when that happens." *If* that happened.

"I'm personally looking forward to the next phase," Violet continued. "I have a friend who claims she couldn't get enough sex, and I know that will thrill

Rafe. Of course, the best part about being pregnant is…" She leaned forward and whispered, "No period."

No period…

The comment prompted Nasira to grab her cell phone from her bag and retrieve the calendar app. After she scanned the dates and did a mental countdown, she was overcome with panic when she should have been overcome with joy.

"Are you all right, Nasira?"

She raised her gaze to Violet. "I… I think…"

"You think what?"

"I might be pregnant."

And if that were true, she could only imagine what that possibility would entail. Perhaps stress had been the cause of her missing her period. Perhaps it would be best to wait a bit longer to find out the truth.

Nine

"You're definitely pregnant, Nasira."

A short while later, Nasira found herself at Rafe and Violet's home, holding the second of two positive pregnancy tests in one hand, steeped in shock. "I cannot believe this."

Violet wrested the plastic stick from her grip and set it on the vanity. "Believe it. I think taking a third is a bit of overkill."

Nasira pinched the bridge of her nose and closed her eyes. "How am I to tell Sebastian?"

"Easy. 'Sebastian, you're going to be a daddy.'"

If only it were that simple. If only he would embrace fatherhood. If only… "He will not be happy about this."

"What makes you believe that?"

Nasira opened her eyes to Violet's concerned expression. "It is very complicated. My husband is complicated."

"I can do complicated, Nasira. Now let's go into the living room and you can explain."

Nasira aimlessly followed her future sister-in-law into the parlor and settled in beside her on the sofa. After taking a cleansing breath, she began the arduous explanation by recounting Sebastian's concerns for her safety, his bittersweet memories of his mother, his reluctance to be like his father. She ended her explanation in a haze of tears, saying, "I am worried he will never accept the news at this point."

"He has no choice," Violet said with certainty. "It might take some time, but after he sees you're totally healthy and happy, he'll get used to the idea. And as soon as he holds your baby the first time, he'll wonder why he wasted so much energy worrying over nothing."

Nasira wished she could be so confident. "I hope you are right, Violet."

"And on the off chance I'm not, what are you going to do?"

Nasira had yet to make any solid decisions in that regard. "I suppose I will wait and see how Sebastian reacts when I deliver the news."

Violet took her hand. "I know it's tempting to put it off as long as possible, but the sooner you tell him, the sooner you'll know how to prepare for the future."

"I would rather hop a plane to Bermuda and bask on the beach."

"And I wish I could wear normal jeans again."

They exchanged a smile and a quick embrace before

Nasira came to her feet. "I so very much appreciate your counsel. Please wish me luck."

"Good luck." Violet stood and drew her into another embrace. "That's what family is for. And if your husband acts like a jerk, you know you always have a place here with us."

"I would never want to impose."

"You wouldn't be imposing. I'm sure Rafe would be thrilled to have his pregnant little sister and wife hanging around, driving him insane with sporadic hormonal outbursts."

Nasira tried to laugh yet it sounded hollow. "That would be the last thing my brother would want, having his younger sibling residing under the same roof while he is in the honeymoon phase with his new bride."

Violet's expression went suddenly serious. "He's very protective of you, Nasira. I'd hate to think what he might do if he knew about Sebastian's attitude toward fatherhood."

The thought made Nasira even more anxious. "Promise me you will not tell him."

"I promise," Violet said. "And you promise me you'll call as soon as Sebastian knows. If he throws a fit, get in the car and come here so he can cool down."

Nasira sincerely wanted to believe that would not be necessary, yet she found comfort in the offer. At least she would not be alone should Sebastian decide to walk out on their marriage. "I will, and thank you for being such a grand friend. I suppose I should go now and face the music."

"Nasira, in my heart of hearts," Violet began, "I believe everything will work out well. Sebastian might be snake-bit in the baby department, but it's obvious he loves you very much."

Nasira wanted to have faith in that as well, but her concerns only increased as they walked out the door into the warm May night.

"One more thing, Nasira," Violet said when they reached the sedan. "Every child is a gift and if Sebastian can't see that, then he's a fool. Don't let him allow you to think this is all your fault."

Nasira touched the place that housed her unborn child. "You are right. This baby is all I have ever wanted." And could be all she would have if her love for Sebastian, and his love for her, proved not to be enough to overcome their differences.

As she drove toward the ranch, Nasira recognized she would need a good dose of courage, and perhaps ammunition, for the upcoming debate she would surely have with her husband. On that thought, she pulled the sedan to the side of the road to make a call that could provide her with the information she needed. A fact-finding mission that could possibly hold the key to the past, and perhaps the fate of her future.

She withdrew the cell to input the number and waited. When she heard the familiar voice, she drew in a deep breath and exhaled slowly. "Stella, this is Nasira. I am in dire need of your help."

"What ever is wrong, dear?"

Everything. "Nothing really. I simply need to know all the details of Sebastian's mother's death."

She was met with momentary silence before Stella spoke again. "I am not at liberty—"

"Please, Stella. This is of the utmost importance. I need to know. Sebastian needs to know."

"Then you will need to speak to James about it."

That posed a grave dilemma. "Do you believe he's able to tell me?"

"Oh yes. He often leaves the present, yet he is very much suspended in the past."

"I do not want this to upset him."

"I assure you, it will. It does every time he goes back to that time, and he does so often."

"I would never want to cause James any distress, but this is very important." Even though going behind Sebastian's back could incur his wrath, and only make matters worse. Still, she had to take that chance in light of learning she was pregnant.

A span of silence passed before Stella spoke again. "All right, but be quick about it, and if he becomes too upset, I implore you to end the conversation."

"I promise I will."

"Then wait a moment and I will bring the phone to him."

Nasira heard indistinguishable sounds then James's careworn voice saying, "Hello, Nasira. Stella tells me you want to talk about my Martha. She was a jewel of a woman…."

She listened patiently as her father-in-law extolled the virtues of his late wife, and with great interest when he finally arrived at the fateful day in question. The information was both stunning and troubling. By the time the conversation ended, Nasira was no less clear on what she should tell Sebastian. The truth could truly set him free, or sever their marriage once and for all.

She had no choice but to reveal everything, every last dreadful detail, and prepare for the predictable fallout after she confessed to him she was pregnant.

Sebastian was beside himself. Nasira hadn't called to say why she had been detained, and her phone was going directly to voice mail. That caused him great concern. He should have given her a ride to the diner. He should have rented a second car. What if she had been in an accident, or at the very least, found herself lost on some dilapidated Texas back road? If she didn't arrive soon, he would contact the law and organize a search party.

After he heard the front door open a few minutes later, though, he finally relaxed…until he noticed the distressed look on Nasira's face when she entered the great room. He shot off the sofa, his nerves on edge. "What happened to you?"

She tossed her bag on the coffee table and collapsed in the club chair across from him. "The meeting with Violet went longer than planned."

It was so unlike his wife to blatantly lie, but she had. "I called Violet. She said you left the diner an hour ago."

Nasira averted her gaze. "I suppose I did at that. I was on the phone and lost track of time."

He was plagued by an immediate surge of jealousy. "Were you talking to that McCallum fellow?"

She nailed him with a glare. "Do not be absurd, Sebastian. I haven't spoken with Mac since the night you arrived."

Only minimally relieved, Sebastian lowered onto the sofa and leaned forward to look for any sign of deception in her eyes. "Who else in town would you be talking to if not him?"

She kicked off her sandals and curled her legs beneath her. "I never said I spoke to anyone from Royal. For your information, I was in touch with London."

He couldn't seem to contain his sarcasm. "It's no wonder the call took so long if you talked to the entire city. Could you possibly be more specific?"

"If you must know, I spoke with Stella."

He worried the news might involve his father, and it might not be good. "What did she want?"

"Actually, I called her."

"To check in on our status?"

"To gather the details of your mother's death, which I did."

He waffled between resentment over the intrusion to borderline anger. "Forgive me if I'm feeling somewhat betrayed. The least you could have done was tell me your plans to contact her."

"I understand, but I felt it was of the utmost importance you know the whole truth."

"I don't see why any of it should matter now."

"It does, Sebastian, and you'll realize why as soon as I tell you what I've learned with your stepmother's assistance."

For some reason, he experienced trepidation over the possible contents of the conversation. "I'm quite surprised Stella would tell you what she knows, if she really knows anything pertinent beyond what I've heard."

"I learned the facts from your father, not Stella."

The revelation took Sebastian aback. "My father doesn't remember what he had for dinner."

"He does still remember the past, and quite well."

Sebastian couldn't argue with that observation. "I'm not certain I care to hear his version of the truth."

"You are going to hear it," she said almost forcefully. "And I believe you will be glad you did."

He believed she would be sorely disappointed. "I'll be the judge of that, but please, continue. I enjoy a good fairy tale now and then."

She shifted her weight slightly, a certain sign of her uneasiness. "First of all, your mother was not pregnant at the time of her death."

"Of course he would say that—"

"She *was* pregnant not long before her death," Nasira proclaimed before he could finish his sentence, then added, "A fact unbeknownst to everyone, including your father."

Sebastian allowed the astonishment to subside and logic to come into the picture. "I have a difficult time believing a straightforward woman like my mother would conceal a pregnancy from anyone, let alone her husband."

A strange look passed over Nasira's face. "She had her reasons, Sebastian. Some might say good reasons under the circumstances."

He saw no excuse for blatant dishonesty, and he had a difficult time believing his own mother—the one he remembered—would engage in serious subterfuge. "And what would those reasons be?"

"She kept the pregnancy hidden because your father was adamant she not have another child due to her multiple miscarriages. He sided with the physicians, not your mother, although he claimed that was agony. He loved her so much he hated not giving her a baby."

He had never known his father to agonize over anything other than the state of the global economy. "Clearly James was not without fault in the matter since I assume he was present when she conceived."

"Yes, but she lied about using birth control because she wanted another baby that badly."

Exactly what Nasira had initially done to him, as if history were bent on repeating itself. "Did the pregnancy directly cause her demise?"

"Indirectly. She apparently had another miscarriage and chose not to tell anyone, including her physician. That led to a lethal infection and subsequently, her untimely death."

He took a few moments to digest the information, then summarily rejected it. "It would be just like my father to twist the truth to relieve himself of all culpability."

"He has no reason to lie, Sebastian. Stella told me he has lived with horrible guilt since the day your mother passed away. He blames himself for her decision to keep quiet about the baby. He believes if he had not been so set against her conceiving, she would have told him about the pregnancy and he could have prevented her death."

He acknowledged the scenario made sense, yet he had trouble trusting the source. "I'm still having a great deal of difficulty believing my father remained totally in the dark."

"Stella suspected you would, so she offered to give you the official certification."

"That only confirms the cause of death, not my father's claims."

Nasira impaled him with a glare the likes of which he'd never witnessed. "If you will stop being such a buffoon and search your soul, you might finally realize that your mother was not a saint, and your father is not Satan."

He suddenly felt extremely drained. "I'll attempt to come to terms with the information, but I cannot promise I will feel any differently."

He could tell by the lift of her chin and the defiance in her eyes she wasn't quite finished with the lecture. "It is high time you call an end to your suspicions and resentment. If you don't, you will possibly regret the decision after it is too late to make amends with James. Believe me, that is a burden you will not want to bear."

Sebastian wanted to debate the pros and cons of forgiveness, but his emotions were too tangled in turmoil. He rested against the sofa and feigned a calm demeanor. "Did you enjoy your time with Violet?"

Nasira's dark eyes widened with disbelief. "You wish to know about my day after what I revealed?"

"I see no point in dwelling on the past."

"I do if it relates to our future, and our present situation."

"This information has no bearing on us, Sira, aside from the fact it does reinforce why it's not wise for you to become pregnant again."

"As I have said before, I am not your mother. I am healthy and able to bear more children. Women have babies every day without incident. Life holds no guarantees and comes with a certain amount of—"

"Risk," he finished for her. "I understand that, but it's a risk I don't care to take with your well-being. And if you don't mind, I would like to move off this subject for now."

She lowered her eyes and clasped her hands tightly in her lap. "I cannot discard my worries, Sebastian. Not after what I discovered today."

Concern came crashing down on him as he braced for confirmation of what he suspected she was about to say. "Please tell me you're not pregnant."

She centered her gaze on his. "I am pregnant, and I am thrilled. I hope you will put aside your fears and celebrate the news."

Celebrate? He came off the couch, laced his hands behind his neck and began to pace like a caged cougar. "How can you expect me to be happy after what you've told me about my mother?"

"I knew I was taking a chance by unveiling the truth, yet I had to be forthright."

He spun around to confront her. "That truth only cements my apprehension."

"Your mother chose to become pregnant against medical advice and your father's protests. She also chose not to seek appropriate treatment after she lost the baby, and in turn inadvertently caused her own death due to her deception. In a way I understand—"

"Of course you would," he said, noticeable anger in his tone. "I imagine you would do the same."

Fury turned her features to stone. "I would not do the same, and I cannot fathom why you would believe I would risk my life to have a baby if I had been told the cost would be so high. But I have not been told that, Sebastian. On the contrary, the doctor said I have every reason to believe this time will be different."

"And what if it's not? What if you lose another child? Worse still, what if you lose your life?"

She finally rose from the sofa. "I refuse to buy into your pessimism and fears. I choose to be optimistic and hopeful. If you cannot join me in that optimism, then there is no hope for us at all."

He experienced a different fear. "What are you saying?"

"I am saying go back to London, Sebastian. If you do not want this child, and clearly you do not, then I cannot be with a man who will not support me during my pregnancy. I would prefer to be surrounded by people who will be happy to provide that support. I have that here with Rafe and Violet."

"I need time to think." Time to assess the possibilities.

She picked up her purse, withdrew the bracelet with the rattle charm he had given her all those months ago and laid it on the table before him, as if she was bent on wounding him further. "Then think, but I warn you not to take too long. In the meantime, I am going to stay with Rafe until you decide what you want. I respectfully request you not attempt to contact me until you've made up your mind. I will have someone return the car later this evening."

As he watched his wife walk away, Sebastian experienced a strong sense of déjà vu. Her departure from London a brief month ago had come with the same demand not to contact her. Then, too, he had suffered an emotional pain that stole his breath and his resolve. With his overriding fear of losing Nasira, he had definitely cemented that self-fulfilling prophecy he'd been so concerned about.

He wasn't the kind of man who would abandon his child, provided that child came to be, yet he worried his wife had already abandoned any expectations of salvaging their marriage.

If he did not come to terms with impending fatherhood, and learn to embrace it, he risked saying goodbye to his beautiful Nasira for good.

He had too much to consider, and too little time.

"Have you heard from your worthless husband?"

Seated in the chair next to the window, Nasira glanced up from the book she was pretending to read, steeling herself against her brother's consternation. "Have I?"

He moved from the doorway and perched on the bench at the end of the bed. "If I knew, I would not have asked."

"If my memory serves me correctly, you failed to tell me Sebastian called when I arrived here. How can

I trust that you have not thwarted his attempts to contact me this time?"

"I assure you he has not called and if he had, I would have informed you immediately. I have learned my lesson in that regard."

She highly doubted that. "I truly do not want you to worry about my situation during what should be a joyous time for you and Violet. Are you looking forward to the wedding tomorrow?"

"I am looking forward to having Violet back in my bed. I do not understand the tradition involving withholding the bride from the groom before the wedding."

"It is believed that sleeping with the bride the night before the wedding will invite bad luck."

"It only invites sexual frustration."

Spoken like a man. "Has she left yet?"

"No. She is still packing her suitcases while Mac remains downstairs, growing increasingly impatient. What will you do if Sebastian returns to London without contacting you?"

Nasira refused to give up on him yet. "I am trying not to entertain that possibility."

"Regardless, I will contact Nolan Dane after Violet and I return from our honeymoon. He's a lawyer here in Royal who used to work for me."

"I do not need a barrister." At least not presently.

"You might in the future. He will provide a reference for a family law attorney should you decide to pursue a divorce. Preferably a high-profile attorney to ensure you will receive an equitable share of your husband's assets. One who has experience dealing with international divorce."

She tossed her book onto the side table and sighed. "I do not need Sebastian's money, Rafe. I have more than enough left of my inheritance."

"That is your decision."

"Yes, it is."

"At the very least he should be required to support the child."

She should not be surprised that Violet had told Rafe about the baby. Somewhat disappointed, yes, but not at all shocked. "I see you have been talking to your fiancée."

"Do not blame Violet, Nasira. I pressed her for information when you arrived on our doorstep, looking as though you had lost your dearest friend. She had no choice but to reveal the details to put my mind at ease, although she did not accomplish that goal."

"You need not worry, brother," Nasira said. "I will manage on my own if necessary."

Rafe took on an angry guise. "I would like to seek out Sebastian and tell him—"

"You will not say a word, Rafiq. This is not your concern."

"You have always been my concern, my petite pearl."

She smiled at the brotherly term of endearment. "I am no longer your life, Rafe. Violet is. Your unborn child is."

He rose from the bench, crossed the space between them and pressed a kiss to her forehead. "You will always be a part of my life. I will always be there to protect you if your husband refuses to do so."

She had to learn to accept that Sebastian could be absent from her world forever. That she might never converse with him again. Hold him again. Make love with him again…

The shrill of the doorbell thrust her thoughts back to the present. The sound of the deep, endearing voice demanding he see her sent her shattered heart on a sprint.

Had he come to tell her he intended to stay, or to say farewell for all eternity?

Ten

As his brother-in-law descended the staircase, stood in the opening to the parlor Sebastian prepared to be thrown out on his arse. Yet when Nasira followed not far behind, sporting a plain cotton blouse, light blue slacks and a champion scowl, he sensed she would prefer to do the honors herself. He would accept that fate. He deserved it.

He glanced to his right to see Violet and her brother, Mac, Sebastian's former nemesis, seated on the sofa as if they planned to preside over a kangaroo court with him playing the defendant. Rafe brushed past him and claimed the overstuffed chair adjacent to the settee, not bothering to hide his disdain for his sister's spouse.

Nasira remained in the foyer, her arms folded beneath her breasts, looking every bit the hanging judge. "Well?"

"May I speak with you in private, Sira?" he asked with forced civility. "It's extremely important."

She regarded the curious onlookers before bringing her attention back to him. "Whatever you need to say, you may say it in front of my family and friends."

She had turned his privacy plan on its proverbial ear, and he would have to accept it, even if it meant an unwelcome audience. "You're absolutely right. Your friends and family are most welcome to witness what I have to say. I only hope they support my decision."

Her shoulders immediately tensed. "I assume that decision involves your return to London."

Wrong. He took both her hands in his. "I'm not going anywhere without you. I'm here to humbly ask you to forgive all my faults."

"Such as?"

He'd compiled a laundry list that was too long to recite now, so he would concentrate on those which would matter most to her. "Forgive me for periodically leaving my towel on the floor after I shower. Forgive me for leading you to believe that I think you're not capable of being involved in the business, because you are, and I welcome your input. Above all, I beg you to forgive me for being such a bloody, controlling coward."

"I have never said you are a coward."

A point in his favor. "Perhaps not, but I wouldn't blame you if you thought it." He paused to draw a breath. "The truth of the matter is, I have fought with men twice my size—"

"Seriously?" Violet interjected.

"I'd believe it," Mac added.

Rafe cleared his throat. "Let the man continue. Violet needs her rest and at this rate, we will be here until midnight."

Violet leaned over and patted her husband's cheek. "Thank you, honey."

"As I was saying," Sebastian continued, "I've been in several situations that required bravery, but the thought of being responsible for a tiny, helpless creature frankly scares the hell out of me."

He studied Nasira's eyes and saw a glimpse of understanding, or so he assumed. "Sebastian, you are in charge of a major corporation. I am confident you can handle fatherhood with the same aplomb."

"Except for the dirty diapers maybe," Mac said, earning him a look from Rafe.

"I can only promise I will try," Sebastian said sincerely. "But what I lack in skill, I will make up in the willingness to learn."

Instead of falling into his arms, she frowned. "Why the sudden turnaround, Sebastian?"

He should have realized she wouldn't make this easy on him. "I spent hours thinking about what you said. Life isn't without risk, but I'm willing to take that risk with you in light of the reward. I've also spoken with Stella and my father. I've come to the conclusion that I've wasted many years resenting a man without just cause, and I will never know true peace unless I learn to forgive his faults. And I hope you forgive mine. In reality, I'm very much like him, and only part of that is learned behavior. The other part is genetic."

He couldn't seem to even coax a slight smile from her. "Will you be able to love our baby?"

More than she would know. More than he could express. "I vow to love our child as much as I love our child's mother."

When he pulled the bracelet from his pocket in an effort to confirm his commitment, and placed it on Nasira's wrist, his wife finally smiled. "That is all I needed to know. And I love you, too. I forgive you all your faults, if you will forgive mine as well."

His spirits soared like a hawk. "You're perfect, Sira. But I need to warn you, you'll have to be patient with me. I'm going to worry about you every moment of every day during your pregnancy. I'm definitely going to be ridiculously overprotective and I'll be gauging your every move—"

"Shut up and kiss me, Sebastian."

She would get no argument from him. As he took her in his arms and kissed her soundly, for the first time in many years, he felt entirely at peace. Once they parted, he realized the room had cleared out as though he was a randy rock star giving a bad performance. "Would you care to accompany me back to our rented ranch?"

She hid a yawn behind her hand. "Gladly. I am so exhausted. I could not sleep without you by my side."

Neither could he. "Rest assured I will respect your need for sleep. You will have to get more of it to remain healthy."

She slid her arms around his waist and sent him a sly grin. "Actually, I am not that tired, nor am I fragile."

No, she was not, and he realized he had known that all along. "Well then, Mrs. Edwards, let us away to our borrowed bed."

"That sounds like a very good plan, Mr. Edwards."

They made love once during the night, and again in the morning. As the first light of dawn streamed through the slightly parted curtains, Nasira rested her cheek on Sebastian's chest and listened to the strong beat of his heart as she basked in the afterglow of re-markable lovemaking…and much-needed hope for their future together.

Sebastian's steady strokes on her back threatened to lull her to sleep, but she awoke completely when he shifted slightly. "You know what I like best about your pregnancy?" he asked.

"I know what I like best," she murmured. "I can avoid tight clothing for nine months."

"You would look good in a gunny sack, Nasira. I personally enjoy not having to wear another bloody raincoat."

She shifted onto her back and stretched her arms above her head. "What do you mean? We are not in London, Sebastian. Today you will not need a rain-coat. The forecast calls for an abundance of sunshine."

He chuckled. "I meant raincoat as in *condoms*. I've had enough of those annoying rubber ducks to last a lifetime. Sheer torture, I tell you."

The description made her smile. "The reference to a bath toy presents quite a grand visual."

He rolled to his side, bent his elbow for support and propped his jaw on his palm. "What time do we have to be at the wedding?"

"Noon. I have to assist Violet with her dress."

He lowered the sheet, baring Nasira's torso, and laid his cheek beneath her breasts. "I'm certain she has several ladies-in-waiting who will come to her aid."

"Perhaps, but I would like to be a part of the process."

Using a fingertip, he drew circles around her belly. "Then you should definitely get some rest."

"How can I rest with you touching me this way?"

"I am trying to connect with our child."

And that proclamation moved Nasira in unexpected and wonderful ways. "Do you wish for a boy or a girl?"

His hand came to a stop on her belly. "I'm still getting use to the fatherhood idea. I haven't had time to consider the gender."

She stroked his hair. "I personally have no preference, although I could see you with a daughter. She would have you wrapped around her finger in an instant."

"That would mean she's exactly like her mother." He pressed a kiss on her belly then rose up slightly and began to speak softly, sincerely. "Hello there, baby Edwards. This is your old dad. I wanted to introduce myself even though some might believe I've taken total leave of my senses, talking to a tadpole who undoubtedly won't remember this conversation."

He sent Nasira a grin before giving his consideration back to his unborn child. "In the future, beyond your toddler years, you're most likely going to be frustrated with me, and perhaps during your teens, you're going to despise me. At times I might be strict, but you never need to doubt how much I love you, and how much I love this wonderful woman who is currently giving you a safe haven in which to grow. But whatever you decide to become, be it a businessman or a butler, please know I will always be proud of you, and I promise I will always forgive your faults."

Overwhelmed by the sweetness of his words, Nasira battled tears. This time, tears of joy. Of blessed relief. "You will be an amazing father."

He returned to her side and kissed her cheek. "I will be the best father I can be."

"Sebastian, my love, I know in my soul you will be the very best."

Nasira had finally been granted her heart's desire—the gift of a precious baby and the love a good man. She felt as if she were the most fortunate woman in the world. And before she drifted off again, she wished that same good fortune on Rafe and Violet on this day when their life together would truly begin....

"With the power vested in me by the great State of Texas, I now pronounce you husband and wife. Now give that little gal a kiss."

Nothing was more boring than sitting through a wedding, especially when the man presiding over the nuptials was clearly a repressed comedian. Yet Sebastian admittedly enjoyed Nasira squeezing his hand during the vows. And he reluctantly acknowledged that Violet and Rafe's pledge to each other had been rather moving at times.

Bloody hell. He had turned into a lovesick sap. But he wouldn't want it any other way.

After the bride and groom vacated the makeshift altar, Sebastian took his wife by the hand and led her through the hordes of humanity. He had no idea so many people resided in this spot-in-the-road town of Royal.

"I'm going to congratulate Violet and Rafe," Nasira said when they managed to find a small space to stand without bumping into guests. "Are you coming with me?"

Sebastian peered out over the crowd and noticed the lengthy reception line near the white tent. He also spotted one man he needed to speak with out of his wife's earshot. "If you don't mind, I believe I'll find a waiter and get a drink. I'll catch up with you in a bit."

She brushed a kiss across his cheek. "All right, but please hurry. I do not want anyone to assume I put you on a plane to London without me."

He frowned. "Why would anyone assume that?"

"This is a very small town, Sebastian. Gossip travels at the speed of lightning, according to Violet."

Nothing he hadn't encountered in the jolly old town of London. "I'll be along briefly."

After Nasira disappeared in the sea of people, Sebastian set out for Mac McCallum, who was standing near the bar bedecked in white bunting. He could now kill two birds with one stone.

As soon as he reached the drink station, he addressed the bartender, tip in hand. "I need a scotch, neat. The best scotch you have, actually."

The man poured the drink and set it before him. "It's free."

Did he think he was so socially inept that he didn't understand the concept of an open bar? "I realize that," he said as he tossed the fifty-dollar bill on the counter. "This is a tip."

"Thanks a heap, mister."

"You're most welcome, barkeep."

He grabbed the drink, approached Mac and looked around before he began asking questions. Realizing the coast was crystal clear, he addressed the cowboy. "Did you make the arrangements?" he asked in a lowered voice.

"Yeah, I did. Delivered the funds personally."

"What timeline should I expect?"

Mac swiped a hand over his jaw. "You're going completely custom, so I estimate at least a year, maybe a bit longer."

That would allow enough time to finalize the deal before the birth of their child. Odd that only a few weeks ago, he would not allow himself to believe he could continue the Edwards legacy. "I appreciate your help. And by the way, who are all these people?"

Mac leaned back against the bar. "Most are Texas Cattleman's Club members, old and new, and their significant others. The man over there is Ben Rassad, Darin Shakir's cousin. And that guy over there is Gavin McNeal."

"I met the former sheriff at the festival a few weeks ago."

"Yeah, he's part of the old guard. The man standing near him is the new Texas Cattleman's Club president, Case Baxter and his wife, Mellie. I'm surprised he bothered to show up, but I guess he's decided to bury the hatchet. And right over there is the current sheriff, Nathan Battle."

Sebastian sensed a story coming on. "Does this Baxter fellow have a problem with the bride and groom?"

Mac set his empty beer aside and straightened. "It's a long story, but Case was very angry with Rafe for secretly trying to buy up the town, including Mellie's land where the club sits. But all's been settled now that Rafe decided not to get revenge on me for his assumption I defiled your wife a long time ago, and as you probably know, that led to Rafe's torture and confinement by your deceased father-in-law."

The unbelievable story, laid out in such a manner, reeked of a made-for-TV movie plot. And although he now knew the details, and that Mac had no designs on Nasira, he still wasn't pleased with the man using *defiled* and *his wife* in the same sentence. "Regardless, I'm glad the situation has been resolved."

He was also glad to see his spouse weaving through the masses, heading his way. When she arrived, he slipped his arm around her slender waist. "Did you give the happy couple my regards?"

"Unfortunately I could not reach them. Fortunately we have time to visit with them before our flight departs tonight." She turned her smile on Mac. "I spoke with Andrea a few moments ago. I believe she is searching for you."

The man's expression lit up like a livewire. "She's probably wondering about the documents I left her yesterday. You folks enjoy the rest of the day, and have a safe flight."

Nasira laughed as soon as Mac left the immediate premises. "Did you notice how quickly he left when I mentioned his assistant's name?"

"I did. Obviously she is very efficient."

She frowned. "She is very attractive, and Mac is completely smitten. I would not be surprised to learn they are the next couple to wed in Royal."

Honestly, Sebastian didn't care about anyone other than the woman standing next to him, looking stunning in her coral chiffon gown and matching heels. He crooked his finger in invitation. "I would greatly appreciate some alone time with my wife."

She took a moment to survey the frantic scene. "That could be difficult to come by unless I borrow a cattle prod to clear the crowd."

Cattle prod? Obviously his wife had resided in Texas long enough to adopt the classic cowboy colloquialisms. "I don't see anyone milling about that massive statue of the woman Gavin McNeal mentioned at the fair."

Nasira peered off into the distance. "Oh, yes, the statue of Jess Golden, his wife's distant relative. If we hurry, perhaps we might steal some privacy, although we will have ample alone time on the plane."

He liked the sound of that, yet he refused to wait until they boarded the jet to let her in on his secret plan. He felt like an impetuous schoolboy on Christmas Eve as he guided her toward the legendary figure from Texas Cattleman's Club's past. Once they arrived, he gave his beautiful bride a kiss and as an added bonus, a pat on her shapely bottom.

"I spoke with Mac earlier today," he began, "and he told me that at one time, the Texas Cattleman's Club members engaged in missions bordering on espionage. Apparently it was quite the rage back then."

She favored him with an endearing smile. "You cannot believe everything you hear, although I admit, I have heard the same. However, clearly times have changed."

He looked lovingly at Nasira and in that moment recognized the value of family and love. "I'd personally like to believe that men of honor still have the capacity to come to the rescue of their fair maidens."

She touched his face with reverence. "They do. After all, you have rescued me from a life without a child, fathered by the man I love with all my heart and soul."

"You have done the same for me. I want nothing more than to have you as the mother of our children, my love. And to reward you for your efforts, I have a gift to present you."

Her sunny expression melted into a frown. "You have already given me the best gift I could have ever wished for. Our baby-to-be."

She had given him more than he could express. "This will be something we can all enjoy as a family."

"Is it bigger than a music box?"

"Much bigger."

"Where is it?"

"It is being built as of tomorrow."

She looked entirely confused. "Sebastian, I have the Bentley. I do not need another car."

"It's not a car, sweetheart. It's a house."

She appeared unimpressed. "We already own two houses."

"And we shall have three, only this one is a vacation home and will not be located in the UK."

"Tahiti?"

"No. Royal."

Worried that he might have permanently rendered her speechless, he waited for her shock to subside. "Why? Where?"

"In the gated golf community of Pine Valley. I selected a lot and I met with the architect after you left me to return to Rafe's. It's a place we can call home when we return next year on holiday."

Her eyes brightened. "Oh, Sebastian, that would be marvelous. By that time, we will have our baby and we can introduce him or her to its new cousin."

Knowing he had pleased her pleased Sebastian greatly. "I vow to make this home as extravagant as you like."

She wrapped her arms around his neck and held him tightly for a time. "My dear sweet love, my home is anywhere you are."

This incredible woman, his wife, the mother of his child, had changed him in ways he had never believed possible. "And I promise you this day, beneath this historic statue and this symbol of bygone days, I will be there for you and our children through good times and bad."

She pulled away and stared at him. "Children?"

"Certainly. At least five. However, you do realize that will require quite a bit of practice, beginning tonight in the sleeping quarters on the plane."

"I am already pregnant, Sebastian."

"My dear, practice does make perfect."

As they rejoined the celebrants and sought out the bride and groom, Sebastian Edwards realized that perfection was in his reach. He had a remarkable wife, the promise of a bright future and a love he had resisted out of fear. He had learned to forgive when forgiveness had not come easily for him, yet he had his lovely bride to thank for that. The moment he returned home, he would seek out his father and afford him the benevolence Nasira had taught him, before it was too late to mend their relationship.

Ten years ago, the confirmed bachelor and billionaire had entered into a convenient marriage with an exotic stranger. He had done so to produce the requisite heir but had abandoned that plan and refused to entertain the idea of having children when she'd miscarried. For her part, Nasira had married to escape a life dictated by her father's belief she wasn't worthy to choose her own mate. Never in a million years would Sebastian have believed this arrangement would result in undeniable, unconditional love.

Life was good, and he predicted it would only grow better with each passing day. Forgiveness was his for the taking, and love would forever be the constant that ruled his life. Not business. Not gold. Only Nasira.

Always Nasira.

*****

A BRIDE FOR
THE BOSS

MAUREEN CHILD

To all of the wonderful writers
in this fabulous continuity series—
it's been an honor working with all of you.

And to Charles Griemsman,
thanks for being such a great editor and for
not tearing your hair out during this process!

One

"What do you mean, *you quit*?" David "Mac" McCallum stared at his assistant and shook his head. "If this is a joke, it's not funny."

Andrea Beaumont took a deep breath, then said sharply, "Not a joke, Mac. I'm dead serious."

He could see that, and he didn't much care for it. Usually when Andi stepped into his office, it was to remind him of a meeting or a phone call, or to tell him she'd come up with some new way to organize his life and business.

But at the moment, she had angry glints firing in her normally placid gray eyes, and he'd do well to pay attention. Having a younger sister had taught him early to watch his step around women. Violet had a temper that could peel paint, and Mac knew that a wise man stayed out of range when a woman got a certain look about her.

Right now, Andi—his calm, cool, organized executive assistant—appeared to be ready for battle.

Andi looked the same as always, even though she was in the middle of tossing his well-ordered world upside down. June sunlight slipped through the wide windows at Mac's back and poured over her like molten gold. Her long, straight, dark brown hair hung past the shoulders of the pale blue blazer she wore over a white dress shirt and dark blue jeans. Black boots, shined to a mirror gleam, finished off the outfit. Her storm-gray eyes were fixed on him unblinkingly and her full, generous mouth was pinched into a grim slash of determination.

Looked like they were about to have a "discussion."

Mac braced himself. Whatever she had in mind just wasn't going to fly. He couldn't afford to lose her. Hell, running McCallum Enterprises was a full-time job for ten men and damned if he'd let the woman who knew his business as well as he did simply walk away.

She'd been his right-hand man—woman—*person*— for the last six years and Mac couldn't imagine being without her. When something needed doing, Andi got it done. Mac didn't have to look over her shoulder, making sure things were handled. He could tell her what he needed and not worry about it. Andi had a knack for seeing a problem and figuring out the best way to take care of it.

She could smooth talk anyone, and if that didn't work, he'd seen her give an opponent a cool-eyed glare that could turn their blood cold. There'd been plenty of times when Mac had actually enjoyed watching her stare down an adversary. But he had to say, being on the receiving end of that icy look wasn't nearly as enjoyable.

What had brought this on?

"Why don't you take a seat and tell me what's got you so angry."

"I don't want a seat," she said. "And I don't want to be soothed like you do those horses you love so much…"

He frowned. "Then what exactly do you want?"

"I already told you. I want to quit."

"Why the hell would you want to do that?"

Her gray eyes went wide, as if she couldn't believe he even had to ask that question. But as far as Mac knew, everything was just as it should be. They'd closed the Donaldson deal the day before and now McCallum Enterprises could add Double D Energy Services to its ledgers. And Andi'd had a lot to do with getting David Donaldson to sign on the dotted line.

"I just gave you a raise last night for your work on the energy project."

"I know," she said. "And I earned it. That deal was not pretty."

"So what's the problem?"

"You told me to take over the planning for Violet's baby shower."

He drew his head back and narrowed his eyes on her in shocked surprise. With her talent for list making and organization, Andi should be able to handle that shower in a finger snap. "That's a problem? I thought you and Vi were friends."

"We *are*," she countered, throwing both hands high. "Of course we are. That's not the point."

"What *is* the point, then?" Mac dropped into his chair and, lifting his booted feet, crossed them at the ankle on the edge of the desk. "Spit it out already and let's get back to work."

"For one, *you* don't decide on Vi's baby shower. For heaven's sake, you stick your nose into everything."

"Excuse me?"

"But my main point is," she said, setting both hands at her hips, "I'm tired of being taken for granted."

"Who does that?" he asked, sincerely confused.

"*You* do!"

"Now, that's just not so," he argued. "Let's remember that raise yesterday and—"

"In the last day or so, you had me arrange for the new horse trailer to be dropped off at the ranch. I called Big Mike at the garage to get him to give your car a tune-up before the weekend, then I saw to it that the new horses you bought will be delivered to the ranch tomorrow afternoon."

Scowling now, Mac bit back on what he wanted to say and simply let her get it all out.

"I drew up the plans for the kitchen garden your cook wants for behind the house and I made sure the new baby furniture you're giving Vi was delivered on time." Andi paused only long enough to take a breath. Her eyes flashed, her mouth tightened as she continued. "Then I called Sheriff Battle to make sure he cleared the road for the delivery of the last of the cattle water tanks."

"Had to clear the road—"

"Not finished," she said, holding up one hand to keep him quiet. "After that, I bought and had delivered the standard half-carat diamond bracelet and the it's-not-you-it's-me farewell note to the model who can't string ten words together without hyperventilating…"

Mac snorted. All right, she had a point about Jezebel Fontaine. Still, in his defense, Jez was seriously built enough that he'd overlooked her lack of brain cells for the past month. But even he had his limits.

"You're my assistant, aren't you?"

"I am and a darn good one," she countered. "I've kept your life running on schedule for the last six years, Mac. No matter what you throw at me, I handle it and add it into the mix I'm already juggling."

"You're a damn fine juggler, too," he said.

She kept talking as if he hadn't said a thing.

"Then when I asked you for this afternoon off so I could go see my nephew's baseball game, you said you had to *think* about it. *Think about it?*"

"I appreciate a good Little League game as much as the next man," Mac said slowly, keeping his gaze fixed on hers, "but we've still got some details to be ironed out on the Double D deal and—"

"That's my point, Mac." His eyes widened when she interrupted him. "There's always *something* that needs to be handled and I'm so busy taking care of those things I haven't had time to find a *life*."

"You've got a pretty good life from where I'm standing," he argued, pushing up from his desk. "Great job, terrific boss—" He paused, waiting for a smile that didn't come, then tried to continue, but he couldn't come up with a third thing.

"Uh-huh. Job. Boss. No life." She took a deep breath. "And that stops today."

"Okay," he said flatly. "If it's that important to you, go. See your nephew's game. Have some popcorn. Hell, have a beer. We'll talk more tomorrow morning when you come in."

"I won't be in," she said, shaking her head. "It's time for a change, Mac. For both of us. I've gotten too comfortable here and so have you."

He laughed abruptly. "You call dealing with what all that's been going on around here *comfortable*?"

She nodded. "There've been problems, sure, but we handled them and things are slowly getting back to normal. Or, as normal as life gets around here."

Mac sure as hell hoped so. It had been a wild time in Royal, Texas, over the past couple of years. A lot of turmoil, more than their share of trouble. There was the tornado, of course, then the drought that held most of Texas in a tight, sweaty fist and then a man he used to think of as one of his oldest friends, Rafiq "Rafe" bin Saleed, had come to town with the express purpose of ruining Mac's reputation, his business and his family. And he'd come damn close to pulling it off.

Remembering that was still enough to leave Mac a little shaken. Hell, he'd trusted Rafe and had almost lost everything because of it. Sure, they'd worked everything out, and now Rafe was even his brother-in-law, since he and Mac's sister, Violet, were married and having a baby.

But there were still moments when Mac wondered how he could have missed the fact that Rafe was on a misguided quest for revenge.

Without Andi to help him through and talk him down when he was so damned angry he could hardly see straight, Mac didn't know if the situation would have resolved itself so quickly.

So why, when life was settling down again, had she chosen *now* to talk about quitting? Mac had no idea what had brought this nonsense on, but he'd nip it in the bud, fast. Now that things were calming down in Royal, Mac had plans to spend more time actually working and even expanding the family ranch, which Violet used to handle. With his sister focusing on the place Rafe had bought for them, Mac wanted to get back to his roots: being on a horse, overseeing the day-to-day decisions of ranch life and working out of a home office to keep his wildly divergent business interests growing.

Life was damn busy and Andi was just going to have to stay right where she was to help him run things—the way she always had.

"Where's this coming from, Andi?" he asked, leaning one hip against the corner of his desk.

"The fact that you can even ask me that is astonishing," she replied.

He gave her a slow grin, the very same smile that worked to sway women across Texas into agreeing with anything he said. Of course, Andrea Beaumont had always been a tougher sell, but he'd use whatever weapons he had to hand. "Now, Andi," he said, "we've worked together too long for you to get snippy so easily."

"Snippy?" Her eyes fired up again and Mac thought for a second or two that she might reach up and yank at her hair. "That is the most insulting thing…"

She took another deep breath and Mac idly noticed how those heavy breaths she kept taking made her small, perfect breasts rise and fall rhythmically. For such a tiny woman, she had curves in all the right places. Funny he'd really not taken the time to notice that before.

Andi was simply *there.* She kept on top of everything. Nothing ever slipped past her. But apparently *this* had slipped past *him.*

"This is coming out of the blue and I think you owe me some sort of explanation."

"It's *not* out of the blue, Mac," she said, throwing both hands high. "That's the point. I've worked for you for six years."

"I know that."

"Uh-huh. And did you notice I didn't even take a vacation the last two years?"

His frown deepened. No, he hadn't noticed. Probably should have, though, since every damn time she *did* take some time off, he ended up hunting her down, getting her to solve some damn problem or other. The fact that she'd stayed here, working, had only made his life continue on its smooth, well-planned path, so he hadn't had to think about it.

"Is that what this is about?" He pushed off the desk, braced his feet wide apart and folded his arms across his chest. "You want a vacation?"

Her mouth flattened into a straight, grim line. "No. I want a life. To get that life, I have to quit. So, I'm giving you my two weeks' notice."

"I don't accept that."

"You don't get a vote, Mac."

"See," he said tightly, "that doesn't fly with me, either."

It was like talking to two brick walls, Andrea thought, staring up at the man who had been her focus for the past six years. About six foot one, he had short, dark blond hair that in another month or so would be shot through with sun streaks. His summer-green eyes were cool, clear and always held a sort of calculating gleam his competitors usually took for affability. He was lean but strong, his build almost deceptively lanky.

Mac McCallum was the stuff women's dreams were made of. Sadly, that was true of Andi's dreams, too.

Six years she'd worked for him. She wasn't sure exactly when she'd made the supreme mistake of falling in love with her boss, but it seemed as if those feelings had always been with her. A part of her had always hoped that one day he might open his eyes and really *see* her—but the more rational, reasonable part of Andi knew that was never going to happen.

To Mac, she would always be good ol' Andi. She knew he saw her as he did the new laser printer in the office. Efficient, able to get the job done and nearly invisible. The raise he'd given her notwithstanding, he didn't really appreciate just how hard she worked to keep McCallum Enterprises running smoothly—he just expected it. Well, it had taken her a long time to reach this point, but she really wanted a life. And as long as she was here, mooning after a man she couldn't have, that wouldn't happen. Andi had been working up to quitting for a long while now, and today had finally given her the last little nudge she'd needed.

It was liberation day.

"Go on, Andi. Go to your nephew's game. Enjoy the rest of the day and we'll talk about this again when you calm down."

He still didn't get it, and she knew that she had to make herself clear. "I'm completely calm, Mac. I'm just done."

A slow, disbelieving smile curved his mouth, and Andi told herself to stay strong. Stay resolved. There was no future for her here. But watching him, she realized that he would spend her two weeks'-notice time doing everything he could to change her mind. Knowing just how charming he could be was enough to convince her to say, "I haven't had a vacation in two years. So I'm going to take my vacation time for the next two weeks."

"You're just going to leave the office flat?" Stunned now, he stared at her as if she had two heads. "What about the contracts for the Stevenson deal? Or the negotiations on the Franklin Heating project?"

"Laura's up-to-date on all of it and if she needs me," Andi said firmly, "she can call and I'll be happy to walk her through whatever problem she's having."

"Laura's the office manager."

True, Andi thought, and though the woman had been with the company for only a couple of years, she was bright, ambitious and a hard worker. And as a newly-wed, she wouldn't be spinning romantic fantasies about her boss.

"You're serious?" he asked, dumbfounded. *"Now?"*

"Right now," Andi told him and felt a faint flutter of excitement tangled with just a touch of fear.

She was really going to do it. Going to quit the job she'd dedicated herself to for years. Going to walk away from the man who had a hold on her heart whether he knew it or not. She was going out into the world to find herself a life.

With that thought firmly in mind, she turned and headed for the door before Mac could talk her out of leaving.

"I don't believe this," he muttered.

Can't really blame him, she thought. This was the first time since she'd met Mac that she was doing something for herself.

Andi paused in the doorway and glanced back over her shoulder for one last look at him. He was everything she'd ever wanted and she'd finally accepted that she would never have him. "Goodbye, Mac."

Outside, the June sunlight streamed down from a brassy blue sky. Summer was coming and it seemed in a hurry to get here. Andi's footsteps crunched on the gravel of the employee parking area behind the office.

With every step, she felt a little more certain that what she was doing was right. Sure, it was hard, and likely to get harder because Andi would miss seeing Mac every day. But hadn't she spent enough time mooning over him? How would she ever find a man to spend her life with if she spent all her time around the one man she couldn't have?

"Just keep walking, Andi. You'll be glad of it later." Much later, of course. Because at the moment, she felt as if she couldn't breathe.

What she needed was affirmation and she knew just where to find it. When she got to her car, Andi opened the door and slid into the dark blue compact. Then she pulled her cell phone from her purse, hit the speed dial and waited through five rings before a familiar voice answered.

"Thank God you called," her sister, Jolene, said. "Tom's shift ended two hours ago and now that he's home, he says he needs to unwind…"

Andi laughed and it felt good. "So which wall is he tearing down?"

Jolene sighed. "The one between the living room and the kitchen."

While her sister talked, Andi could picture exactly what was happening in the old Victorian on the far side of Royal. Her brother-in-law, Tom, was a fireman who relaxed by working on his house. Last year, after a brush-fire that had kept him working for more than a week, he built a new powder room on the first floor.

"It's a good thing you bought a fixer-upper," Andi said when her older sister had wound down.

"I know." Laughing, Jolene added, "I swear the man's crazy. But he's all mine."

Andi smiled sadly, caught her expression in the rearview mirror and silently chastised herself for feeling even the slightest twinge of envy. Jolene and Tom had been married for ten years and had three kids, with another on the way. Their family was a sort of talisman for Andi. Seeing her sister happy and settled with her family made Andi want the same for herself.

Which was just one of the reasons she'd had to quit her job. Before it was too late for her to find what her heart craved. Love. Family.

"And," Jolene was saying, "I love that my kitchen's about to get a lot bigger. But oh, Lord, the noise. Hang on, I'm headed out to the front porch so I can hear you."

Andi listened to the crashing and banging in the background fade as her sister walked farther away from the demolition zone.

"Okay, backyard. That's better," Jolene said. "So, what's going on, little sister?"

"I did it." Andi blew out a breath and rolled her car windows down to let the warm Texas wind slide past her. "I quit."

"Holy…" Jolene paused and Andi imagined her sister's shocked expression. "Really? You quit your job?"

"I did." Andi slapped one hand to her chest to keep her pounding heart from leaping out. "Walked right out before I could change my mind."

"I can't believe it."

"You and me both," Andi said. "Oh, God. I'm *unemployed*."

Jolene laughed. "It's not like you're living on the streets, Andi. You've got a house you hardly ever see, a vacation fund that you've never used and a rainy-day savings account that has enough in it to keep you safe through the next biblical flood."

"You're right, you're right." Nodding, Andi took a few deep breaths and told herself to calm down. "It's just, I haven't been unemployed since I was sixteen."

The reality of the situation was hitting home and it came like a fist to the solar plexus. If this kept up, she might faint and wouldn't that be embarrassing, having Mac come out to the parking lot and find her stretched out across her car seats?

She'd quit her job.

What would she do every day? How would she live? Sure, she'd had a few ideas over the past few months about what she might want to do, but none of it was carved in stone. She hadn't looked into the logistics of anything, she hadn't made even the first list of what she'd need do before moving on one of her ideas, so it was all too nebulous to even think about.

She had time. Plenty of time to consider her future, to look at her ideas objectively. She would need plans. Purpose. Goals. But she wasn't going to have those right away, so it was time to take a breath. No point in making herself totally insane. Jolene was right. Andi had a big savings account—Mac was a generous employer if nothing else—and it wasn't as if she'd had time to spend that generous salary. Now she did.

"This is so great, Andi."

"Easy for you to say."

Jolene laughed again, then shouted, "Jilly, don't push your sister into the pool."

Anyone else hearing that would immediately think built-in, very deep pool. In reality, Andi knew the kids were jumping in and out of a two-foot-deep wading pool. Shallow enough to be safe and wet enough to give relief from the early Texas heat.

"Jacob's game still at five today?" Andi asked abruptly.

"Sure. You're coming?"

Of course she was going to the game. She'd quit her job so she'd be able to see her family. She smiled at her reflection as she imagined the look on Jacob's little face when she showed up at the town baseball field. "You couldn't keep me away."

"Look at that—only been unemployed like a second and already you're getting a life."

Andi rolled her eyes. Jolene had been on her to quit for the past few years, insisting that standing still meant stagnating. As it turned out, she had a point. Andi had given Mac all she could give. If she stayed, she'd only end up resenting him and infuriated with herself. So it was no doubt past time to go. Move on.

And on her first official day of freedom, she was going to the Royal Little League field to watch her nephew's game. "I'm just going home to change and I'll meet you at the field in an hour or so."

"We'll be there. Jacob will be so excited. And after the game, you'll come back here. Tom will grill us all some steaks to go with the bottle of champagne I'm making a point of picking up. You can drink my share."

Andi forced a smile into her voice. "Champagne and steaks. Sounds like a plan."

But after she hung up with her sister, Andi had to ask herself why, instead of celebrating, she felt more like going home for a good cry.

Two

Andi went to the baseball game. Jolene had been right: eight-year-old Jacob was thrilled that his aunt was there, cheering for him alongside his parents. Of course, six-year-old Jilly and three-year-old Jenna were delighted to share their bag of gummy bears with Andi, and made plans for a tea party later in the week.

It had felt odd to be there, in the bleachers with family and friends, when normally she would have been at work. But it was good, too, she kept telling herself.

After the game, she had dinner with her family and every time her mind drifted to thoughts of Mac, Andi forced it away again. Instead, she focused on the kids, her sister and the booming laugh of her brother-in-law as he flipped steaks on a smoking grill.

By the following morning, she told herself that if she'd stayed with Mac and kept the job that had consumed her life, she wouldn't have had that lazy, easy afternoon and evening. But still she had doubts. Even though she'd enjoyed herself, the whole thing had been so far out of her comfort zone, Andi knew she'd have to do some fine-tuning of her relaxation skills. But at least now she had the time to try.

Sitting on her front porch swing, cradling a cup of coffee in her hands, Andi looked up at the early-morning sky and saw her own nebulous future staring back at her. Normally by this time she was already at the office, brewing the first of many pots of coffee, going over her and Mac's calendars and setting up conference calls and meetings. There would already be the kind of tension she used to live for as she worked to keep one step ahead of everything.

Now? She took another sip of coffee and sighed. The quiet crowded in on her until it felt as though she could hear her own heartbeat in the silence. Relaxation turned to tension in a finger snap. She was unemployed and, for the first time since she was a kid, had nowhere in particular to be.

It was both liberating and a little terrifying. She was a woman who thrived on schedules, preferred order and generally needed a plan for anything she was going to do. Even as a kid, she'd had her closet tidy, her homework done early and her bookcases in her room alphabetized for easy reference.

While Jolene's bedroom had been chaotic, Andi's was an island of peace and calm. A place for everything, everything in its place. Some might call that compulsive. She called it organized. And maybe that was just what she needed to do now. Organize her new world. Channel energies she would normally be using for Mac and his business into her own life. She was smart, capable and tenacious. There was nothing she couldn't do.

"So." After that inner pep talk, she drew her feet up under her on the thick, deep blue cushion. "I'll make a plan. Starting," she said, needing the sound of her own voice in the otherwise still air, "with finally getting my house in shape."

She'd bought the run-down farmhouse a year ago and hadn't even had the time to unpack most of the boxes stacked in the second bedroom. The walls hadn't been painted, there were no pictures hung, no rugs scattered across the worn, scarred floor. It pretty much looked as lonely and abandoned as it had when she first bought it. And wasn't that all kinds of sad and depressing?

Until a year ago, Andi had lived in a tiny condo that was, in its own way, as impersonal and unfinished as this house. She'd rented it furnished and had never had the time—or the inclination—to put her own stamp on the place. Working for Mac had meant that she was on duty practically twenty-four hours a day. So when was she supposed to be able to carve out time for herself? But in spite of everything, Andi had wanted a home of her own. And in the back of her mind, maybe she'd been planning even then on leaving McCallum Enterprises.

Leaving Mac.

It was the only explanation for her buying a house that she had known going in would need a lot of renovation. Sure, she could have hired a crew to come in and fix it all up. And she had had a new roof put on, the plumbing upgraded and the electrical brought up to code. But there were still the yards to take care of, the floors to be sanded, the walls to be painted and furniture to be bought.

"And that starts today," she said, pushing off the swing. With one more look around the wide front yard, she turned and opened the screen door, smiling as it screeched in protest. Inside, she took another long glance at her home before heading into the kitchen to do what she did best. Make a list.

She knew where she'd start. The walls should be painted before she brought in sanders for the floors, and they'd probably need a couple of coats of paint to cover the shadow images of long-missing paintings.

In the kitchen she sat at a tiny table and started making notes. She'd go at her home exactly as she would have a new project at McCallum. Priorities. It was all about priorities.

An hour later, she had several lists and the beginnings of a plan.

"There's a lot to do," she said, her voice echoing in the old, empty house. "Might as well get started."

She worked for hours, sweeping, dusting, mopping, before heading into Royal to buy several gallons of paint. Of course, shopping in town was never as easy as entering a store, getting what you wanted and then leaving again. There were people to chat with, gossip to listen to and, as long as she was there, she stopped in at the diner for some tea and a salad she didn't have to make herself.

The air conditioning felt wonderful against her skin, and Andi knew if it was this hot in early June, summer was going to be a misery. She made a mental note to put in a call to Joe Bennet at Bennet Heating and Cooling. If she was going to survive a Texas summer, she was going to need her own air conditioning. Fast.

"So," Amanda Battle said as she gave Andi a refill on

her iced tea. "I hear you quit your job and you're running off to Jamaica with your secret lover."

Andi choked on a cherry tomato and, when she got her breath back, reached for her tea and took a long drink. Looking up at Amanda, wife of Sheriff Nathan Battle and owner of the diner, she saw humor shining in her friend's eyes.

"Jamaica?"

Amanda grinned. "Sally Hartsfield told me, swears that Margie Fontenot got the story direct from Laura, who used to work with you at Mac's. Well, Laura's cousin's husband's sister got the story started and that is good enough to keep the grapevine humming for a while."

Direct was probably not the right word to describe that line of communication, but Andi knew all too well how the gossip chain worked in town. It was only mildly irritating to find out that she was now the most interesting link in that chain. For the moment.

But Jamaica? How did people come up with this stuff? she wondered, and only briefly considered taking her first vacation in years, if only to make that rumor true. Still, if she went to Jamaica, it would be a lot more fun if she could make the secret-lover part of the gossip true, too.

"Secret lover?" If only, she thought wistfully as an image of Mac rose up in her mind.

"Oooh. I like how your eyes got all shiny there for a second. Tells me there might be something to this particular rumor. Something you'd like to share with a pal? Wait." Amanda held up one finger. "Gotta fill some coffee cups. Don't go anywhere until I get back."

While she was gone, Andi concentrated on the sounds and scents of the Royal Diner. Everything was so familiar; sitting there was like being wrapped up in a cozy blanket. Even when you knew that everyone in town was now talking about *you*. Royal had had plenty of things to chew over the past couple years. From the tornado to an actual *sheikh* working a revenge plot against Mac, local tongues had been kept wagging.

And the diner was gossip central—well, here and the Texas Cattleman's Club. But since the club was limited to members only, Andi figured the diner was the big winner in the grapevine contest.

She looked around and pretended not to notice when other customers quickly shifted their gazes. The black-and-white-tile floor was spotless, the red vinyl booths and counter stools were shiny and clean, and the place, as always, was packed.

God, she hated knowing that mostly everyone in there was now talking and speculating about her. But short of burying her head in the sand or locking herself in her own house, there was no way to avoid any of it.

Amanda worked the counter while her sister, Pamela, and Ruby Fowler worked the tables. Conversations rose and fell like the tides, and the accompanying sounds of silverware against plates and the clink of glasses added a sort of background music to the pulse of life.

When Amanda finally came back, Andi mused, "Where did Laura come up with Jamaica, I wonder?"

"Nothing on the secret lover then?" Amanda asked.

Andi snorted. "Who has time for a lover?"

Amanda gave her a sympathetic look, reached out and patted her hand. "Honey, that's so sad. You've got to make time."

She would if she had the option of the lover she wanted. But since she didn't, why bother with anyone else? "How can I when I'm going to Jamaica? But again, why Jamaica?"

"Maybe wishful thinking," Amanda said with a shrug, leaning down to brace folded arms on the counter. "Heaven knows, lying on a beach having somebody bring me lovely alcoholic drinks while I cuddle with my honey sounds pretty good to me most days."

"Okay, sounds pretty good to me, too," Andi said. If she *had* a honey. "Instead, I'm headed home to start painting."

Amanda straightened up. "You're planning on painting your place on your own? It'll take you weeks."

"As the gossip chain informed you already," she said wryly, "I'm unemployed, so I've got some time."

"Well," Amanda said, walking to the register to ring up Andi's bill, "using that time to paint rather than find yourself that secret lover seems a waste to me. And, if you change your mind, there's any number of kids around town who would paint for you. Summer jobs are hard to come by in a small town."

"I'll keep it in mind. Thanks." Andi paid, slung her purse over her shoulder and said, "Say hi to Nathan for me."

"I'll do that. And say hi to Jamaica for me." Amanda gave her a wink, then went off to check on her customers again.

Several hours later, Andi knew she should have been tired. Instead, she was energized, and by the end of her first day as a free woman, the living room was painted a cool, rich green the color of the Texas hills in springtime. It would need another coat, but even now she saw the potential and loved it. She had a sense of accomplishment, of simple satisfaction, which she hadn't felt in far too long. Yes, she'd been successful in her career, but that was Mac's business. His empire. This little farmhouse, abandoned for years, was all *hers*. And she was going to bring it back to life. Make it shine as it had to some long-gone family.

"And maybe by the time it's whole and happy again, I will be, too," she said.

"Talking to yourself?" a female voice said from the front porch. "Not a good sign."

Andi spun around and grinned. "Violet! Come on in."

Mac's sister opened the screen door and let it slap closed behind her. Being nearly seven months pregnant hadn't stopped Vi from dressing like the rancher she was. She wore a pale yellow T-shirt that clung to her rounded belly, a pair of faded blue jeans and the dusty brown boots she preferred to anything else.

Her auburn hair was pulled into a high ponytail at the back of her head and her clear green eyes swept the freshly painted walls in approval. When she looked back at Andi, she nodded. "Nice job. Really. Love the darker green as trim, too. Makes the whole thing pop."

"Thanks." Andi took another long look and sighed. "I'll go over it again tomorrow. But I love it. This color makes the room feel cool, you know? And with summer coming…"

"It's already hot," Vi said. "You are getting air conditioning put in, right?"

"Oh, yeah. Called them at about eight this morning, as soon as the sun came up and started sizzling. They're backed up, though, so it'll be a week or two before they can come out here."

"Well," Vi said, walking into the kitchen as comfortably as she would at her own house. "If you start melting before then, you can come and stay with Rafe and me at the ranch."

"Ah, yes," Andi said, following her friend into her kitchen—which was comfortably stuck in the 1950s. "What a good time. I can be the third wheel with the newlyweds."

"We don't have sex in front of people, you know," Vi told her with a laugh. "We tried, but the housekeeper Rafe hired disapproved."

She stuck her head in the refrigerator, pulled out a pitcher of tea and sighed with pleasure. "Knew I could count on you to have tea all ready to go. You get glasses. Do you have any cookies?"

"Some Oreos." They'd been friends for so long, they worked in tandem. "In the pantry."

"Thank God."

Laughing, Andi filled two glasses with ice, then poured each of them some tea as Vi hurried into the walk-in pantry and came back out already eating a cookie. She sighed, rolled her eyes and moaned, "God, these are so good."

Still chuckling, Andi took a seat at the tiny table and watched her friend dig into the cookie bag for another. "Rafe still watching what you eat?"

Vi dropped into the chair opposite her, picked up her tea and took a long drink. "Like a hawk. He found my stash of Hershey's bars, so they're gone." She ate the next cookie with as much relish as she had the first. "I love the man like crazy but he's making me a little nuts. Although, one thing I'll say for him, he does keep ice cream stocked for me."

"Well, that's something," Andi agreed, taking a seat opposite her.

"But, wow, I miss cookies. And cake. And brownies. The only bad part about moving to the Wild Aces when I married Rafe? Leaving the Double M and our housekeeper Teresa's brownies. I swear they're magic." Vi sighed and reached for another cookie. "You want to make a batch of brownies?"

Andi really hated to quash the hopeful look on her friend's face, but said, "Oven doesn't work." Andi turned to look at the pastel pink gas stove. The burners worked fine, but the oven had been dead for years, she was willing to bet. "And it's too hot in here to bake anything."

"True." Vi turned her tea glass on the narrow kitchen table, studying the water ring it left behind. "And I didn't really come here to raid your pantry, either, in spite of the fact that I'm eating all of your Oreos."

"Okay, then why are you here?"

"I'm a spy," Violet said, laughing. "And I'm here to report that Mac is really twisted up about you quitting."

"Is he?" Well, that felt good, didn't it? She had long known that she was indispensable in the office. Now he knew it, too, and that thought brought her an immense wave of satisfaction. Instantly, a ping of guilt began to echo inside her, but Andi shut it down quickly. After all, it wasn't as if she *wanted* Mac to have a hard time. She was only taking the opportunity to enjoy the fact that he was. "How do you know?"

"Well, spy work isn't easy," Violet admitted. "We pregnant operatives must rely on information from reliable sources."

Andi laughed shortly. "You mean gossip."

"I resent that term," Violet said with an indignant

sniff. Then she shrugged and took another cookie. "Although, it's accurate. Mac hasn't actually said anything to me directly. *Yet.* But Laura called a couple hours ago practically in tears."

"What happened?" Andi asked. "Mac's not the kind of man to bring a woman to tears."

"I don't know," Violet said, smiling. "He's made me cry a few times."

"Angry tears don't count."

"Then Laura's tears don't count, either," Vi told her. "She was really mad—at *you* for leaving her alone in the office."

"Probably why she made up the Jamaica story," Andi muttered.

"Jamaica?"

"Never mind." She waved one hand to brush that away. "What did Mac do?"

"Nothing new. Just the same old crabby attitude you've been dealing with for years. Laura just doesn't know how to deal with it yet."

Okay, now she felt a little guilty. Mac could be…difficult. And maybe she should have used her two weeks' notice to prepare Laura for handling him. But damn it, *she'd* learned on her own, hadn't she? Laura was just going to have to suck it up and deal.

"Anyway," Vi continued, "I told her the best thing to do was stay out of his way when he starts grumbling under his breath. She said that's exactly what he was doing already and that the office was too small for her to effectively disappear."

Andi chuckled because she could imagine the woman trying to hunch into invisibility behind her desk. "Poor Laura. I really shouldn't laugh, though, should I? I sort of left her holding the bag, so to speak, and now she's having to put up with not only Mac's demands but the fact that I'm not there to take the heat off."

"Laura's tough. She can take it." Vi picked up a fourth cookie and sighed a little as she bit in. "Or she won't. Either way, her choice. And if she walks out, too? An even better lesson for Mac."

"You think?"

"Absolutely," his sister said, waving her cookie for emphasis before popping it into her mouth and talking around it while she chewed. "The man thinks he's the center of the universe and all the rest of us are just moons orbiting him.

"Maybe it really started when our parents died and he had to step up. You know, he's only six years older than me, but he went from big brother to overbearing father figure in a finger snap." She frowned a little, remembering. "We butted heads a lot, but in the end, Mac always found a way to win."

Andi knew most of this family history. Over the years, Mac had talked to her about the private plane crash that had claimed his parents and how he'd worked to make sure that Violet felt safe and secure despite the tragedy that had rocked their family. He'd done it, too. Violet was not only a successful, happy adult, she was married and about to become a mother.

Maybe he had been overbearing—and knowing Mac, she really had no doubt of that—but he'd protected his sister, kept the family ranch and even managed to build on the business his parents had left behind until McCallum Enterprises was one of the biggest, most diversified companies in the country.

In all fairness to him, Andi had to say, "Looks to me like he did a good job."

Violet shrugged and nodded. "Yeah, he did. But the thing is, he's so used to people snapping to attention whenever he walks into a room, I think it's good for him that you quit. That he's finding out he can't *always* win. It'll be a growth moment for him."

But Andi knew that growth wasn't always easy. She also knew she should feel bad about being glad that Mac would have a hard time without her.

Apparently, though, she wasn't that good a person.

She still wasn't there.

From the moment Mac walked into the office that morning, a part of him had fully expected to find Andi right where she belonged, at her desk. But she hadn't been.

Except for a few times when he'd had no other choice, Mac had spent most of the day ignoring Laura as she hunched behind her computer, pretending to be invisible. No doubt she'd been worried how the day would go without Andi there to take care of things.

Well, hell, he had been, too.

As it turned out, with reason.

"This day just couldn't get worse."

Mac left his office and fired a hard look at Laura. "I need the Franklin contracts. I tried to pull up the pdf and it's not where it's supposed to be. Bob Franklin just called, he's got some questions and—" He noticed the wide-eyed expression on Laura's face and told himself it was pointless to hammer at her.

This was Andi's territory. Turning, he stomped into the back of the building where Andi had stored hard copies of each of their in-progress deals in old-fashioned file cabinets. Of course, their records were mostly digitized and stored in the cloud, with several redundant backup sites so nothing could be lost. But there was something to say for holding a hard copy of a contract in your hands. It was immediate and more convenient, in his mind, than scrolling up and down a computer screen looking for a particular clause. Especially when you couldn't find the damn digital copy.

"And now I have to hunt down the stupid contract the hard way." He yanked open the top file drawer and started flipping through the manila separators. He made it through the *F*s and didn't find the Franklin takeover.

Shaking his head, he told himself that he was the damn *boss*. It wasn't up to him to find a damn contract on a damn deal they'd done only three weeks ago. The problem was it was *Andi's* job and she wasn't here to do it.

Laura was good at what she did and he had no doubt that in time she might grow to be even a third as good as Andi at the job. But for now, the woman was an office manager suddenly tossed into the deep end. There were a couple of part-time interns, too, but neither of them could find their way out of a paper bag without a flashlight and a map.

"So bottom line?" he muttered, slamming the drawer and then opening another one. "I'm screwed."

Normally, this late in the afternoon, he and Andi were huddled around his desk, talking about the day's work and what was coming up on the schedule. He really didn't want to admit how much he missed just talking to her. Having her there to bounce ideas off of. To help him strategize upcoming jobs.

"Plus, she would know exactly where the stupid contract is," he muttered.

Mac hated this. Hated having his life disrupted, his business interfered with—hell, his *world* set off balance. Worse, Andi had to have known this would happen when she walked out and, no doubt, she was sitting on a beach in Bimini right now, smiling at the thought of him trying to set things right again on his own.

"Take a vacation. Who the hell has time for a vacation?" he asked the empty file room. "If you love what you do, *work* is vacation enough, isn't it?" He slammed the second drawer shut and yanked the third open. What the hell kind of filing system was she using, anyway?

"She loved her work, too," he muttered. "Can't tell me otherwise. In charge of every damn thing here, wasn't she? Even setting up the damn filing system in some weird way that I can't figure out now. If she thinks I'm going to let this damn office crumble to the ground then she's got another damn think or two coming to her because damned if I will, damn it!"

Temper spiking, he slammed the third drawer shut and then just stood there, hands on his hips, and did a slow turn, taking in the eight filing cabinets and the dust-free work table and chairs in the center of the room.

"Why the hell is she on a beach when I need her help?"

His brain dredged up a dreamlike image of Andi, lying back on some lounge, beneath a wide umbrella. She sipped at a frothy drink and behind huge sunglasses, her eyes smiled. Some cabana boy hovered nearby enjoying the view of Andi in a tiny yellow bikini that Mac's mind assured him was filled out perfectly.

Mac scowled and shut down that mental image because he sure as hell didn't need it. "Why is she off enjoying herself when I'm here trying to figure out what she did?"

But even as he complained, he knew it wasn't the filing that bothered him. Given enough time, he'd find whatever he needed to find. It was being here. In the office. Without Andi.

All day he'd felt slightly off balance. One step out of rhythm. It had started when he got there early as usual and didn't smell coffee. Andi had always beat him to work and had the coffee going for both of them. Then she'd carry two cups into his office and they'd go over the day's schedule and the plans that were constantly in motion.

Not today, though. He'd made his own damn coffee— he wasn't a moron after all—then had carried it to his desk and sat there alone, going over schedules that *she* had set up. She wasn't there to talk to. She wasn't there to remind him to keep on track and not to go spinning off into tangents—so his brain had taken one of those side roads and he'd lost two hours of time while researching an idea on the internet. So the rest of the day he was behind schedule and that was her fault, too.

"What the hell is she doing in Bimini? Or Tahiti or wherever it is she went looking to relax?" Shaking his head, he walked to the window and stared out as the twilight sky deepened into lavender and the first stars winked into existence.

In the distance, he could see the fields of his home ranch, the Double M, freshly planted and only waiting for summer heat to grow and thrive and become a sea of waving, deep, rich green alfalfa. Beyond those fields lay miles of open prairie, where his cattle wandered freely and the horses he wanted to focus on raising and breeding raced across open ground, tails and manes flying.

This was his place. His home. His empire.

He'd taken over from his father when his parents died and Mac liked to think they'd have been proud of what he'd done with their legacy. He'd improved it, built on it and had plans that would continue to make it grow and thrive.

"And it would be a helluva lot easier to do if Andi hadn't chucked it all for the beach and a margarita."

When his phone rang, he reached for it, digging it out of his pocket. Seeing his sister's name pop up didn't put a smile on his face. "What is it, Vi?"

"Well, hello to you, too," she said, laughing in his ear. "Nothing like family to give you that warm, fuzzy feeling."

He sighed, scraped one hand across his face and searched for patience. He and Vi had been at odds most of their lives, especially since he had been in charge of her and Vi didn't take kindly to anyone giving her orders. Through it all, though, they'd remained close, which he was grateful for.

Usually.

Already annoyed, he didn't need much of a push to pass right into irritated. "What is it, Vi? I'm busy."

"Wow, I'm just choking up with all this sentiment. Must be all these hormones from being pregnant with your first niece or nephew."

Reluctantly, Mac smiled. Shaking his head, he leaned back against the nearest cabinet and said, "Point made. Okay then, what's going on, little sister?"

"Oh, nothing much. Just wanted to see how you were

holding up—you know," she added in a sly tone, "with Andi gone and all."

"Heard about that, did you?" Hadn't taken long, Mac thought. But then the only thing that moved faster than a Texas tornado was gossip in Royal. He hated knowing that the whole town was talking about him.

Again. During that mess with Rafe, the McCallum family had been pretty much front and center on everyone's radar. With that settled, he'd expected life to go back to normal. Which it would have if Andi hadn't gotten a wild hair up her—

"Of course I heard," Vi was saying, and he could tell by her voice she was enjoying herself. "People all over town are talking about it and I figured Laura could use some advice on how to defuse your temper."

"Temper?" He scowled and shifted his gaze back to the view out the window. He realized it was later than he thought, as he watched Laura hurrying across the parking lot to her car. He sighed when she glanced back at the building uneasily. Hell, he'd be lucky if Laura didn't desert him, too. Still, he felt as though he had to defend himself. "I don't have a temper—"

Violet laughed and the sound rolled on and on until she was nearly gasping for breath. "Oh my, Mac. That was a good one."

He scowled a little as Laura drove out of the lot, then he shifted his gaze to the twilight just creeping across the sky. "Glad you're having a fine time."

"Well, come on," she said, laughter still evident in her tone. "Don't you remember the roof-raising shouting you used to do at me when I was a kid?"

"Shouting's not temper," he argued, "that's communication."

"Okay, sure," she said, chuckling. "Anyway, how's it going in the office without Andi there riding herd on everything?"

"It's *my* business, Vi," he reminded her. "I think I can take care of it on my own."

"That bad, huh?"

His back teeth ground together and he took a tight grip on the shout that wanted to erupt from his throat. It would only prove his sister right about his temper. And yeah, she was right about Andi being gone, too. It wasn't easy. Harder, frankly, than he'd thought it would be. But he wouldn't admit it. Wouldn't say so to Vi and for damn sure wouldn't be calling Andi to ask for help while she sat on some beach sipping cocktails. She'd made her choice, he told himself. Walked away from her responsibilities—from *him*—without a backward glance.

"Well, when I saw Andi earlier, she was doing just fine, in case you were interested..."

He came to attention. "You *saw* her? Where?"

"Her house."

Mac frowned out the window at the darkening sky. "She said she was taking her vacation time."

"And she's using it to fix up the house she's barely seen since she bought it."

He heard the dig in there and he wouldn't apologize for working so much. And as his assistant, Andi had been expected to spend as much time as he did at the job—and she'd never complained until now.

"With what I pay her as my executive assistant," he argued, "Andi could have hired crews of men to pull that house together at any point in the last year."

"Speaking of points," his sister said, "you're missing

Andi's entirely. She wants a *life*, Mac. Something you should think about, too."

"My life is just fine."

"Right. It's why you're living in the big ranch house all by yourself and the last date you had was with that airhead model who had trouble spelling her own name."

Mac snorted. She had a point about Jez. But when a man dated a woman like that, he wasn't worrying about her IQ.

"You realize you're supposed to be on *my* side in this?"

"Strangely enough, I am on your side, Mac. You're the most hardheaded man I've ever known—and that includes my darling husband, Rafe."

"Thanks very much," he muttered.

"I'm just saying," Vi went on, "maybe you could learn something from Andi on this."

"You want me to quit, too? You ready to take over?"

She laughed and he could almost see her rolling her eyes. "A vacation isn't the end of the world, Mac. Even for you."

While Vi talked, telling him all about the new nursery she and Rafe were having designed, Mac's mind once again focused on Andi.

Why in hell she'd all of a sudden gone off the rails, he still didn't understand. But if she was here in Texas and not being waited on by hot-and-cold-running cabana boys, maybe he could find out.

He smiled to himself. And maybe, he could convince her that quitting this job was the biggest mistake she'd ever made.

Three

It had been a long day, but a good one.

Andi was feeling pretty smug about her decision to quit and was deliberately ignoring the occasional twinges of regret. She'd done the right thing, leaving her job and—though it pained her—Mac behind. In fact, she should have done it three years ago. As soon as she realized that she was in love with a man who would never see her as more than a piece of office equipment.

Her heart ached a little, but she took another sip of wine and deliberately drowned that pain. Once she was free of her idle daydreams of Mac, she'd be able to look around, find a man to be with. To help her build the life she wanted so badly. A house. Children. A job that didn't eat up every moment of her time until it was all she could do to squeeze out a few minutes for a shower every day.

Shaking her head clear of any thoughts at all, she

sipped her wine and focused on the TV. The old movie playing was one of her favorites. And *The Money Pit* seemed particularly apt at this moment. The house needed a lot of work, but now she had the time and the money to put into it. It occurred to her that she was actually nesting and she liked it. The smell of fresh paint wafted through the room, even with the windows open to catch whatever the early-summer breeze might stir up. It was a warm night, but Andi was too tired to care. Her arms ached from wielding a roller all day, but it felt good. So good, in fact, she didn't even grumble when someone knocked on the front door, disturbing her relaxation period.

Wineglass in hand, she answered the door and jolted when she saw Mac smiling at her from across the threshold. He was absolutely the last person she would have expected to find on her porch.

"Mac? What're you doing here?"

"Hello to you, too," he said and stepped past her, unasked, into the house.

All she could do was close the door and follow him into the living room.

He turned a slow circle, taking in the room, and she looked at her house through his eyes. The living room had scarred wooden floors, a couch and coffee table and a small end table with a lamp, turned on now against the twilight gloom. The attached dining room was empty but for the old built-in china cabinet, and the open doorway into the kitchen showed off that room's flaws to perfection.

The whole house looked like a badly furnished rental, not like someone's home. But then, in her defense, she hadn't had the opportunity before now to really make a difference in the old house. Still, her newly painted soft green walls looked great.

He sniffed. "Been painting."

"Good guess."

He turned around, gave her a quick smile that had her stomach jittering before she could quash her automatic response. "I can smell it. The color's good."

"Thanks. Mac, why are you here?"

"First off," he said, "where the hell did you file the Franklin contracts?"

She hadn't been expecting that. "Alphabetically in the cabinet marked *T* for *takeovers*. There's also a *B* for *buyouts* and *M* for *mergers*."

He whipped his hat off and ran his fingers through his hair. "Of course there is."

"Laura could have told you this."

"Laura's not speaking to me."

"You scared her, didn't you," Andi said, shaking her head.

"I'm not scary."

"You don't scare *me*."

"Maybe I should," he muttered, then shrugged. "I'm also here because I wanted to get a look at what you left me for."

"You make it sound like I'm your cheating wife." She sighed. "I didn't leave you. I left my job."

But she *had* left him, Mac thought. It didn't feel like an employee walking out, but a betrayal. Damn it, she'd taught him over the years to count on her. To depend on her for too many things—and then she was gone. How the hell else was he supposed to feel?

"Same thing." His gaze fixed on her and for the first time he noticed that she wore a tiny tank top and a silky pair of drawstring pants. Her feet were bare and her toe-nails were painted a soft, blush pink. Her hair was long and loose over her shoulders, just skimming the tops of her breasts.

Mac took a breath and wondered where that flash of heat swamping him had come from. He'd been with Andi nearly every day for the past six years and he'd never reacted to her like this before. Sure, she was pretty, but she was his assistant. The one stable, organized, effi-cient woman in his life and he'd never taken the time to notice that she was so much more than that.

Now it was all he could notice.

Dragging his gaze from her, he took a deep breath and looked down the short hall toward the back of the house. "Do I get a tour?"

"No." She really wanted him out of there. He had to wonder why. "I painted all day. I'm tired. So—"

He looked back at her and thought she didn't look tired to him. She looked downright edible. "You don't have to do it all yourself, Andi. I could have a crew out here tomorrow and they'd be done with the whole place by the end of the week."

"I enjoy painting."

He shot her a speculative look. "You enjoy hacking your way through jungles, too? A team of gardeners could tear out those briars growing wild by the front porch."

"I don't want to hire someone—"

"I said I would hire them."

"No."

"Why the hell not?" He could understand stub-bornness. Hell, he sort of admired it. But this was pure mule-headedness. There was no reason for her to work herself into the ground trying to prove a point. "People who own houses hire people to work on them all the time."

"You don't get it, Mac," she said. "I want to do the work."

"You obviously need the help." He gave another quick look around. He could see what his sister had meant. The house did seem to be practically void of any kind of personal decoration or warmth. "You've been here—what? A year? As organized as you are, it shouldn't have taken you nearly that long to whip this place into shape. But it looks like you've hardly touched it."

Insult shot through her tone. "Seriously? When was I supposed to do any of that? I spend—spent—all of my time at the office. And on those extremely rare—I'm talking bigfoot-sighting rare—occasions when I did get an entire weekend off, I tried to squeeze in a little family time. See people. Go outside."

Mac rubbed one hand across the back of his neck and wished he could argue with her, but he knew she was right. He had pretty much monopolized her every waking moment for the past six years. But it wasn't as if he'd held her hostage. She'd made a hell of a lot of money thanks to the job she'd walked away from so easily.

"You don't have to make it sound like you were in prison," he pointed out in his own defense. "You love the work as much as I do."

"I do enjoy the work, and I'm good at it," she added as if he needed reminding. "But I want more out of life than closeting myself up in an office."

"And painting your house yourself, digging out briars and a mountain of weeds like I've never seen before, is 'more'?"

She frowned and he felt her irritation coming at him in thick waves. "For now, yes."

"You really must be desperate if you call painting and gardening a vacation," he said, watching her. "I really expected the rumor about you and Jamaica was true and you were off having silly drinks in coconut shells."

That mental image of Andi in a bathing suit rose up in his mind again, and now, thanks to seeing her out of her normal buttoned-down attire, his imagination was doing a much better job of filling out that dream bikini.

She huffed out a breath, folded her arms over her middle, unconsciously lifting her breasts high enough that he got a peek at the tops of them thanks to the scoop-necked tank she wore. A buzz of electricity zapped Mac and he had to work to keep his own hormones in line. How had he spent six years with this woman and *not* noticed how nicely she was put together?

She'd always worn her long, straight brown hair pulled back in a businesslike knot or ponytail, so until tonight he never would have guessed that it was wavy when she let it down around her shoulders—or that lamplight brought out hidden golden streaks among the dark brown. Andi had always worn sensible, straitlaced clothing on the job, so seeing her in that sleeveless tank and loose, silky sleep pants was a jolt to his system. Not to mention the fact that her upper arms were sleekly muscled and tanned. Where did she get that tan?

"Do I really strike you as the kind of woman who would enjoy lounging on a beach for two weeks?"

"Yesterday," he told her, "I would have said no way. But today—" he paused and let his gaze sweep up and down the length of her in an appreciative glance "—maybe."

She seemed to realize what she was wearing and he thought he actually caught a flush of color fill her cheeks briefly. *Andi blushing?* How many more surprises could a man take?

"You should go," she said simply.

Yeah, he probably should. But not yet. He could see that she was nesting or some damn thing here and until she'd gotten it out of her system, nothing would budge her out of this tiny, unfinished house. So the quickest way to get things back to normal would be for him to help her. Besides, if he really had kept her so busy she couldn't even unpack over the past year, maybe he owed it to her.

Whether Andi knew it or not, she was going to be bored senseless with nothing more to do than paint and mow the yard and whatever the hell else needed doing around here. Her mind was too sharp, her organizational skills too well honed for her to be happy puttering around the house. The sooner she realized that, the better for all of them.

"Tell you what," he announced. "I'll take the next two weeks off, too."

"What? Why? What?" She shook her head as if she hadn't heard him clearly, and who could blame her?

Mac couldn't remember when he'd last taken time off. He'd always been reluctant to leave the business in anyone's hands but his own. Not even his vice president's, and there weren't many people Mac trusted more than Tim Flanagan.

Now, with both Mac and Andi out of the office, and Tim off investigating another possible business move, there'd be no one there but Laura and a couple of interns. But it wasn't as though he was leaving the country, he told himself. He was right here in Royal, so if Laura ran into problems, he was completely reachable. Besides, two weeks would be over in a blink and everything would get back to normal.

"You quit your job so you'd have time to do stuff like this, right?"

Andi's lips pursed for a second before she nodded. "In a nutshell, yes."

"Fine. Then I'll be here for the next two weeks, helping you slap this place into shape." He curled his fingers over the brim of his hat. "Once we're done, if you still want to quit, fine."

"I will," she told him. "In fact, I already *have* quit."

He shrugged. "You can always change your mind."

"Not going to happen."

"We'll just think of these next two weeks as a sort of trial period," he said as if she hadn't spoken at all. "You can see what it's like to be out of the office and still have a chance to call off your resignation."

"Mac, you're making this harder than it has to be."

Yeah, he thought, recognizing the stubborn set to her chin, the flash in her eyes. Her mind was set. But then, he reassured himself, so was his. And when Mac McCallum made a decision, it was set in stone. In short order, he was going to prove to Andi that she wasn't the kind of woman to walk away from a high-powered job. She liked the responsibility. Thrived on it.

He had no doubt at all who was going to come out the winner in their little contest of wills. And by the time Andi had spent two weeks doing nothing but nesting, she'd be yearning to get back to the office and dive right in.

Giving her a slow smile, he said, "Tomorrow morning, I'll go in, take care of a couple things, tie up some loose ends and then I'm all yours."

"Mine?"

His smile deepened. Maybe it was small of Mac, but he enjoyed seeing her confused and just a little flustered. That almost never happened. Andi was too controlled. Too organized. Too on top of every damn thing that entered her universe. Being able to throw her for a loop, he decided, was fun.

"Yeah," he said, hooking his thumbs in the front pockets of his jeans. "Like I said, I'll be here, helping you. So for the next two weeks, you're the boss and I'm the employee."

"I'm the boss?"

He winked. "Like the sound of that, don't you?"

While she stared at him, he shifted his gaze around the room, checking out the freshly painted walls. "You did a nice job in here—"

"Gee, thanks."

"—*but*," he added as if she hadn't spoken, "the ceiling could use another coat. Hard for you to reach it I guess, since you're not all that tall."

"I used a ladder—"

"I won't need one to go over it tomorrow. Then we'll do the trim."

"I don't want your help."

His gaze immediately locked on hers. "Maybe not. But you need it."

She opened her mouth, then shut it again and took a breath before speaking. "Mac, I appreciate the offer…"

"No, you don't." In fact, her storm-gray eyes were smoldering. Typical Andi—she'd never admit there was something she couldn't do on her own.

Her lips twitched. "Okay, no, I don't. But then, you don't really want to take time away from the office to paint my house, either."

Mac thought about it for a minute. Ordinarily no, he wouldn't. His company had been his life for so many years now, he couldn't really imagine taking two weeks away from it. But if he wanted to keep Andi working for him—and he did—then he'd have to invest the time to convince her to stay. So he shrugged off her comment as if it meant nothing. "When I was a kid, my dad had me out on the ranch painting the barn, the stables, the fence around my mother's garden. I'm damn good with a paintbrush. And at woodworking. The ranch carpenter taught me a lot back then. I've got a fair hand at plumbing, too, though that can be iffy."

"Why would you want to use your no doubt impressive skills on my house?"

Here he gave her a grin and a wink. "What kind of Texan would I be if I didn't ride to the rescue?"

Her head snapped back. "*Rescue?* I don't need to be rescued, Mac. And now's a good time to remind you that for the last six years, I'm the one who's done most of the rescuing."

He laughed. Her outrage put fire in her eyes and a rush of color in her cheeks. Her breath was coming fast and furious and her breasts hitched even higher beneath that skimpy tank top. He'd have to remember to make her furious more often.

"Okay," he said, "I'll give you that. You've been riding herd on the business and keeping things moving for six years. So now it's time I paid that back."

She shook her head. "I don't need you to pay me back for doing my job."

"Maybe it's not about what you need," he said, and felt tension crawl through him as he stared into her gray eyes, where the fire was now banked, simmering low. This woman had been a central part of his life for years and he wasn't ready for that to end yet. Now that he was here, with her, in this nearly empty house with the dark settling around them, he wanted that even less than when he'd first come here.

"We'll work together and at the end of two weeks, if you still want to walk away, so be it." Sounded reasonable, though Mac had no intention of letting her go. "This is my decision, Andi. And you should know better than anyone else, once I make a call, I stick to it."

A second or two passed before she blew out a breath. "You're impossible."

"You set this in motion, Andi," he told her, shaking his head. "I'm just riding your wave."

Until, he told himself, he could get her back to the office, where she belonged. In the end, he would have his way and his life and the office would get back to normal. He and Andi would be working together again. Because Mac McCallum never accepted less than exactly what he wanted.

She shouldn't have been nervous, but she was.

Andi got up the next morning and her stomach was a twist of knots in anticipation of Mac's arrival. Why was he making this so hard? Why couldn't he just accept her resignation and let her go? For six years he'd treated her as if she were nothing more than an efficient, invisible worker bee.

Why was he noticing her now?

Andi poured herself a cup of coffee and carried it out

to the front porch. She sat down on the top step, cradled her cup between her palms and stared out at the gnarled oaks and the fields that surrounded her small house. But her mind wasn't on the view. Instead, every thought she had was for Mac. He might think she'd change her mind and go back to work, but she wouldn't.

Yes, dealing with Mac when he was determined to do something was a little like being a wave pounding away at a boulder. But over time, she assured herself, water won. It wore the rock away until only the water remained.

So she would be a wave. Relentless. Taking a deep breath, she looked up at the wide sweep of deep blue sky and told herself that it was a good thing Mac was coming over. When he realized she wouldn't change her mind, they could both move on.

And, she didn't believe for a minute that he'd last the entire two weeks. But maybe while he *was* here, she could help him discover how to relax. Turn off his big brain and think about something other than McCallum Enterprises. The man had been working nonstop since he was a teenager and needed a break even more than she did. If she could help him find it while getting her house in shape, then she'd do it. It was one last thing she could do for him. She just hoped she'd survive having him so close and so out of reach all at the same time.

He showed up an hour later, dressed in battered jeans, a stained University of Texas T-shirt and the scarred, worn boots she knew he wore for working on the ranch. His dark blond hair ruffled in a hot breeze when he yanked his hat off and grinned at her. "Ready to work?"

What was it about the man's smile that could tangle

her stomach up into twisted threads of desire? Just that simple curve of his mouth was enough, though when it was matched with his deep voice and lazy way of speaking, he was her kryptonite.

"Ready?" she asked, lifting her coffee cup. "I'm on a break. Already started."

He winked and walked past her. "Then I'd best start catching up."

She followed him into the house, her gaze dropping unerringly to his butt, covered with soft, faded denim. Oh, this was such a bad idea.

"The living room needed another coat," she said, clearing her throat, "so I started in there."

"Yeah, I can see that." He tipped his head back, studied what she'd done so far and what still needed doing. Tossing his hat to the couch, he turned and asked, "Where's your roller? I'll get the ceiling and the walls while you cut in against the trim."

"Who put you in charge?"

He winked. "Honey, when a McCallum's around, they're just naturally in charge."

"Oh, for—" Irritating, yes, she admitted silently, but he made her laugh, too. He always had. She watched him pick up the roller with the extension pole and swipe it through a tray of paint. As much as it pained her to admit it, she really could use his help on the stupid ceiling. Her neck had hurt all night from straining and looking up for hours the day before.

He glanced over his shoulder at her and there was a knowing smile in his eyes. "So, you gonna start painting again or are you just going to stare at me?"

"Paint. I'm going to paint," she said firmly, not sure

if she was convincing him or herself. "Just go. Be in charge."

"Always easier when they acquiesce so quickly."

Andi snorted and deliberately ignored him as she started painting. It wasn't easy. She could *feel* him in the room. *Hear* him breathing her air. If she looked over her shoulder, would he be looking at her, too? Wow, she was way too old for these junior high school thoughts.

"It's a good color," he said, that deep voice of his reverberating in the room before rumbling up her spine.

She shrugged the sensation off and concentrated on laying down a wide path of paint. "Yeah, it feels cool and in summer, that'll help."

"You've got air conditioning, right?"

"Not yet," she admitted and sighed a little. It was already hot and she knew it was going to get ugly by afternoon. Last night had been a long, private misery. She'd kept her bedroom windows open, hoping a breeze would find its way in, but it hadn't helped.

"Bet it's number one on your list," he said.

"My list?" She turned to look at him.

He was grinning and his gaze fixed on her briefly as he said, "Andi, you make so many lists, you have a master list to keep track of them all."

Did he really know her that well? He turned back to work and probably didn't see evidence of the surprise that flickered inside her, then changed to something else the longer she watched him. Heat that had nothing to do with the weather pumped through her as she watched the play of muscles across his back and shoulders. Mac moved the roller smoothly, applying even swaths of paint with much more ease than she had the day before.

But it wasn't paint that interested her at the moment.

It was the man standing so close, so tall, so...*there*. Mesmerizing really, she thought, the ripple and flow of those muscles was just—

"Andi? Hey, you all right?"

She shook her head, forcing herself out of the hormonal stupor she'd slipped into. "What? Yes. Fine. What?"

He grinned and dipped the roller into the tray for more paint. "Daydreaming won't get the work done."

"Right." *Idiot.* Six years she'd worked with him and hadn't once betrayed anything she felt for him. Darned if she'd start now. She went to work, determined to concentrate on the task at hand.

"I asked if it was Bennet Heating and Cooling you called about the AC."

"Yes," she said, not bothering to turn around to look at him. "But they're backed up. It seems everyone in the county is getting their air worked on or installing new units. Won't get out here for another week or two."

He didn't answer, so she figured the conversation was over. Easier to keep her mind on painting when she could pretend he wasn't in the room with her, anyway. Then he started talking again—but not to her. Andi turned around to face him.

"Hey, Joe, it's Mac McCallum." He smiled at her and kept talking into his cell phone. "Yeah, I'm over at Andi Beaumont's place and she tells me you can't get out to install air conditioning for a week or two. That right?"

It was that whole "take charge" thing again. He couldn't seem to help himself. She started to tell him to butt out, but he actually held one finger up in the air in a sign for quiet. So Andi did a slow, silent burn.

"Yeah, that's not going to work for me. How about

you get your boys out here tomorrow? Damn hot in here and we're painting and fixing the place up." He winked at Andi then said more softly, "Now, Joe, I don't want to wait for this, understand me? I'd consider it a personal favor if you could handle this tomorrow."

Personal favor. Everyone in town was eager to do favors for Mac because he never forgot, and if Joe Bennet ever needed help down the line, Mac would be there to return the "favor."

Nodding, he said, "That's good news. I'll tell Andi you'll be here tomorrow then. Oh, and how about installing some of those new units where you don't need to put in all the duct work? Like you installed at my office? That way we get that puppy up and running soon as we can. Hotter than the halls of hell in here, Joe." Mac laughed, then nodded. "Good. Good, we'll see you then. Appreciate it."

He shut his phone off, stuck it in his pocket and said cheerfully, "There I go, rescuing you again."

"I didn't ask to be rescued," she reminded him.

"A good rescuer doesn't wait to be asked."

"You shouldn't have done that, Mac." He was rich, powerful and so damn likable with it, most people went along just because he'd charmed them. It was well-known in Royal that Mac McCallum got what he wanted when he wanted it, and as far as she knew, no one had ever told him no. At least, not for long.

His eyebrows lifted. "Want me to call him back, then? Tell him there's no hurry? You're fine with the heat?"

She bit down on her bottom lip. He had her and he knew it. No, she didn't need rescuing, but she'd be spiting herself if she turned down help when it was offered. What would she prove by doing that?

"No."

"Good."

"You still shouldn't have."

"You're welcome."

"I didn't say thank-you."

"I'm willing to look past that shameful lack of grati-tude." He winked again. "And if I get a sandwich and some cold tea out of this deal I'll forgive you completely."

"You'll forgive *me*?" She choked out a laugh. "You're impossible."

"Can't be impossible," he said as he worked the paint roller smoothly. "Here I stand."

"The question is, why are you standing *here*?"

He lowered the roller, turned to look at her and said, "Because we're not done, Andi. I'm not willing to let you go, and I think over the next couple weeks we're both going to learn a thing or two."

Her stomach shivered and her mouth went dry. "If you really want to take time off—which is hard to believe—why not Paris? London? Jamaica?"

His eyes burned into hers. "You're not there, are you? Besides," he added, "why would I want to leave Texas?"

"You're making me a little crazy," she admitted, shak-ing her head.

"Nothing wrong with being a little crazy," he said. "It's the *lot* of crazy you have to watch out for."

He started painting again and Andi could only stare at him. He'd pretty much been the center of her business life for six years and now he was steamrolling his way through her personal life. Andi had deliberately taken these two weeks so she could get some space between herself and Mac.

How could she get over him if she was *with* him? But

she was forced to admit that she was glad she'd have
two more weeks with him. It was probably foolish, but
maybe while he was here, she really could help him find
a way to relax. To turn off that sharp, brilliant mind long
enough to enjoy his life a little. Except for the rare times
when he went out on a date or two with some gorgeous
yet dim model, actress or flight attendant, Mac was as
relaxation-deprived as she was.

Then she remembered what Amanda had said only
yesterday about *making* the time to have a secret lover
in her life. She shot Mac a sidelong look and let her gaze
sweep over him.

And suddenly, the next two weeks looked a lot more
interesting.

Four

"Where have you been hiding the last few days?"

Mac looked across the table at one of his oldest friends. Rafiq "Rafe" bin Saleed no longer looked the part of a Harvard-educated sheikh. Between moving here to Royal and marrying Mac's sister, Vi, Rafe had been transformed into an honorary Texan.

Since he'd had to go by the office and take care of a couple of things—how did people go on vacations?—Mac had called Rafe to meet him at the Royal Diner. They were sharing a booth in the back, and Mac caught a couple of the other customers shooting them curious glances. He ignored them and lifted his coffee cup for a sip of the dark, hot brew.

"Thought for sure Vi would have told you. I've been at Andi's house, helping her put it together." He shrugged. "It's really why I called. I've spent most of my time here lately talking to no one but women. Andi. Laura. Your wife."

"Your sister," Rafe reminded him. "And why are you helping Andi fix up that old house?"

In that clipped, well-bred accent, the question sounded more demanding than inquisitory. Mac chuckled. "You may not be a sheikh anymore, but you've still got that do-as-I-say thing in your voice."

Rafe smiled and sipped at his own coffee. "I believe the correct phrase here would be 'it takes one to know one.'"

"Okay. Touché." Easing back in the booth, Mac glanced out the windows at Main Street. Shoppers hurried up and down the sidewalks, carrying bags and herding toddlers. Cars crawled along the street, mindful of the speed limit. Rivers of colorful flowers spilled from baskets hanging from the streetlights. It was Main Street, USA, out there—just the way Mac liked it.

"Did Vi tell you about Andi quitting her job?"

"She did." Rafe, too, looked out the window briefly before shifting his gaze back to his friend. "And that you're trying to change her mind. My friend, you should know that a woman is difficult to manage."

He snorted. "Manage? Nobody manages Andi." He admired that about her even as that personality trait was working against him at the moment. Grinning at Rafe, he said, "And I'd truly love to be there when Vi finds out you think you're *managing* her."

Rafe shivered. "A wise man never lets that information slip."

"True." While the diner filled with customers who went about their business, Mac looked at his old friend and took a moment to realize how glad he was that they had managed to put their friendship back together. "Off the fascinating subject of women for a minute," he said abruptly, "have you given any more thought to officially joining the Texas Cattleman's Club?"

"I have," Rafe said softly. "And I actually wanted to ask if you would be the one to support my application."

A wide, satisfied smile stretched across Mac's face as he held one hand out across the table. When Rafe took it in a hard, firm shake, Mac said, "My pleasure. Really."

"I appreciate that. It's good to be here with you like this, Mac." Rafe took a breath and let it out. "When I let myself think about what I almost lost, almost threw away, by refusing to see the truth—"

"Almost doesn't mean a damn, Rafe. What matters is that you did see it. Finally," he added, and laughed when his friend winced at the reminder. "I'm glad to have you back, too. Plus, you married my sister, you poor dumb fool…"

"She's wonderful and you know it."

"Yeah," Mac allowed. "But don't tell her I said so." Shaking his head again, he said, "Wish to hell Andi was as easy to read as Violet."

"I wouldn't say your sister is 'easy' to understand."

Mac brushed that comment aside. "But Andi's always been easy to be around. She's a hell of a taskmaster. Kept the business running without a bump for years. Hell, Rafe, I thought I *knew* her. And all of a sudden, she's turned everything around on me. I feel like this is a woman I don't know at all."

"Maybe you don't," Rafe mused. "A work relationship is entirely different from life on the outside."

"Yeah, but people are who they are."

"Not always. When you're not wheeling and dealing,

you like being on a horse and speaking as if you're in an old Western movie."

Mac snorted. "Why was I glad to see you again?"

"Because everyone needs an honest friend." Rafe lifted his coffee cup in a salute.

"Maybe. And maybe you're right, too, about the work thing. Andi's determined to quit, damn it, and I can't let that happen."

"It may be that you won't be able to stop it."

Mac shot him a hard look. "Whose side are you on?"

Rafe held up both hands in mock surrender. "Yours, my friend. Of course. But as I have learned in dealing with your sister, I can say that a woman's mind is a tricky, always evolving thing."

"So I've noticed." He took another drink of coffee.

"And I've noticed," Rafe said with a cautious glance around, "that some in Royal are still unsure about me."

Mac sighed a little. "Well, this is one of the reasons I wanted you to meet me here. The more people see us together, as friends, the more they'll move on from what happened before. They'll all figure out that the hatchet's been buried and there's no hard feelings. Folks in Royal aren't the type to hold grudges, Rafe. They'll get past it—just like I did."

Rafe smiled. "Thank you for that, my friend. With you and Violet on my side, I'm sure all will be well."

"Wish I was as sure of my own situation as I am of yours," Mac said.

"How are my two most handsome customers doing?" Amanda Battle walked up to their table and gave each of them a wide smile.

"Coffee's good and so's the ambience," Mac said, smiling back.

"It's what I like to hear," Amanda said. "Now, Rafe, you tell Violet I expect her to come around soon. I want to keep an eye on that baby bump of hers."

"I will do it," he agreed, pleasure shining in his dark eyes.

"As for you," Amanda said, giving Mac a wink, "you tell Andi I said to remember that 'secret' we were talking about."

"Okay," Mac said warily.

She gave them their check, told them to hurry back, then walked away to say hello to more of her customers.

"Now, what do you suppose that was about?" Mac asked. "What 'secret'?"

"I have already said, my friend," Rafe told him as he picked up the check and headed for the cash register. "A woman's mind is a tricky and evolving thing."

"Yeah," Mac muttered as he followed his friend. "Just what I need. Tricky women with secrets."

For the next couple of days, Mac and Andi worked together on the old house. The amount of renovation that still needed to be done was staggering, though, and Mac had a twinge or two of guilt a couple times. It was because of him and his business that Andi hadn't had time to take care of her house before. But he didn't let regret take too big a chunk out of him because damned if he'd feel bad for hiring her, handing over responsibilities and coming to count on her for too damn much.

If she hadn't wanted to become irreplaceable, then she shouldn't have been so good at her job.

"She's not walking away. Not from the office. Not from *me*," he swore quietly. He'd figure out a way past all of this. It was what he did.

He'd still like to know what "secret" Amanda Battle had been talking about. Especially because when he'd mentioned it to Andi, she'd blushed a fiery red and smiled to herself. And if that wasn't enough to make a man wonder, he didn't know what would. But she'd refused to tell him, and just got to work stripping old wallpaper off the dining room walls so they, too, could be painted.

Now while she was in there, here he was, head and shoulders under her first-floor powder room sink. When Mac had arrived, she was about to call a plumber to fix a leaking pipe and he'd insisted on doing it himself. If she needed help then he'd damn well provide it. He was going to make himself as irreplaceable to her as she was to him.

Mac wielded a pipe wrench on the joist that was tight enough to have been welded on, and when the damn wrench slipped free, he scraped his knuckles on the old copper pipes. He hissed in a breath and let it go on a string of muffled curses. Then he jolted when his cell phone rang and rapped his head on the underside of the sink and briefly saw stars. Cursing a bit louder now, he wiggled out, reached for the phone and muttered, "What?"

"Hey, boss, good talking to you, too."

Reaching up, Mac rubbed the growing knot on top of his head then glared at the raw scrape on his knuckles. "Tim. What's going on?"

Tim Flanagan, a friend since college, was now Mac's vice president. He was currently in Montana going over the details of a ranch takeover. The Gilroy ranch was being swallowed by McCallum Enterprises and would soon be stocked with prime cattle.

"I called the office looking for you," Tim said. "Laura

told me you haven't been in for a few days." He paused. "Somebody die?"

Snorting, Mac shook his head, drew one knee up and rested his forearm on it. His gaze shot around the incredibly tiny first-floor powder room. Whoever the last owner had been, they'd painted it a dark brick red, making the room seem even smaller than it actually was. And to top it off, they'd used gold paint for the trim. It looked as if it belonged in a bordello. Not a particularly exclusive one, either. Naturally, Andi had plans for it, but first thing was getting the plumbing working right—such as making it so the sink would drain.

"Yeah, nobody's dead. I'm taking a few days is all." He rested his head against the bottom of the old sink and let the cool of the porcelain seep into his body. Thanks to the newly installed air conditioning, he wasn't dying of heat, but a man could still work up a sweat when wrestling with stubborn pipes.

"I heard Andi quit," Tim said. "What's up with that?"

Mac shot a glance out the door to make sure the woman in question wasn't in earshot. Then he said, "I'm working on it."

"Good," Tim told him with a slight laugh. "Because without her as a buffer I probably would have killed you five, six years ago."

Mac's mouth twitched in a smile. "You would have tried. So, is there some reason in particular you're calling or was it just to harass me?"

"There's a reason. Harassment's just a bonus. Old man Gilroy's wanting to hold back ten acres, claiming it's in the contract for him to get the allowance for a hay field."

Frowning now, Mac said, "I don't remember it that way." They'd made allowances for the Gilroy ranch house and the surrounding five acres to remain in their name, as a courtesy since the Gilroys had been on the land more than a hundred years.

But the truth was, the old man couldn't run the ranch on his own anymore and his kids weren't interested in being ranchers. They loved the land and wanted at least some of it to remain in the family, but the younger Gilroys all had jobs that took them off the ranch. McCallum Enterprises was paying fair market value for the land and Mac wasn't about to hand out favors. That just wasn't how you ran a business.

"Call the office, have Laura pull up the contract and get the details," Mac said. "We want to be sure of our standing here and—"

"What's going on?" Andi stepped into the doorway and leaned one shoulder against the jamb.

Mac looked up at her and damn, she looked good. No woman should look as fine when she'd been ripping away at dirty old wallpaper. He gave his head a shake, reminding himself to focus, then told Tim to hang on and explained, "Tim says Mr. Gilroy in Montana is insisting that we agreed to an extra ten acres set aside for him in the contract and I don't—"

"You did," she said, then reached down and plucked the phone from his hand. "Hi, Tim, it's Andi. The original contract called for just the house and the surrounding five acres to remain in Gilroy hands. But we renegotiated several points about two weeks into the deal and Mac agreed to a ten-acre plot behind the main ranch house. Mr. Gilroy wants his daughter and her husband to be able to build near the main house. And they want to grow enough hay for the animals they're keeping."

Mac watched her. She had pulled that information out

of her computerlike brain, and damned if he didn't find that sexy as hell. A woman with a mind like that didn't waste herself. She needed challenge. Needed the kind of work she'd been doing for six years. Why the hell did she think she could be happy without it?

"Sure," Andi said and grinned. "It's no problem, Tim. Happy to help. Okay, here's Mac again."

She handed him back the phone. "Problem solved."

"Yeah," he said, still watching her. "I see that. You always were impressive."

"Thanks." She left a second later but he continued to look after her. Then he spoke into the phone. "Everything straightened out now?"

"Yeah," Tim said. "She is *good*. With all the things we have going on concurrently, it amazes me that she could just remember details like that. What the hell are we going to do without her?"

Mac shifted his gaze to the ceiling when he heard her footsteps pass overhead. He wondered briefly what she was doing up there. Then he realized that if she left, he'd spend the rest of his life wondering what she was up to. That was unacceptable. "We're never gonna have to find out."

Two hours later, Andi set two sandwiches on her tiny kitchen table and poured two tall glasses of iced tea. If it felt odd serving Mac lunch, she brushed it off, knowing that with all the work he'd done around there the past few days, the least she owed him was a meal.

He walked into the kitchen and grinned at her. "I didn't even know you could cook."

"A ham and cheese sandwich is not cooking," she said, and took a seat. Picking up a potato chip, she bit in and chewed. "However, I'm a darn good cook—when I have the time."

He winced and sat down opposite her at the table. "Time again. Point made."

She shrugged and smiled. "It's not all you and the job," she admitted as she looked around the room. "This kitchen is not exactly conducive to creative cookery. Plus, the oven doesn't work."

He looked behind him and laughed. "A pink stove?"

"It might come back in style," she said, not sure why she was bothering to defend the appliance she had every intention of replacing. When he just gave her a you've-got-to-be-kidding look, she said, "Fine. It's terrible. But getting a new one is low on my list right now. Anyway, you bought pizza yesterday, so it's only fair I take care of lunch today."

"Always about what's fair, aren't you?"

"Something wrong with that?"

"Not a thing," he assured her and picked up half his sandwich. "But if you're so fired up about being 'fair' you might want to rethink walking out on a business that needs you."

Andi watched him, and though she felt that rush of knowing he didn't want to lose her, she knew it was still the only answer for her. Being around him so much the past few days had been so hard. Her heart ached for what she couldn't have, and if she stayed working for him, that ache would eventually swallow her whole.

"You were doing fine before me and you'll do fine without me," she said, taking a bite herself.

"Fine's one thing," he said, waving his sandwich at her. "Great's another. And you know damn well that to-gether, we were doing great."

"There's more to life than work, Mac." At least she hoped there was. And she fully intended to find out.

"If you love what you do, you'll never work a day in your life. My dad told me that when I was a kid," Mac said. "Someone famous said it, I think. Anyway, turns out Dad was right. Work is *fun*, Andi, and you know it."

She had enjoyed her job, keeping on top of problems, working out strategies and plans for the future. It was exciting and fulfilling and everything a good career should be. But to be honest, doing all of that *with Mac* was what had really been the best part for her.

With his free hand, he pulled his phone out of his shirt pocket and scrolled through, checking email. Andi shook her head. Even during lunch, he couldn't stop working. "This is exactly what I'm talking about."

"Huh? What?" He didn't look at her. Instead, he tapped out an answer, hit Send, then checked for incoming texts and missed calls.

"Look at you. You can't even stop working long enough to eat a sandwich."

"Multitasking," he argued, shooting her a quick look. "Contrary to what women believe, men are capable of doing more than one thing at once. Besides, I'm just—"

Before he could finish, she interrupted. "Twenty dollars says you can't go an hour without checking your phone."

"What?" His cool green eyes shone with bemusement.

"It's a bet, Mac." She braced her forearms on the table and gave him a rueful smile.

"Yeah, I know that," he said, setting the phone at his elbow. "But I don't feel right about taking your money."

His phone vibrated and he glanced at the readout. When he looked back at her, her eyebrows were arched and there was a definite smirk on her mouth. "Oh, I think my money's safe enough. Especially since I don't think you'll take the bet, because you know you'd lose."

Frowning, he picked up the phone and tapped out an answer to the text from Laura. "I've got a business to run, you know."

"That's *all* you've got, Mac," she said as he set the phone aside again. "It's all I had until I quit."

His mouth tightened and she watched a muscle in his jaw twitch as if he had plenty to say but was holding the words back.

It took a couple of seconds, but he finally put his sandwich down, tipped his head to one side and asked, "And you really believe you had to walk out to find more?"

"Yeah." She took a sip of her tea because her throat was suddenly dry and tight. "Look at you. You said you were going to be here, working on the house for two weeks. But you haven't really left the office at all."

He grabbed a chip, tossed it into his mouth and crunched viciously. "What's that supposed to mean?"

"It means that you can take the boy out of the office, but you can't take the office out of the boy." She shook her head, sad to realize that she'd been right to leave. Mac didn't need a woman in his life. He had his *work*. "All the while you're painting or fixing the broken tiles or unclogging a sink, you're checking your phone. Answering emails. Texts. Checking with Laura about the situation at the office."

"What's wrong with that?"

"Nothing if it's all you want. Heck, until I quit, I was doing the same thing." Andi looked down at her own empty hands and said, "I was almost convinced my phone was an extension of my hand. Every waking moment revolved around the business and all of the minutiae involved with keeping it running. It was getting crazy, Mac. I was practically *showering* with my phone. That's when it hit me that not only did I want more, but I *deserved* more. And you do, too."

"This is all because I check my phone?"

"Because you can't *stop* checking your phone."

It vibrated on the table again and instinctively he started to reach for it—then stopped, curling his fingers into his palm. He locked his gaze with hers. "Twenty bucks?"

"Only if you can go an entire hour without checking your phone—or responding to a call." He'd never be able to do it, Andi told herself. Right now, she could see it was *killing* him to not answer whoever had called or texted.

He thought about it for a long moment, then seemed to come to a decision. "You're on, but first—" he hedged as he picked up his phone "—I send one text to Laura telling her to go to Tim with any questions."

Andi met his gaze and nodded. "Agreed. But after that, it's one hour. No phone."

Mac texted Laura at the office, put the phone in his pocket and held out one hand to her. "Deal."

The instant his hand closed around hers, Andi felt a rush of heat that raced up her arm to settle in the middle of her chest. As if he, too, felt that zip of something wicked, he held on to her hand a little longer than necessary. She couldn't look away from his eyes. The sharp, cool green of them drew her in even when she knew she should resist the fall. With the touch of his hand against hers, though, it was so hard to think about caution.

When he finally let her go, Andi could still feel the

warmth of his skin, and clasped her hands together in her lap to hang on to that feeling as long as she could.

"What do I get when I win?" he asked.

Was it her imagination or was his voice deeper, more intimate than it had been only a moment ago? Quickly, she picked up her glass of tea and took a long drink before answering.

"The prize is twenty dollars. But you won't win."

"Uh-huh." One corner of his mouth curved up and Andi tightened her grip on the tea glass in response.

"When I win," he said, "I'm going to need a little more than a paltry twenty dollars."

She swallowed hard. "Is that right?"

"Oh, yeah." He picked up his sandwich again and gave her a teasing smile over it.

Well, when Mac's eyes gleamed like that, Andi knew he had something up his sleeve. Over the years, she'd watched him back opponents into corners or wheedle exactly what he wanted out of a deal in spite of the odds being against him. And it was always heralded by that smile.

So warily, she asked, "What did you have in mind?"

"Well, now," he mused, taking another bite, "I believe that after this amazing sandwich, we're going to be needing dinner."

"And?" she prompted.

"And, the two of us. Dinner. The club."

"The TCC?" she asked, surprised.

Mac, like his father before him, was a member of the Texas Cattleman's Club, a members-only private organization that had only recently begun to welcome women as full members. The club was legendary in Royal, with most people going their whole lives and never seeing the inside of the place. "Why would you want to do that?"

"They serve a great steak," he said with a careless shrug that she didn't believe for a minute.

Whatever his reasons for suggesting they go out on a real dinner date—he was suggesting a *date*, wasn't he? Oh, God, why was he asking her on a date? Because he knew he'd never have to go through with it, that's why, she thought an instant later. He couldn't win this bet and he knew it.

"Okay," she said, agreeing in the same spirit he'd asked. "Deal. Dinner at the TCC if you win. Which you won't."

"Seem awful sure of yourself," he mused.

"You'll never be able to go without answering your phone," she said, taking a bite of her sandwich.

"Never say never, darlin'."

Five

The first half hour just about drove him out of his mind. He couldn't count how often he actually went to reach for his phone before stopping himself just in time. Whenever his phone rang, Andi watched him, one eyebrow lifted high as she waited for him to surrender to the inevitable. But he didn't do it. Mostly because she was so sure he would and that just annoyed the hell out of him. So he held out and poured his concentration into painting, and humming along with the country tunes on the radio.

He and Andi talked and worked together as well as they always had, and before Mac knew it, three hours had gone by. He hadn't checked his phone once, he realized, and the world hadn't ended. His business was still up and running and there were no signs of a coming apocalypse. Even more than that—after the first agonizing half hour, he'd actually enjoyed not grabbing for the phone whenever it beeped or vibrated.

"You did it," Andi said, with just a hint of surprised admiration in her voice. "I didn't think you'd make it, but you did."

"You should have learned by now not to doubt me," he said, taking a step back to survey the job they'd done. "Looks good, Andi."

"It does," she said, turning in a circle to admire the room now that it was finished. "We make a good team."

"Always did," he agreed, then kept talking before she could back away from that one simple truth. "So, if it's okay with you, think I'll use my phone now and make us a reservation at the TCC. Then I'll use that twenty bucks you owe me to put gas in my truck."

Her head tipped to one side. "You want to have dinner with me?"

"I guess I do." He wanted a lot more than dinner, too. But a man had to start somewhere. He pulled his phone from his pocket and hit the speed dial. When she started to speak again, he held up one finger for quiet and watched her quietly steam. It was probably wrong how much he enjoyed doing that.

"Afternoon, James. This is Mac McCallum. I'll be bringing a guest in for dinner tonight. Around eight. Thanks. Appreciate it." He hung up and looked at her. "They're holding my favorite table."

"Of course they are."

"Problem?" he asked.

"You always get what you want, don't you?"

"Damn straight."

"I shouldn't even be surprised when people snap to attention when you speak, should I?"

"I've never seen you jump when I speak," he said.

Her mouth curved. "True."

"Always liked that about you," he admitted. That stiffness in her spine, the determined gleam in her eyes and the defiant tilt to her chin all rolled together to make her one amazing woman. "From that first day you came in to interview for the job. You let me know from the start that you'd work your butt off, but you wouldn't be a yes woman."

"You didn't need one more person kowtowing to you."

Amusement filled him. "Kowtow?"

"It's an appropriate word."

His eyebrows lifted as he considered it. He supposed she had a point, in spite of that snotty tone. However everyone else treated him, Andi had always given him an honest opinion. No matter what. He had always known that she'd tell him straight and wouldn't hold back. And he was only now seeing how much he'd come to rely on that trait over the years.

He could still see her as she had been that first day. He'd interviewed three people for the job before her, but the moment she walked into the office, all starch and precision, he'd known she would be the one. She'd had a great résumé, a firm demeanor and he liked how she had stood right up to him.

Now she wanted to leave. Was it any wonder he was trying so hard to keep her?

He studied her for a second or two, and in her eyes he saw more than his trusted assistant. More than the woman who'd made his work life run like a Swiss watch. He saw a woman he enjoyed being around. A woman who made his skin sizzle with a touch and irritated him and intrigued him all at once. Why had he never opened his eyes to the possibilities before this?

Looked as though he was just going to have to make up for lost time.

"So," he said, cutting his own thoughts off. "Dinner tonight. I'll pick you up at eight."

He looked at her steadily, silently daring her to say no. Just when it seemed she might, she said, "Fine. Eight."

Nodding, Mac started talking again before she could change her mind. "I'll finish with this sink, then head home to clean up, take care of some things."

She was standing close. So close he could smell her shampoo. Why had he never noticed that soft, flowery scent before? Her T-shirt was tight, clinging to her breasts and her narrow waist. Her cutoff denim shorts were cuffed high on her thighs and those pale pink toes looked too damn sexy.

His breath labored in his lungs, and every square inch of his body tightened until he felt as if a giant fist was wrapped around him, squeezing. They stared at each other for several long seconds, and then Andi broke away, shattering whatever thread had been stretched between them. Mac took a deep breath, thinking to settle himself, but all it did was make him appreciate her scent that much more.

"Um, okay then. I'll get back to the hideous cabbage rose wallpaper and—" She half turned and he stopped her.

"Wait," he said tightly. She tensed up. He could see it and he enjoyed knowing that she was feeling as twisted up as he was. Reaching out, he pulled flakes of wallpaper out of her hair, then held them out to her with a smile.

"Isn't that perfect?" she muttered. Taking them, her fingers brushed against his and sent another quick snap of sensation between them. "Thanks. I'll be sure to wash my hair before dinner."

Well, now he was imagining her in the shower, soap suds and water running over her bare skin, hair slicked back from her flushed face to hang down her back in heavy, wet strands… Oh, man. He rubbed one hand across his mouth, hoping he wasn't drooling.

She gave him a long look out of those storm-gray eyes that had his insides fisting. He fought down an urge to grab her, pull her close and hold on to her. Because if he held her, he'd have to kiss her. Taste the mouth that was suddenly more tempting to him than anything he'd ever seen before. But if he did that, it would change their relationship completely and, knowing her, Andi would only use that shift between them as another reason to leave her job. So he wouldn't risk it. Not yet, anyway.

When she turned to the hall, this time he let her go.

"A date? Seriously? You're going on a date with Mac?"

Jolene and the kids had stopped by on their way home from baseball practice and now Andi and her sister were sitting in the kitchen, keeping an eye on Jacob, Jilly and Jenna playing in the backyard. She had less than two hours before Mac picked her up for their not-a-date.

"It's not a date," Andi insisted, as she had been telling herself all afternoon.

"Really?" Jolene reached out and tapped her fingernail against the window until her son looked up. She wagged her finger at him and Jacob got the message, immediately letting go of his baby sister's doll. The little girl's shrieks broke off instantly. Satisfied, Jolene turned back to Andi.

"If it's not a date, what's the word they use to describe it these days?"

"Funny," Andi told her. She sliced a couple of apples into wedges, then added squares of cheese to a plate before carrying it all to the table and sitting down opposite her sister. "Really, I don't know what it is. But he's never thought about me *that* way, so I know it's not a date."

"Uh-huh." Jolene took a sip of her tea and flicked another glance out the window to make sure no one was killing anybody. "Sounds to me like he's thinking of you 'that' way now."

"No, he's not. Is he?" She worried her bottom lip as she considered, then rejected the whole idea. "No, he's not."

"Things change," Jolene said, snatching a slice of apple and crunching into it. "Let us pause to remember that after my first date with my beloved Tom I told him I never wanted to see him again."

"That's because he took you fly-fishing."

"He really was an idiot," Jolene murmured with a smile. Rubbing one hand over her belly, she said, "But look at us now."

"Okay, you have a point. Things have already changed." In the past few days, there had been a kind of *shift* in her relationship with Mac. Always before, they'd been friendly, but she'd been determined to maintain that cool separation of boss and assistant. But here, away from the office, that barrier had dropped and they'd both reached across it.

What that meant, she had no idea.

"What're you going to wear?" Jolene asked.

"Oh, God." She dropped her head to the table and only groaned when her sister laughed.

* * *

Andi swiveled her head from side to side and didn't even care that she must look like a tourist on their first visit to New York City. It was how she felt. She'd never been inside the Texas Cattleman's Club before, so this was a real moment for her. She didn't want to miss a thing—and not only because Jolene had demanded a full description.

The building itself was stone and wood and boasted a tall slate roof that afforded the rooms in the club with nearly-cathedral ceilings. The paneled walls were dotted with hunting trophies and pieces of the history of Royal, Texas. Old photos of stern-looking men glaring at the camera were interspersed with other Texas memorabilia. Andi took it all in as Mac led her toward the dining room.

"I feel like we should have had to use a secret password to get in here," she said, keeping her voice low as if she were in a library.

"Ah, we use code signals. Much more stealthy." He leaned his head toward hers. "Did you see how I tipped my hat to the right when I took it off? There you go."

Her lips twitched. A playful Mac was a dangerous Mac. At least to her heart. "This is exciting. To finally see it all."

Mac tucked her arm through his. "Well, the dancing girls are only here Tuesdays and Thursdays, and the harem's closed to female guests, so you'll have to make do with the dining room."

She tipped her head up to give him a sardonic look. "Aren't you the funny one?"

"Charm, Andi. It's called charm."

"There's a less attractive name for it, as well," she told him.

He laughed. "You're quick. I like it. Always did. So what do you think of the place?"

"I feel like we should be whispering," she confessed, lowering her voice again as she looked at the old framed letters on her left and nearly gasped when she saw one signed by Sam Houston himself.

"The place has got plenty of history," he said, "but it's moving with the times, too."

She raised an eyebrow at that.

"Okay, turtle speed," he allowed. "But we are moving. We even have a day care center here now and I thought that was going to send a couple of the older members into heart attacks."

She chuckled, but realized he was probably right. The arguments over the day care center had kept the town talking for weeks. But oh, she remembered well how infuriated the old guard of the club had been to grudgingly accept female members.

In a way, she felt sort of sorry for the poor old dinosaurs. Their world was changing and they couldn't stop it.

"Of course," Mac was saying as he shifted his gaze to the ceiling, "the building suffered some damage during the tornado. But I like what they did when they repaired it. There's a little more light in here—makes it seem less like a paneled cave when you walk through."

"I love it." She tipped her head back to look up at him. "I've always had a mental image of what the inside of this place might look like and, surprisingly enough, I was pretty close. But you've fulfilled a childhood dream by bringing me here. So thank you."

"Absolutely my pleasure," he assured her. Then he covered her hand on his arm with his own. The closeness to him was exhilarating and made her head swim. She liked it.

He looked wonderful, though she had to admit that he always looked far too good. Tonight, he wore black slacks, black boots, a white collared shirt and a black jacket. He carried his black dress Stetson in his free hand and his sharp green eyes surveyed every inch of his surroundings.

He *fit* in this building that was so much a combination of past and present. She could completely see Mac McCallum a hundred and fifty years ago, still having that steely gaze, carving out an empire in the Old West.

As if he felt her watching him, he turned his head, looked down into her eyes and asked, "What's going on in your mind right now?"

"Too many things I don't want to talk about."

"Intriguing."

She sighed a little. "I'm not trying to be intriguing."

"Maybe that's why you are," he said, voice low, a caress of sound in the hushed atmosphere. Well, that should keep her system humming for a while, she thought as he led her into the main dining room.

Here, the tables were square, covered in white linen then draped with deep red cloths. There were candles and tall, fragile vases, each holding a single yellow rose. It made her smile.

Leaning toward him, she whispered, "The yellow rose of Texas?"

He grinned, as if pleased she'd caught it. "Nobody has traditions like Texas."

She'd been so nervous about coming here with him,

worried about what it might mean, what would happen. And now she was enjoying herself too much. It wasn't good, she thought. She couldn't allow her feelings for him to keep growing. If she did, walking away would be even harder than it had to be.

"Stop thinking."

Andi blinked and shook her head as if coming up out of a trance. "What?"

"I can see you're starting to second-guess tonight." Mac dropped one hand to the small of her back. "Why not just let it roll on and see where it takes us instead?"

Ignoring the burst of warmth that bloomed from his touch, she sat down and kept her gaze on his as he took the seat beside her at the table for four. "You hired me for my organizational skills, for my ability to think everything through from every angle."

"As you're continually reminding me," he said with a quick smile, "we're not at work."

If they were, Andi would know where she stood. As it was now, she felt a little off balance—a not altogether uncomfortable feeling.

"Right. Okay. Just enjoy." She looked around the dining room. There were several other people at the tables scattered across the gleaming wood floor. She recognized most of them and nodded to Joe Bennet, who excused himself to his wife and headed across the room toward them.

He and Mac shook hands, then Joe turned to Andi and asked, "How's that new air conditioning system I installed working out for you?"

Here she had no trouble knowing exactly what to say. Giving him a wide smile, she said, "It's wonderful, Joe.

I can't thank you enough. It's lovely being able to sleep at night without gasping for air."

His wide, plain face beamed with pleasure. "Happy to hear it. Now, if you have any problems at all, you let me know, all right?"

"I will."

"You enjoy your night, you two." He gave Mac a conspiratorial wink, then walked back to his own table.

"Oh, boy." That man-to-man wink was a sure sign that she and Mac were about to be the hot topic of conversation tomorrow in Royal.

"Yeah," Mac said, nodding. "I know what you mean. Joe's a good guy, but the man gossips like an old woman. Did you know he spent a half hour telling me how the Grainger boy's scholarship to UT came at the right time. His dad was so proud he forgot all about the boy crashing the family car."

"Did he?" Amused, Andi listened.

"And when he'd finished with that tale, he moved right on to Sylvia Cooper and how her husband, Buck, bought her a shiny new cast-iron skillet for their twenty-fifth anniversary—and she promptly bounced it off his forehead."

She cringed. "Oh!"

"Yeah," he said with a wince. "Have to say, though, I think Buck had that one coming. Anyway, twenty stitches and a mild concussion later, Buck saw the light, bought two tickets to Paris and the lovebirds leave next week."

Andi laughed, enjoying herself as Mac continued.

"Then Joe went on a rant about Pastor Stevens and how he preaches against gambling but made a bet on a horse race last Friday night and won—without telling his old friend Joe about the tip he got before the race."

She was having fun. Andi hadn't expected to, not really. There was too much tension between them.

The quiet of the restaurant, the efficient smoothness of the waiters moving from table to table and the intimacy of the candlelight flickering in his eyes made her want to hug this moment close. Watching his easy smile slide across his face had her returning it and saying, "So Joe's a big gossip, is he?"

Mac laughed, then shrugged off the obvious dig. "Must be contagious."

"I think it is," she agreed and looked around at the people shooting them interested glances. "And by tomorrow afternoon, everyone in town will know we were out to dinner together."

"That bothers you?"

Her shoulder blades itched as though people were staring. "I don't like being talked about."

He laughed again and the sound was low and deep. "Don't know how you could avoid it around here. You know how it is in small towns. You've lived in Royal all your life just like me."

True, they had grown up just a few miles apart, but their lives were so different they could have been on separate planets. Mac had been the golden boy. Football team captain, star baseball player. His parents were wealthy, he lived on one of the biggest ranches in the state and everything he touched turned to gold. Until his parents died, leaving him to care for Violet and find his own way alone.

Andi and Jolene had grown up in town, in a nice middle-class home with two parents who doted on them and loved each other. She and her sister had worked hard at after-school jobs, not leaving much time for activities like cheerleading or drill team or band.

So, though they had both grown up here, and she had of course known who Mac was, Andi had never met him until the day she applied for a job with his company. She'd thought she'd come to know him very well over the years, but the past few days had shown her a new side of him, and it was fascinating to discover there was still so much more of him to know.

He was staring at her as if he could delve into her mind and read her every thought. Just in case he could, she spoke up quickly. "Vi seems really happy."

Mac nodded as if accepting her change of subject. "She is. Rafe loves her, which I'm grateful for, as I'd hate to have to pound on one of my best friends. And right now, she's driving the poor guy nuts with trying to get the nursery ready for the baby."

"He's loving it and you know it," Andi said.

"Okay, he is. It's only me she's driving nuts."

The waiter arrived, took their order and Andi listened as once again Mac took charge. She gave him this one, since, being a Texan, she liked a good steak now and then. The wine he ordered was served a few minutes later and, after being sampled, was poured. Then the two of them were alone again and she took a long sip of that wonderful red, just to ease the twisting knots in her stomach.

"Do you spend a lot of time here at the club?" she asked.

Mac winked. "Lately, it's been pointed out to me repeatedly that the only place I spend a *lot* of time is at work…"

She nodded at his implication.

"But yes," he said, glancing around the dark, intimate dining room. With a shrug, he added, "Food's good. If I want company, it's here, if I don't, I get left alone. Not much point in making Teresa dirty up the kitchen at home cooking just for me."

His housekeeper, Teresa Mooney, was a fifty-year-old widow who, Andi guessed, would love to be allowed to fuss over her employer. But typically enough, Mac made that call for her, not bothering to find out how she felt about it.

"You do that a lot, you know?" she said.

"What's that?"

"Make decisions for people."

"What're you talking about?"

"I ran into Teresa at the grocery store a few weeks ago. She was looking at a huge pot roast and bemoaning the fact that you don't want her to cook for you."

"Really?" He frowned a little, took a sip of wine.

"Yes, really." Andi sighed. "People like to feel needed. Useful. You're taking that away from her."

"Bad analogy," he said, shaking his head. "*You* felt needed and useful at the office and yet you walked away."

She shifted uneasily in her chair. "That's different."

"Not so much," he said, drinking his wine, then thoughtfully staring at her over the rim of the glass. "You're leaving *because* you were needed."

"It's not only that."

"Then what else?"

Okay, she wasn't about to admit that she'd left because she loved him and knew her dreams were doomed to die. "It doesn't matter," she said, evading the question she couldn't answer.

"Well," he said, setting his glass down as their meal arrived, "once you're back in the office where you belong, I'll have plenty of time to find out what's really bothering you."

She glanced up at the waiter and smiled as he served her dinner, waiting until the man was gone again to speak. When she did, she leaned in close enough that Mac could hear her whisper, "You're not going to convince me to come back."

"You didn't think I'd win our bet today either, but here we are." Smiling to himself, he cut into his steak.

Andi sat there quietly simmering, wondering just when it was she'd lost control of the situation. She'd quit her job, yet now she was half convinced that Mac was right. He would find a way to get her back.

Six

Mac didn't want the night to end yet—though he wasn't interested in asking himself why. It was enough to keep her with him awhile longer. After dinner, he coaxed her into taking a walk down Main Street. With the summer just getting started, the night was warm, but the breeze was cool and just strong enough to lift the hem of the dark red dress she wore and flutter it above her knees.

He was forced to admit that he'd felt staggered from the moment he picked her up at her house tonight. Over the past few days, Mac had been seeing Andi in a whole new light and it was just a little disconcerting. And to-night, she'd kicked it up several notches.

She had her hair pulled back at the sides so that it tumbled down her back in a waving mass that tempted a man to sink his hands into it. Her red dress had thin, narrow straps and a bodice that dipped low enough that he got another peek at the breasts she had apparently been hiding from him for six years. The fabric then nipped in at a waist so narrow he was willing to bet he could encircle it with his hands, then sloped down over rounded hips and clung there, just to torment him further. Not to mention, he thought with an inner groan, the heels. Black, shiny, four inches at least, with a cut-out toe that showed off the dark red polish on her nails.

She'd practically killed him right there on her front porch.

Every man at the club had watched her pass by and for the first time ever jealousy stirred through Mac. He'd never been possessive about a woman. Never cared if other men looked at her or even if she looked back. Until now. Admitting that to himself was damned unsettling.

At work, she had always been the personification of professionalism. Tidy, businesslike, she'd never once hinted at the woman beneath the veneer, and right now he figured that was a good thing. If she had, he might have fired her so he could date her and would never have been able to appreciate what she could bring to the business. And now, he thought, work was the furthest thing from his mind.

Her scent wafted to him on a sigh of wind and he inhaled it deeply, drawing it into him until he could practically taste her. Which was just what he wanted to do.

"It's a pretty little town, isn't it?" she asked when they got back to the car. She'd turned to look back down Main, and the expression on her face was soft and dreamy.

He turned to face the town he'd grown up in and saw it as she did. Street lamps formed globes of yellow light that were reflected in puddles on the sidewalk. Tubs and hanging baskets of flowers brightened the scene and the shop windows were ablaze with light, welcoming customers to come in and browse.

Mac had lived in Houston for a while, but he hadn't lasted long. Big cities were fun to go to for a few days, but his heart would always draw him back here. He liked the slower pace, the familiar faces and the views out his own windows. He liked knowing every inch of his surroundings and he enjoyed being in a place where everyone and their uncles and cousins made it their business to know yours.

"It's changed a lot from when we were kids," Andi mused, "but somehow it stays the same, too." She turned her head to look up at him. "You know what I mean? The heart of Royal is still small-town beautiful."

"Yeah, it is," he finally said, shifting his gaze to hers. Those gray eyes shone a little brighter with the gleam of lamplight reflected in their depths. It was enough to stop a man's heart if he wasn't careful. Which Mac generally was.

"You know," he said abruptly, "it's early yet. How about you come with me to the ranch? I can show you that mare you had to make all the travel arrangements for."

She bit down on her bottom lip as she considered it, and he tried not to watch. "I don't know. I've got a lot of things to do tomorrow and—"

"Being alone with me scare you a little?" he asked in a whispered hush.

Her gaze snapped to his. "I told you before, you don't scare me."

But she was nervous. He could see it. And that gave him the nudge to push her into coming out to his place. Maybe it wasn't a smart move, but right now he wasn't interested in being "smart." "Then there's no problem, is there?"

He'd delivered her a direct challenge, one she wouldn't be able to resist. He knew her as well as she did him, so Mac realized that she'd never say no. Because she wouldn't want him to think she was as uneasy as she obviously was.

Damn. His thoughts were starting to circle like a merry-go-round in a tornado. What was the woman doing to him?

"All right," she said, shaking him out of his own head, for which he was grateful. "But after you show me the mare, you take me home. Deal?"

He took her hand but instead of shaking it, lifted it to his mouth. Keeping his eyes on hers, he kissed her knuckles and saw the flare of heat flash across that cool, gray surface. Her skin was soft, smooth, and the scent of her pooled in his gut and began to burn. "We're making a lot of deals here lately, Andi."

She pulled her hand from his, and damned if he didn't miss the feel of her. "Just remember this one, okay? Horse, then home."

"Oh, I'll remember."

He opened the car door for her, then closed it firmly and smiled to himself. He didn't say how *long* it would be after she saw the horse that he would take her home. For a woman as organized and detail-oriented as she was, she'd really overlooked that particular loophole.

He smiled all the way to the ranch.

The twenty minute drive from town to the Double M ranch seemed to pass in seconds. Andi couldn't even enjoy the scenery they passed, with the moonlight washing over it all in a pale, cool light. She was way too tense to appreciate the view, for heaven's sake.

The ride in Mac's Range Rover was smooth, and quiet but for the Southern blues pumping from the stereo. She hardly spoke because she had too many thoughts racing through her mind. Mac didn't have much to say, she was guessing by his smug smile, because he'd already gotten his way by getting her to go to his ranch with him.

Why was she going with him?

He had kissed her hand.

That one small, sexy action had pulled her in and made it impossible for her to say no. Darn it, Mac was being sweet and seductive and she felt herself weakening. She'd loved him for years, wanted him for years, and now, for whatever reason, he'd turned his charm onto her and she was slipping. Slipping down a slope that was going to be so hard to climb back up.

At the edge of the McCallum ranch land, they passed the office where she'd worked for six years. There were low lights burning in the windows and the gravel parking lot was empty in the moonlight. A huge chunk of her life had been spent there and a part of her was sorry to see it go—the part that wanted to be with Mac, no matter what.

Andi's stomach pitched and she shot him a careful look from the corner of her eyes. He was smiling to himself and that only increased the anxiety already pumping through her. What was he thinking? Heck, what was he planning?

How strange. She had believed she knew Mac better than anyone in the world. For years, she had anticipated his every professional need and rushed to meet it. But the Mac who kissed her hand and gave her wicked smiles over a shared bottle of wine while firelight shone in his eyes was a whole new ball game. She wasn't sure of her next move.

Frankly, she wasn't sure of much at the moment. But Amanda's words kept whispering through her mind. *Make time for a secret lover.* Is that what she was doing?

Heat zipped through her, head-to-toe, at the thought, leaving a lingering burn that sizzled somewhere in the middle. Going to bed with Mac was a bad idea and yet...

They turned off the main road and drove beneath the Double M gates, which swung open, then closed with a touch of a remote button. The land seemed to stretch out for miles, while the long drive to the ranch house was lined with oaks, their gnarled, twisting branches reaching for each other across the graveled drive. In full summer, this drive would be a shaded lane. Right now, there were still some bare branches that allowed moonlight to slip through and lie in silvered patches on the ground in front of them. At the end of the drive, the house waited.

A sprawling affair, it was two stories, built of stone and wood with wings that spread out from the center. More oaks stood sentinel at the corners of the house and the flower beds were a riot of color that even in the moonlit darkness looked cheerful and welcoming. The windows were lit, creating squares of gold across the front of the house, and the yard lights blinked on as Mac pulled up and parked.

Now what?

He hopped out of the car, came around to her side and opened the door, giving her a hand down. She appreciated it, since the heels she was currently teetering on weren't made for climbing. Or walking, when it came to it, which was why she winced when he took her hand and led her toward the stables.

"You know, I'm not really dressed for a barn visit—"

Mac glanced at her and one corner of his mouth tipped up. "It's okay. Next time you can dress up."

"What? Oh, for—"

He winked at her and kept walking.

That charm of his kept tugging at her and she was pretty sure he knew it. Andi huffed out a breath because clearly the man was not going to be dissuaded. Hurrying her steps to keep up with his much longer strides, she asked, "Is this a race?"

"Sorry," he said, and slowed down, never letting go of her hand. Not that she wanted him to. She liked the feel of his hard, calloused palm pressed close to hers.

That was the problem.

Every step they took crunched out into the country quiet. The soft breeze was still blowing and felt cool against her skin. Mac was a tall, solid presence at her side, and as they walked together in the moonlight, she had a hard time holding her all-too-eager heart back from taking a tumble to land at his feet.

"Soon enough, it'll be steaming hot here, but for now, it's a nice night for a walk."

She looked up at him. "It is. If you're wearing the right shoes."

"If you can't walk in them," he said, giving her heels a quick glance, "why wear them?"

"They're not for walking," she said. "They're for making my legs look great."

He took another look, a slow, lengthy one this time, then met her eyes with a smile. "Mission accomplished."

"Thanks." Her heart started that tumble again and she

steeled herself against giving in. She already loved the man. And the Mac she knew would run like a scalded cat if he knew it. In the past, any woman who'd started getting what he called the "white-fences gleam" in her eye had been set aside so fast their heads were probably still spinning.

If Andi didn't keep a grip on her feelings, she really would wind up lying alone in a dark room with nothing but her pain for company. So instead of concentrating on the man at her side, she looked around as they neared the stable.

The corral fences were painted white and stood out against the darkness like ghostly barricades. The stable itself was moon-washed and looked like a deeper shadow against the night. The barn farther off to the right was bigger, wider, to accommodate all of the equipment needed to keep a ranch of this size running. There were other outbuildings, too. A house for the ranch manager and his wife, a barracks of sorts where unmarried employees lived and a separate storage building where winter feed could be kept until it was needed.

Mac McCallum might be a wildly successful businessman, but at the core of him, Mac was a rancher. He would always love this land, this place, the horses and cattle he ran and the wide-open stretch of sky that seemed as if it went on forever. This ranch was in his blood, it was bred in his bones, and whether he acknowledged it or not, this place was the beating of his heart.

"You went quiet all of a sudden," he said. "A sure sign you're thinking too much again."

She laughed and shook her head. "Since when do you notice what I'm doing?"

"I always noticed, Andi," he said softly, and his voice

slipped inside her to caress every last nerve ending. "Though I'll admit, I just took you for granted before."

"Really?"

He glanced at her and smiled. "Don't be so surprised. Even I can grow some."

How was she supposed to fall *out* of love with a man who could say something like that?

"I figured," he continued, "that you'd always be there when I needed you. In my own defense, though, you're the one who caused me to believe it."

Wryly, she shook her head and smiled. "So it's my fault."

"Absolutely."

She laughed again. "Well, then, I'm so very sorry."

"Don't be," he said and drew them to a stop. Hands on her arms, he turned her to face him. "I wouldn't change a damn thing, except for the idea of you quitting."

"It's not an idea. It's fact. You can't change it, Mac. It already happened."

"Don't count me out just yet," he warned, one corner of his mouth lifting into that half smile that did amazing things to the pit of her stomach.

It was a scene built for romance. If she wasn't living it, Andi would have thought it was like being in the pages of a romance novel. Moonlight, soft breezes, stars glittering overhead and a tall, gorgeous man looking down at her as if she were the center of the universe.

Just for a moment, for the length of a single heartbeat, Andi wished it were true. Wished she and Mac were a couple. That they were here on *their* home ranch, taking a walk in the moonlight before going upstairs together.

Then the moment passed and reality came crashing

back down on her. "Um, you going to show me that mare?"

"You bet," he said, then in one smooth move bent down, scooped one arm under her legs and swung her up against him.

So surprised she could hardly speak, Andi just gaped at him. Whether he knew it or not, he was really filling in the blanks on her romantic fantasy.

"Mac!" She pushed ineffectually at his chest and wasn't surprised at all when she didn't make a dent. "What are you doing?"

"Look there," he said, jerking his head to a spot just ahead of them.

She did, and saw a mud puddle that stretched from the stable fence to nearly the back of the ranch house. "Oh."

"That's right." He looked down at her. "Those pretty shoes of yours would never make it through the mud. A shame to ruin them."

"Or," she said, squirming a little in his hard, tight grasp, "I just won't go see the horse tonight. Put me down."

"Nope, we had a deal. I'll carry you to the stable." He started walking and then added, "Guess I just have to rescue you again. How many does that make now?" he wondered aloud. "Are you keeping count?"

"This isn't a rescue," she said, not completely able to hide the exasperated laughter bubbling from her throat as she wrapped her arms around his neck. "This is a kidnapping."

"Is that right?" He shrugged and hefted her just a little higher in his arms. "Well, it's my first."

"Congratulations."

"Thanks." He looked at her again. "I'm having a hell of a good time."

"Strangely enough," she said wistfully, "so am I."

He stopped, stared down into her eyes. "Good to know."

A couple of humming, electrical seconds passed while they stared at each other and the soft, early summer breeze wrapped itself around them. She was in so much trouble, Andi told herself.

Finally, he went on, carrying her across the muddy water and into the stable, where the scents of fresh hay and horses greeted them. It was quiet but for the occasional stamp of a hoof against the floor. Slowly, Mac set her on her feet, but caught her hand in his and held tight.

"Come on," he said, "I'll show you the mare."

They walked the length of the freshly swept aisle between stalls and as they passed horses poked their heads out as if to say hello. Mac had a moment with each of them, stroking noses, murmuring soft words to the animals until Andi was half convinced they were actually communicating.

At the last stall, he stopped and smiled at a gray horse with a blond mane as the animal reached out her nose toward him. "Andi, this is Moonlight."

"She's beautiful." She stroked the horse's neck and jaw, loving the soft, sturdy feel of the friendly mare.

"Yeah," Mac said, shifting his gaze from the mare to her. "She is. And this pretty girl's going to produce some beautiful children over the next few years."

"Who's the proud father-to-be?"

"Ah," he said, giving the mare one last pat before turning and pointing to a stall twice as big as the other animals had. "That would be Apollo."

The stallion was a dark, sleek brown with a black mane and tail, and he held his head high and aloof as if he knew just how important he was.

"He looks as if he thinks of himself as a god, so, appropriate name," Andi said.

"For a stallion, he's got a great temperament, too." They walked closer and the big horse shook his head and snorted.

"Yeah, I can see he's really friendly," Andi said, laughing nervously.

"He just doesn't like being tied down. He'd rather be out in the corral kicking up his heels than shut down for the night."

"So he's definitely male."

One eyebrow lifted. "Is that a slur against my gender?"

"Not a slur. An observation," she said, walking back up the aisle, pausing now and again to say hello to one of the horses or to stroke or pat.

"Based on your vast experience?" he teased from just a step behind her.

She looked over her shoulder at him. "I've known a few who've taken off for the hills as soon as anything remotely serious pops up. Take you, for example."

"Me?" He slapped one hand to his chest as if deeply wounded.

She laughed again, enjoying herself in the quiet, dimly lit stable. "Please. How many times have I purchased the see-you-later-thanks-for-the-memories bracelets?"

He winced and that only made her laugh harder. "Admit it, Mac. It's not only when you get bored with a woman that you move on. It's also when she starts getting stars in her eyes over you. Much like your stallion over there, you prefer running free. The only real commitment you've ever made was to the business."

"Maybe," he said, taking her arm and pulling her around to face him, "it's because I haven't met the right woman yet."

"Not for lack of trying," she said wryly.

He grinned and shrugged that off. "I'm no quitter."

He slid his hands up her arms to cup her face between his work-roughened palms. His thumbs stroked her cheekbones as his gaze met hers and held, warming the longer he looked at her. "You're confusing me, Andi," he said so softly she wasn't sure she'd heard him correctly.

Andi felt that rush of heat she'd come to expect from his touch, then her breath caught when the heat exploded into an inferno as he leaned down, bringing his mouth just inches from hers. If she had a single working brain cell, she would move back, keep a distance between them. A kiss from Mac was going to lead to places she really shouldn't consider going.

But she couldn't think. What woman could under the same circumstances? Her heartbeat sounded like a bass drum in her own ears. Breathe, she reminded herself. *Breathe.*

He smiled, a slow, slight curve of his mouth. "What's the matter, Andi? Feeling a little nervous after all?"

"No." *Liar.* Nerves, yes. Excitement, oh yes. Worry? She should be worried. Instead there was a tiny, faint voice crying out for caution, trying to be heard over the clamor of need screaming in her head.

She licked her lips and watched his eyes flare at the motion.

"Seduction in a stable, Mac?"

"The horses won't mind," he assured her.

"Maybe not," she whispered, her gaze dropping briefly to his mouth before meeting his again. "But I should."

His hands stilled as he stared into her eyes. "Do you?"

"No."

"Thank God."

She leaned into him and he moved quickly, laying his mouth over hers. Andi thought she heard herself groan, but that was the last thought she had. It was impossible to think when so many sensations were awakening, demanding to be relished, explored.

He pulled her tight against him, his arms coming around her like a vise, squeezing as though he thought she might try to escape his hold. But that was the last thing Andi wanted. This was probably a mistake and no doubt she'd come to regret it at some point, but at the moment, all she could think was *yes. Touch me. Hold me. Be with me.*

For six years, she'd loved him. For six years, she'd hidden everything she felt. Now finally, if only for this one night, she would be with the man she loved. Know what it was like to hold his body close to hers. To take him inside. And she wouldn't give up that chance for any amount of logic and reason.

He drew his head back and looked down at her, eyes wide, flashing with emotions that changed too quickly for her to read. But maybe that was for the best.

"Man," he whispered. "Should have done that a long time ago."

"Now is good, too," she said, though her voice sounded breathy and so unlike her she hardly recognized it. Her whole body was humming with impatience, with need. She was practically vibrating with the tension coiled tight in the pit of her stomach.

"Now is *great*," he amended, then swept her up into his arms again.

"What are you doing?"

"Just another rescue," he said, and headed out of the stable. But instead of going toward his car, Mac made a right turn and started for the ranch house. "This time, though," he told her, "I'm saving us both."

Seven

Andi held on, then leaned up and kissed the side of his neck. Her decision was made. There would be no turning back now. Tonight, she would make memories that years from now she'd relive and remember. "Hurry."

A low, throaty growl rolled from his throat, but he did exactly as she ordered, his long legs eating up the distance to the house in a few minutes. Overhead, the sky was black with a wide sweep of stars impossible to see unless you were outside a city, away from the lights. A nearly full moon glowed against the blackness and sent that wash of light over everything like a blessing. The warm June wind wrapped itself around them and swept them on toward the lamplit house ahead of them.

He opened the door, stepped through and kicked it shut behind him. The kitchen lay empty and still in the glow of a stove light, but Mac didn't stop to admire the elegantly remodeled space.

Andi barely had a chance to admire it, even if she'd been interested, before he was across the room and striding down a long hallway. They passed a dining room, Mac's study and the great room at the front of the house before he came to the wide oak staircase, where he suddenly stopped.

Surprised, Andi tore her gaze away from the massive iron and wood chandelier hanging from the cathedral ceiling over the foyer to look into his eyes. A view she preferred.

"What is it? What's wrong?" Her heart galloped in her chest as his hands held her in a proprietary grasp.

Keeping her pressed tightly against him, Mac said, "Nothing's wrong as far as I'm concerned. I'm just checking one last time."

She smiled and trailed the tips of her fingers along his jaw and throat. He shivered, then sucked in a gulp of air like a drowning man tasting hope.

She smiled, loving his response. And she knew exactly what he was doing now. Mac being Mac, he was giving her one last chance to change her mind about what was about to happen. He was charming, gorgeous and had a sense of honor that not enough men these days possessed. How could she resist him?

But still she asked innocently, "Checking what?"

"God help me," Mac said, letting his head fall back helplessly. "Yes or no, Andi. Don't make me beg."

"It's a big step," she teased. "I just don't know…"

He narrowed his eyes on her and gave her a hard squeeze. "Woman, you're treading on thin ice here."

She smiled and asked, "How fast can you take these stairs?"

His grin flashed bright. "We're about to find out."

Probably silly, Andi thought as her heart raced, to feel such a wild rush of pleasure at the man she loved holding her close and sprinting up a staircase.

She'd been in the house before, to see Vi when she'd lived in the west wing. But Andi now caught glimpses of Mac's side of the house when he made a sharp right at the top of the stairs. She couldn't have been less interested in the decor, but noted the Western paintings on the cream-colored walls as he passed. She saw the heavy, dark beams on the ceiling and heard every muffled boot step on the carpet runner along the hall. Then he turned into his bedroom and Andi focused only on him.

He swung her to her feet, but didn't let her go. Instead, he cradled her close to his chest, lowered his head to hers and kissed her breathless.

There was no slow slide into delight here; this was like a fall on a roller coaster. A whoosh of sensation that rushed through the blood and then gave you just enough time to breathe before starting all over again.

His hands, those big, strong hands, were everywhere at once—sliding up and down her spine, around to cup her breasts and then up to touch her face, fingers spearing through her hair, tipping her head first one way then the other as he deepened a kiss that was already searing her soul.

"I've been wanting my hands on you," he murmured when he tore his mouth from hers.

"I've been wanting that, too." *For so long.*

"Glad to hear it," he said, giving her the wicked half smile that never failed to send jolts of anticipation rocketing through her. And now, that sensation was going to have a payoff. At last.

He turned her around, her back to his front, and

tugged her zipper down slowly. She sighed, air sliding from her lungs on a half moan at the touch of his fingers against her back.

The bed in front of her was huge. Like an adult play-ground, with a midnight-blue duvet and a dozen pillows propped at the headboard. Across the room, there were French doors that led out onto the second-story balcony and a door on the right of the room that no doubt led to a bathroom suite. A cold hearth stood on one side of the room and there were two matching leather comfy chairs in front of it.

She wasn't feeling comfy at the moment, though; she was on edge, every nerve in her body tingling with ex-pectation. Mac slid the shoulder straps of her dress down her arms and followed the motion with his mouth. Lips, teeth, tongue trailed over her skin and made her shiver. She couldn't believe this was happening. After six long years of loving, she was finally *being* loved by the man she'd thought she could never have.

And even if this was only one night, it was one she would always remember. She would etch it into her mem-ory so she could replay it over and over again. Relish every touch, every breath, every sigh—and regret that it hadn't lasted longer than one night.

"I wanted slow and seductive," he admitted as he turned her to face him and watched as the bodice of her dress dropped to her waist, displaying a strapless black lace bra. His eyes went wide and hot as he lifted his gaze to hers. "But I find I'm too hungry for you to take my time."

"Me, too, Mac." She'd wanted for so long, needed so much; this was no time for lazy caresses and tenderness.

This was a rush to fulfillment. To ease the aches they both felt. And she was ready.

Andi reached for the buttons on his shirt even as he shrugged off his jacket and let it fall. When the shirt lay open, she splayed her hands on his hard, muscled chest and felt his heart pound in time with her own. His eyes caught hers and locked, passion glittering bright and sharp in those green depths. He kissed her again, long and deep, eliciting another groan from her as he tumbled her back onto the bed and followed her down. He tore his own shirt off, then came back to her, sliding her dress down her hips and taking her black lace panties with it. He pushed them off and onto the floor.

The duvet felt silky and cool against her back, adding contrasting layers to the sizzling warmth pumping through her. Andi unhooked her bra and watched his eyes as her breasts were bared to him. Heat flashed in his gaze just before he lowered his head to take, first, one rigid nipple, then the other into his mouth. His tongue lapped at her, his lips and teeth tugged and suckled at her, and in seconds, Andi was writhing beneath him, moving with the need erupting like lava in her blood. She held his head to her and watched him, and her mind spun out into sparkle-splashed darkness. There was nothing in the world but the two of them. This moment. This bed. This...wonder.

Then he moved up her body and took her mouth again, their tongues tangling together in a frenzied dance of passion that fed the fires already burning inside them both.

His right hand swept down her length and into the heat of her. She was wound so tight, had waited so long, that that first intimate touch was enough to make her shatter in tiny, helpless waves of pleasure that flickered and shone like lit sparklers just beneath her skin. "Mac…"

"Just getting started, darlin'," he promised, and delved deep, his fingers stroking, caressing already sensitive skin until she lifted her hips into his hand, hoping to ease the sudden burst of need that continued to build.

"I can't do this again so soon." Proud of herself for getting the words out, she clutched at his shoulders and held on as her body did things she hadn't expected it could.

Always before, sex had been a soft, almost sweet release of tension. A gentle ripple that drifted through her body on a tender sigh of completion.

This was different. That soft ripple had already washed away in a rising tide of fresh need that swamped everything that had come before.

He kissed her mouth, her shoulders, her breasts; he touched her deeply, intimately, and watched her every reaction. She gave him everything she had. She showed him everything she felt. Andi held nothing back because she'd waited too long to feel it all.

His touch was fire. His eyes were magic. She felt her own body jumping out of her control and she let it go.

Another climax hit her, stronger than the last, and she cried out his name as her body trembled and shook beneath his hands. But he wasn't finished, she realized as she lay there, struggling for air, trying to make her mind clear enough to appreciate just where she was.

She opened her eyes and saw him slide off the bed, strip off the rest of his clothes. Her eyes went wide as she looked at his amazing body, so lean and strong and sculpted. And for tonight at least…hers.

He joined her on the bed again, this time covering her

body with his, sliding up the length of her. Andi's hands and nails scraped up and down his back. Her legs parted, lifted, welcoming him to her, and when he entered her, she gasped and arched at the swift invasion. He felt so good. So right. So big. He filled her until it seemed as though they'd joined on much more than a physical level.

In this moment, they were one unit, and as she moved with him, she stared up into his eyes and lost herself in the wild gleam she saw there. He plunged into her heat, and unbelievably, she responded by tightening into another fiercer ball of tension deep inside. She felt the now familiar buildup and knew that this time, when he pushed her over the edge, it would be shattering. She couldn't wait.

So when he pulled away from her, Andi nearly whimpered with the boiling need clawing at her. But he paused only long enough to dig into the bedside table drawer and grab a condom.

"Damn," he said, glancing at her. "I was so caught up in you I almost forgot protection."

"You're not alone in that. I can't believe it, but I wasn't thinking—"

"Who needs to think?" he asked, and in a second he was back, buried inside her, and the two of them raced toward the finish line.

She held him, hooked her legs around his waist even as he reached under her with one hand and lifted her hips. Andi struggled to breathe, gave up any attempt to hang on to sanity and threw herself into the moment with an abandon she'd never experienced before.

Here was the difference, she thought wildly, between sparklers and skyrockets. Pleasure slammed into her with a crash, making it hard to breathe and harder to care. As the first incredible eruptions exploded inside her, she cupped his face between her hands and looked deeply into the green of his eyes as she jumped into the void.

She was still holding him when his eyes glazed over, his hips pumped against her and he tumbled into the same starlit darkness with her.

Minutes, hours, heck, maybe *weeks* later, Andi's brain started working again. She simply lay there, completely spent. She loved the feel of Mac lying on top of her and would have been perfectly content to stay in just that position from now until whenever. But even as that thought slipped through her mind, he was rolling to one side of her. He kept one arm wrapped around her, though, and pulled her in close, nestling her head on his chest. She heard the frantic pounding of his heart and knew her own was racing, as well.

God, she'd never been through anything like that before. Every other sexual experience she'd had in her life paled alongside what she'd just lived through. The man was…gifted.

"That was," he whispered into the darkness, "well, I don't think I can find a word for it."

"Yeah," she agreed. "Me, either."

He rolled her over onto her back and levered himself up until he was looking down into her eyes. "Can't believe it took us six years to do that."

"It was worth the wait," she told him.

"And then some," he agreed, pushing her hair off her shoulder, dipping his head to kiss that warm curve at the base of her throat.

Andi shivered again. Oh, she was in so much trouble. When she'd first decided that going to bed with Mac was a good idea, there'd been a small part of her convinced that if she did, it might help her get over him. Get past the feelings she had for him so she could move on with her own life. Instead, she was in even deeper trouble than she had been before.

He hadn't made love only to her body, but to her heart, too. Love welled up and spilled over. She wasn't going to get over him. Ever. And that was a thought designed for misery. Because he didn't love her back. And there was just no lonelier feeling in the world than loving someone who didn't love you.

He lifted his head, smiled down at her and said, "Hope you're up for a repeat performance, because I don't think I'm done with you yet."

She loved hearing that, and there was nothing she'd like more. The idea of staying right there in that big bed with Mac was more appealing than she could admit. She wanted to watch the sunrise with him. Wanted to be here again in the evening and spend her nights wrapped around him.

But none of that was going to happen.

Andi had already indulged herself; now it was time to start protecting herself. For her own good.

"That's probably not a good idea," she said.

"Why the hell not?" he demanded, tightening his hold on her as if she might try to get out of bed.

Which she really should.

"Because this—between us—it's not going anywhere, Mac, so what's the point?"

He laughed. "You can ask me that after what we just shared? Andi, that was incredible."

"It was," she said, starting to feel the chill of the room on her skin. "And now we're done."

"Don't have to be," he told her, bending down to kiss her once, twice, just a brush of her lips with his. "Andi, this just proves what I've been saying all along. We make a great team."

"A team?" The chill she felt deepened as she waited for him to continue.

"Yeah." Idly, he ran one hand over her skin until he finally cupped one of her breasts. As he talked, his fingertips caressed her.

A new wash of heat swept over her, but was lost in the chill when he continued.

"We're a team, Andi. At the office. Clearly, in bed." He dropped his head, kissed her briefly, then looked at her, satisfaction shining in his eyes. "You've got to come back to work now. Can't you see what a mistake it would be to walk away from everything we have together?"

Okay. The chill was now icy. Her heart was full of love and all he could think about was using sex to get her back to the office? She brushed his hand aside and scooted back from him. Her own nudity didn't bother her; she was much too consumed by a temper that bubbled and frothed in the pit of her stomach to worry about being naked.

She knew he'd felt what she had when they came together. He couldn't have been immune to the incredible sense of "rightness" that had lit up between them. Could he? Could he have experienced just what she had and explain it all away as *teamwork*?

Sad, that's what it was. Just sad. But anger was better than sorrow, so she gave herself over to it.

"Seriously?" she asked, shaking her hair back from her face. "You think promising me more sex will keep me as your assistant?"

"Why not?" He grinned again, clearly not picking up on the ice in her tone. "Honey, we just made the world tremble. I don't know about you, but I've never experienced anything even remotely like it before. Why the hell wouldn't we do that again? As often as possible?"

He couldn't see why and she couldn't tell him. So they were at an impasse. One that wasn't going to be maneuvered around. Before she could say anything, he started talking again, clearly enthused with his idea.

"As long as no one at the office knows what's going on between us, we can go on being lovers and work together just like we did before."

He reached for her, but she shook her head. "Just like before."

"Yeah." His smile slipped a little as if he were beginning to pick up on the fact that she wasn't all that enthused with his "plan." But still, he kept going. "We work together, each have our own homes and we share amazing sex."

"So we're boss and assistant at the office and bed buddies once that door's closed."

He frowned. "Bed buddies seems a little—"

"Accurate?"

"Okay, something's bothering you."

She laughed shortly and the sound of it scraped across her throat. "Yeah. Something."

God, she was an idiot. Yes, she had the memory of this night to cling to, but now, she'd also have the memory of this conversation to color it. How could he be so smart and so stupid all at once? And how could she have walked right into this situation, a smile on her face and eagerness in her heart?

"It's the best of all possible worlds, Andi," he said, voice deep, low. "What could be better?"

So many things, she thought. Love. Commitment. Marriage. Family. The offer he'd just made her paled in comparison. She couldn't say any of that, of course. For him, love had never entered the picture and damned if she'd shove it through the door now.

"No." Shaking her head, she scooted off the bed and grabbed her dress off the floor.

"No?" he echoed, sitting up to stare at her. "That's all you've got to say? Just…no?"

"Just no." Stepping into the dress, she pulled it up, then fought with the zipper. Andi was so done. She needed to get out of there. Fast. Before she said too much of what she was thinking. Problem? She didn't have her car. She'd be trapped in his all the way back to town. Nearly groaning in frustration now, she tugged again at the *stupid* zipper, which remained stuck.

Still, psychologically, she felt much more able to have a fight if she at least wasn't naked.

"Why no, Andi?" He came off the bed, too, and went to grab her shoulders before she slipped away. His eyes fired. "Is there someone else? Some guy I don't know about? Is that what this is?"

She looked at him in disbelief. "Are you kidding? *When* could I possibly have found a guy, Mac?" She whipped her hair behind her shoulders, tugged at the damned zipper again and knew she'd snagged it in the fabric. Letting her arms fall to her sides, she glared at him as if even the zipper was his fault. "Until several days ago I was pretty much an indentured servant. I had no life outside that office."

"Servant?" His eyes flashed and this time it was anger

pumping from him, not sexual energy. "A damn well-paid servant if you're asking me."

"I'm not," she countered.

"Well, you should." He shoved one hand through his hair and gritted his teeth.

"Sure, I made a great salary—and had zero chance to spend any of it." Andi met his anger with her own and stood her ground, just as she always had. "How do you think I can afford to quit? I've got everything you ever paid me sitting in a bank account."

"That's great." He threw his hands up and let them fall again. "So I'm *paying* you to leave me."

"In a nutshell." She looked around wildly, searching for her shoes. He'd carried her in here, and right now that little romantic moment felt light-years away. Had she kicked them off? Had he pulled them off? Did it matter?

"There!" She spotted one of her heels under a chair near the fireplace. Surely the other one would be close. "What're you doing?"

"It should be obvious." She picked up one shoe and continued the search for the other. "I'm getting dressed. I need to go home."

"You can't leave in the middle of a fight."

She saw the other shoe and snatched it. "Watch me."

"How?"

God, she was so done. Andi couldn't believe that what had started out as an amazing evening had devolved into a battle. And what was she fighting for? He didn't want to be won. He wanted his assistant back—with fringe benefits. How humiliating was that?

"How what?" She pulled her shoes on, straightened up and glanced at Mac.

"How are you going to leave?" He was still blissfully

naked and it was a struggle to keep her hormones from jumping up and down just from looking at him. His arms were folded across his chest, his green eyes were narrowed. "It's a hell of a long hike from the ranch to town. Especially in those heels."

Here was the problem she'd noted earlier. "Damn it, you have to drive me."

"When we're done talking," Mac said.

"Oh," Andi told him, nodding, "trust me, we're done."

"You can't tell me that what just happened between us didn't change something."

"It changed *everything*," she said, wishing she'd suddenly sprout wings so she could just jump off his balcony and get herself home. Now. "That's the point."

"And my point is, that change doesn't have to be a bad one."

If he only knew. "Mac…"

He pulled her in close and though she was still pretty angry, she didn't fight him on it. Tipping her head back, she looked into his eyes and wished things were different. Wished she didn't love him so damn much. Wished he felt even a touch of what she felt.

"Don't say no so fast, Andi," he whispered, tucking a stray lock of her hair behind her ear. She shivered at the gentle touch and knew that something inside her was melting in spite of everything. What kind of fool did that make her?

"Wait," he said. "See." He winked. "I've still got most of the two weeks I took off left to help you set up your house. Get it in order. Let's see where we are at the end of it. Okay?"

At the end of the two weeks, they would be in the same damn place, only she'd be even more twisted up and torn over it. There was no way to win in this particular battle. When it was over they would both lose something, and she couldn't prevent that, even if it ended tonight.

So did she take the rest of those two weeks, torment herself with dreams that had no basis in reality? Or did she end it now, while she was cold and empty and sad?

"Give us the time, Andi," he urged, and caressed her cheek with the backs of his fingers. "Let's find out together where we are at the end of it."

"I know where we'll be," she said, shaking her head.

"You can't, because I don't." His gaze moved over her face and Andi felt it as she would have a touch.

"Give it a chance," he said. "Don't end it now."

Fool, she told herself. *Don't be an idiot*, her brain warned. *Step back now and make it a clean break*, her heart shouted.

But she looked up into his eyes and didn't listen to any of it.

"Okay."

Eight

Mac didn't have his phone on him and realized that it was the first time in years he'd been completely disconnected from the rest of the world. He owed Andi for that. For making him see just how attached he'd gotten to the damn thing. Now, he could go hours without even thinking about his phone, and wasn't that amazing?

As thoughts of Andi rose up in his mind, though, he forgot about his phone and wondered what she was doing. Where she was. He hadn't been able to stop thinking about her since he dropped her off at her place the night before. Who could blame him? He never would have guessed at the woman behind the cool, professional demeanor. She'd hidden that from him so well, it had to make him wonder what other secrets she had. For the first time in his life, he wanted to know more about a woman, not less. And for the first time in his life, the woman wasn't interested.

"How the hell can she not be?" he muttered, scrawling his signature across the bottom of a contract. He tossed the papers to one side and reached for the next stack.

Last night with Andi had been a revelation. He'd been with his share of women over the years, but nothing he'd ever experienced had come close to what had happened between them. Being locked inside her body had taken him higher than ever before. Her every breath, every sigh had somehow drifted within him, taking root and blossoming so richly he'd hardly been able to breathe. Touching her had awakened a tenderness in him he hadn't been aware of. Need hadn't been satisfied. If anything, it had grown, until now he felt as if he were choking with it.

He'd wanted her to stay with him last night. Another first. He didn't usually take women to his home, and on the rare occasions he had, he'd hustled them back out again as quickly as possible. But this time, it had been Andi who'd drawn a line in the sand.

Mac could admit, at least to himself, that when she'd jumped out of bed with the idea of closing things off between them, he'd felt—not panic, he assured himself—more like a sense of being rattled. He'd thought that after what they'd shared, she'd turn cuddly and, damn it, *agreeable*. Instead, she'd refused to see reason and had almost cut him off.

That had never happened before.

He didn't like it.

Pausing in his work, he tightened his grip on the sterling silver pen and stared blindly at the wall opposite, not seeing his office but the woman currently driving him around the bend.

When he dropped her off at her place, they'd agreed

to take the next day apart, to catch up on things that had to be done—but more than that, they'd both needed some time to come to grips with what had happened between them. So Mac was here, signing off on the contracts his lawyers had approved and Andi was…where?

Damn it.

He grabbed his desk phone, punched in a number and waited while it rang. When a familiar voice answered, Mac said, "Rafe. You open for lunch today?"

Mac needed to talk to another guy. A man would understand. Women were just too damned confusing.

"Yes," Rafe said. "I'm free. Is there something wrong?"

"Damned if I know," Mac muttered. "I was sort of hoping you could help me figure that out."

"Well, now I wouldn't miss lunch for anything. The diner then? About one?"

"That'll work." Mac hung up and got back to the business at hand.

Thoughts of Andi nibbled at his mind, of course. The office seemed empty without the sound of her voice or the click of her sensible black pumps on the floor. He kept expecting her to give her perfunctory knock before throwing his door open to tell him where he needed to be.

Instead, he had a neatly typed-up schedule from Laura—with no notations like *be on time* written in red ink in the margins. His office was running along and he had to admit they seemed to be managing without him fairly well.

Tim would be back next week and, meanwhile, phone calls between Laura and him were keeping everything going while Mac was gone. He didn't know how he felt about that, to be honest.

Finished signing the stack of papers, he tossed his pen

onto the desk and leaned back in his leather chair. He swiveled to look out a window at the spread of McCallum land and told himself that he should be pleased. Work was getting done. Clients were happy. Papers were being filed. It seemed his company didn't need his 24/7 dedication after all. Exactly what Andi had been trying to tell him.

So had he just been wasting his life locked away here in this building? He'd devoted himself to his job, to the exclusion of everything else only to find that the business ran just fine without him. What the hell did that say?

To him, it said that he couldn't sit here anymore. Why the hell did he agree to take this time away from Andi when all he really wanted was to be with her?

Disgusted with his own company, Mac picked up the contracts and carried them out to the main office. Dumping them all on Laura's desk, he said, "These are ready to go out."

"I'll take care of it right away," she assured him.

Mac noticed she still looked wary of him, so he made the effort to drop the brusqueness from his tone. "You're doing a great job, Laura. It's appreciated."

Surprised, she blinked up at him and a shy smile curved her mouth. "Thanks, Mr. McCallum."

He nodded. "Call me Mac. And if you've got any questions, you give Tim a call, all right?"

"I will." As he pushed open the door, he heard her call out, "Have a good day, Mac."

Not much chance of that.

"Thanks for coming out with me today, Violet."

"Are you kidding?" Vi held up several bags. "I love shopping here."

The Courtyard was just a few miles west of downtown Royal. It had begun as a ranch, then was taken over and renovated to become a bustling collection of eclectic shops. There were antiques, yarn and fabric stores, an artisan cheese maker and most Saturday mornings there was a farmer's market. You could get all the local produce you wanted, along with fresh flowers, not to mention the food stands that popped up to feed the hungry shoppers.

Since it was a long drive from Royal into the big city, having the Courtyard here was a real bonus to everyone for miles around. But as popular a spot as it was, Andi hadn't had the chance to really explore it as much as she'd wanted to. Working nonstop for Mac had kept her from doing a lot of things. But how could she regret time spent with him now that it was over?

"Anything in particular you're looking for?"

"Well, I do have a house to finally furnish," Andi said wistfully.

"Fun," Vi said. "And I'd like to stop in at the soap makers, then pop into Priceless. Raina's holding an antique rocking chair for me."

Raina Patterson Dane ran the antiques store, but she'd made it so much more by also offering craft classes in the back. Still, the furniture and wild mix of decor items had made Priceless *the* place to find different kinds of things for your house. Plus her new husband, Nolan, was opening his law office in the loft space above Priceless, so it really was a family affair.

"Sure," Andi said, turning to head over there. "I wanted to look there for the furniture, anyway."

"Good idea," Vi said as they walked side by side. "Priceless has so many nice things, I always need a truck to haul it all home when I'm finished in there. I swear every time I tell Rafe I'm going shopping, I can almost hear him thinking, *Please, not Priceless.*"

Andi didn't believe her for a minute. Vi's husband was so in love with her, he supported everything she said or did. "Rafe wants you happy."

"He really does," Vi said, and ran one hand over her belly. "And I am. Completely. God, I didn't think I'd ever get to this place, you know? Things were so muddled with Rafe for a while, I was afraid we were going to lose what we'd found together."

Andi knew just how she felt. The only difference between them was that Andi *knew* she was going to lose what was most important to her. It was just a matter of time. Less than two weeks now, to be exact.

"I'm really glad," she finally said, trying to keep that twinge of envy she felt to herself.

"Oh man." Vi came to an abrupt stop and stared at Andi. "I'm so insensitive, I should be horsewhipped. There's something wrong, isn't there? That's why the spontaneous shopping invitation today. What happened?" Her shoulders slumped and she winced. "Did Mac do something? Should I have *him* horsewhipped?"

"Thanks for the offer." Andi laughed and reached out to hug her friend. "But no, you don't have to go after your brother. I swear, Vi, I don't know what I'd do without you and Jolene."

"Well, you don't have to know, do you?" She frowned. "Speaking of Jolene, why isn't she with us on this expedition?"

Andi had called her sister first thing that morning and told her everything—about her amazing night with Mac and then how it had ended not in joy, but with a whimper. Naturally Jolene had been thrilled, then sad, then furious on her behalf. How did people live without a sister to bitch to? Since Jolene hadn't been able to join Andi and Vi today, she'd made Andi give a solemn promise to come by later with more information. "She couldn't come. Jacob had a ball game."

"That's so nice." Vi's eyes went misty as she rubbed her belly again. "We'll have ball games, too, won't we, baby?"

"What if it's a girl?"

"Well, we'll find out soon," Vi reminded her, "And if it is a girl, I'll have to say that I was the starting shortstop on my Little League team."

"I stand corrected."

"Okay, but can we do it sitting down for a minute?" Vi pointed to several cushioned iron tables and chairs positioned close to the bakery. "Maybe get a scone and some tea?"

"Great idea." Once Andi had Vi sitting down comfortably, she said, "You stay here and watch our bags. I'll get the food and drinks."

It wasn't long before Andi was carrying a tray with two iced teas and two blueberry scones back to the table. The minute she set it down, Vi snatched at a scone. "Sorry I'm so greedy, but the baby's hungry all the time."

Wistful, Andi sighed a little. She had nieces and a nephew she loved. She could watch her best friend hurrying toward motherhood. But the chances of Andi ever having a child of her own were slim to none, since the only man she wanted to father her children couldn't be less interested.

"Now that I'm sitting down—thank you for that—and

baby's getting a scone…tell me, what's got that puckered-up look on your face?"

"My what?"

"You know." Vi wrinkled her brow and pursed her lips.

"Oh fine," Andi muttered and deliberately evened out her features.

"It's Mac, isn't it?" Vi set down the scone and took a sip of tea. "No one can wrinkle a woman's forehead like my brother."

"Sad, but true." Andi took a quick look around to make sure no one was close enough to overhear. But there were only a few other people taking a break and they were seated a couple of tables over.

Shoppers wandered, a toddler whined for a toy and a busy mom pushed a stroller at a fast trot while she kept a tight grip on a five-year-old. Everything was so ordinary. So normal. But Andi's world had been knocked completely out of whack.

She looked at Vi. "I slept with him."

"Mac?" Her friend's eyes popped wide and her mouth dropped open. "You slept with my brother?"

Hunching her shoulders a little, Andi whispered, "Could you maybe not shout it loud enough to spread it through town like a brushfire?"

"Sorry, sorry." Vi winced and leaned in over the table. "This is so great, Andi. I mean really. I've hoped and hoped you two would get together and finally it's happened. Tell me everything. Well, not everything, but you know. When? Why? No, never mind why. I know why, you're nuts about him, which could just make you literally nuts, but never mind. When?"

"Last night and yes, I probably am nuts." She was

glad that Vi was so happy about the situation. Andi only wished she could be. Breaking off a tiny piece of her scone, she nibbled at it. "I don't know what I was thinking."

"If it's like what happened with Rafe and I, you weren't thinking at all." Vi sat back, took another bite of her scone. "I don't think you're *supposed* to think about something that big. You're supposed to *feel* it."

Oh, there had been lots of feeling. Sadly, it had been all on her side. "Well, fine. But I have to think now, don't I?"

Violet sighed. "Yes, being you, I guess so."

"Thanks," Andi said wryly.

"Oh, honey, I love you, but you really do think too much. Couldn't you just relax and enjoy it for a while?"

"No, because he doesn't want what I want."

"Not yet, anyway."

"Not ever, Vi." Andi had to remember that. No point in setting herself up for more crushing blows. She had to take what was left of their two weeks together and then turn her back on the past and force herself to find a future. A future that wouldn't include Mac. Damn it.

"What he wants," she said, "is to get me back into his bed and back to my job. I'm not even sure if that's the order he'd prefer it in."

"He just doesn't know what he really wants." Vi reached across the table and took Andi's hand. "It was the same with Rafe, I swear. Men can be completely clueless about this stuff. It's as if they can't admit to feeling more for a woman because it tears little chunks of their manhood off or something. But *love*, to most men, is a terrifying word. The big dummies."

"I don't know that Mac is scared of love, Vi," she said

after a moment's pause. "I just know that he doesn't feel it for me. He talked about being a great team. About how when I go back to the office, we can each have our own places and meet up for sex and nobody has to know."

"Oh, God." Vi's chin dropped to her chest. "I'm related to an idiot. It's mortifying."

Andi had to chuckle and it felt good, letting go a little of the misery crouched in the corner of her heart. Knowing Vi was on her side helped a lot. It just didn't change anything.

"I can't go back to work for him. And I've agreed to keep spending time with him until the two weeks are up, but how am I going to be able to stand it? It's not as if I can sleep with him again."

"Why the hell not?"

Andi laughed. "That's exactly what he said."

"For once, my brother was right. So why not?"

Andi took a drink of her tea to ease a suddenly desert-dry throat. "Because it'll only make it harder on me when it ends if I keep getting drawn into a fantasy that will never come true."

"You could make it true." Vi took another bite of her scone and moaned softly in appreciation.

"Fantasies, by their very definition, are just that."

"Doesn't mean you can't do something about them."

"Really?" Intrigued, Andi watched her friend's sly smile and felt only a small niggle of worry in reaction. "How?"

"Easy." Vi shrugged. "You have to dump him."

Andi blew out a pent-up breath. "Dump him? We're not together—how can I dump him?"

"You said it yourself. You spend time with him, but

you don't let him close. Do exactly what you were going to do. Don't sleep with him again. It'll drive him crazy."

Andi would like to think so, but Mac had an amazing ability to rebound from women. Why should she be any different from the legions he'd moved on from in the past?

"Think about it," Vi said. "What did Mac do when you quit your job?"

"Argued with me."

"Well, sure, but then?" She picked up her scone and gestured with it. "Mac went after you. Went to your house. Talked you into this two-week thing."

"True."

"Dump him and he'll come after you again," Violet pronounced. "I know my brother. And he won't be able to stand you walking away from him."

That did sound like Mac, Andi admitted. But coming after her because he didn't like to lose didn't mean anything, did it? That would just be him responding to a direct challenge. It wouldn't mean he cared. Briefly, she remembered how it had been between the two of them the night before and she felt a flush sweep over her in response. But letting herself be drawn into a wave of hope only to be crushed didn't sound appealing.

"I don't know," she said, shaking her head and breaking off another piece of her scone. "I'd be tricking him."

Violet gave a long, dramatic sigh. "And your point is?"

Andi laughed.

"All's fair in love and war, right?"

"He doesn't love me," Andi said.

"I wouldn't be so sure," Vi replied thoughtfully.

* * *

The Royal Diner was bustling with the usual lunch crowd, plus a handful of tourists thrown into the mix. Conversations flowed fast and furious, orders were called into the kitchen and the cook stacked finished meals on the counter, waiting for them to be picked up.

The place smelled like hamburgers and good, rich coffee and felt as comfortable as Mac's own living room. Which was why he didn't mind getting there early enough to snag a booth and people-watch until Rafe arrived.

Mac knew mostly everyone in town, really. It was nice to see Nolan and his wife, Raina, laughing together in a booth on the far side of the room. Then there were Joe Bennet and his foreman talking business over apple pie and coffee. And Sheriff Nathan Battle getting a kiss from his wife, Amanda, before taking his to-go lunch out the door with him.

Rafe came in as Nathan left, and Mac waved a hand in the air to get his friend's attention.

Sliding onto the bench seat opposite him, Rafe leaned back and said, "Thank you for the lunch invitation. I've been working since five this morning and really needed to take a break."

"Five?"

"Calls to London, Shanghai. You know how it is, dealing with international businesses."

"I do, but you know what? I've discovered something recently that you should try. Relaxing."

The other man laughed, set his phone on the table in front of him and signaled Amanda for a cup of coffee. "You are going to teach me how to relax? This is a joke, right?"

"No joke. Ironic, maybe. But not a joke." Mac glanced at his friend's phone. "You don't see me checking my phone, do you?"

Rafe frowned. "No, I do not. Where is it?"

"In the truck." Mac shrugged it off. "I'm learning to put the damn thing down. You should, too."

"Here you go, Rafe," Amanda said as she set the coffee in front of him. "What can I get you two?"

They ordered and when she moved off into the crowd again Rafe asked, "Just who is teaching you how to relax? Would it be Andrea?"

Mac nodded. "It would. Funny, but in the last few days, she's taught me a lot." *Especially last night*, he thought but didn't say. There were some things a man didn't talk about, even with his friends. What had happened between Andi and him was private and would remain that way.

"So Violet tells me. You're painting now? Repairing sinks and tile floors? Have you decided to go into the home construction business as a sideline?"

"Not exactly." Mac smiled when Amanda set his turkey sandwich in front of him and grabbed a french fry. Shaking it at Rafe, he said, "I'm helping her get her house into shape." *And stealing time with her.* "But being there with her, working alongside her, she's got me thinking."

"Please. Don't keep me waiting." Rafe took a bite of his fish sandwich and kept quiet.

"Okay. The way I see it, Andi and I are good together." He took a bite of his own sandwich, then added, "We've always worked well together and it turns out we're a great team…outside of the office, too."

Rafe lifted a dark eyebrow. "Go on."

"I want her." Three simple words that seemed to suddenly be filled with a lot more meaning than he'd expected. Yes, he wanted her back at the office, he wanted her back in his bed, but the bottom line was, he just *wanted* her. Period.

That thought was heavy enough to make him scowl down at his sandwich.

"You seem to have her," Rafe mused. "So what's the problem?"

"She's determined to back away, that's the damn problem." It irritated him to even say it. "I need to find a way to keep her."

"Do you love her?"

He jerked back. "No one said anything about love."

"Maybe you should."

Mac frowned at him. "You're feeling awful damn easy with that word. Not too long ago, it was different. You remember that?"

Rafe's eyes went dark. "Yes, all too well. I almost lost your sister to my own pride and stubborn refusal to see the truth of my own feelings. Will you let that happen to you as well, my friend? Or will you learn from my mistakes?"

"It's different," Mac insisted, grabbing a fry and popping it into his mouth. "You loved Violet."

"Well, if you do not love Andi, then let her go. Let her find a man who *will* love her as she deserves to be."

"What man?" Mac demanded, leaning over the table. "Is there some guy in town with his eye on Andi?"

Rafe blew out a laugh. "Any number of them, I should imagine. She's a lovely woman."

Scowling now, Mac snapped, "You're married to my sister, so you shouldn't be noticing things like that."

"I'm married, not dead."

"That could be arranged," Mac muttered, but Rafe only laughed.

"It seems to me that for a man who claims to not be in love, you're very territorial."

"I don't share," Mac grumbled. "Doesn't mean anything more than that."

"And so she should make herself available to you as your assistant, your mistress, your companion?"

Mac scowled again and couldn't find the appetite for more of his damn lunch. "Aren't you supposed to be on my side?"

"I am," Rafe assured him.

"Doesn't look like it from this side of the fence."

"I'm only trying to make you see that Andi deserves more than being your convenience."

"Never said she was convenient. A more argumentative woman I've never known. Except for my sister," he amended.

"I will agree that my wife is very opinionated."

Mac snorted a laugh. For all the times Rafe had made him furious over the years, for all the trouble he'd tried to stir up when he first blew into Royal, he was surely paying for it with the woman he loved. Violet had never been an easy woman, so Mac knew that Rafe's life was colorful, to say the least.

But Violet and Rafe were a team.

As he and Andi were. Or could be. If she would only see that he was right about this.

"You're walking a fine line here, Mac," Rafe said, taking a sip of his coffee. "If you step wrong, you could lose everything. I know."

Worry flickered in the back of his mind, but Mac

quashed it fast. There wasn't a damn thing Mac McCallum couldn't get once he'd made up his mind.

And his sights were set on Andi.

"I'll watch my step," he said, and picked up his sandwich again. "I know what I'm doing."

"I hope so, my friend," Rafe said with a shake of his head. "I do hope so."

Nine

Andi had never really planned to stay for so long, working for Mac.

When she started, it had seemed like a good place for her. After growing up in Royal, she'd left town, gone to college and, with her business degree, she'd headed to California. Working in LA had been exciting; living there had been less so. The crowds, the noise, the inability to look up at the sky and see more than a small square of smog-tinted blue had eventually begun wearing on her. At her core, she was a small-town girl and when she accepted that truth and moved back to Royal, things had fallen into place for her. She'd reconnected with her sister, found a fast and true friend in Violet and fallen stupidly in love with her boss.

"Okay, so not everything worked out," she muttered, setting some of her books onto the built-in shelves along one wall of her tiny living room. The house was coming together, the two weeks with Mac would soon be over and she had to do some thinking about her life.

The job with McCallum Enterprises had been good for her, though. She'd loved the energy, the rush of helping to run an international company with a great reputation. But it wasn't *hers*. Just like Mac, that company would never belong to her, and Andi wanted something of her own. To build a life and find what she was missing. To build a business from the ground up and watch it grow. She just didn't know what.

"Thank God you had tea made," Jolene said as she came into the living room carrying two tall ice-filled glasses with a small plate of cookies balanced on top of one of them. "I swear, summer's coming along too early for me."

"It's not that hot." Andi reached up to take the cookies and her glass of tea.

"Not in here, bless the air conditioning gods." Jolene eased down to the floor, maneuvering her belly as if it were a separate entity. "Oh, I should have gone shopping with you and Vi. It would have been much more relaxing, not to mention cooler. That baseball field will kill you. Blazing sun, the shouting, the crying—and that's just the parents…"

Andi laughed.

"Good," Jolene said with a brisk nod. "You can still do that."

"Of course I can. It's just, there's not a lot to laugh about right now."

"I could get Tom to go over and kick Mac's butt for you."

"No, but thanks for the thought."

Jolene shrugged. "Just as well. Tom really likes Mac."

"So do I." Andi grumbled as she bit into a cookie. "That's the problem."

"Damn it, I was so sure that once you'd had sex with the man it would either shatter your illusions or make him realize just how great you are. Numskull man."

"It's not his fault, Jolene," Andi said, taking a cookie she didn't really want and biting in, anyway. "I'm the one who fell in love."

"That's not a crime."

"No, but stupid should be."

"Honey, there aren't nearly enough jails if stupid turns out to be a crime."

"True." Taking a sip of her tea, Andi looked at her sister. "How did I live without you when I was in LA?"

"Beats hell out of me."

Andi grinned. "I was just sitting here thinking how glad I was that I moved back home. I've got you and Tom and your kids and I'll be here for the new baby's birth…"

"You bet you will. What if Tom gets called out to a fire? You're my backup."

Smiling still, Andi finished, "California just wasn't for me."

"No, but you figured that out, came home and found a job you loved. You'll do it again. As soon as you're ready."

"I think I am. Ready, I mean," Andi said as her idea solidified in her mind and settled in to stay. "But I've been doing a lot of thinking about this and I don't want a job, Jolene. I want my own business."

"Really? Great! What're you planning?"

"I'm going to be a professional organizer." It had been bumping along in her brain for a few months now and she'd toyed with it, even while she worked for Mac. She supposed that a part of her had realized that she couldn't stay at McCallum Enterprises forever, and her subconscious had been busily at work plotting her next move. She was going to organize people's homes, their businesses, heck, *garages*. She was great at finding order in chaos, so why shouldn't she make a living doing what she was so good at?

"That is the most brilliant idea you've had in years." Jolene had a wide smile on her face as she lifted her tea glass in a toast. "Honestly, I'll be your first customer. I'll expect the pregnant sister discount, of course, but you could come through and get my kids' bedrooms straightened out. Do you know I found an overlooked Easter egg in Jacob's room last week? I probably would have found it sooner, but I thought the smell coming from there was just from his discarded socks. Like usual."

Andi laughed. "Jacob's room may defeat me, but I'm willing to try."

"Then there's my kitchen and, God help you, Tom's workshop." Jolene reached out, took her sister's hand and squeezed. "It's a great idea and you'll be a huge success at it. Guaranteed."

"Thanks, I think I will, too. And God knows I've got the time to pour into it."

"But not like a workaholic again, right?" Concern shadowed Jolene's eyes briefly. "You're not going to turn into a stranger again while you bury yourself in work, right?"

"Absolutely. I want my own business," Andi said firmly, "but I want a *life*, too. And I'm going to find one, Jolene."

While her sister talked about the possibilities, Andi

thought about the night before, being in Mac's arms, the magic of the moment. A whisper of regret echoed in her heart, for all the hopes and dreams that would never be realized. Then she deliberately erased those images from her mind because it was time she started training herself to have that life she craved so much.

Without Mac.

The following day, Mac took her horseback riding.

She tried to regret agreeing to finish out the two weeks they'd originally decided on, but it wasn't easy. Because their remaining time together was really a gift to herself. When this time was up, Andi would have to walk away for her own sake, no matter what it might cost her. And in spite of what his sister might think or hope, Mac wouldn't follow her again. He didn't like losing.

These two weeks were his attempt to win her back. When that failed, Mac would move on—as he had so many times before.

Dumping him as Vi had suggested wouldn't work. And even if it would, Andi wasn't going to play games. If she had to trick Mac or trap him, he wouldn't be worth catching, would he? The heck of it was, Andi knew that if she told him the truth, admitted to loving him, it would throw him so hard, he'd walk away long before the two weeks were up. He wasn't interested in love.

But even knowing that she would be free of him if she just confessed, Andi couldn't do it. She still had her pride and damned if her last memory would be of Mac looking at her with pity shining in his eyes just before he turned away from her.

Those worries were for later. Today, they were here together, riding across open ranch land as if they were the only two people in the world. The Double M was a huge ranch, stretching out for miles. A stand of wild oaks straggled along the river and Mac led her in that direction. The sun was heating up and in another month, this ride would be downright miserable. But today was clear and just warm enough to remind you that summer was coming.

"You're thinking again," Mac said from beside her. "I can hear you from here."

"You've something against thinking?" She pulled the brim of her borrowed hat down lower over her eyes to cut the glare from the sun.

"On a day like today, while it's just us and the horses? Yeah, I do." He gave her a brief smile and nudged his horse closer to hers. "You know I didn't bring my phone with me?"

She laughed, delighted. So this time with her had changed him—if only a little. "I'm so proud."

"You should be," he said. "Without you, I'd be hunkered over in the saddle, checking stock reports, catching up with Tim and making sure Laura sent out the contracts due to be mailed today. Instead, thanks to you, I'm spending time on my ranch alongside a beautiful woman. And at the moment, I don't give two damns what's happening back at the office."

She smiled; how could she help it? The man was charming and darn near irresistible. Sadly, he knew it.

"So, are you going to show me where they set up the last water tank?"

"Interested in ranch life, are you?" The twinkle in his eye sparkled in the sunlight.

"Interested in seeing the tank I had to get road clearance approval on to bring in," she countered.

Ranchers kept huge water tanks stationed around their property to be filled by rainwater or, in times of serious drought, by water trucks brought in for that purpose. There were stock ponds, of course, natural watering holes for the animals, but they could go dry in a blistering hot Texas summer and you had to be able to refill them when necessary. The tanks were one sure way of accomplishing that. But several of them had come down during the big storm, and Mac had had to replace them. Now they were in place, only waiting to be filled before the start of summer.

Thankfully, they'd already had a good-sized storm at the beginning of the month and more were being predicted. In fact, she thought as she peered up at the sky to see gray-and-black clouds huddling together as if forming an attack strategy, it looked like another storm was headed this way so fast, Andi and Mac might get wet themselves before this ride was over.

"It's this way." He tugged on the reins and his horse moved in that direction. Nudging Apollo into a trot, Mac looked back to make sure Andi was following him. She was, and waved to him in reassurance. The gelding she rode was in no particular hurry, which was just as well. It had been a couple of years since she had been riding and she knew her muscles would be screaming by tomorrow.

Despite the heat of the sun, a brisk breeze blew, bringing the scent of the storm with it. Andi pulled her hat down hard so it wouldn't blow away and followed after Mac, determined to keep up. It was another twenty minutes to the stock pond and the water tank that stood alongside it.

"The pond looks good." She dismounted with a quiet sigh of relief.

"It's early yet," Mac said, squinting into the sun, watching a few lazy cattle meander down to the water's edge for a drink. "But yeah. Last year, the water level was only half as much at this point in the season. A couple more good storms," he said, checking out the sky, "and we'll be set. Tanks and ponds."

"It's a lot, Mac," she said softly, letting her gaze sweep across miles of grazing land. Cattle dotted the countryside, and here and there a few horses were sprinkled in as added interest. "Running your business, and the ranch, it's a lot. Do you ever want to hand the reins over to someone else? Step back from it?"

For a second, it looked as though he might give her a wink and a grin and the kind of quick, smooth answer he was best known for. But then his features evened out and he took another long look around him before turning back to her. "No. I don't. Though I'll say, if I ever had to make a choice—either the business or the ranch—the ranch would win hands down." He bent over, scooped up a handful of dirt and grass and then turned his hand over, letting it all drift to earth again. "I love this place. Every blade of grass and clod of dirt. Every stupid steer, every irritation. The worry about not enough water, too much water, calves being born, losing some to coyotes..." He stood up again and shook his head. "It's McCallum land and I guess it's in me."

She heard it in his voice, saw it in his eyes. The business he'd taken over when his parents died was something he'd built, defined, expanded because he'd needed to prove something. To his father. Himself. Maybe even the world. But this ranch was the soul of him. What kept him going, what drove him. His love for the land and the continuity of caring for it.

Her heart turned over in her chest as he looked at her, and Andi wondered how much more she could possibly love him. How could the feeling inside her keep growing, filling her up until she thought she must be glowing with it?

He tipped his head to one side, stared at her. "What is it? You've got this weird expression your face."

She smiled and walked toward him. Just when she thought she had come to grips with everything, he threw her for a loop again. Seeing him like this, standing tall and arrogant and proud on land his family had owned for generations, made her want to tell him everything. Confess her love, let him know what she thought and felt. She couldn't, though, any more than she could turn from him now and pretend she'd heard and felt nothing.

"You just...surprise me sometimes, that's all," she said, walking close enough that she could reach up and cup his cheek in her palm. Heat flowed from his body to hers and back again. "You're kind of wonderful."

Pleasure shone in his eyes. He covered her hand with his and, as their gazes locked, she felt a shift in the emotions charging around them. Passion burned just beneath the surface, a reminder that what was between them was powerful, difficult to ignore or deny.

"If I'd known it would have this effect on you," he whispered, "I'd have brought you out to the water tank before."

She laughed and shook her head. "You're also impossible."

"So it's been said." He pulled her in close until she had to tip her head back to look up at him.

"What am I doing here?" she murmured, more to herself than to him.

He took her hat off, smoothed her hair back from her face, dipped his head and whispered, "Driving me crazy."

Lightning flashed in the distance and thunder rolled toward them like an approaching army. Then he kissed her and the storm erupted around them, pelting them with rain they didn't even notice.

When the storm rushed in and lightning began to slash at the ground much closer to them, they broke apart and climbed onto the horses.

Drenched and laughing like loons, they outpaced the storm, rode up to the ranch house and turned the horses over to the stable hands. Then racing for the house, Mac and Andi ran into the kitchen and gratefully took the towels Teresa offered them.

"Couple of crazy people is what you are," she muttered, with a half smile tugging at her lips. Her short, gray-streaked brown hair hugged her head like a cap. Her lipstick was bright red and her nails were painted to match. She wore jeans, boots and a long-sleeved blue-and-white-checked shirt. "Could have been struck by lightning out in this storm. You're lucky you're just half-drowned instead."

"Thank you, Teresa," Andi said, running the towel over her hair and toeing her boots off one at a time. "We're messing up your floor. I'm so sorry."

Mac glanced behind them and saw the muddy foot-prints and small river of water that had followed them in. He cringed a little and added his own apology. He might own the house, but Teresa ruled it, and everyone on the ranch knew it. "We gave you more work to do, didn't we?"

Impatiently, Teresa waved that away. "Don't have

nearly enough to do around here to keep me busy, so don't worry about that. You two go on up now and get out of those wet clothes. I'll throw everything in the dryer as soon as you do."

"I'll bring our clothes down in a couple minutes." Barefoot now, Mac took Andi's hand and pulled her along with him, though she came reluctantly. He had to assume it was because she was embarrassed that Teresa knew the two of them would soon be naked together. But she'd just have to get over that or risk pneumonia. Already, she was shivering from the effects of being soaking wet and the air conditioning blowing through the house. So reluctant or not, she followed after him, down the hall, up the stairs and to his bedroom.

"Come on, get out of those wet clothes," he urged as he stripped himself.

"You're just trying to get me out of my panties again." Her voice trembled with cold.

"You caught on to my nefarious scheme. Make a woman so damn cold she turns blue, then have my way with her."

She laughed shortly. Her hands shook as she undid buttons and then pulled off her shirt, jeans and underwear. He tried not to look because the point here was getting her warm again, not jumping her the minute she was vulnerable. Once they were both finished, he tossed her his robe, then pulled on a pair of dry jeans without bothering with boxers beneath them.

Bundling up the sodden mess of clothes, he opened the bedroom door. "I'll just take these to Teresa and be right back."

"Take your time. This is so humiliating," she murmured, sitting on the edge of his bed, shaking her head.

"Yeah, getting caught in a storm is a real embarrassment." He grinned at her then bolted back down the stairs. He knew she wasn't going anywhere, but he wanted to get back to her quickly.

Teresa was waiting for him. "I'll get those dry. You take up that tray I fixed for the two of you. Get some of that hot coffee into Andi before she turns into an icicle."

"I will." Mac spotted the tray on the kitchen table and couldn't stop the smile of appreciation. There was leftover fried chicken, potato salad, a half-dozen cookies, two mugs and a small carafe of coffee.

Impulsively, he kissed her cheek and was shocked to see her blush. "You are a wonder," he said softly. "And I don't think I tell you that often enough. Thanks, Teresa. I appreciate it."

"Well, now, you two need some warming up—and food and coffee are just one of the ways to get that done." She slid him a sly smile. "I imagine you can think of another way."

He winked at her. "Oh, one or two come to mind."

Back upstairs, he found Andi just where he'd left her. Her hair was dark and wet and she was looking a little less sure of herself, which was, he told himself, a good thing. He wanted her as off balance as he'd been lately. Damn it, all he could think about was her. From the first day of their two-week agreement, she'd been front and center in his mind. And if anything, it had only gotten worse the more time they spent together. Her laugh haunted him, her eyes filled his dreams and the scent of her seemed to always be in the air. Andi had somehow become a part of him and he wasn't quite sure what to do about that.

Oh, he'd once thought about a future wife and children

in a vague, maybe-one-day kind of way. But that was a long time ago. Before he'd had responsibility thrust on him by his parents' deaths.

Then it had been not only the family ranch—that had been in McCallum hands for generations—and the business his father had been building, but there had also been Violet, his teenage sister he had to protect and look after. He and Vi had butted heads time and again, which was to be expected, but being brother *and* father to her had made keeping their relationship tight that much harder.

So he'd buried himself in work because at least there, he was sure of his footing. Slowly, over time, he'd lost all sense of a future because his present was packed with far too much already.

Mac's parents had been happy. He and Vi had been raised by people who loved each other and them. But when they died, it was as if Mac had shut down that loving side of himself. The part that remembered family and laughter and the ease of just being happy. He hadn't had time for happiness back then. It had all been about saving his father's company. Keeping the ranch together. Diversifying. Building on a fortune to make sure that Violet would never have to worry. He'd expanded the ranch beyond his father's dreams and he'd built a company that was larger and more successful than anyone could have imagined. And somewhere along the line, he realized, he'd lost himself.

In the past ten days or so, he'd begun to find the man he used to be. He'd laughed more, talked more and done less work than he had in ten years. But who he was now was ingrained in his soul. Wasn't it too late to go backward? To try to reclaim permanently the younger version of himself? The one that had plans beyond running a successful company? If he tried, didn't he run the risk of losing everything he'd built?

"Mac?" Andi's voice cut into his thoughts and brought him back from the meandering road his mind had taken. "You okay?"

"Yeah," he said, focusing on her and letting the rest go. For now, anyway. "Fine. Look. I bring supplies."

She smiled. "I can't imagine what Teresa's thinking right now."

"I can." He grinned and carried the tray to the table set between the two cozy chairs in front of the hearth. "She's thinking, *Look at all that mud and water. He's a lucky man to have a girl like Andrea Beaumont give him a second glance when he drags her through a thunderstorm on horseback.*"

Andi laughed as he'd meant her to.

"Come over here," he urged. "I'm gonna start a fire, get us both warmed up while we eat."

She stood up and he saw she was dwarfed by his dark red robe. The hem of it hung to well below her knees and her hands had disappeared into the sleeves. But she didn't look as pale and cold as she had before. While she took a seat, picked up one of the coffee mugs and took a sip, Mac built a fire in the hearth.

He supposed it really wasn't cold enough to warrant it. And it was completely illogical to have a fire going while the air conditioner was running. But the flames already licking at the kindling and snapping up along the stacked logs were comforting. Romantic. With a naked Andi within arm's reach, romantic was a very good thing.

"I love a fireplace," she said softly, staring at the blaze as the flickering light washed over her features. "I wish my house had one."

He took the chair beside hers, relishing the feel of the heat rushing toward him from the hearth. "Feel free to come and use mine any time you want."

"Thanks." She tipped her head to one side and smiled at him. "Maybe I will."

They ate cold chicken and talked about the town, their families, their friends, studiously avoiding all mention of what was between them. Tension coiled in the air and snapped as hungrily as the flames on wood.

By unspoken agreement, they hadn't had sex since that first time, but whenever he tried to sleep, Mac relived that night over and over again. The taste of her. The feel of her beneath his hands. The hot damp core of her that took him in and held him. Before Andi, after he'd had a woman, she retreated from his mind, as if with the need satisfied, he was content to move on to whatever— or whoever—came next.

With Andi, though, it was just the opposite. He wanted his hands on her again. Wanted to lay claim to all that she was. Wanted to hear her sighs and watch those storm-gray eyes of hers glaze over with passion then flash with completion when he took her.

Hell. He just *wanted* her. All the damn time. More than his next breath. More than anything.

"Um," she said, as if reading his mind and the quick, hungry thoughts racing through it, "we should see if our clothes are dry. Or maybe I could borrow something of yours just to get home in and—"

She was backing away. Sitting right there beside him and pulling back from him and he wasn't going to let her. Need drove him out of his chair. Want had him kneeling on the floor in front of her, staring up into gray eyes that would, he was sure, continue to haunt him for years to come.

"Or," Mac said, as he came up on his knees, "there are other options."

She took a deep breath and shook her head, making her still-damp hair swing about her face. "Mac, we shouldn't—"

"Miss a golden opportunity," he finished for her. Reaching out, he untied the robe belt at her waist, then spread the fabric apart. She shivered and her eyes went glassy as his hands skimmed over her body with sure, long strokes.

"Oh, Mac…"

She sighed and he knew he had her. Knew she wouldn't say no, wouldn't turn away from what they could find together. Running his hands up her body, he cupped her breasts and pulled gently at her rigid nipples. He loved watching that dazed expression come into her eyes. Loved the sound of her breath hitching in her lungs. Loved…

He parted her thighs, spreading her legs wide, then leaned in, covered her with his mouth and devoured her. Her quick gasp of surprise, then desperation, filled his head. Her sighs, her whimpers, her jerky movements as he pleasured her body, fed him, pushed him on. He licked, nibbled, suckled at her until she lifted her hips off the chair and threaded her fingers through his hair, holding his head to her as her cries became pleas.

She was frantic now for what he could give her and her need fueled his own. She cried out his name and the sound became a choked-off scream of release as the first explosions rocketed through her.

He continued to push, to torment her even as her body

splintered in his grasp. And before the last of the tremors shook her, he pulled her from the chair, laid her out on the rug in front of the fire and buried himself deep inside her.

The tight, damp heat of her surrounded him, and Mac paused long enough to savor the sensation of being close enough to become a part of her. He threw his head back and practically roared his satisfaction. Then she moved, arching into him, rocking her hips, urging him on.

"More, Mac," she whispered harshly. "Give me more. *Take* more of me." Her head tipped back, exposing the line of her throat, and he tucked his face into that curve, kissing her, feeling the beat of her heart in the pulse that pounded against his mouth.

His mind fogged, his heart raced. Together they rushed to completion, bodies joined in an ancient dance that felt new and wondrous. All other thoughts fled, dissolving in the wide, deep ocean of sensation they were sinking into. He felt her body tighten around his, her legs lock around his middle and even as she called his name brokenly, he joined her in the fall, giving her everything he was.

Ten

It wasn't until later, as they lay wrapped together in a blissful haze, that Mac suddenly snapped back to reality. When he realized what had just happened, he groaned, closed his eyes and muttered, "Damn it."

"What?" It came on a sigh, as if she really couldn't bring herself to care what was wrong. She slid one hand down his back and her touch felt like fire-wrapped velvet.

No way to do this an easy way. Just say it. Lifting his head, he stared down into her eyes and said, "I didn't use protection."

Well, he thought, watching her eyes flash wide with apprehension, that was dropping a lead balloon on the festivities.

"Oh, God." She covered her eyes with one hand.

He pulled away from her but didn't move far. Her skin

gleamed like fine porcelain in the firelight. Her eyes flashed and changed as emotions, like the firelit shadows, danced in them. "My fault," he said tightly. "Can't believe I did that. It's never happened before. Swear to God, you are the only woman I've ever met who could shut down my brain so completely."

She worked up a pitiful smile at that halfhearted compliment. She sat up, grabbed her blanket and drew it around her shoulders before huddling deeply into it.

"It's okay," she said firmly, as if trying to convince herself as well as him. "It was just the once. I'm sure it's fine."

Mac snorted, disgusted with himself for losing control and amused at her attempt at a positive attitude. "Yeah, I'm guessing couples have been telling each other that for centuries."

"Couples?" she repeated softly, then shook her head. "Doesn't matter. It's fine, I'm sure."

Couples. Was that what they were? For so long, they'd been colleagues. Boss and assistant. Friends. Had they worked around to where they were a couple now? When did that happen? What the hell should he do about it?

Too many things to think about when most of his blood supply was situated well below his brain. "We'll find out soon enough, won't we?" He propped his back against the closest chair, then dragged her up next to him despite her attempt to squirm away. She was stiff with tension, and he knew her mind had to be racing through every imaginable scenario and there was nothing he could do to make it easier.

He stared into the fire and tried to do some thinking of his own. The first rush of panic and self-directed fury was easing now, and Mac indulged himself in exploring a few of those future possibilities. If Andi wasn't pregnant, they could go on as they always had. Surprisingly enough, that notion wasn't as appealing as it had been even two short weeks ago.

If there was no baby and she still wanted to quit her job, he'd have to find a way to deal with that. He couldn't force her to stay if she was determined to leave. Mac frowned at the fire as Andi shifted in his grasp, probably uneasy with her thoughts. And he really couldn't blame her.

If she was pregnant, well, that opened up a whole new road. She would be carrying *his* child, so she wouldn't be walking away from him no matter what she wanted to believe.

A baby. He rubbed one hand across his face, took a deep breath and released it slowly, waiting for another wave of panic.

It didn't come.

Hell, he thought, if Andi was pregnant, she'd marry him, live here at the ranch. They'd work together, raise their kid and have great sex. The two of them would have the best of all possible worlds. That sounded pretty good to him.

The hard part would be hog-tying her until she agreed with him.

"Mac?"

"Yeah?" He tightened his hold on her in case she tried to bolt.

But she only turned her face up to his, her gray eyes stormy. "This doesn't change anything between us. It can't."

He tucked her head onto his shoulder, rested his chin on top of her head and stared into the fire blazing in the river-stone hearth. "Guess we're gonna find out about that, aren't we?"

A few days later, they still hadn't really talked about what had happened and the possible repercussions. Andi simply refused to think about it because she knew that if a part of her would really love to be pregnant with Mac's baby—it would never happen. If she were terrified at the possibility, it was almost guaranteed she'd be pregnant.

That's just the way life worked and she accepted it.

Mac, though, had been acting differently for days. She couldn't really identify what he was thinking, but she knew there was a change in him. Was it panic at the thought of perhaps being a father? Or was it something…else?

A flutter of hope tangled with anticipation in the pit of her stomach. Maybe he had come to care for her. Maybe he was looking at what the two of them had and seeing it for what it could be. Maybe.

"I bring pizza," he announced as he came in from her kitchen. He was balancing a large butcher-block cutting board that held a steaming sausage-and-mushroom pie.

All day, they'd worked on the pink room, with Mac helping the appliance delivery guy install her new black-and-chrome range. They'd tried out her new oven with a bake-it-yourself pizza she'd picked up at the market, and judging by the delicious scents wafting to her, it had worked great.

Smiling in spite of the turmoil bubbling inside her, Andi held up two glasses of dark red wine. "And I've already poured, so that's great timing."

He frowned a little as he set the pizza down on her tiny coffee table. "Maybe you shouldn't be drinking wine."

Andi sighed. "I'm not pregnant, Mac."

"We don't know that."

"Well, until we do, cheers." One glass wasn't going to hurt her or the baby if there was one. And being here with Mac, in the twilight of an early summer evening, she needed the wine.

He shrugged, served them each a slice and handed her a plate as he took a seat beside her on the floor. Andi took a bite, then waved a hand at her mouth in an attempt to cool it off.

"Yep," he said, "new oven works great. What's convection?"

"I should know that," she admitted as she huffed out a breath trying to cool the molten cheese currently burning the roof of her mouth. "But I don't."

"That makes me feel better," he admitted with a grin. Taking a sip of his wine, he looked around the living room. "We did a really good job in here, didn't we?"

"We did."

"Great team."

"Don't start."

"I'm not starting," he told her with a wink, "I'm continuing. There's a difference."

Mac being charming was hard to resist, and still, she had to. She picked up her wine for a sip.

"Andi, we've got something great." His gaze locked on to hers. "Don't walk away from it."

Sighing a little, she shook her head. "I told you, Mac, I can't keep working for you. I want a life."

"Well, so do I now." He set his glass down, then

plucked hers from her hand and set it aside, too. Taking her hands in his, he rubbed his thumbs across her knuckles while he looked deeply into her eyes. "Over the last couple of weeks, I've discovered a few things."

That flutter of hope beat a little faster in her stomach. "Such as?"

Nodding, he said, "Such as, I forgot just how good it felt to take my horse out and ride the ranch myself instead of just relying on reports from my foreman."

"I'm glad." Remembering the look on his face when he told her about what the ranch meant to him, she smiled. Maybe she had gotten through to him. At least a little.

"And," he added with a quick grin, "I learned that not answering my phone doesn't mean instant death."

Laughing, she said, "Also good."

"Mostly, though," he said, and his voice dropped to a low, throaty hush that seemed to ripple along her nerve endings, "I learned what we have."

"Mac—"

"Just wait," he said and held on to her hands when she tried to tug free. "Look, I admit, I was doing all of this to get you to come back to the office. Couldn't see how I'd run the place without you. But it's more now."

There went that flutter of hope again. "More?" She held her breath, watched his eyes.

"We're great together." He said it flatly, brooking no argument even if she'd been inclined to try. "Hell, we have *fun* together. The sex is incredible and damn it, Andi, if we can have it all, why shouldn't we?"

And the hope died.

This was only what he'd said before. Teamwork. Come

back to the office. Be his trusty sidekick. Keep separate homes. Have sex with him. Don't let anyone know.

"If it turns out you are pregnant," he was saying, and Andi warned herself to pay attention, no matter what pain it cost, "we can get married and live out at the ranch." He gave her that smile filled with charm as if that would be enough to smooth over the jagged edges of her heart. "Closer commute for both of us. And Teresa's there to take care of the baby while we're at work."

The last remaining remnants of that hope burned to a cinder and the ashes blew away.

God, she was an idiot.

Before she could tell him to leave, his phone rang. "You mind?" he asked after glancing at the readout.

"No, go ahead." It would give her another moment or two to find the right words to end this. God. How could she be so cold?

"Right… Okay, Tim… Yeah, I know you could. But I'll feel better if I meet you. Twenty minutes?" He hung up, slid the phone into his pocket and looked at Andi. "We've got to finish this later. I have to get to the office. The Brinkman deal is faltering."

Brinkman. She flipped through her mental files. "Oh. Brinkman Auto Industries."

"Right." He stood up, then leaned over and took a last bite of his now cool pizza. Still chewing, he told her, "There are a few things to be done before Hal Brinkman panics and backs out entirely."

"Why are you going in?" Sitting on the floor, she stared up at him and said, "Tim was point person on that deal. No one knows Brinkman better than he does."

"Yeah, but it's my company. Buck stops with me." He narrowed his eyes on her. "And you. Come to the office with me, Andi. You did all the prelim work on those contracts. With your mind, you remember every single detail."

Her heart actually *hurt*. "No, Mac."

Frowning, he stared at her. "What do you mean, 'no'?"

"I mean, I quit, Mac. Two weeks ago. And if that doesn't help, I quit again. This time, it's final." Mac was ready to race out the door even though this wasn't an emergency. Andi had to recognize that she simply wasn't a priority to him. Never would be.

How could he not see it? Despite everything they'd shared the past two weeks, nothing had changed. He wanted her. Back in the office. Back in his bed. And for nothing else. It hurt to accept. To realize that Mac hadn't changed. Not really. His company was still the most important thing to him.

Even now, when he was trying to finagle her back into his life, he was willing to put that conversation on hold so he could race to the office to deal with something his vice president was completely capable of handling.

"I'm done, Mac." Slowly, Andi stood up, because if she was going to stand her ground metaphorically, then she'd do it literally, too. "You're running back to the office when they don't even need you to."

"It's business," he said as if that explained everything.

"And Tim can handle it, but you won't let him. You have to be there." She shook her head sadly and looked at him as if etching this memory into her mind forever. It would help, she told herself, while she worked to get over him. "I thought your heart was really in the ranch, but I was wrong. It's in that office. In the computers and the files and the phone calls and hustle of the day. But mine's not, Mac. It's not what I want."

"What the hell *do* you want, Andi?"

She laughed quietly, sadly. "I want Easter eggs that smell like little boys' sweaty socks. I want little girls who have tea parties with their hamsters. Little League games and cheerleading practice."

He looked so confused, it broke her heart. He'd never understand so she wouldn't bother trying to explain.

"Mostly, I want love, Mac. I want to be loved like I love you."

"You—" His head jerked back as if she'd slapped him.

"Yeah," she said softly, sadly, as hope dissolved into dead dreams and left her feeling hollowed out from the inside. She'd had to say it, if only once. She didn't want his pity, but damn it, she deserved the opportunity to tell the man she loved him, even if she shouldn't. "But don't hold it against me. I'll get over it eventually."

"What the hell am I supposed to do with that?"

"If you have to ask," she said, "then I can't explain it."

"Okay." He shook his head, hard. "Leaving that aside for a second, you've known me long enough that you should understand what that company means to me. Hell, it meant a lot to you, too, once."

It had. But those days were gone. "Not as much as having a life, Mac. That means more."

"So you can just walk away? From me? From what we've had for years? What we had the last two weeks?"

"I have to," she said simply.

"You love me so much you can't get away fast enough?" He laughed shortly and there was fury and pain shining in his eyes. "What the hell kind of love is that?"

She sighed and her heart broke a little more. "The kind I can recover from. I hope."

* * *

The next two weeks were a lot less interesting than the previous ones. Mac fell back on his default settings and buried himself in work. The office. The ranch. He kept himself so damn busy he didn't have time to sleep. Because he couldn't risk dreaming.

Tim was now generally stationed at the office and working with Laura to run down new leads on failing companies that might be suitable takeover material. The Brinkman contract problems had been solved readily enough and looking back Mac could see that Andi had been right. Tim could have handled it. But the point was, this was Mac's business and his responsibility. So of course he'd had to go in. Supervise. Give his opinion and monitor the situation until it was settled. There was zero reason for him to feel guilty about doing what he had to.

So why did he?

She loved him.

A cold, tight fist squeezed his heart. Why the hell would she tell him that and then toss him out of her damn house? That was love? He rubbed at the center of his chest as if he could ease the ache that had settled in there the night he'd last walked away from Andi's house.

She loved him.

Well, if she loved him, why wasn't she *there*? You can't say you love someone and then say, *But I don't like you doing this and this. You should do that instead.* What the hell kind of love was that?

He kept remembering Andi's face, the expression in her eyes. The…disappointment he'd read there. And he didn't like it. Didn't care to remember that she'd told him to leave. That he'd never change. Hell, he had changed.

He'd asked her to come back to work for him, hadn't he? He hadn't demanded it.

Pushing up out of his chair, Mac paced the confines of his office like a tiger looking for an escape route out of his cage. That thought brought him up short. Made him frown as he looked out the window to a wide sweep of McCallum land. The office wasn't a cage. It was... what? The heart of him, as Andi had said?

"No, damned if it is," he muttered. Stalking to the window, he slapped both hands on either side of the glass and leaned toward it.

Outside, the sun was heating up. July was just around the corner and summer was settling in to stay for a while. On the ranch, they'd be moving the herd to a new pasture. The sky looked brassy and there wasn't a cloud in sight. But he didn't really care what kind of view he was staring at. "Why the hell is she being so stubborn?"

He missed her, damn it. What did sweaty Easter eggs have to do with anything?

"That's it, you're gonna snap soon. Talking to yourself." He shoved away from the window and went back to pacing. "You start answering your own questions and you're done, son."

He kicked his desk and gritted his teeth against the pain. He didn't want to miss her, but he couldn't deny that without Andi in his life, it felt as though he was missing a limb.

He'd interviewed a half dozen people for the executive assistant job and not one of them had been able to read his mind the way Andi could. Being at the office wasn't enjoyable anymore. He didn't want to be here, but he couldn't find any damn peace at his own house, either.

Every time he walked in the door, Teresa gave him a cool, disapproving look. And when he tried to sleep in his own bed, visions of Andi rose up and kept sleep at bay while his body burned. He couldn't even look at the hearth in his room without remembering those moments in the firelight with Andi. She'd changed everything on him. And now it felt as if nothing fit quite right.

The buzzer on his desk phone sounded and he glared at it. No damn peace. Three long strides had him at his desk. He hit a button and snapped, "What is it?"

"Sorry, Mac," Laura said coolly and he winced in response. "Tim's on line one."

"Fine. Thanks." His vice president was in Northern California to foster a deal on a tech company. Mac picked up, turned to look out the window again and said, "Yeah, Tim. How's it going?"

"Not good." Tim sounded hesitant—the kind of tone people used when they were about to break bad news and really wished they didn't have to. "Jackson Tully made a deal with someone else last week. We lost out, Mac. Sorry, there was nothing I could do. Tully wanted his business to stay in California."

Mac heard but was barely listening. He realized that a couple of months ago, that news would have made him furious. They'd put in a lot of time, working up strategies for the Tully takeover. The tech company was on its last legs and Mac had figured to pick it up cheap, restructure, then sell it for a profit within eighteen months. Now that plan was shot.

And he didn't care. Scrubbing one hand across the back of his neck, he acknowledged that the blown deal didn't mean anything to him. Because Andi wasn't there. She was gone so nothing else mattered.

What the hell had she done to him?

He rubbed his eyes. "It's all right, Tim. Come on home. Time to move on to something else."

"If it's okay with you," he said, "I'll stay a couple more days. Have a lead on a sinking computer company. I figure it's worth a look."

"Sure. Keep me posted."

Mac hung up, thinking that a month ago, he'd have been all over that news, eager to carve another notch in McCallum Enterprises' belt.

But what the hell did success mean when you didn't have anyone to share it with? When you didn't have the *one* person who mattered. Always before, he and Andi had celebrated every deal together, congratulated each other on the maneuvering, the planning and the final win.

But she was gone and he'd just have to get the hell over it. He wasn't going to go after her again. A man had to hang on to some of his pride, didn't he?

"I didn't know I could be this bored." Andi slumped into one of her new kitchen chairs and propped both elbows on the table. Staring at Vi, she said, "The house is painted. The new furniture's here. There's nothing left for me to *do*."

"What about starting your business?" Vi asked, reaching for an Oreo. "Isn't that on the agenda?"

"It should be," Andi mused, turning her coffee cup around and around between her palms. "But there's no hurry and I'm just not feeling real motivated, you know?"

It had been three weeks since Mac walked out of her house for the last time. July had arrived and her sister was insisting she attend the Royal Fourth of July celebration. She couldn't have felt less like being around people who would expect her to smile and mean it.

Violet sighed, dunked her cookie in her coffee and said, "Mac is being stupid."

"He's being Mac."

"That's what I said." Vi bit her cookie and muffled a groan.

Andi laughed a little, but her heart wasn't in it. Those two weeks with Mac had gone too quickly. She'd thought she was building memories, but what she'd really constructed were personalized torture devices. Whenever she closed her eyes, he was there. How was she supposed to get over him, get past this feeling, when her own subconscious was working against her?

She had to find a way because Andi knew Mac wouldn't be coming back. She'd done the unthinkable and told him no. He'd let her go and called it a lesson learned, because his pride wouldn't allow him to come for her again.

"You know," Vi spoke up again. "Mac's just as miserable as you are."

"He is?" Ridiculous how that thought cheered her up. It seemed misery did love company after all.

"That's got to make you feel a little better."

"It does." Andi got up, went to her new French-door refrigerator and got more tea to refill their glasses. "But you know, rather than the two of us being sad and gloomy apart, I'd rather we were happy. Together." She poured the tea, offered her friend more Oreos, then said, "But it's over, Vi. I can't go back to the office. I love him, so working with him every day would be a nightmare. And I can't jump back into his bed—same reason. The problem is, I haven't figured out yet how I'm supposed to live without him."

"I don't think you're going to have to," Vi said quietly.

Andi looked at her. "Why?"

Smiling, Vi said, "If there's one thing I know, it's my brother. Mac loves you, sweetie. He just hasn't figured it out yet."

"I wish I could believe that." Andi shook her head, and lifted her chin. She had to protect herself. She couldn't keep building hopes on a shaky foundation and not expect them to crash down around her. So instead of giving in to the urge to pin her dreams on Vi's words, Andi said quietly, "I can't take the chance, Vi. I can't wait and hope and keep my fingers crossed. I love Mac, but I'm not going to put my life on hold just on the chance he might wake up and realize that he loves me."

"Oh, Andi…"

"No." Taking a deep breath, Andi said, "Living without him will be the hardest thing I've ever had to do. But I've got to find a way to do it."

Eleven

Mac was working a horse in the corral when his sister found him. He was in no mood for company. Hell, hadn't he bolted from the office because he wanted to be left alone? Feeling surly, he dismounted, tossed the reins to the nearest ranch hand and crossed the dirt enclosure to where his sister waited just outside the fence.

The heat was steaming, making him even more irritable, which he wouldn't have believed possible. Snatching his hat off, he raked his fingers through his hair, then slapped the brim of the hat against his jeans to get rid of at least some of the dirt he'd managed to collect. He opened the gate, stepped through and secured it again. Only then did Mac look at his sister.

"Violet, what are you doing here?"

"It's still my home as much as yours," she reminded him.

"Bet that's news to Rafe." He tugged his hat back on. "Go home, Violet."

"Not until we have a talk," she said.

"Not in the mood."

"Too bad."

"Not a good day for this, Violet." He turned and headed for the stable, but she was right behind him, though she had to hurry her steps just to keep up.

"Pregnant here, not as fast as I used to be," she called out, and that made him stop. He couldn't risk her falling and injuring herself or the baby.

He faced her, his arms crossed over his chest, feet planted wide apart. Squinting into the sun, he glared at her. "Fine. Talk."

"What is wrong with you?" she demanded.

He gritted his teeth and sucked air in through his nose. His temper was dangerously close to erupting so he made a deliberate attempt to hold it down. "Not a damn thing except for an interfering little sister."

Poking her index finger against his chest, she asked, "Don't you see that Andi is the best thing that ever happened to you?"

Of course he saw that. Was he blind? But Andi was the one who'd ended things. "If that's all you came to talk about, this meeting is over."

Damned if he'd stand here and be lectured to by his younger sister. He had stuff to do. And he figured if he kept himself busy enough, he wouldn't have the room or the time to think about Andi.

"You're an idiot."

Mac shook his head. He'd had about enough of women lately. "Great. Thanks for stopping by. Say hi to Rafe."

"I'm not done."

"Yeah," he nearly growled. "You're done. I don't want to share my feelings, Vi. I'm not looking for a soft shoulder or a stern talking-to. You can butt the hell out because this is none of your business, understand?"

"We're *family*, you knot-head," she snapped, and leading with her prodigious belly, encroached on his personal space. "If you think you can scare me off with that nasty streak of yours, you can forget it. I'm only here because I love you."

He had already been pushed way past the edge of his control. The woman he wanted insisted she loved him, but didn't want him. His company didn't interest him. He couldn't even work up any concentration for the horses he loved. The heat was boiling his brain and his little sister dropping in to insult him was just the icing on his damn cake.

Scrubbing his hand through his hair, he muttered darkly, "Suddenly I've got women who love me giving me nothing but grief."

"That's right. Andi *loves* you. What're you going to do about it?"

He frowned at her, eyes narrowing in suspicion. "Does Rafe know you have Oreo breath?"

Vi jerked back, looked embarrassed, then shook it off and argued, "This isn't about me."

One eyebrow lifted. "So my life is up for grabs, but yours is private?"

"Yes," Vi said, lifting her chin to glare at him. "Because I'm not currently being an idiot."

Mac scowled at her. "You're not exactly endearing yourself to me."

Sighing, Violet moved in closer, gave him a hard hug and whispered, "I love you, Mac. I want you happy. So I'm asking you to try some personal growth. Fast."

He hugged her back, then released her. "It's over, Vi. Let it go."

"She's pregnant," Violet blurted out.

"What?"

"Andi. She's pregnant."

Ears ringing, heart slamming in his chest, Mac was staggered. Pregnant? Why hadn't she told him? What the hell kind of love was it that made you leave *and* hide a child? Breath caught in his chest until it felt as if he might just explode. Instantly, images, thoughts, emotions chased each other through his mind. Panic was there, naturally, along with pride, excitement, anger and a sense of satisfaction. Pregnant. Andi was carrying his child. His baby.

Mac examined exactly what he was feeling and realized the one underlying emotion that was strongest was also the most unfamiliar. Happiness. Hell, it had been so long since he'd really been completely happy, no wonder he hardly recognized it.

"Mac? You okay?"

He came up out of his thoughts like a diver breaking the water's surface. "I'm better than okay."

Giving his sister a hard kiss, he grinned at her and said, "This may never be true again, so listen up. Thank you for interfering. For sticking your nose in. For loving me."

Violet smiled up at him. "It was my pleasure."

"I know it."

"So, since you're so grateful to me, we don't have to say anything to Rafe about the cookies, right?"

He only smiled. He loved her, but his little sister could just go home and worry that she'd be ratted out. It would do her good. Leaving her there by the corral, he headed

for the house. He had to change, get to town, then go see
the woman who was currently driving him nuts.

Andi couldn't take boredom for long. By the following day, she had been to the Royal nursery and come
home with a plan.

She had a half-dozen bags of red cedar mulch, flats
of petunias and gerbera daisies and a few bags of peat
moss. She didn't know much about gardening, so she also
bought a book that promised to teach garden-challenged
people to grow beautiful flowers. She just wanted to
know enough not to kill the jewel-colored blooms.

For an hour, she worked steadily, digging holes, planting flowers, laying mulch. The sun blasted down on her,
making her feel as if her blood was boiling. Didn't help
that there was no breeze at all and the oaks in her yard
were busily shading the area where she wasn't.

She liked knowing she was continuing to make her
house beautiful. But the downside to gardening was you
had too much time to think. Naturally, her thoughts kept
spinning back to the man who held her heart and didn't
want it.

"Way to go, Andi," she muttered, patting the dirt in
around a bright red petunia. "You're doing great on the
not-thinking-about-Mac thing."

Disgusted with herself, she sat back on her heels to
admire her work and gave a small sigh of satisfaction.
The flowers were red, white and blue, and with the red
mulch it looked patriotic and fresh and beautiful. Now
all she had to do was find some other chore around the
house to keep her busy. Gathering up her tools and the
empty bags of mulch, she stood up and wished for a moment or two that she had a pool to jump into.

Her cutoff jeans shorts were filthy, her white tank top was sticking to her skin and her ponytail was slipping free, with tendrils of hair hanging down on either side of her face. She wanted a shower, a glass of wine and maybe to lie prostrate on the cool, tiled floor of her kitchen while the air conditioner blew directly onto her.

She might have wished she was out at the ranch with Mac, maybe swimming in the pond behind the house. Skinny-dipping would have been fun on a hot summer day. But that wasn't going to happen, so she let it go on a sigh. Carrying all of her things into the garage, she heard a truck pull into her driveway. The thought of having to be polite and welcoming to a visitor right now made her tired.

Andi wanted some time alone. Time to sulk and brood and enjoy a little self-pity with her glass of cold white wine. So, if it was Vi or Jolene, she'd send them home. The two women had been tag teaming her lately, each of them taking turns to check in with Andi and make sure she wasn't lonely. Well, she *needed* a little lonely at the moment.

With her arguments ready, she came around the corner of the house and stopped dead. Mac. His huge black truck sat in the drive, sunlight glinting off the chrome. The man himself was walking toward her house, looking so good Andi wanted to bolt back into the garage and close the door after her.

She looked *hideous*. Why did he finally decide to come to her when she was hot and sweaty and covered in garden dirt? Quickly, she gathered up her hair, tightened the ponytail, checked out her reflection in the side mirror of her car and brushed spots of dirt off her cheeks. She wasn't wearing makeup because her thought that morning had been, *who needed mascara to plant flowers?* So getting rid of the dirt on her face was really the best she could do and wasn't that all kinds of sad?

She closed her eyes and took a breath. Why had he come here? Was this just another attempt to get her back to the office? Well, she thought, why else would he have come? The man didn't like to lose; Andi knew that better than most. So he'd come back to try to convince her. Again.

Steeling herself for another argument with him, Andi walked out to meet him.

He gave her that wide, slow grin when he saw her and Andi's heart jumped in response. The man would always have that effect on her, she knew. It just wasn't fair that he could score a direct hit on her heart without even trying.

"Flowers are nice," he said.

"Thanks." She tucked her hands into her shorts pockets. To resist the urge to reach for him? Probably. "What're you doing here, Mac?"

"We have to talk." His expression unreadable, Andi thought about it for a few seconds, then nodded. If this really did turn out to be a futile attempt to get her back to the office, it would be better to deal with it. To finally and at last make him see that she wasn't going back. No matter what.

"Okay, fine. Come inside, though. It's too hot out here. And I need something cold to drink."

"Should you be outside working in the heat that way?"

She tossed a quizzical glance at him over her shoulder. "The flower beds are outside, Mac. Hard to plant from the living room."

"I'm just saying, you should be more careful."

Well, that was weird. She headed down the hall toward the kitchen, with Mac right behind her. Andi went straight to the fridge and opened it, relishing the rush of cold air that swept out to greet her. "Tea? Beer?"

"No beer. I'm driving. Listen, Andi—"

"I'm going to stop you right there, Mac. If this is about the office, you can save your breath." She poured two glasses of tea and handed him one. After she took a long drink of her own, she said, "I'm not going over the same old ground again just because you can't accept no for an answer."

"It's not that." He set his tea down, then plucked her glass from her hand and set it aside, too.

The air in the room was cool, but he was standing so near to her that Andi felt the heat of him reach out for her. She'd wished to see him again, but now that he was here, it was painful to be so close to him and yet still so far away.

"Why are you here, Mac?"

He dropped both hands onto her shoulders, looked down into her eyes and said, "It's time you married me."

"What?" This was the last thing she'd expected. A proposal? Granted, not the most romantic proposal in the world, but that didn't matter so much. Demanding she marry him was very Mac after all. But the fact that he was proposing at all was so stunning, Andi felt shaken. Was it possible that he really meant it? Were her dreams about to come true?

He let go of her long enough to dip one hand into his jacket pocket and come up with a small, square ring box. He snapped open the deep red velvet to reveal a round cut diamond so big that when the sunlight caught it, the glare almost blinded her.

She slapped one hand to her chest as if she were trying to keep her heart where it belonged. Slowly, she lifted her gaze from the ring to Mac's eyes.

"Marry me, Andi," he urged, eyes bright, determination stamped on his features. "Right away. We can do it this weekend, if you want. I'll call the mayor, he'll fix us up with a license and it'll be all taken care of."

"This weekend?"

He leaned in and planted a fast, hungry kiss on her mouth. "I think that's best. Look, I don't know why you haven't told me yet, but you should know that Violet spoiled the surprise. She told me about the baby."

Andi's mind went blank. She stared at him and tried to get past the knot of emotion lodged in her throat. For a second or two, she couldn't even draw a breath. *Of course.* This was why he'd proposed to her and was insisting on a hurried wedding. It wasn't about love at all. He hadn't had an epiphany. Hadn't realized that she was what he wanted. Mac was only doing what he would consider his "duty."

"No." Andi pushed away from him and took a step backward for extra measure. "Violet lied. There's no baby. I'm not pregnant, Mac."

He looked as though someone had punched him in the stomach. "Why would she lie?"

"I don't know." Andi threw both hands up and let them fall again. Sorrow fought with anger and the sorrow won. Logically, she knew her friend, Mac's sister, had done all of this to bring the two of them together. But emotionally, she had to wonder what Vi had been thinking to play games like this with people's hearts. "She's a romantic," Andi finally said, her voice soft and tinged with a sigh. "She wants us together and probably thought that this was a sure way to make that happen. And I'm sorry but I may have to kill her."

"Get in line," he grumbled, staring down at the ring in his hand before snapping the box closed with what sounded like permanence.

Her heart aching, tears she refused to allow to fall burning her eyes, Andi whispered brokenly, "The point is, I'm not pregnant. At least I don't think so—"

His head came up and his gaze pinned her.

"—but even if it turns out I am," Andi qualified, lifting one hand for emphasis, "that doesn't mean I would marry you just because of a baby. I'm capable of raising a child on my own and I won't get married unless it's for love."

And that was never going to happen, she thought, at least not with Mac. Why was the one man she wanted also the one man she couldn't have? Spinning around, she stomped to the kitchen window, then spun back.

Furious with Violet, Andi blinked hard to keep those tears choking her at bay. For one all-too-brief moment, she'd thought that Mac had come to her because he wanted her. Instead, they were both being dragged over the coals again. And there was just no reason for it.

"Just take the diamond and go, Mac." *Please go*, she prayed silently. Before she cried.

He opened the jeweler's box, looked down at the ring, shining so brightly on its bed of red velvet, and he shook his head. "No." Shifting his gaze to her, he started toward her with long, slow steps.

Andi groaned, and naturally backed up until she hit the wall. Then she had no choice but to hold her ground and try to keep it together until he left again. *Please let that be soon.*

"I'm not going anywhere." His gaze moved over her face, her hair, her mouth, then settled on her eyes again. "When you just said there was no baby, you know what I felt?"

She huffed out a breath, then firmed her bottom lip when it trembled. "Relief?"

He shook his head. "Disappointment."

Andi blinked at him and apparently he read the surprise on her face.

"Yeah, caught me off guard, too." He laughed softly to himself. "Trust me when I say that my little sister and I are going to be having a talk about this."

"Get in line." She repeated his earlier words and he grinned.

"But," he added, moving in on her, crowding her until she couldn't draw a breath without his scent surrounding her, invading her, "it's because of Vi that I'm here. It's just the push I needed, though I doubt I'll be admitting that much to her. Being here with you, thinking about us being married and having a family, made me realize something important."

Andi swallowed hard and whispered, "What's that?"

"It wasn't a baby that had me proposing, Andi. It was *you*." He smiled, stroked her hair back from her face with the tips of his fingers. "A pregnancy gave me the excuse I thought I needed to come here again. To look at you and admit to both of us that it's you I want, Andi. You I need."

"Mac..." Thank God her back was against a wall. Otherwise, her liquefied knees just might have her slumping onto the floor.

"Not done," he said, winking. "I love you, Andi, and I'm just as surprised by that statement as I see you are."

His expression went tender, soft, as he tipped her chin up with his finger to close her mouth. "The thing is, I've counted on you being a part of my life for so long, I never noticed that you had *become* my life."

A single tear escaped and slid along her cheek. He kissed it away.

"Without you, nothing's fun anymore," he whispered, gaze roaming over her features, voice thick. "Not work. Not relaxation. Not the ranch or a damn picnic or anything. I need you, Andi, and more than that, I need you to believe me."

"Mac, I want to. I really do. More than anything." Her heart in her throat, blood rushing through her veins, she couldn't look away from those green eyes of his.

"Then do it." He cupped her face in his palms. "I'm mad at Vi, but I'm grateful to her, too. Her lie gave me the push to come here. To find my life. To do what I should have done years ago."

Confused, shaken, so touched she could hardly see through the blur of those sneaky tears in her eyes, Andi could only watch as he dropped to one knee in front of her.

"Since I'm only doing this once in my life, I'm going to do it right." He took her hand, slid the ring onto her finger and kissed it. Then looking up at her, he said, "I love you, Andrea Beaumont. Maybe I always have. I know I always will. And if you're not pregnant now, I hope you are soon. I want a houseful of kids running around the ranch."

Her free hand covering her mouth, Andi looked down at him and nodded, unable to speak past the growing knot of emotion clogging her throat.

"I'm taking that as a yes."

"Yes." Slowly, Andi sank to her knees beside him. "I love you, too, Mac. So yes, I'll marry you and have babies with you and ride horses and have picnics—"

"And sweaty Easter eggs?" he asked, his smile shining in his beautiful eyes.

Andi threw her head back and laughed. "God, yes. Sweaty Easter eggs."

"And you'll explain that to me at some point, right? Been driving me crazy trying to figure it out."

She laughed again and felt the easing of hurt and disappointment and regret as all of the negative emotions drained away leaving behind nothing but hope. And joy.

"I promise."

"Come home with me, Andi."

"I will." She looked around her shiny new kitchen and knew she'd miss it. Though Mac's ranch house was wonderful and she knew the life they would build there would be amazing, there would always be a place in her heart for this tiny house. Because it was this place that had brought her and Mac together. The hours they'd spent working on it were memories she'd never part with.

As if reading her mind, Mac whispered, "Let's keep this house. You can use it as an escape route the next time I make you mad. Then I'll always know where to find you so I can come get you and bring you home again."

How lovely to have a man know her so well and love her, anyway. Yes, there would be times they'd fight, argue, and she might storm off and come here. Where she would wait for him to come after her to take her home. *Home.* A home and a family with Mac.

"That sounds just right," she said. Then drawing her head back, she looked up at him and asked, "So, is this another rescue?"

"Yeah," he said softly, wrapping his arms tightly around her. "But this time, *you* rescued *me*."

And he kissed her to seal the promise of their future.

Epilogue

Five months later

A Christmas party at the Texas Cattleman's Club was not to be missed. It looked as though half the town of Royal was gathered to celebrate.

There were five Christmas trees, decorated with multicolored lights and ornaments gathered and collected over the years, placed around the room and at the entrance to the club. Strings of tiny white lights were draped along the walls, and the scattering of tables were covered in red and green cloths. Pine boughs jutted up from vases and lay across the tops of framed paintings, with silvery threads of tinsel hanging from them, catching the light and dazzling the eye. Christmas carols were piped through the overhead speakers and champagne flowed like water.

"You're late," Violet said, coming up to Andi for a hug.

"We're always late now." Andi rubbed her belly and gave a small, sweet smile. Turned out Violet hadn't been lying when she'd sent Mac to Andi all those months ago. Of course, she hadn't known it at the time. It had been a wild guess—although Vi liked to pretend she'd had a psychic moment of intuition. Their baby girl would be born in three months and Andi woke every morning grateful for the love in her life.

"The baby's not here yet. It's not her fault," Violet said, threading her arm through Andi's to steer her through the crowd.

"But we start talking about her and making plans and today we were painting her room," Andi admitted wryly.

"Again? I thought you were sticking with the soft peach."

"I was, but it just seemed as though it would feel hot in there in summer," Andi confessed, "so Mac's painting it that pale green it was before."

Violet laughed. "It's so good to see Mac getting all twisted up over his yet-to-be-born daughter."

"Yes," Andi said, "because Rafe is so la-di-da over your son."

Vi grinned. "I have new pictures to show you of your baby's cousin." She sighed and slapped one hand to her heart. "I swear, I never suspected you could love this much. But Rafe and I are so crazy about our baby boy, we're already talking about expanding the family."

"Good," Andi said, chuckling, "because Mac still has plans to fill every bedroom in the ranch house."

Vi blinked. "There are eight of them."

"I know." Andi sighed. "Isn't it great?"

"Hey, there you are." Mac came up behind Andi, put his arms around her and let his hands come to rest on the swell of their child. He was always touching her, touching their baby. It was as if he couldn't stand to be away from her, and Andi was loving every minute of it.

"I missed you. How you doing? Tired? You want anything?"

"Not tired," she said, "but water would be great, thank you." He kissed the side of her neck, winked at Vi, then headed for the bar.

"I'm so happy for you guys," Violet said on a sigh. "I've never seen Mac so relaxed, so…well, happy."

"I am, too." Andi took a deep breath of the pine-scented air and added, "My life is officially perfect."

She had Mac, their baby, their families and friends. Life was just *wonderful.* Looking around the room, Andi let her gaze sweep across the friends and neighbors gathered there. Case and Mellie Baxter looked amazing. She knew Case was planning on running for another term as club president, and Mellie and Andi had made an informal agreement to use their respective businesses to support each other. With Mellie's Keep N Clean, a house-sitting/cleaning business, and Andi's own Put-It-Away, they would each benefit. Andi could pick up new clients and then could recommend Keep N Clean to her customers to help their newly organized homes stay that way.

"It's pretty amazing what Mellie did for the TCC."

"Generous, for sure," Andi agreed. The TCC had decided it wanted to own the land it sat on instead of keeping the long-term lease they already had going with Mellie's family. So they'd officially made an offer for the property. Which she had promptly turned down. Then, with the agreement of her father, who was now back from rehab and doing much better, Mellie had gone ahead and made a gift of the land to the club.

So, this party was not just for Christmas, but a celebration for the Texas Cattleman's Club.

And the party was a huge success. With Christmas only two weeks away, everyone was feeling festive. Nolan and Raina Dane were laughing with the sheriff and his wife, Amanda.

Liam and Hadley Wade were married now and expecting twins, which explained why Liam was plopping Harper down into a chair in spite of her protests.

"What's the smile for?" Violet asked.

"Just thinking about all that's happened to our friends and the town in the last several months."

Nodding, Vi looked around, too. "It was crazy a lot of the time, but I think we all came through really well. Oh, look. There's Jolene and Tom!"

Tom veered off for the bar, clearly a man on a mission, and Jolene headed straight for Vi and Andi. Newly svelte, now that her fourth child and second son had been born a few months ago, Jolene looked as happy as Andi felt.

"Hi, you guys. Isn't this party amazing?" She turned her head to take in her sister. "Andi, you look gorgeous. Love the color red on you."

Andi sneaked a quick look to where Mac, Rafe and Tom were all balancing drinks and talking. "Mac likes me in red. Says it reminds him of what I wore on our first date. He surprised me with the dress this afternoon."

And then he'd taken her to bed and proved to her beyond a shadow of a doubt how beautiful he thought she was. Such a gift, she told herself, to have a man's love, to know that he felt what you did. To *know* that he would always be there for you and your children.

As if sensing her thoughts, Mac turned, looked directly at her and winked.

"Aren't our men just gorgeous?" Vi sighed a little and waved to her husband as Rafe smiled at her.

"Oh, yeah," Jolene agreed with a wink of her own for Tom.

Mac had supported her idea for a business of her own. Put-It-Away was building quickly, and Andi had as many clients as she wanted. She was picky, though, refusing to be drawn into another all-work, no-play scenario. Mac, too, had cut back on time at the office, leaving Tim more and more in charge as Mac himself concentrated on their growing family and the ranch that was the center of their lives.

"Look," Andi said, "there's Kyle and Grace Wade. They look great, don't they? Grace tells me the twins are doing so well that Maddie is quickly catching up to Maggie development-wise."

"I know. It's great." Vi nodded toward the far side of the room. "Oh, Parker Reese and Claire just came in. They're so busy planning their wedding, I've hardly seen Claire lately."

"I was sorry to hear Rafe's sister and her husband wouldn't be able to come for Christmas," Jolene said.

"Me, too," Vi murmured. "But with Nasira pregnant, Sebastian has decreed no long flights."

Jolene frowned. "Is everything all right?"

"Everything's great, but Sebastian is being as protective and proud as Mac is of our Andi. And though Nasira really wanted to be here, I think she's enjoying having Sebastian hover and take care of her."

"Well, we all like that," Jolene said, "whether we cry feminist or not."

"True." Andi turned to smile at her husband as the three men rejoined the women. Mac dropped one arm around her and pulled her into his side.

"Having a good time?"

"The best," she said, smiling up into his eyes.

"Have I mentioned lately how much I love you?"

"I believe you have but feel free to repeat yourself," Andi said, a smile twitching at her lips.

"Have Yourself a Merry Little Christmas" piped from the speakers overhead, and as his arms came around her, she knew that every Christmas from now on would be perfect.

"I think we should go home early," Mac whispered, his mouth so close to her ear that his breath brushed warmly against her skin. "Decorate the tree in our bedroom and then make love in front of the fire."

She smiled as her insides tightened. Leaning into him, she turned her head so she could look out over the crowd while enjoying this private moment.

"I think that's a wonderful idea, Mac."

He tipped her face up and gave her a quick, soft kiss. "Merry Christmas, Andi."

"Merry Christmas, Mac." She leaned into him and smiled as her heart filled with the kind of joy that would be with her forever.

* * * * *

THE WIFE
HE COULDN'T
FORGET

YVONNE LINDSAY

This story is dedicated to my fabulous readers,
whose continued support I cherish.

One

She hated hospitals.

Olivia swallowed hard against the acrid taste that settled on her tongue and the fearful memories that whispered through her mind as she entered the main doors and reluctantly scoured the directory for the department she needed.

Needed, ha, now there was a term. The last thing she needed was to reconnect with her estranged husband, even if he'd apparently been asking for her. Xander had made his choices when he left her two years ago, and she'd managed just fine, thank you, since then. Fine. Yeah, a great acronym for freaked out, insecure, neurotic and emotional. That probably summed it up nicely. She didn't really need to even be here, and yet she was.

The elevator pinged, and its doors slid open in front of her. She fought the urge to turn tail and run. Instead, she deliberately placed one foot in front of the other, entering the car and pressing the button for the floor she needed.

Damn, there was that word again. *Need.* Four measly

letters with a wealth of meaning. It was right up there with *want*. On its own insignificant, but when placed in the context of a relationship where two people were heading in distinctly different directions it had all the power in the world to hurt. She'd overcome that hurt. The pain of abandonment. The losses that had almost overwhelmed her completely. At least she'd thought she had, right up until the phone call that had jarred her from sleep this morning.

Olivia gripped the strap of her handbag just that little bit tighter. She didn't have to see Xander if she didn't want to—even if he had apparently woken from a six-week coma last night demanding to see her. Demanding, yes, that would be Xander. Nothing as subtle as a politely worded request. She sighed and stepped forward as the doors opened at her floor, then halted at the reception area.

"Can I help you?" the harried nurse behind the counter asked her, juggling an armful of files.

"Dr. Thomas, is he available? He's expecting me."

"Oh, you're Mrs. Jackson? Sure, follow me."

The nurse showed her into a blandly decorated private waiting room, then left, saying the doctor would be with her shortly.

Unable to sit, Olivia paced. Three steps forward. Three steps back. And again. They really ought to make these rooms bigger, she thought in frustration. The click of the door opening behind her made her spin around. This was the doctor, she assumed, although he looked far too young to be a neurological specialist.

"Mrs. Jackson, thank you for coming."

She nodded and took his proffered hand, noting the contrast between them—his clean, warm and dry, hers paint stained and so cold she'd begun to wonder if she'd lost all circulation since she'd received the news about Xander.

"You said Xander had been in an accident?"

"Yes, he lost control of his car on a wet road. Hit a power pole. His physical injuries have healed as well as could have been expected. Now he's out of the coma, he's been moved from the high-dependency unit and onto a general ward."

"And his accident? I was told it happened six weeks ago? That's a long time to be in a coma, isn't it?"

"Yes, it is. He'd been showing signs of awareness these past few days, and his nerve responses were promising. Then last night he woke fully, asking for you. It caught the staff by surprise. Only his mother was listed as next of kin."

Olivia sank into a chair. Xander? Asking for *her*? On the day he'd left her he'd said they had nothing to say to each other anymore. Were they talking about the same man?

"I...I don't understand," she finally managed.

"His other injuries aside, Mr. Jackson is suffering from post-traumatic amnesia. It's not unusual after a brain injury—in fact, studies show that less than 3 percent of patients experience no memory loss."

"And he's not in that 3 percent."

The doctor shook his head. "Post-traumatic amnesia is a phase people go through following a significant brain injury, when they are confused, disoriented and have trouble with their memory, especially short-term memory loss. Although, Mr. Jackson's case is a little more unusual with some long-term memory loss evident. I take it you were unaware of his accident?"

"I rarely see anyone who is in regular contact with him and I was never particularly close with his mother. I'm not surprised no one told me. I haven't seen Xander since he walked out on our marriage two years ago. We're just waiting for a court date to complete our divorce."

Olivia shuddered. Even now she couldn't keep the bitterness from her voice.

"Ah, I see. That makes things problematic then."

"Problematic?"

"For his release."

"I don't understand." Olivia furrowed her brow as she tried to make sense of the doctor's words.

"He lives alone, does he not?"

"As far as I know."

"He believes he's coming home to you."

Shock held her rigid in her chair. "H-he does?"

"He believes you are still together. It's why he's asking for you. His first words when he woke up were, "Tell my wife I'm okay."

Dr. Thomas began to explain the nature of Xander's injuries, but his words about loss of physical form due to the length of his coma and difficulties with short-term memory on top of the longer-term memory loss barely filtered through. All she could think of was that after all this time, her estranged husband wanted her.

"Excuse me," she interrupted the doctor. "But just how much *does* Xander remember?"

"As far as we can tell, his most recent clear memory is from about six years ago."

"But that was just after we married," she blurted.

That meant he remembered nothing of them finishing renovations on their late 1800s home overlooking Cheltenham Beach, nothing of the birth of their son five years ago.

Nothing of Parker's death just after he turned three.

She struggled to form the words she needed to ask her next question.

"Can he…does he…will he remember?"

The doctor shrugged. "It's possible. It's also possible he may never remember those lost years or that he may only regain parts of them."

She sat silently for a moment, letting the doctor's words sink in; then she drew in a deep breath. She had to do this. "Can I see him now?"

"Certainly. Come with me."

He led Olivia to a large room on the ward. There were four beds, but only one, near the window, was occupied. She steeled herself to move forward. To look at the man she'd once pledged her life to. The man she'd loved more than life itself and who she'd believed loved her equally in return. Her heart caught as she gazed on his all-too-familiar face, and she felt that same tug anew when she saw the similarities to Parker. They'd been like peas in a pod. She rubbed absently at the ache in the center of her chest, as if the motion could relieve the gaping hole there.

"He's sleeping naturally, but he'll probably wake soon," the doctor said at her side after a cursory glance at Xander's notes. "You can sit with him."

"Th-thank you," she replied automatically, lowering herself onto the seat at his bedside, her back to the window and the sunshine that sparkled on the harbor in the distance.

Olivia let her eyes drift over the still figure lying under the light covers. She started at his feet, skimming over the length of his legs and his hips before drifting over his torso and to the face. He'd lost weight and muscle mass—his usually powerful frame now leaner, softer. A light beard covered his normally clean-shaven jaw, and his hair was in dire need of a cut.

She couldn't help it. She ached for him. He would hate being this vulnerable and exposed. Xander was a man used to action, to decisiveness. To acting rather than being acted on. Lying helpless in a hospital bed like this would normally drive him nuts. Olivia started in shock as Xander's eyes opened and irises of piercing gray met hers. Recognition dawned in Xander's gaze, and her heart wrenched as he smiled at her, his eyes shining in genuine delight. She felt the connection between them as if it were a tangible thing—as if it had never been stretched to the breaking point by circumstances beyond both of their control. Her lips automatically curved in response.

How long had it been since she'd seen his smile? Far, far too long. And she'd missed it. She'd missed him. For two awful, lonely years Olivia had tried to fool herself that you could fall out of love with someone just as easily as you had fallen in love with him, if you tried hard enough. But she'd been lying to herself. You couldn't flip a switch on love, and you couldn't simply shove your head in a hole in the ground and pretend someone hadn't been the biggest part of your life from the day you'd met him.

She loved him still.

"Livvy?" Xander's voice cracked a little, as if it was rusty and disused.

"It's me," she replied shakily. "I'm here."

Tears burned in her eyes. Her throat choked up, and she reached out to take his hand. The tears spilled down her cheeks as she felt his fingers close tight around hers. He sighed, and his eyes slid closed again. A few seconds passed before he croaked one word.

"Good."

She fought back the sob that billowed from deep inside. On the other side of the bed Dr. Thomas cleared his throat.

"Xander?"

"Don't worry—he's sleeping again. One of the nurses will be by soon to do observations. He'll probably wake again then. Now, if you'll excuse me…?"

"Oh, yes, sure. Thank you."

She barely noticed the doctor leave, or one of the other patients shuffling into the room with his walker and a physical therapist hovering beside him. No, her concentration was fixed solely on the man in the bed in front of her and on the steady, even breaths that raised his chest and lowered it again.

Her thoughts scattered to and fro, finally settling on the realization that Xander could have died in the accident that had stolen his memory and she might never have known about it. That she might never have had another opportunity to beg him for one more chance. It opened a whole new cavern of hurt inside her until she slammed it closed. He hadn't died, she reminded herself. He'd lived. And he'd forgotten that he'd ever ended things between them.

Xander's fingers were still locked around hers. As if she was his anchor. As if he truly wanted her to be there with him. She leaned forward and gently lifted his hand up against her cheek. He was warm, alive. Hers? She hoped so. In fact she wanted him as deeply and as strongly right now as she had ever wanted him. A tiny kernel of hope germinated deep inside Olivia's mind. Could his loss of memory allow them that second chance he'd so adamantly refused?

Right here, right now, she knew that she'd do anything to have him back.

Anything.

Including pretending the problems in their past had never happened? she asked herself. The resounding answer should have shocked her, but it didn't.

Yes. She'd do even that.

Two

Olivia let herself in the house and closed the door, leaning back against it with a sigh as she tried to release the tension that now gripped her body. It didn't make a difference. Her shoulders were still tight and felt as if they were sitting up around her ears, and the nagging headache that had begun on the drive home from the hospital grew even more persistent.

What on earth had she done?

Was it lying to allow Xander to continue to believe they were still happily married? How could it be a lie when it was what he believed and when it was what she'd never stopped wanting?

You couldn't turn back the clock. You couldn't undo what was done five minutes ago any more than you could undo what happened in the past two years. But you could make a fresh start, and that's what they were going to do, she argued with herself.

It might not be completely ethical to take advantage of his amnesia this way, and she knew that she was running a risk—a huge risk—by doing so. At any moment his memory could return and, with it, Xander's refusal to talk through their problems or lean on her for help of any kind. Yet if there was a chance, any chance that they could be happy again, she had to take it.

She pushed off the door and walked down the hall toward the large entertainer's kitchen they'd had so much fun renovating after they'd moved into the two-story late nineteenth-century home a week after their marriage. She automatically went through the motions, putting the kettle on and boiling water for a pot of chamomile tea. Hopefully that would soothe the headache.

But what would soothe the niggling guilt that plucked at her heart over her decision?

Was she just doing this to resolve her own regrets? Wrapped in her grief over Parker's death and filled with recriminations and remorse, hadn't she found it easier to let Xander go rather than fight for their marriage—hell, fight for *him*? She'd accused him of locking her out of his feelings, but hadn't she done exactly the same thing? And when he'd left, hadn't she let him go? Then, when she'd opened her eyes to what she was letting slip from her life, it was too late. He hadn't wanted to even discuss reconciliation or counseling. It was as if he'd wiped his slate clean—and wiped his life with her right along with it.

It had hurt then and it hurt now, but time and distance had given her some perspective. Had opened her eyes to her own contribution to the demise of their marriage. Mistakes she wouldn't make again.

The kettle began to whistle, momentarily distracting her from her thoughts. Olivia poured the boiling water into the teapot and took her favorite china cup and saucer from the glass-fronted cupboard where she displayed her antique china collection. After putting the tea things on a tray, she carried everything outside. She set the tray down on a table on her paved patio and sank into one of the wood-and-canvas deck chairs. The fabric creaked a little as she shifted into a more comfortable position.

Bathed in the evening summer sun, Olivia closed her eyes and took a moment to relax and listen and let the sounds of her surroundings soak in. Behind the background hum of traffic she could hear the noises of children playing in their backyards. The sound, always bittersweet, was a strong reminder that even after tragedy, other people's lives still carried on. She opened her eyes, surprised to feel the sting of tears once more, and shifted her focus to pouring her tea into her cup. The delicate aroma of the chamomile wafted up toward her. There was something incredibly calming about the ritual of making tea. It was one of the habits she'd developed to ground herself when she'd felt as though she was losing everything—including her mind.

She lifted her cup, taking a long sip of the hot brew and savoring the flavor on her tongue as she thought again about her decision back at the hospital. The risk she was taking loomed large in her mind. So many things could go wrong. But it was still early days. Xander had a long road to recovery ahead, and it would be many days yet, if not weeks, before he was released from hospital. He had yet to walk unaided, and a physical therapy program would need to be undertaken before he could come home again.

Home.

A shiver ran through her. It wasn't the home he'd lived in for the past two years, but it was the home they'd bought together and spent the first year of their marriage enthusiastically renovating. Thank goodness she'd chosen to live with her memories here rather than sell the property and move on. In fact, the decision to stay had very definitely formed a part of her recovery from her grief at Parker's death followed so swiftly by Xander's desertion of her, as well.

She'd found acceptance, of a sort, in her heart and in her mind that her marriage was over, but her love for Xander remained unresolved. A spark of excitement lit within her. This would be their new beginning. After his release from hospital, they'd cocoon themselves back into their life together, the way they had when they'd first married. And if he regained his memory, it would be with new happier memories to overlay the bitterness that had transpired between them before their separation.

Of course, if he regained his memory before coming home with her, it was likely they'd never get the chance to rebuild their marriage on stronger ground. She had to take the risk. She just had to. And she'd cope with Xander's real world later. The world in which he worked and socialized was not hers anymore. Keeping his distance from his friends and colleagues would be easy enough, initially—after all, it's not as if his bedside cabinet had been inundated with cards or flowers. Just a card signed by his team at the investment bank where he worked. Until he was strong enough to return to his office anyway. By then… Well, she'd cross that bridge when they got there.

Xander's doctors had categorically stated he was in no condition to return to work for at least another four weeks, possibly even longer depending on how his therapy progressed. It should be easy enough to fend Xander's colleagues off at the border, so to speak, Olivia thought as she sipped her tea and gazed out at the harbor in the distance. After all, with Xander in the high-dependency unit at the hospital, and with family-only visitation—which she understood equated to the occasional rare visit from his mother who lived several hours north of the city—it wasn't as if they'd be up-to-date beyond the minimal status provided by the hospital. She'd call one of his partners in the next few days and continue to discourage visitors at the same time.

She felt a pang of guilt. His friends had a right to know how he was, and no doubt they'd want to visit him. But a careless word could raise more questions than she was comfortable answering. She daren't take the risk.

It was at least two years late, but Xander's amnesia was offering her another chance, and she was going to fight for him now. She just had to hope that she could successfully rebuild the love they'd shared. The fact that he woke today, obviously still in love with her, was heartening. Hopefully, they would have the rest of their lives to get it right this time.

Xander looked at the door to the hospital room for what felt like the hundredth time that morning. Olivia should be here by now. After a heated debate with Dr. Thomas about whether or not he'd go to a rehab center— a debate Xander had won with his emphatic refusal to go—the doctor had finally relented and said he could go home tomorrow, or maybe even later today. He'd used the mobile phone Olivia had left with him—his had apparently been pulverized in the accident and his laptop, as well, had been smashed beyond repair—to call the house and get her to bring him some clothes. He'd missed her, and she wasn't answering her mobile phone, either.

He'd go home in his pajamas if he had to. He couldn't wait to get out of here and back to their house. He liked to kid himself he could even see its green corrugated iron roof from the hospital window. It gave him a connection to Olivia in the times she wasn't here.

It had been three weeks, but, God, he still remembered that first sight of her when he'd fully woken. The worry on her exquisitely beautiful face, the urge to tell her that everything would be all right. Sleep had claimed him before he could do anything more than smile at her. This damn head injury had a lot to answer for, he cursed inwardly. Not only had it stolen the past six years from his memory but it had left him as weak as a kitten. Not even capable of forming proper sentences on occasion. Each of the therapists he'd seen had told him he was doing great, that his recovery was progressing well, but it wasn't enough. It would never be enough until he could remember again and be the man he was before his crash.

He couldn't wait to be home. Maybe being around his own familiar things in his own environment would hasten the healing process. He looked out the window and cracked a wry smile at his reflection in the glass. At least one thing hadn't changed. His levels of impatience were right up there where he always remembered them being.

Xander caught a sense of someone in the doorway to his shared room. He turned and felt the smile on his face widen as he saw Olivia standing there. Warmth spread through his body. A sense of rightness that was missing when she wasn't with him.

"You're looking happy," Olivia remarked as she came over and kissed him on the cheek.

Her touch was as light as a butterfly. Even so, it awakened a hunger for more from her. He might not be at his physical peak, but the demands of his body still simmered beneath the surface. They'd always had a very intense and physically satisfying relationship, one he couldn't wait to resume. He laughed inwardly at himself. There was that impatience again. One thing at a time, he told himself.

He swung his legs over the edge of the bed. "I might be able to come home today. I tried to call you—"

"Today? Really?"

Was he imagining things or did the smile on her face look a little forced? Xander rejected the thought immediately. Of course she was as genuinely excited as he was. Why wouldn't she be?

"Dr. Thomas just wants to run some final tests this morning. Provided he's happy I should be able to leave here later this afternoon."

"Well, that's great news," Olivia said. "I'll shoot back home and get some things for you."

Xander reached out and caught her hand in his. "In such a hurry to leave me? You just got here. Don't go yet."

Her fingers curled around his, and he turned her hand over before lifting it to place a kiss on her knuckles. He felt the light tremor go through her as his lips lingered on her skin and her fingers tightened, saw the way her pupils dilated and her cheeks flushed ever so slightly.

"I miss you when you're not here," he said simply, then examined the hand he held more closely. Her nails were short and practical, and even though she'd scrubbed at them, he could still see traces of paint embedded in her skin. It made him smile. "I see you're still painting. Good to know some things haven't changed."

She bit her lower lip and turned her head, but not before he saw the emotion reflected in her eyes.

"Livvy?"

"Hmm?"

"Are you okay?"

"Sure, I'm fine. I'm just worried I'm going to have to cart you home in those," she said lightly as she tugged her hand free and pointed at his striped pajamas with a disparaging look on her face. "And yes, I'm still painting. It's in my blood. Always has been, always will be."

He laughed, like she wanted him to, at the line he'd heard her say so many times. He saw the strain around her eyes lift a little.

"Fine, you better go then, but come straight back, okay?"

"Of course. I'll be as quick as I can," she said, bending down to kiss him on the forehead.

Xander leaned back against his pillows and watched her departing back. He couldn't quite put his finger on it, but something wasn't right. They'd talked about him going home for days. Now that the time was finally here, was she afraid? He mulled the idea over in his head. It was possible. He'd been through a lot, and maybe she was worried about how he would cope on his reentry into the real world. She was such a worrier, always had been. He guessed that came with the territory of being the eldest out of four kids growing up on a farm without their mother. His Livvy was used to micromanaging everything around her so that nothing would go wrong.

When he'd married her, he'd silently promised himself that he would never be a burden to her—that he would never make himself one more responsibility she had to shoulder. Even now, he was determined to make certain that his recovery didn't weigh her down. He'd do whatever it took to ensure that the rest of his recuperation went smoothly so that the worry would disappear from her eyes once and for all.

"Nothing will go wrong," he said aloud, earning a look from the guy in the bed opposite his.

Olivia hastened to the car parking building and got into her car. Her hand shook slightly as she pressed the ignition, and she took a moment before putting on her seat belt and putting the car in gear.

He was coming home. It was what she wanted, so why on earth had she run like a startled rabbit the minute he'd told her? She knew why. It meant she would have to stop putting her head in the sand about the life he'd created when he'd left her. It meant taking the set of keys that she'd been given, among the personal effects the hospital had held since his accident—ruined blood-stained clothing included—and going to his apartment to get his things.

She knew she should have done it before now. Should have gathered together what he would expect to find at their home. His wardrobe, his toiletries. Those were pretty much all he'd taken with him when he'd left. There was nothing for it but to steel herself to invade the new home he'd created. At least she knew where he lived. That was about the only thing the legal separation documents had been any good for, she thought grimly as she drove the short distance from Auckland City Hospital to the apartment block in Parnell where Xander had taken a lease.

She parked in one of the two spaces allocated to his apartment and rode the elevator to the top floor. Letting herself in through the door at the end of the corridor, she steeled herself for what she would find on the other side. As she stepped through the entrance hall she found herself strangely disappointed.

It was as if she'd stepped into a decorator's catalogue shoot. Everything perfectly matched and aligned—and totally lacking any character. It certainly didn't look as though anyone actually lived here. There was none of his personality or his love of old things, no warmth or welcome. She walked through the living room and toward a hallway she hoped would lead to his bedroom. It did, and she was surprised to discover the bedroom was in the same pristine, sterile condition. Not so much as a stray sock poking out from the simple valance that skirted the king-size bed. It wasn't like the Xander she'd known at all—a man who was meticulous in all things except what she teasingly referred to as his *floor-drobe*. Maybe he had a cleaning service come through. Or maybe, the thought chilled her, he really had changed this much.

Anyway, she was wasting time. She needed to get his things and take them back to her house on the other side of the harbor bridge and then get back to the hospital again before he began to think she wasn't coming to take him home after all.

In the spare room closet Olivia found a large suitcase, and she quickly grabbed underwear, socks and clothing from the walk-in wardrobe in Xander's bedroom. From the bathroom she grabbed shower gel, cologne and his shaving kit. She wondered briefly if he remembered how to use it. It had been a while since he'd shaved properly. Only last week she'd teased him about the furry growth that ringed his jaw. Privately, she found she quite liked it. It made him seem a bit softer, more approachable than the cold stranger who'd stalked so emphatically out of her life.

She shook her head as if she could rid herself of the memory just as easily and wheeled the case to the front door. Should she check the refrigerator? She cringed a little at the idea of finding nine-week-old leavings rotting inside, but she figured she would have to do it sometime. She poked around in the drawers until she found a plastic garbage bag and then, holding her breath, opened the shiny stainless-steel door of the fridge.

Empty. *How odd*, she thought as she let the door close again. Not even a half bottle of wine stood in the door. If she hadn't taken Xander's things from his bedroom and en suite herself, she would hardly have believed he even lived here. She pulled open a pantry door and was relieved to see neatly labeled containers and a box of his favorite cereal stacked on the shelves. Okay, so maybe whoever had made the apartment look so spick-and-span had cleaned out the fridge, as well. She made a mental note to try and find out from somewhere, perhaps among his personal papers, if he had a cleaning service. If so, she'd need to put their visits on hold indefinitely.

She looked around the open-plan living room and dining area to see where he might keep his personal files and records. There was nothing to suggest a desk or office space in here. Maybe there was another bedroom? Olivia went back down the hall that led to Xander's bedroom, and spied another door. She opened it, stepped inside and immediately came to a halt.

Her heart thumped erratically in her chest as her eyes fixed on the photo on the desk in what was obviously Xander's home office. She recognized the frame as one she'd bought for him for his first Father's Day and in it was the last photo they'd taken of Parker before he died.

Three

Her hand went to her throat as if she could somehow hold back the sob that rose from the deepest recesses of her grief. She hadn't even realized Xander had taken the picture with him when he'd left. He must have hidden it away when, after the funeral, she'd packed up Parker's room and shoved all the boxes in the attic, along with his albums and the framed photos they'd had scattered around the house.

It had hurt too much to see the constant reminders of his all-too-short life.

If only…

Those two words had driven her almost insane. If only Xander hadn't left the gate open, or hadn't thrown the ball quite so vigorously for Bozo, their dog. If only Bozo hadn't run out into the street in pursuit of the ball and—even now, she gasped against the pain from the memory—if only Parker hadn't run out into the street after him. If only she hadn't told Parker to run outside and play with Daddy in the first place, instead of staying safely in the studio with her that day.

Racked with her own guilt and her anger at the world in general and Xander in particular, she'd done the only thing she could to alleviate the searing pain. She'd packed up Parker's short life and hidden it, telling herself she'd look at his things again when she was able. Every piece of clothing, every toy, every photo—hidden away.

All except this one. She reached out a finger and traced the cheeks of her little boy, locked behind the glass. A child forever—never to grow up and go to school, play a sport or meet girls. Never to stretch his wings, push his boundaries or be grounded for some misdemeanor or another.

Her hand dropped back to her side. She stood like that for several minutes before shaking herself loose from the memories and trying to remember why she'd come in here in the first place. Yes, the cleaning service, that was it. Olivia rifled through Xander's filing system—as linear and exact as she remembered—and found the number she was looking for. A quick phone call to suspend services until further notice was all that was required, and then she was on her way.

Before she left the room, though, she lifted the photo from Xander's desk and shoved it in a drawer. It hurt to shut her baby away like that, but if she had to come back here again, she couldn't bear to see the stark reminder of all they'd lost.

Thankfully traffic through the city to the harbor bridge approach was lighter than usual and she made the trip home in good time. She dragged the suitcase up the flight of stairs and into the guest bedroom, and quickly unpacked and hung up Xander's shirts and trousers and a few suits, still in their drycleaner bags, in the closet and shoved his underwear, socks and T-shirts into the small chest of drawers. She put his toiletries in the bathroom across the hall. It wouldn't be a lie to tell him she'd moved his things in there so he could recuperate in his own space. She just wouldn't mention that she'd moved them from across town rather than from down the hall.

Before leaving the house again, she folded a set of clothes and a belt into a small overnight bag for him and then flew out the door. She was jittery with emotional exhaustion and lack of food by the time she got back to the hospital. Xander was standing at the window when, slightly out of breath, she finally arrived.

"I was beginning to think you'd changed your mind about taking me home," he said lightly when she approached him.

Even though his words were teasing, she could hear the underlying censure beneath them. And she understood it; really she did. Under normal circumstances she would have been back here much earlier. But their circumstances were far from normal, even though he didn't know that yet.

"Traffic was a bitch," she said as breezily as she could. "So, are we good to go? I have some clothes for you here, although I'm thinking you'll find everything on the big side for you now. We might need to get you a whole new wardrobe."

Her attempt at deflection seemed to work. "And I know how much you love shopping," he said with a laugh.

She felt her heart skip a beat. He'd always teased her about her shopping style. While she liked getting new things, she hated crowded stores. She had the tendency to decide what she wanted before she left the house and, with no dillydallying, get in, get the product and get right back out again as quickly as possible. No window-shopping or store browsing for her. Unless it was an art supply store, that was.

Olivia told herself it was ridiculous to be surprised that he'd remember that. After all, he hadn't lost all his memory, just the past six years. She forced a laugh and handed him the bag of his things.

"Here you go. Will you need a hand to get dressed?"

He'd had issues with balance and coordination since awakening from his coma. Physical therapy was helping him regain his equilibrium and motor skills, but he still had some way to go.

"I think I can manage," he said with the quiet dignity she had always loved so much about him.

"Just call me if you need me."

Xander looked her straight in the eye and gave her a half smile. "Sure."

She smiled back, feeling a pang deep inside. She knew he wouldn't call her. He was nothing if not independent—and stubborn. Yes, there'd been a time, early in their marriage, when they'd each been the center of the other's world. But that had all changed.

He was so lucky he didn't remember, she thought fiercely. Lucky that he was still locked in the best of their marriage and couldn't remember the worst of them both.

Xander took the bag through to the shared bathroom and closed the door behind him. A tremor ran through his body as he allowed the relief he'd felt when he'd seen Olivia return run through him. Ever since she'd left earlier today he'd been tense and uncomfortable, so much so the nurse preparing his discharge papers had remarked on the spike in his blood pressure.

He couldn't understand it. Olivia was his wife. So why had he suddenly developed this deeply unsettled sensation that things weren't what they should be between them? He shoved off his pajamas and stepped into the shower stall, hissing a little as the water warmed up to a decent temperature. He couldn't wait to be out of here. Even with Olivia's daily visits to break the monotony of sleep, eat, therapy, eat, sleep, over and over again, he wanted to be *home*.

Xander roughly toweled himself off, swearing under his breath as he lost his balance and had to put a hand on the wall to steady himself. His body's slow response to recovery was another thing driving him crazy. It was as if the messages just weren't getting through from his brain to his muscles.

He looked down at his body. Muscles? Well, he remembered having muscles. Now his build was definitely leaner, another thing he needed to work on. He pulled on his clothing and cinched his belt in tight. Olivia had been right. His clothes looked as if they belonged to another man entirely. He couldn't remember buying them, so they had to be something from his lost years, as he now called them.

A light tap at the door caught his attention.

"Xander? Are you okay in there?" Olivia asked from outside.

"Sure, I'll be right out."

He looked at his reflection in the small mirror and rubbed his hand around his jaw, ruffling the beard that had grown during his stay here. He looked like a stranger to himself. Maybe that was part of Olivia's reticence. The beard would have to go when he got home. Xander gathered his things off the floor and shoved them in the bag Olivia had brought and opened the bathroom door.

"I'm ready," he said.

"Let's go then," she answered with that beautiful smile of hers that always did crazy things to his equilibrium.

Had he ever told her how much he loved her smile, or how much he loved to hear her laugh? He couldn't quite remember. Another thing he would have to address in due course.

They stopped at the nurses' station to say goodbye

and collect his discharge papers, and then they began the walk down the corridor toward the elevator. It irked him that Olivia had to slow her steps to match his. It bothered him even more that by the time they reached her car he was exhausted. He dropped into the passenger seat with an audible sigh of relief.

"I'm sorry—I should have gotten you to wait at the front entrance and driven round to get you," Olivia apologized as she got in beside him.

"It's okay. I've had plenty of time to rest. Now it's time to really get better."

"You say that like you haven't been working hard already." She sighed and rested one hand on his thigh. The warmth of her skin penetrated the fabric of his trousers, and he felt her hand as if it were an imprint on him. "Xander, you've come a long way in a very short time. You've had to relearn some things that you took for granted before. Cut yourself some slack, huh? It's going to take time."

He grunted in response. Time. Seemed he had all too much of it. He put his head back against the headrest as Olivia drove them home, taking solace in the things he recognized and ignoring his surprise at the things that had changed from what he remembered. Auckland was a busy, ever-changing, ever-growing city, but it still disturbed him to see the occasional gaping hole where, in his mind at least, a building used to stand.

"Did the school mind about you taking time off to spend with me?" he asked.

"I don't work at the school anymore," Olivia replied. "I stopped before—"

"Before what?" he prompted.

"Before they drove me completely mad," she said with a laugh that came out a bit forced. "Seriously, I quit there just over five years ago, but I've been doing really well with my paintings since. You'd be proud. I've had several shows, and I'm actually doing quite well out of it."

"But it was never about the money, right?" he said, parroting something Olivia had frequently said to him whenever he'd teased her about not producing a more commercial style of work.

"Of course not," she answered, and this time her smile was genuine.

By the time they arrived at the house he felt about a hundred years old, not that he'd admit it to Olivia, who, to his chagrin, had to help him from the car and up the front stairs to the house.

As she inserted a key into the lock and swung the door open he couldn't help but twist his lips into a rueful smile.

"Seems like not that long ago I was carrying you across that threshold. Now you're more likely to have to carry me."

He regretted his attempt at humor the moment he saw the concern and fear on her face.

"Are you okay?" she said, slipping an arm around his back and tucking herself under his arm so she supported his weight. "You should rest downstairs for a while before tackling the stairs to the bedroom. Or maybe I should just get a bed set up down here for you until you're stronger."

"No," he said with grim determination as they entered the hall. "I'm sleeping upstairs tonight. I'll manage okay."

She guided him into the sitting room and onto one of the sofas.

"Cup of coffee?"

"Yeah, thanks."

While she was gone he looked around, taking in the changes from what he remembered. French doors opened out onto a wooden veranda—they were new, he noted. There'd been a sash window there before and—he looked down at the highly polished floorboards—there'd been some ancient and hideous floral carpet tacked onto the floor. Seems they'd done quite a bit of work around the place.

Xander levered himself to his feet and walked around the room, trailing his hand over the furniture and the top of the ornate mantel over the fireplace, which was flanked by wingback chairs. Had they sat here on a winter's evening, enjoying the warmth of the fire? He shook his head in frustration. He didn't know. He sat in one of the chairs to see if it triggered anything, but his mind remained an impenetrable blank.

"Here you are," Olivia said brightly as she came back into the room. "Oh, you've found your chair. Would you like the papers?"

"No, thanks. Just the coffee."

"Still struggling with concentration?"

He nodded and accepted the mug she handed him. His fingers curled around the handle with familiarity and he stared for a while at the mug. This, he knew. He'd bought it at the Pearl Harbor memorial when they went to Hawaii for their honeymoon. He took a sip and leaned back in the chair.

"That's good—so much better than the stuff they serve in the hospital." He sighed happily and looked around the room again. "I guess we did it all, huh? Our plans for the house?"

Olivia nodded. "It wasn't easy, but we completed it in just over a year. We…um…we got impatient to finish and hired contractors to handle a lot of it. I wish you could remember haggling for those French doors. It was a sight worth seeing."

He must have pulled a face because she was on her knees at his side in a minute. She reached up to cup his cheek with one hand and turned his face to hers.

"Xander, don't worry. It'll come back in its own good

time. And if it doesn't, then we'll fill that clever mind of yours with new memories, okay?"

Was it his imagination or did she sound more emphatic about the new memories than him remembering his old ones? No, he was just being oversensitive. And overtired, he thought as he felt another wave of exhaustion sweep through him. It was one thing to feel relatively strong while in the hospital, when there were so many people in worse condition he could compare himself with. Quite another to feel the same in your home environment, where you were used to being strong and capable.

He turned his face into her palm and kissed her hand. "Thanks," he said simply.

She pulled away, a worried frown creasing her brow. "We'll get through this, Xander."

"I know we will."

She got up and smoothed her hands down her jeans. "I'll go and start dinner for us, okay? We should probably eat early tonight."

He must have fallen asleep when she left the room because before he knew it he was awoken with another of those featherlight kisses on his forehead.

"I made spaghetti Bolognese, your favorite."

She helped him stand and they walked arm in arm into the dining room. It looked vastly different from the drop-cloth-covered space he remembered. He looked up at the antique painted glass and polished brass library lamp that was suspended from the ceiling.

"I see you got your way on the prisms," he commented as he took his seat.

"Not without a battle. I had to concede to the ugliest partner desk in all history for the study upstairs to get this," she said with a laugh.

He smiled in response. There it was. The laugh he felt had been missing from his life for so long. Odd, when it had only been nine weeks since his accident. It felt so much longer.

After dinner Xander propped himself against the kitchen counter while Olivia cleaned up. He tried to help, but after a plate slipped from his fingers and shattered on the tile floor, he retreated in exasperation to the sidelines to watch.

"Stop pushing yourself," Olivia admonished as she swept up the last of the splinters of china on the floor with a dustpan and brush.

"I can't help it. I want to be my old self again."

She straightened up from depositing the mess in the kitchen trash bin. "You are your old self—don't worry so much."

"With Swiss cheese for brains," he grumbled.

"Like I said before, we can plug those holes with new memories, Xander. We don't have to live in the past."

Her words had a poignant ring to them, and he felt as if she wanted to say more. Instead, she continued tidying up. When she was done, she looked at him with a weary smile. Instantly he felt guilty. She'd been doing a lot of driving back and forth from here to the hospital and helping when she could with his physical therapy. And he knew that when she was painting, she'd often work late into the night without eating or taking a break. Why hadn't he noticed the bluish bruises of exhaustion under her eyes? Silently he cursed his weakness and his part in putting those marks there.

"I don't know about you, but I'm ready for an early night," Olivia said with a barely stifled yawn.

"I thought you'd never ask," he teased.

Together, they ascended to the next floor, too slowly for Xander's liking but an unfortunate necessity as his tiredness played havoc with his coordination.

"Did we change bedrooms?" he asked as Olivia led him to the guest room at the top of the stairs.

"No," she answered, a little breathlessly. "I thought you'd be more comfortable in here. I've become a restless sleeper, and I don't want to disturb you."

"Livvy, I've been sleeping too long without you already. I'm home now. We're sleeping in the same bed."

Four

Sleep in the same bed?

Olivia froze in the doorway of the guest bedroom and watched as Xander made his way carefully down the hall to the master suite. She followed, then halted again as she watched Xander strip off his clothes and tumble, naked, into the side of the bed that had always been his. He was asleep in seconds. She watched him for a full five minutes, unsure of what to do. In the end, she grabbed her nightgown from under her pillow and slipped into the en suite bathroom to get ready for bed. By the time she'd washed her face and brushed her teeth her heart was pounding a million miles a minute.

He'd done so many things automatically in the few short hours since they'd returned to the house. It had been reassuring and frightening at the same time. It showed the damage from his injury hadn't destroyed everything in his mind, but it certainly raised questions, for her at least, about how long she'd have before he might remember everything.

Olivia gingerly slid under the bedsheets, trying not to disturb Xander, and rolled onto her side—taking care to stay well clear of him—so she could watch him sleep. She listened to one long deep breath after another, finding it hard to believe he was actually here. His breathing pattern changed, and he suddenly rolled over to face her.

"What are you doing all the way over there on the edge? I've missed you next to me long enough already." His voice was thick with sleep; he reached an arm around her to pull her toward him and snuggled her into his bare chest. "You *can* touch me. I'm not made of spun glass, you know."

And with that, he was asleep again.

Olivia could barely draw a breath. Every cell in her body urged her to allow her body to sink into his, to let herself soak up his warmth, his comfort. He felt so familiar and yet different at the same time. But the steady heartbeat beneath her ear was the same. And, right now, that heart beat for her. How could she not simply relish the moment, take pleasure in it, accept it for what it was worth?

Gold. Spun gold. Jewels beyond compare.

How many achingly lonely nights had she lain here in this very bed since he left her? Made futile wish after wish that they could lie here together, just like this, again? Far, far too many. And now, here he was. All her dreams come true, on the surface at least.

They said you couldn't turn back time, but isn't that effectively what his accident had done?

She sighed and relaxed a little. The moment she did so her mind began to work overtime. If his memory came back, would he forgive her this deception? Could he? She'd basically kidnapped him from the life he'd been leading before the accident. Brought him here to resume a life he'd chosen to leave behind.

She'd never been a deceitful person, and now it felt as if a giant weight hovered above her, held back by nothing more than a slowly fraying thread. One wrong step and she would be crushed; she knew it. Doing this, bringing him home, acting as if nothing bad had ever happened to them? It was all a lie. She felt it was worth telling—would he feel the same way? Only time would tell.

Olivia drew in a deep breath through her nose, her senses responding to the familiar scent of the man she'd already lost once in her life. She wasn't prepared to lose him again. She had to fight with all her might this time. Somehow she had to make this work.

She shifted a little and felt Xander's arm close more tightly around her, as if now he had her in his arms he wouldn't let her go, either. It gave her hope. Tentative, fragile hope, but hope nonetheless. If, in his subconscious mind, he could hold her like this, then maybe, just maybe, he could love her again, too.

Olivia woke to an empty bed in the morning and the sight of Xander standing naked in front of their wardrobe with the doors spread wide-open.

"Xander?" she asked sleepily. "You okay?"

"Where are my clothes?" he asked, still searching through the rails and the built-in drawers.

"I put them in the spare room when I thought you'd be convalescing there."

He made a sound of disgust. "Convalescing is for invalids. I'm not an invalid."

Olivia sat up and dropped her legs over the edge of the bed. "I know you're not," she said patiently. "But you aren't at full strength, either. What is it that you want? I'll see if I can find it for you."

At least she hoped she'd be able to find it for him. She hadn't brought everything of his from the apartment.

What if he had something he particularly wanted to wear and she'd left it behind? Now he was home it would be a lot harder to go back to his apartment and get more of his things. She castigated herself for not thinking about that sooner.

"I want my old uni sweatshirt and a pair of Levi's," Xander said, turning around.

Olivia's eyes raked his body. He'd lost definition, but he was still an incredibly fine figure of a man. There was a scar on his abdomen, pink and thin, where his spleen had been removed after the crash. The sight of it made something tug hard deep inside her. He could so easily have died in that accident and she wouldn't have this chance with him. It was frightening. She already knew how fragile life could be. How quickly it could be stolen from you.

Her gaze lingered on his chest where she'd pillowed her head for most the night. Beneath her stare she saw his nipples tighten and felt a corresponding response in her own. She sighed softly. It had been so very long since they'd been intimate and yet her body still responded to him as if they'd never been apart. And his, too, by the looks of things.

"Why don't you grab your shower and I'll go get your clothes," she suggested, pushing herself up to stand and heading for the spare room.

The sheer need that pulled at her right now was more than she could take. She had to put some distance between them before she did something crazy—like drag him back to bed and slake two years of hunger. As if he read her mind, he spoke.

"Why don't you grab it with me?" Xander said with a smile that make her muscles tighten.

"I'm not sure you've been cleared for that just yet," she said as lightly as she could.

Before he could respond, she headed into the hallway and hesitated, waiting until she heard the en suite door close and the shower start. Then she went to the narrow spiral wooden staircase that led to the attic. Her foot faltered on the first step, and she had to mentally gird herself to keep putting one foot on each step after another.

Somewhere along the line, the attic had become the repository for the things she didn't want to face. But right now she had no choice. She closed her eyes before pushing open the narrow door that led into the storage area lit only by two small diamond-shaped multipaned windows set in at each end. Another deep breath and she stepped inside.

Keeping her line of sight directly where she had stored the large plastic box of clothing that Xander had left behind, she traversed the bare wooden floor and quickly unsnapped the lid, digging through the items until she found the jeans and sweatshirt he'd been talking about.

She dragged the fabric to her nose and inhaled deeply, worried there might be a mustiness about them that would give away where they'd been stored, but it seemed the lavender she'd layered in with his clothing had done its job. There was just a faint drift of the scent of the dried flowers clinging to the clothing. With a satisfied nod, Olivia jammed the lid back on the storage box and fled down the stairs. She'd have to come back later and get the rest of Xander's clothes. She certainly couldn't just take a box down to their bedroom right now because she didn't want to invent explanations for why his things were stored away, either.

In her bedroom—*their* bedroom, she corrected herself—Olivia laid the jeans and sweatshirt on the bed and was getting her own clothing together when Xander came out of the en suite wrapped in a towel, a bloom of steam following him.

"I see we got the hot water problems fixed," he said, coming toward her.

"Yeah, we ended up installing a small hot water heater just for our bathroom." Olivia nodded. "Did you leave any for me?"

"I invited you to share," Xander said with a wink.

She huffed a small laugh, but even so her heart twinged just a little. He sounded so like his old self. The self he'd been before they realized they were expecting a baby and would be dropping to one income for a while. While they'd never been exactly poor, and her income as a high school art teacher had mostly been used to provide the extras they needed for the renovations, it had still been a daunting prospect. Of course, since then, Xander's star had risen to dizzying heights with the investment banking firm he now was a partner in. And with that meteoric rise, his income had hit stratospheric levels, too.

"Hey," Xander said as he walked over to the bed and picked up his clothes. "You expecting me to go commando?"

"Oh, heavens, I didn't think. Hang on a sec."

Olivia shot into the guest bedroom and grabbed a pair of the designer boxer briefs she'd brought back from his apartment. She tossed them at him as she came back in the door.

"There you are. I'll grab my shower quickly. Then I'll get some breakfast together for us, okay?"

Xander caught the briefs she'd thrown at him and nodded. "Yeah, sounds good."

The bathroom door closed behind her, and he sat down on the edge of the bed, suddenly feeling weak again. Damn, but this was getting old, he thought in exasperation as he pulled on his boxers and stood up to slide on his jeans. They dropped an indecent distance on his hips.

He stepped over to the chest of drawers and opened the one where he kept his belts. He was surprised to find the drawer filled with Olivia's lingerie instead. Maybe he'd misjudged, he thought, opening another drawer and then another—discovering that the entire bureau was filled with her things. That wasn't right, was it? It was as if he didn't share a room with her anymore. She said she'd moved his clothes to the guest room, but it seemed odd that she'd have moved everything. And shouldn't there be empty spaces left behind where his things had been?

Xander spied the pair of trousers he'd worn yesterday, lying on the floor. He picked them up and tugged the belt free from its loops. As he fed the belt through his Levi's he wondered what else he'd forgotten. What else was so completely out of sync in this world he'd woken up to? Even Olivia was different from how he remembered her. There was a wariness there he'd never known her to have before. As if she now guarded her words, not to mention herself, very carefully.

Olivia came through from the bathroom, and his nostrils flared as he picked up the gentle waft of scent that came through with her. A tingling began deep in his gut. She always had that effect on him. Had right from the first moment he'd laid eyes on her. So how was it that he could remember that day as if it was yesterday, yet his brain had switched off an entire chunk of their life together?

They went downstairs—Olivia tucked under his shoulder with her arm around his back, he with one hand on the rail and taking one step at a time. His balance and coordination were still not quite there, and he fought to suppress his irritation at being so ridiculously helpless and having to depend on his wife to do such a simple thing. He normally flew down these stairs, didn't he?

"What would you like for breakfast?" Olivia asked when they reached the kitchen.

"Anything but hospital food," he replied with a smile. "How about your homemade muesli?"

She looked startled at his request. "I haven't made that in years, but I have store-bought."

He shook his head. "No, it's okay. I'll just have some toast. I can get that myself."

Olivia gently pushed him onto a stool by the counter. "Oh no you won't. Your first morning home, I'm making you a nice breakfast. How about scrambled eggs and smoked salmon?"

His mouth watered. "That sounds much better. Thanks."

He watched her as she moved around the kitchen, envying how she knew where everything was. None of it was familiar to him. The kitchen was different to the poorly fitted cupboards and temperamental old stove that had been here when they'd bought the property in a deceased estate auction. The place had been like a time capsule. The same family had owned it since it had been built. The last of the family line, an elderly spinster, had lived only on the ground floor in her later years, and nothing had been done to modernize the property since the early 1960s.

The aroma of coffee began to fill the room. Feeling uncharacteristically useless, Xander rose to get a couple of mugs from the glass-fronted cupboard. At least he could see where they were kept, he thought grimly. Automatically he put a heaping spoon of sugar in each mug.

"Oh, no sugar for me," Olivia said, whipping one of the mugs away and pouring the sugar back in the bowl before putting the mug back down again.

"Since when?"

"A couple of years ago, at least."

Just how many of the nuances of their day-to-day life did he need to relearn, he thought as he picked up the mugs and moved toward the coffee machine. She must have seen the look that crossed his face at the news.

"It's okay, Xander. Whether I take sugar or not isn't the end of the world."

"It might not be, but what about important stuff? The things we've done together, the plans we've made in the past few years? What if I never remember? Hell, I don't even remember the accident that caused me to lose my memory, let alone what car I was driving."

His voice had risen to a shout, and Olivia's face, always a window to her emotions, crumpled into a worried frown—her eyes reflecting her distress.

"Xander, none of those things are important. What's important is that you're alive and that you're *here*. *With me*."

She closed the distance between them and slid her arms around his waist, laying her head on his shoulder and squeezing him tight as if she would never let him go. He closed his eyes and took in a deep breath, trying hard to put a lid on the anger that had boiled up within him at something so simple, so stupid, as misremembering whether or not his wife took sugar in her coffee.

"I'm sorry," he said, pressing a kiss on the top of her head. "I just feel so bloody lost right now."

"But you're not lost," Olivia affirmed with another squeeze of her arms. "You're here with me. Right where you belong."

The words made sense, but Xander struggled with accepting them. Right now he didn't feel as if he belonged here at all. And the idea was beginning to scare him.

Five

Olivia could feel him mentally withdrawing from her and it made her want to hold on to him all the harder. The medical team had warned her that Xander would experience mood swings. It was all part and parcel of what he'd been through and what his brain was doing to heal itself. She gave him one more squeeze and then let him go.

"Shall we eat breakfast out on the patio?" she asked as brightly as she could. "Why don't you pour our coffees, and then maybe you could set the table out there for me while I finish making breakfast."

Without waiting for a response, she busied herself getting place mats and cutlery and putting them on a large wooden tray with raised edges so that if he faltered nothing would slide off. She couldn't mollycoddle him all the time, but no one said she couldn't try to make things easier for him, either. She went ahead and opened the doors that led onto the patio, ensuring that the way was clear for him with nothing to trip over.

"There, I'll be out in a minute or two," she said after

he'd filled both mugs with coffee. He seemed to hesitate. "Something the matter, Xander?"

"I didn't notice yesterday if you still take milk or not."

His voice was flat, with an air of defeat she'd never heard from him before. Not even after Parker died.

"I do, thanks."

She turned around to the stove and poured the beaten eggs into the pan rather than let him see the pity that she knew would be on her face. As she stirred the egg in the pan, she listened, feeling her entire body relax when he picked up the tray and slowly began to move out of the kitchen. When the eggs were almost done, she sprinkled in some chopped chives from her herb garden and stirred the egg mixture one last time before loading the steaming mix onto warmed plates. She garnished the egg with some dots of sour cream, another sprinkle of chives and some cracked pepper, then added the smoked salmon shavings on the side. Satisfied the meal looked suitably appealing, she carried the plates out to the patio.

Xander was standing on the edge of the pavers, staring at the cherry blossom tree he'd planted when they moved in.

"It's grown, hasn't it?" Olivia remarked as she put the plates down on the table. "The tree. Do you remember the day we planted it?"

"Yeah, I do. It was a good day," he said simply.

His words didn't do justice to the fun they'd had completing the raised brick bed and then filling it with barrow loads of the soil and compost that had been delivered. After they'd planted the tree, they'd celebrated with a bottle of imported champagne and a picnic on the grass. Then, later, made love long into the night.

"Come and have breakfast before it gets cold," Olivia said, her voice suddenly thick with emotion.

They'd made so many plans for the garden that day,

some of which they'd undertaken before their marriage fell apart. She hadn't had the time or the energy to tackle the jobs they'd left undone on her own. In fact, she'd even debated keeping the house at all. Together with the separate one-bedroom cottage on the other side of the patio, where she had her studio, the property was far too big for one person alone.

But now he was home again, the place already felt better. As if a missing link had been slotted back in where it belonged. She pasted a smile on her face and took a sip of her coffee.

Xander desultorily applied himself to his plate of eggs.

"Is it not to your liking?" Olivia asked.

"It's good," he replied, taking another bite. "I don't feel hungry anymore, that's all."

"Are you hurting? They said you'd have headaches. Do you want me to get your painkillers?"

"Livvy, please! Stop fussing," he snapped before throwing down his fork and pushing up from his seat.

Olivia watched as he walked past the garden and out onto the lawn. His body was rigid, and he stood with his hands on his hips, feet braced slightly apart, as if he was challenging some invisible force in front of him.

She stared down at her plate and pushed her breakfast around with her fork, her own appetite also dwindling as the enormity of what she'd done began to hit home. He wasn't a man to be pushed or manipulated; she'd learned that years ago. She'd made decisions before that had angered him. Like the day she brought Bozo home from the pound without discussing it with him first. And the day she stopped taking her birth control.

A shadow hovered over her, blocking the light. Xander's hand, warm and strong and achingly familiar, settled on her shoulder.

"I'm sorry. I shouldn't have reacted like that."

She placed a hand on top of his. "It's okay. I guess I am fussing. I'll try to keep a lid on it. It's just that I love you so much, Xander. Hearing about your accident terrified me. Thinking that I could have lost you…" Her voice choked up again.

"Oh, Livvy. What are we going to do?" he said wearily, wiping a stray tear from her cheek with his thumb.

She shook her head slightly. "I don't know. Just take one day at a time, I guess."

"Yeah." He nodded. "I guess that's all we can do."

He sat back down at the table and finished his breakfast. Afterward, he looked weary, as if every muscle in his body was dragging. Olivia gestured to the hammock she'd only recently strung up beneath the covered rafters.

"You want to test-drive the hammock for me while I tidy up?"

"Still fussing, Livvy," he said, but it came with a smile. "But yeah, that sounds like a good idea."

She gave him a small smile in return and gathered up their things to load the tray he'd brought out earlier.

"Do you want another coffee?" she asked.

"Maybe later, okay?"

She nodded and went back inside. After she'd stacked the dishwasher she intended to tackle the hand washing, but all of a sudden she was overwhelmed with the enormity of the road ahead. She closed her eyes and gripped the front of the countertop until her fingers ached and turned white. For a moment there, outside, when he was staring at the garden, she'd been afraid he'd remember that fateful day when he'd been playing with Bozo and Parker in the yard. She still remembered his shout at Parker to stop. There'd been something in his voice that had made her drop her paintbrush, leaving it to splatter on the floor as she'd turned and run outside in time to hear the sickening screech of tires.

A shudder ran through her body, and she pushed the memory aside. She'd dealt with all of that. Dealt with it and put it away in a filing cabinet in her mind and locked the drawers as effectively as she'd taped the boxes of Parker's things closed before hiding them in the darkest recess of the attic.

Olivia opened her eyes and applied herself to scrubbing her cast-iron pan clean and wiping the stove top and the benches down until they gleamed. She cast a glance outside to where Xander lay in the hammock, asleep. Maybe now would be a good time to bring his clothes down from the attic and filter them in among the items she'd brought from his apartment. *And* put the whole lot back in their bedroom where he believed they belonged.

And they did belong there, she affirmed silently. Just as he belonged here, with her.

Mindful that she might not have much time, Olivia moved quickly. This time she managed to avoid looking at the boxes of Parker's things altogether, right up until she turned around with the storage box and headed back to the door. She had to pass the shadowy nook where she'd put her child's entire history. If only it could be as easy to put away the pain that crept out whenever she least expected it and attacked her heart and soul with rabid teeth.

The all-too-familiar burn of tears stung at the back of her eyes, and Olivia forced herself to keep moving toward the stairs. She wouldn't cry. *Not now. Not now. Not now*, she repeated down each step on the spiral staircase. In her bedroom—*their* bedroom, she corrected herself again—she shoved her things to her side of the wardrobe and, after grabbing a few extra hangers, she shook out and hung up the clothes that had been packed in the box. Then she went to the spare room and transferred all the things she'd put in there to the bedroom, clearing the bureau drawers that she'd taken over and putting his clothing away.

It didn't look as though he had much. Certainly not as much as she'd left behind at the apartment. Would he notice? Probably. She *was* talking about Xander, after all. A man who was precise and who took planning to exceptional levels. Detail was his middle name. It was part of why he was so good at what he did and why he'd rocketed through the company ranks. She doubted she'd be able to sneak another visit to his apartment now he was home, not for a while anyway. And if she did that, it would only cause more problems when he discovered she'd added more clothing to his existing wardrobe. No, she'd just have to stick with what she'd already done.

And hope like crazy that it would be enough.

Xander woke abruptly. At first confused as to his surroundings, he let his body relax when he realized he was home, lying in the hammock in the garden. He let his gaze drift around him, taking in the familiar and cataloguing the changes that they'd obviously made over time. They'd done a good job, he had to admit—if only he could remember actually doing any of it, then maybe he'd feel less like a stranger in his own home and more as if he belonged here.

Carefully, he levered himself to a sitting position and lowered his legs to the ground. He wondered where Olivia had got to. He couldn't see her through the kitchen window. He got up and shuffled a few steps forward. Then, as if his brain had taken a little longer to wake up and join the rest of him, he moved with more confidence.

"Livvy?" he called as he went back inside the house.

The creak of floorboards sounded overhead, followed by her rapid footsteps on the stairs.

"Xander? Are you okay?" she called before she reached the hallway where he stood.

He watched as she did a quick inventory of him and suppressed the surge of irritation that she'd immediately jump to the conclusion there was something wrong. It wasn't fair of him to be annoyed with her, he told himself. This was all as new and as intimidating for her as it was for him.

"I'm fine," he said calmly. "Just wondering what you were up to."

"I put your things back in our bedroom," she said breathlessly. "It took me a little longer than I expected. Sorry."

"Don't apologize. You don't have to be at my beck and call."

Some of his irritation leaked out into the tone of his voice, and he wished the words back almost immediately as he saw their impact on her face and in her expressive eyes.

"I might want to be at your beck and call, Xander. Have you considered that? It…it's been a while since I've had you here."

He felt like a fool. Once again he'd hurt her and all because she cared. He reached out and grabbed her hand before tugging her toward him. He felt the resistance in her body and looped his arms around her, pulling her even closer.

"I guess when we promised the 'in sickness and in health' thing we didn't think it would ever really apply to us," he said, pressing a kiss to the top of her head.

He felt her body stiffen, then begin to relax until she was resting against him, her head tucked into his shoulder and her breath a soft caress on his throat. His arms tightened, trying to say with a physical touch what he couldn't seem to say with words. After a few minutes, Olivia pulled away.

"What did you want to do today? Go for a drive maybe?" she asked. "We may as well make the most of it today because your physical therapist will begin home visits tomorrow."

She smoothed her hands down her jeans, making him wonder what she was nervous about. The action had always been her "tell" when something made her uncomfortable. Had it been their embrace? Surely not. They'd always been a physically demonstrative couple. In private anyway. Memories of just how demonstrative they'd been filled his mind and teased his libido into life. Good to know not everything was faulty, he thought cynically.

But even though that part of his body appeared to be in working order, it was as though there was some kind of a barrier between him and Olivia right now.

"Xander?" she prompted, and he realized he must have looked as if he'd zoned out for a while—and probably had.

"You know, I'd like to stay home today. I tire all too damn easily for my liking. How about you show me what you've been working on in your studio lately?"

Her face brightened. "Sure. Come with me."

She slid an arm around his waist—apparently more comfortable with aiding him than accepting physical comfort from him, he noted—and they walked outside and across to the small cottage on the property.

The cottage was one of the reasons they'd bought the property in the first place. He knew that it was Olivia's dream to give up teaching and paint full-time, and if he had it in his power to help her achieve that dream, well he'd been prepared to do whatever he could to see her do it.

Stepping over the threshold and into what was originally an open-plan living/dining area but was now the main part of Olivia's studio almost made him feel as if he were trespassing. This was very much her space, and she'd made it so right from the start.

He could understand it in some ways. In her childhood, she'd never had a space to call her own. Instead she'd been too busy caring for her siblings, supporting her father where she could, right up until she'd graduated high school and come to Auckland for her degree. Even then she'd lived in a shared-flat situation with ten students in a dilapidated old house.

"You've made some changes," he commented as they stepped inside.

"Not recent—" she started, then sighed. "Oh, I'm sorry. That was insensitive of me."

"Not insensitive," he said, looking around at the canvases she had stacked on the walls. "Don't worry about it."

He walked over to the paintings and gestured toward them. "Can I look?"

"Of course you can. I'm doing this harbor series for a gallery showing a bit closer to Christmas."

"Your style has changed," he commented. "Matured, I think."

"I'll take that as a compliment," Olivia said from behind him as he lifted one canvas and held it at arm's length.

"It's meant as one. You've always been talented, Livvy, but these…they're something else. It's like you've transformed from a very hungry caterpillar into a butterfly."

"That's a beautiful thing to say, thank you."

"I mean it. No wonder you gave up teaching."

She ducked her head, her hair—loose today—fell forward, obscuring the blush he caught a hint of as it bloomed across her cheeks.

* * *

Olivia kept her face hidden so he wouldn't see her sudden change of expression. She'd given up teaching six weeks before Parker was born. It had nothing to do with her art. Keeping up this facade was as difficult as it was emotionally draining.

"Do you miss it? The teaching?" Xander asked, oblivious to the turmoil that occupied her mind. He gave a snort of irritation. "I feel like I should know all this. I'm sorry if we're going over old ground."

She lifted her head and looked him straight in the eye. "Don't apologize, Xander. You don't need to. You didn't ask for this to happen—neither of us did. We both have some adjusting to do."

Not least of which was his casual reference to Parker's favorite book. When Xander had likened her improvement in her painting to that of a very hungry caterpillar morphing into a butterfly, she'd wondered if he recognized the reference. Wondered if, deep down inside that clever mind of his, he still could recite, verbatim, the book he'd read to Parker every night.

Six

"Is this what you're working on right now?" Xander asked, coming to a halt in his traverse of her studio to stand in front of a large canvas she had on her easel.

It was a broad watercolor of Cheltenham Beach, only a block down the hill from their house. A place where she usually took daily walks to blow away the cobwebs of the past that continued to stubbornly cling to the recesses of her mind.

"It is. I'm nearly done," she replied, watching him as he stared at the picture.

Would he remember the times they'd taken Bozo for a run on the white sand, laughing as he'd chased seagulls—his short legs and long hairy body no match for the svelte grace of the birds? Or when they'd taken Parker to the beach for his first swim in the sea? Their son had been such a water baby. Crawling flat out on his pudgy hands and chubby little knees to get back to the water every chance he could. In the end they'd had to bundle him into his stroller and take him home, amid much protesting.

Her heart gave a sharp twist. This was going to shred her into tiny pieces—this wondering, the waiting, the fear that he'd remember and the hope that he might not. But was that entirely fair—to hope that he would never recall the past? He'd been a loving father and a good, if initially reluctant, dad. Was it fair that he shouldn't remember all that he'd been to Parker and the love that had been returned from child to father?

"I like it," Xander said, interrupting her thoughts. "Do you have to sell it? It would be perfect over the mantel in the sitting room, don't you think?"

She'd thought that very thing. And there it was. The synchronicity she and Xander had shared from the day they'd met. Just when had they lost it so completely? she wondered.

"I don't have to sell it," she said carefully. "But it's the focal point of the collection."

"Maybe I'll need to buy it myself," Xander said with a wink that reminded her all too much of the reasons she'd fallen in love with him in the first place.

She laughed. "I hope you have deep pockets. It'll command a good price."

"Maybe I have an 'in' with the artist," he said suggestively. "We might be able to come to reciprocal agreement."

Her body tightened on a wave of desire so sharp and bittersweet she almost cried out. It had been so long since they'd bantered like this. So long since it had led to its inevitable satisfying and deeply physical conclusion.

"We'll have to see about that," she said noncommittally and stepped away just when Xander would have reached for her. "I was thinking of baking cheese scones for lunch. You keen?"

"I shouldn't be hungry after that breakfast, but I am,"

Xander conceded but not before she saw the hint of regret in his eyes.

Had he wanted her in that moment when they were teasing? She'd certainly wanted him. She wished she had the courage to act on it. The doctors hadn't said outright that they shouldn't resume normal marital relations. Thing was, theirs was no longer a normal marriage. She'd be taking even greater advantage of him, wouldn't she, if she gave in to the fierce physical pull between them?

Of course she would, she told herself. No matter how much she might wish it to the contrary, it would be lying to him. *Like you are already?* that cynical voice in the back of her mind intruded. *How much worse would it be?*

She shook her head slightly, as if she could rid herself of the temptation that way.

"Come on," Olivia said firmly, slipping her arm around Xander's waist in a totally nonsexual way and turning him away from the painting. "You can do battle with the coffee machine for me while I whip up those scones. We can discuss the painting later."

Two weeks later saw them settled into a more comfortable routine. The physical therapist came to the house twice a week, putting Xander through his paces and working with him to improve his balance and coordination. In between his visits, Olivia helped him through his exercises. She realized, with regular home-cooked meals and the physical exercise, he was slowly returning to normal. Physically, at least.

Mentally, he was still adrift in the past and none too pleased about it. He'd taken to spending a bit of time in his office upstairs each day, familiarizing himself with his client backgrounds all over again. Olivia was thankful he was nowhere near ready to return to work yet, but eventually he would be. She wouldn't be able to cocoon him within their home forever.

It occurred to her that at some point in time, if his memory didn't show any signs of returning, she'd have to tell him they'd had a child. It was too risky not to. Someone at his office could just as easily raise the subject when he returned to work, and she needed to head that train wreck off at the pass if she could. But now wasn't the time. He had enough to cope with, relearning everything in their current world.

Olivia picked up her palette, squeezed some colors onto the board and selected a brush to work with. She tried to force her mind to the small canvas she'd started this morning when Xander had been with the therapist, but her mind continued to drift back to her husband. To the man she loved.

She'd never struggled to focus on her work before. On the contrary, in the two years since Xander had left her, it had been an escape she'd sought with grateful abandon. Even before their separation, she'd guarded her alone time with a single-minded purpose and actively discouraged him from sharing her creative space. But now the gift of his return to her life made her want to spend every moment she could with him.

She put down her brush and palette and took them over to the small kitchen to clean. It was useless to keep trying to work today when all she wanted was to be near him. After she'd tidied up she walked across her studio to the bedroom on the other side. It was a large room, longer than it was wide. Its southerly aspect didn't allow for the best of light, which had made it useless to her as a work space, but it would work well for Xander as an office. He could even access it through a separate door so as not to disturb her when she was working, if he wanted to. And if they relocated his things down here, she'd be able to be near him as she felt she needed to be.

She tried to kid herself that this new overwhelming need to keep an eye on him was nothing more than that of a concerned wife for her recuperating husband, but in all honesty the need was pure selfishness on her part. Sure, she would worry less about him possibly losing his balance on the stairs if he was here in the single-level dwelling with her while she worked. But worry wasn't the only thing that drove her to consider the change. No, it was much more than that. It had more to do with grabbing this second chance at happiness and holding it close. Nurturing it. Feeding it. And never letting him go again.

Fired up by her decision, she went into the main house and straight up the stairs to the room Xander had set up as his office when they'd moved in. The door was open. When she noticed Xander, she hesitated in the doorway, her hand ready to knock gently on the frame.

He was slumped in his chair, his elbows on his desk and his head resting in his hands.

"Xander?" Olivia flew to his side. "Are you okay?"

"Just another of these damn headaches," he said.

"I'll get your pills."

Less than a minute later she was back at his side with the bottle of heavy-duty painkillers the hospital had prescribed and a glass of water to knock them back with.

"Here," she said, spilling the tablets into the palm of his hand. "Take these and I'll help you to our room. You've been pushing yourself again, haven't you?"

He'd already had a therapy session that morning and, for the past two hours after lunch, had been up here in his office. It was more than his tired body and damaged brain could handle—that much was obvious to her if not to her stubborn husband.

"Maybe," Xander grunted.

His admission told her more than he probably wanted to admit, which, in itself, worried her even more. He grew paler as she helped him to his feet and for once he made no pretense about not needing her support as they slowly made their way across the hall to their bedroom.

Xander lay down on the bed with a groan, and Olivia hastened to draw the drapes and cast the room into soft half light. She brushed a light kiss on his forehead and turned to leave the room. But Xander had a different idea.

"Come lie with me, Livvy, please?"

It was the "please" that did it for her. Carefully, she eased her body on the bed next to him and curled to face him—one hand lifting to gently tousle his hair and massage his scalp. Beneath her fingertips she felt the scar tissue that had formed as he'd healed during his coma. It both shocked and frightened her, and she started to pull her hand away.

"Don't stop. That feels great," Xander protested.

It felt ridiculously good to her to be needed by him. Most of the time since he'd been home he'd fought for independence—begrudgingly accepting her help only when he had to or when she insisted. But here, now? Well, it made her decision to bring him home all the sweeter. To be able to fill a need for him, in the home they'd created together rather than know he was alone in that barren and soulless apartment he'd been living in, gave her a stronger sense of purpose than she'd felt in a long time.

The first thing Olivia became aware of when she woke was Xander's face immediately in front of hers. His eyes were open, and his face so serious, so still, that for a split second she was afraid he'd remembered. But then his eyes warmed and he gave her that special half smile of his.

"Livvy?" he asked, lifting a hand to push a hank of hair off her face.

"Mm-mmm?"

"I love you."

Her eyes widened and her heart went into overdrive. How long had it been since she'd heard those precious words from Xander's lips? Far too long.

She turned her head so she could place a kiss in his palm. "I love you, too."

She snuggled up closer to him, loving the fact she could.

"I mean it," he said. "I was thinking about the accident and wondering when the last time was that I told you how much you mean to me. It frightened me to think it might have been a very long time ago, and that I might have died without ever telling you again."

She was lost for words.

Xander continued. "And I wanted to thank you."

"Thank me? Why? I'm still your wife." She gasped in a sharp breath. Would he pick up on the slip she'd made, referring to herself as *still* being his wife?

"You've been so patient with me since I was released from the hospital. I appreciate it."

He leaned in a little closer until his lips touched hers in the sweetest of kisses. Olivia felt her body unfurl with response to his touch—her senses coming to aching life. She couldn't help it; she kissed him back. Their lips melded to each other as if they had never been apart at all, their tongues—at first tentative, then more hungrily—meeting, touching and tasting. Rediscovering the joy of each other.

Xander's hands skimmed her body, lingering on the curve of her waist, touching the swell of her breasts. Her skin grew tight, her nipples aching points of need pressing against the thin fabric of her bra. He palmed them, and fire licked along her veins. And with it an awareness that doing this with him was perpetuating another lie.

With a groan of regret, Olivia caught at his hands and gently eased them from her aching body. She wriggled away from him and swung herself into an upright position. Drawing in a deep breath, she cast a smile at him across her shoulder.

"If that's how you show your appreciation, remind me to do more for you," she said, injecting a note of flippancy into her voice that she was far from feeling.

"Come back," he urged.

She looked at him, took in the languorous look in his eyes, the fire behind them that burned just for her. Even in their darkest days, they'd still had this physical connection between them. A spark that wouldn't be doused. A need that only each other could fulfil.

"I wish I could, but I've got work to do," she said, getting to her feet and straightening her clothing. "You stay in bed though. You're still a bit too pale for my liking. How's the head?"

"It's fine," Xander replied, also getting up.

As Olivia went to leave the room, he stepped in front of her. "Livvy, stop. You won't break me if we make love."

"I know, and I...I want to—don't get me wrong. I just think it's too soon for you, and on top of your headache, as well—" She broke off as the phone rang.

Grateful beyond belief for the interruption, she dived for the phone next to the bed.

"It's the gallery," she whispered to Xander, covering the mouthpiece once she identified who it was. "I'll be a while."

He gave her a piercing look, one that reminded her all too much of the determined man he'd been, and then turned and left the room. Olivia sagged back onto the edge of the bed, her pulse still beating erratically, her mind only half engaged with the gallery owner's conversation. She must have said all the right things in all the right places because the twenty-minute call seemed to satisfy the gallery owner's queries.

After replacing the phone on the bedside table, Olivia reached out and smoothed the covers of the bed. The indentations of where they'd been lying together were easily erased. If only it was as easy to erase the demand that beat like an insistent drum through her body. Sure, she could have given in to him, but the sense of right and wrong that had made her pull away still reared up in the back of her mind.

It would be unfair to make love with him when he didn't know about their past—about the problems that had driven them apart two years ago. She'd been a fool to think she could live in a make-believe world where the past never happened and everything was still perfect between them. She did love him, deeply, and that was more than half the problem. If she didn't, she would have been able to take advantage of his overture to make love, would have been able to lose herself in his skillful touch and the delirium of his possession without guilt holding her back.

She'd been nuts to think she could just bring him home from hospital and keep him at arm's length and not have to face a situation like this. He'd always had a high sex drive, and hers had mirrored his. It had been a long time since they'd found their special brand of perfection together.

Not for the first time, she felt strong misgivings about what she'd undertaken. She'd wanted to give their marriage a second chance. But once he knew what she'd done, how she'd used him and taken advantage of his injuries, where would that leave her?

Where would that leave either of them?

Seven

As she exited the bedroom she heard Xander back in his office. She crossed the hall and leaned against the doorjamb.

"You're supposed to be taking it easy," she said.

He swiveled around in his chair to face her. "I need to do something. Aside from the memory loss, I've started feeling better. I'm bored. With you working on your paintings, I was thinking about calling the office and seeing if I could go in for a few hours a week. Ease in gently, y'know?"

A fist of ice formed around Olivia's heart. If he did that, it wouldn't be long before he'd learn about her deception. And what chance would she have with him after that?

"You haven't been cleared by the doctor yet. Why don't you give it another week or two? See what he says when you go for your checkup?

"Look, I know I need to be working, but there's no reason why you can't be familiarizing yourself with the markets and what's been happening while I'm painting. Why don't we relocate your office to the bedroom off the studio? That way you can work and I won't have to worry about you. We can keep the single bed that's in there so that if you get another headache, or simply need to rest, you can just lie down."

"And you can keep hovering over me like a mother hen?" he asked with a raised brow.

She pulled a face. "If you want to call it that. I prefer to think of it as caring. Besides, at least that way you won't be bored and we can keep an eye on each other."

He inclined his head. "Okay, when you put it that way. You always lose track of time when you're painting, anyway. I'll be able to make sure *you* keep to *your* breaks."

"So, is it a deal?"

He stood up and brushed her lips with his. "It's a deal."

"Let's go and work out where we'll put everything," she said, turning to leave the room.

He followed close behind, and she hesitated to allow him to catch up so she could walk down the stairs with him. Yes, he was getting stronger every day, but she still worried.

"Y'know, I'm kind of surprised you're willing to give up your space to me," Xander commented as they hit the ground floor and started toward the doors that led out to the cottage.

"Why's that?" Olivia asked, although she had an idea she knew where this was heading.

"You've always protected your work space. I don't remember you ever suggesting we share it before."

She shrugged. "A lot can change in a few years. Would you rather not move your office down here? We don't have to."

"No, I'd prefer it. We can always use an extra bedroom upstairs for when we have those kids we've obviously kept putting off having."

Olivia stumbled as weakness flooded her body at his words. They hadn't put off having kids. Would things have been better if they had? Would they have been spared all that suffering if she'd stuck with the five-year plan Xander had painstakingly created for them? He hadn't thought they were ready to be parents—but she'd wanted a baby so badly. She could never regret the time they'd had with Parker, but if they'd waited…if she'd been a few years older, a few years wiser when she became a mother, would she have made better decisions? Would it have changed anything if Xander had been given more time to adjust and prepare himself to become a father?

She'd taken the decision out of their hands when she'd gone off her birth control pills without telling him. He'd been angry at first, when she'd told him she was pregnant, but he'd eventually warmed to the idea. Although she'd always suspected that in many ways he held a bit of himself back. As if he was afraid to love Parker too much. She'd even accused him of loving their son less, in those immediate dark days after Parker had died.

"Hey, you okay?" Xander said, putting a hand to her elbow. "I thought I was supposed to be the clumsy one."

"I'm okay," she insisted, focusing on her every step even as her mind whirled in circles.

"About those kids?" Xander started. "I think we should do something about that as soon as we can. Life's too short and too precious to waste. If my car wreck has taught me nothing else, it has taught me that. I'd like us to start trying."

Outside the cottage Olivia hesitated. "Are you sure about that, Xander? You've only just begun your recovery. Do you really think having children right away is a good idea?"

She didn't even know if she wanted another baby, ever. Was her heart strong enough to take that risk? Loving Xander was one thing, and she'd lost him figuratively the day he'd left their home and she'd almost lost him literally in the wreck that had stolen his memories.

"Aren't you the one who usually accuses me of putting things off too long? Why the change of heart? Talk to me, Livvy."

"Xander, can't we just wait until you're better? You've never wanted to rush into this before."

"But what if I never get *better*? What if my memory doesn't return and those years stay locked away forever?"

There was a part of her that wanted that to happen. But Olivia knew that wouldn't be fair to him or to her. If they were to truly make this marriage work, there couldn't be any secrets between them. Even so, she couldn't bring herself to raise the subject of their separation or the tragedy that had triggered it with him just yet. Not when she was still unsure how he would react.

She'd learned as a child that it was best not to face the pain of loss—it was far better to tuck it away where it couldn't be felt. Her father had taught her that. After her mother had died, her dad had told Olivia that looking after "the wee ones," as he'd called her siblings, was up to her now. And then he'd thrown himself into his farm work with a single-mindedness that didn't allow for grieving.

Whenever Olivia had felt the overwhelming loss of her mother, she'd just buttoned it down and turned to the work she had at hand—whether it was her schoolwork or helping her siblings with theirs. And there were always chores to do around the farm and the house. Following her father's staunch example, she'd never allowed herself time to think about her loss or the pain she felt. And that's exactly how she'd coped after Parker's death.

"Livvy?" Xander prompted.

"We'll cross that bridge when we get there," she said stoically. "Right now the things that matter are getting you strong again and being happy together. And if having you here, sharing my space, means I can stop you from reaching the breaking point like you did earlier today, then that's all to the good."

"And vice versa," he reiterated, lifting a finger to trace the circles she knew were under her eyes. "You work too hard yourself."

She cracked a wry smile. "Pot, meet kettle."

Xander laughed, and Olivia felt some of the weight that had settled in her heart ease a little. They'd discuss the issue of children later. Much later. Which reminded her, she needed to go back on the Pill.

Inside the cottage they debated the best way to set up the bedroom to serve Xander's needs. She'd have to contact a contractor to run the separate phone line Xander had to his office upstairs, to the cottage, as well. The Wi-Fi proved patchy, so that was another thing to be looked into. Privately she was relieved that his access to the internet would be a little restricted here initially. What if he took it into his head to do a search on himself or her? There was bound to be some archived newspaper article that would spring up with the details of the speeding driver who had killed their son and their pet with one careless act. Again Olivia accepted that she'd have to tell him about that dreadful day at some stage, but as long as she could put it off, she would.

"How are we going to get my desk in here?" Xander asked as they surveyed the space. "I'd like it under the window, but I doubt we'll be able to manhandle it between the two of us."

"Wouldn't you rather get a new desk?" Olivia asked hopefully.

She hated the behemoth he'd insisted on installing upstairs in the early days of their marriage. It had been their only bone of contention back then.

"Don't think I don't remember how much you dislike my desk. But I love it, and if I'm moving in here, it's moving with me," Xander said with mock severity.

Olivia sighed theatrically. "Well, if you insist. Mrs. Ackerman next door has a couple of university students boarding with her. They might like to earn a few extra dollars manhandling it down the stairs and into here. With any luck, they might even drop it."

She added the last with a giggle that saw Xander reach for her and wrap her tightly in his arms. "I've missed that sound," he said before tickling her. "But I'm afraid I'm going to have to punish you for that comment."

By the time she'd managed to extricate herself from his hold she was weak with laughter and it felt good. She could almost believe that everything was going to be okay after all.

The next morning, Xander moped around the house at a complete loss for what to do with himself that he knew was at odds with his old self. Olivia had gone out to do some shopping while he was busy with the physical therapist. She'd been gone several hours now. Since he was alone in the house, he decided to use the time for some exploring. He went through each room, starting downstairs, poking through the kitchen cupboards and then examining every item in the living room, dining room and formal lounge. Some things spoke to him; others held their silence. No matter what, he felt as if something vital was missing, and he hated it. He wanted his life back. Hell, he wanted himself back.

On a more positive note, the weakness that had plagued him since awakening from the coma was re-

ceding, and his physical therapist was extremely pleased
with his progress to date. Olivia had suggested turning
the tool room, which only had access from outside on
the ground floor, into a home gym. With his physical
therapist's suggestions it had been outfitted so that he
could keep up his program every single day without fail.

Pushing himself felt good but wasn't without its own
problems. It often left him shaking and struggling to
stay upright under the weight of yet another of those
wretched headaches.

He picked up a silver-framed photo that had been
taken of him and Olivia on their wedding day, and he
felt a strong tug of desire as he studied her face and the
creamy curve of her shoulders, exposed by the strapless
figure-hugging beaded gown she'd worn. At least that
continued to remain the same, he thought as he replaced
the picture on its shelf. The bond between them was as
strong as ever. She'd been of immeasurable support to
him, even if she was still shy about making love. Those
barriers would come down eventually. Their relationship had always been too well-founded and their attraction too strong to allow something like his brain injury
to keep them apart for very long.

The sound of footsteps coming up the front path
caught his attention. A visitor? They'd had no one since
he'd come home from hospital. He'd had little to no contact with anyone else, even his mother, who lived in the
far north. He'd called her once, to tell her he'd been released from hospital, but their conversation had been as
short as it always was. He was fine, she was fine—end of
conversation. The prospect of a fresh face was instantly
appealing, and he was at the front door and ready to open
it before the doorbell could even be rung. He felt his face
drop as he recognized the uniform of the courier standing with his finger poised to press the bell.

"Package for Mrs. Olivia Jackson. Could you sign for me, please?"

The courier handed his electronic device and stylus over to Xander for his signature, then passed Xander the large flat envelope he'd had tucked under his arm. With a cheery "Thanks" and a wave, he was gone.

Xander slowly closed the front door and turned the envelope over in his hands. "Oxford Clement & Gurney" was printed on the envelope. Family law specialists. A frown furrowed his brow as he stared at the black print on the white background. He repeated the name of the firm out loud, knowing that there was something about it that was familiar. But no matter how hard he reached for the key in his mind to open that particular door, it remained firmly closed and out of reach.

Family law specialists—what on earth would Olivia be needing them for? The envelope was poorly sealed, just a slip of tape holding it down in the center of the flap. One small tug would be all it took to open it and check the contents inside. Maybe he'd find something that would fill in some of the gaps in his Swiss cheese for brains. But what if he didn't like what he discovered? And how would he explain to Olivia that he'd been prying in her personal mail? There was no question it was addressed to her and not to him.

Maybe something had been going wrong in their marriage before his accident. Maybe things weren't as he remembered and that was why Olivia remained cagey about the past six years. He hadn't pressed her too hard for any of it, and he now wondered if that wasn't in self-preservation. Were there things he really didn't want to know? Things he was actively suppressing?

The doctors said there was no permanent damage to his brain from the accident and only time would tell if the amnesia would be permanent or not. It was vague and frustrating as hell to know that he had no timeline to full recovery. But perhaps he didn't want to remember. If things hadn't been good between him and Olivia, to the extent that she'd been talking to lawyers, then could he have chosen to forget?

Even as he chewed the thoughts over and over in his mind, he couldn't believe that could be true. Or was it simply that he didn't *want* to believe? Without his memory, without her, what did he have left?

"Argh!" he exclaimed and tossed the envelope onto the hall table in disgust. "It's in there somewhere—I know it is," he raged.

He went through to the kitchen, poured himself a glass of cold water and downed it quickly. His hand shook as he put the glass back down on the counter and grimaced against the all-too-familiar shooting pain in his temple that was the precursor to another headache. He reached for the painkillers Olivia kept on the counter for convenience's sake and quickly threw a couple of them down with another drink of water, then went and lay down on one of the large couches in the sitting room. He'd learned the hard way that the only thing that would rid him of the headache was painkillers and sleep. With any luck, when he awoke, Olivia would be back home with some answers for him about the envelope that had arrived.

Eight

Olivia came in through the back door and was surprised to find the house silent. Had Xander gone out for a walk by himself? Fear clutched at her throat. They'd discussed this and agreed that he wouldn't go out on his own just yet. Even his physical therapist had agreed it probably wasn't a great idea until he was a bit stronger, at least not without a stick and Xander had flat-out refused to use one of those.

"Livvy? I'm in the sitting room," he called out. Olivia felt her entire body sag in relief.

"Coming," she answered, putting down the few extra grocery items she'd bought to cook a special dinner with before going to find him.

He was reclining on the largest of the couches in the sitting room, late-afternoon sunlight spilling over him and, no doubt, responsible for the flush on his cheeks. Even so, she automatically put a hand to his forehead to check for fever. Xander's hand closed around hers.

"Still expecting the worst, Livvy? I'm just a little

warm from the sun. That's all." He sat up and tugged
her into his lap. Catching her chin between his fingers,
he turned her face for a kiss. "Now, that's the proper way
to say hello to your husband," he chided gently.

Her lips pulled into a smile and she kissed him again.
"If you say so, husband. So, have you been behaving
while I've been gone? No wild parties? No undesirable
behavior?"

"All of the above," he answered with a cheeky grin.
"I wish."

His expression changed under her watchful gaze.
"What is it? Did something happen? Did you hurt yourself?"

He rolled his eyes at her. "No, I did not. But there was
a delivery for you. An envelope from some law firm in
town."

Olivia stiffened and got up from his lap, her movements jerky and tight. "An envelope?"

She turned away from him and closed her eyes. Hoping against hope that the thing hadn't triggered any memories for him.

"I left it on the hall table." He rubbed at his eyes.
"Man, I feel so groggy after these naps. They're going
to have to stop."

"Did you have a headache?"

"Yeah."

"Then you know the naps are the only thing to really
get rid of them. Maybe it's the painkillers that leave you
feeling dopey. We can talk to the doctor about it if you
like, maybe ask about lowering the dosage?"

"Good idea."

He got up from the couch and walked through to the
kitchen. She heard him pour water into a glass. While
he was there, she quickly went into the hall and retrieved
the envelope.

"I'm just going upstairs to have a quick shower and get changed," she called out. "I'll be back down in a few minutes."

Without waiting for a response she flew up the stairs and into the bedroom. She grabbed some jeans and a long-sleeved T-shirt and carried them and the envelope into the bathroom, where she closed and locked the door. She turned on the shower, then sat down on the closed toilet seat and tugged open the envelope, allowing the contents to slide into her lap. Her heart hammered an erratic beat as a quick scan of the letter from her lawyer confirmed that the two-year separation that was required under New Zealand law before a couple's marriage could be dissolved had passed. Also enclosed was a joint application for a dissolution order for her signature. It had already been signed in advance by Xander.

Olivia looked at the date he'd signed the paper. It was the same date he'd crashed his car. That meant the document had been lying around somewhere, waiting to be actioned. A shiver ran down her spine. What would have happened if it had been sent to her more promptly? If she'd received it before Xander had woken from his coma and asked for her? She'd probably have signed it and returned it to her lawyer and it would have been duly processed through the court.

She reread the cover letter more carefully. In it, her lawyer apologized for the delay in getting the documentation to her. Apparently a changeover in staff had meant it was overlooked. Just like that, her life could have been so drastically different. She and Xander could already be divorced, rather than still very much married.

Bile rose in her throat, and she swallowed hard against the bitterness. She had to put a stop to the divorce proceedings somehow, but how? She couldn't instruct Xander's lawyers for him. How on earth was she going to get around this? Not signing the papers was a start. She shoved them roughly back into the envelope and folded it in half as if making it smaller would diminish the importance of its contents, too.

She'd have to hide it somewhere where Xander would never think to look. She opened the drawer on the bathroom vanity where she kept her sanitary items and slid it into the bottom. There they'd be safe and he certainly wouldn't accidentally come across them.

She quickly shed her clothing and dipped under the spray of the shower before snapping the faucet off and drying and dressing to go downstairs.

"Good shower?" Xander asked as she came into the kitchen. "I started scrubbing the potatoes, by the way. Earning my keep."

"Thanks," she answered as breezily as she could manage given how she'd rushed through everything. "Good to see you have your uses."

And so it began anew, the teasing. The easy banter that had been one of the threads that had bound them together through the days before they'd become parents. Before everything had become so serious. Before they'd been driven apart.

A light spring rain meant they couldn't eat outside tonight, so Olivia laid the table in the dining room, setting it with their best cutlery and the crystal candleholders they'd received as a wedding gift from her father. Her fingers lingered on them, remembering how they'd originally been a gift to her parents for their wedding and, in particular, remembering the words her father had shared with her when he given them.

"I know your mum would have wanted you to have these, and I hope you and Xander can be as happy together as your mother and I were. We didn't have as long as we should have had, and I regret not telling her every single day that I loved her, but you can't turn back time. Don't leave love unsaid between you and Xander, Olivia. Tell him, every single day."

Recalling his words brought tears to her eyes as she leaned forward and lit the candles. She'd gotten out of the habit of telling Xander she'd loved him, long before Parker had died. She'd been so absorbed in her work at the high school and their renovations on the house. Then her pregnancy and subsequently their new baby. Loving Xander had never stopped, but telling him had.

"I'm sorry, Dad," she whispered as she blew out the match she'd been using. "I let us all down, but I'm not going to do that again. This time I *will* make it work. I promise."

And, later that night, when they went to bed, she curled up against Xander's back and whispered to him in the darkness.

"I love you."

His response was blurred with weariness as he mumbled the same words in return, but it was enough—for now.

The rain had cleared by morning. After breakfast, Olivia suggested they go for a walk on the beach. With Xander's balance and strength improving daily and his coordination almost back to normal, she was sure they'd be able to tackle the softer sand areas. If it proved too much, at least they were only a block away from home. Worst-case scenario, she'd leave him on a bench seat, get the car and pick him up. Not that he'd admit defeat or even let her consider doing something like that, she thought to herself as she finished stacking the dishwasher.

"Ready?" she asked as she straightened from her task.

Olivia looked at Xander, who was leaning up against the counter, watching her.

"Never more so," he said. "It'll be good to get out. Home is great, but I think I'm beginning to suffer a bit of cabin fever."

She'd expected as much, and dreaded it. Living as they had, cocooned together on their property, had been remarkably simple. Her brief weekly updates to Xander's boss, and her reiteration that he wasn't up to visitors or calls just yet, had meant his colleagues hadn't called to talk to him. And with Xander not being cleared to drive yet, his independence had been severely curtailed. Making it all the easier to keep up the pretense that their marriage was in healthy working order.

But was it a pretense? It didn't feel like it. Not when they spent their nights wrapped in each other's arms, their days either in the cottage together or with her painting while he did his physical therapy. She knew this was an idyll that couldn't last forever. Real life would have to intrude eventually, even more quickly if, or when, he began to recall the years he'd lost. She'd have to talk to him soon. She'd have to find a way to present the truth without all the ugliness or the pain or the accusations.

The downhill walk to the beach was a gentle one, the last few hundred meters on level ground. Getting back up the hill toward the house might be another story, but she decided to tackle that when it was time. A bit of an example of how she lived everything in her life right now, she realized.

A brisk breeze blew along the beach, so there weren't too many people about. Just a few hardy souls like themselves, wrapped in light jackets and enjoying the fresh air.

"I forgot how good it feels to be out on the beach,"

Xander commented as they strolled slowly along, arm in arm. "Although I miss running along here like I used to."

His eyes were wistful as he watched a guy power along the beach with long graceful strides, his leashed dog running right alongside him, tongue lolling in its mouth.

"You'll get that back, I'm sure," Olivia said with a squeeze of his arm.

"We should get a dog," Xander said, his eyes on the retreating figure of the runner. "In fact, didn't we have a dog?"

Olivia felt a chill go through her that had nothing to do with the wind that tugged like a mischievous child at her hair. And here it was, the moment she'd been dreading. Having to tell him the truth, or at least a part of the truth about a returning memory from the time he'd lost.

She took a deep breath before answering. "Yes, we did have a dog."

"Bozo?"

"You weren't too impressed with the name, but that's what he came home from the pound with."

A smile spread across Xander's handsome face, and his gray eyes glinted with satisfaction. "I remember him. But what happened? He was young, wasn't he?"

Yes, he was young. Only a year older than their son had been when they'd both been hit by the speeding driver.

"Yeah, he was just a puppy when I brought him home. He was only four when he died."

She held her breath, fearfully wondering if he would press her for more details and praying that he wouldn't at the same time. Her prayers were answered.

"We should get another dog. It'll be good for me, get me out of the house to exercise regularly—and you, too," he said with a wink as he hugged her in close to his body. "I know you—when you're working on your paintings nothing else exists, right? You neglect yourself when you're working."

Olivia swallowed against the lump in her throat. She'd been working the day Parker had died. She'd sent him out of the studio because he was playing havoc with her concentration. If she'd only allowed him to play around her, he would still be alive today.

She'd found it hard to get beyond that guilt. In fact, she doubted she ever would completely. Logically she knew it was a combination of events that led to tragedy that day, and that no single action was at fault, but it didn't stop her wondering how things could have been different.

"Speaking of neglecting yourself. How are you doing? Not too tired? Maybe we should head back," she said, turning the subject back to Xander. It was far easier than allowing the focus to be on her.

When Xander agreed to turn back she was surprised. It wasn't like him to concede anything—and it worried her. Back at the house she went to make them coffee while he rested in the hammock on the patio. When she came out again, he was asleep. He'd pushed himself too hard on the sand, she thought as she settled down at the table and watched him. He was still a little pale, but his cheekbones were less prominent than they'd been when he'd come home from the hospital, his shoulders a little heavier.

Slowly, he was gaining weight and condition again, but he still had a long way to go. The body's ability to heal never failed to amaze her. It was his mind that remained an unknown. The sense that she was living on borrowed time bore down on her. She just knew she'd have to find a way to tell him the truth soon.

It was the small hours of the next morning when Olivia woke in her bed with a sense that something was very wrong. She reached out for Xander and only felt the space where he should have been sleeping. In the gloom, she could see their bedroom door was open. She quickly got up from the bed and flew to the door. She could hear Xander, his voice indistinct as he muttered something over and over again.

Where was he? She followed the sound, feeling her heart pound in her chest as she realized he was in the bedroom that had been Parker's. What had driven him there? At the doorway she hesitated, wondering what she should do. Turn on the light? Wake Xander? But if she did that, it might leave him asking questions she had no wish to answer right now.

Cautiously she stepped into the room.

"Xander?" she said softly and placed a hand on his arm.

He muttered something under his breath, and she strained to hear it—her blood running cold in her veins as she made out the words.

"Something's not right. Something's missing."

His head swiveled from side to side. Even though his eyes were open, she knew he was still asleep.

"Everything's all right, Xander. Come back to bed," she urged gently and took his hand to lead him back to their room.

At first he resisted, repeating the words again, but then she felt his body ease and he followed her back down the hall and into their bed. She lay on the mattress, tension holding her body in its grip as Xander slid deeply back into a restful sleep. She didn't know how long it was before she managed to drift off herself. All she did know was that the writing was on the wall.

While his conscious memory was fractured and had wiped the slate clean of all memories of their son, his subconscious was another matter entirely. Deep down he knew something was out of sync with their life, which begged the question: How much longer did she have before he realized exactly what it was?

Nine

Xander watched through the studio's French doors as Olivia worked, lost in concentration and in the composition of another piece for her exhibition. He loved observing her when she was unaware of his scrutiny. It gave him a chance to see her as she really was and not the face she projected to him each morning and through each day.

Something was obviously worrying her—deeply, he suspected—but she was a master at hiding how she felt about things. When they'd first met, he'd actually admired that about her, had recognized her resilience and strength and found them incredibly appealing. Olivia never showed weakness or dependency, but he'd learned that in itself wasn't necessarily a good thing. He knew she had to feel weakness at times—she just refused to show it. Refused to let him help. Marriage was about sharing those loads. Meeting problems head-on, together.

So what was playing on her mind now and how on earth would he get her to share it with him? Was it something to do with the envelope that had been delivered from those lawyers a couple of weeks ago? The envelope that had magically disappeared and that she hadn't discussed at all? He'd searched the name of the firm online and discovered that they were specialists in divorce and relationship property laws. The knowledge had left him with more questions than answers.

Was there something wrong in their marriage that she couldn't bring herself to discuss? Was this existence they now shared just some facade for a crueler reality? Somehow he had to find out. From the moment he'd seen her at his bedside at the hospital, he'd been assailed with a complex mix of disconnection and rightness. Logically he knew a lot of it could be put down to the head injury he'd sustained and the amnesia, but a little voice kept telling him that there was more he should know. Something vitally important.

But if it was so important, why then was Olivia holding back? He could sense it in her. The words that she bit off on occasion, the sudden sad expression in her eyes when she thought he wasn't looking. Even the furrows in her brow, such as she had right now, implied she was worried about something.

He would give her another few days and then he'd push her to find out what it was. Maybe the missing information was the key to his memory; maybe it wasn't. One thing he knew for certain, he'd be stuck in this limbo forever if he didn't get to the bottom of it.

He moved toward the studio doors. Olivia must have seen him because she turned to face him, her features composed in a welcoming smile that didn't quite reach those beautiful blue eyes of hers. She had some paint in her hair, another proof of her distraction. Sure, she was never immaculately tidy and controlled when she worked, but today she looked pressured, distracted even. Until she put on her face for him, that was.

"It's getting late," Xander said as Olivia put down her brush. "You should call it a day."

"I'm inclined to agree with you," she admitted, stretching out her shoulders and shaking out her hands. "Nothing's going right today."

"Clean up and come inside the house. I have a surprise for you."

"A surprise?"

Her eyes sparkled with interest, and he smiled in response.

"Don't get your hopes up too high. It's nothing spectacular. I'll see you back at the house. Five minutes, no more," he cautioned.

"I'll be there," she promised.

True to her word, on his allotted deadline he heard the back door open and then her footsteps coming toward the kitchen.

"Something smells amazing," she said, coming into the room. "Did you cook for me?"

"I did," he said, bending down to lift the dish he'd made from the oven.

"Oh my, did you make your moussaka?" she asked, coming closer and inhaling deeply. "I haven't had that since—"

And there it was again. That sudden halt in her train of thought. The words she left unspoken. He wondered what she'd have continued to say if she'd left herself unchecked.

"Since?" he prompted.

"Since you made it last, which was a while ago," she replied smoothly. "I'm looking forward to it. Shall I set the table?"

"All done."

"Wow, you're organized tonight."

"You were busy, and I didn't have anything else urgently claiming my attention," he joked. "Come on—we're eating in the dining room."

Carrying the dish, he led the way to the room he'd prepared with fresh-cut spring flowers and their best crockery and cutlery. A bottle of sparkling wine chilled in an ice bucket and tall crystal flutes reflected the glint of the light from above.

"Are we celebrating?" she asked.

"I've been home a month, I thought it appropriate."

"I feel like I should change," Olivia said, plucking at her paint-spattered shirt and jeans. "You've gone to so much bother."

"It wasn't a bother and—" he let his gaze sweep her body "—you look perfect to me."

A flush rose on her throat and her cheeks. "Thank you," she said quietly.

Xander put the dish on the table and took a step toward her. He raised one hand, cupped her jaw and tilted her face to meet his. "I mean it. You're perfect for me."

Then he kissed her. It started out gentle but swiftly deepened into something much more intense. His arms closed around her, and her body molded to his, igniting a sense of rightness that swept over him like a drenching wave. Needs that had been suppressed for weeks unfurled, sending hunger hurtling through his veins that had nothing to do with the meal waiting on the table for them and everything to do with this woman here in his arms.

Xander wanted nothing more than to push all the accoutrements from the table and lay Olivia on its surface. To feast on her and slake the appetite that demanded satiation. But he wanted their first time back together since his accident to be special, and he'd been planning this all day long. He was nothing if not a planner, and he knew that the long-term satisfaction gained would be all the sweeter for not rushing a single moment.

Slowly, gently, he eased back on the passion—loosening his hold on her and taking her lips now in tiny sipping kisses. After a few seconds he rested his forehead on hers. His breath was as unsteady as his hands, and desire for her still clamored from deep within his body.

"Now we've had our appetizer, perhaps we should move to the main course," he suggested, aiming for a light note that—judging by the languorous look in Olivia's eyes—he may have missed entirely.

"If you still cook as good as you kiss, dinner is going to be wonderful," Olivia said dreamily.

"Still?"

There was that hint of something he was missing again. They'd always taken turns cooking and often cooked together. But something in the way she said it made it sound as though she hadn't eaten his cooking in a long time.

"Oh, you know," she said with a flutter of her hand and stepped away from him, her gaze averted. "You've forgotten a lot of things—what if cooking is one of them?"

As an attempt at humor it fell decidedly flat, but Xander chose not to pursue it right now. Instead he tucked it away in the back of his mind, along with the other inconsistencies, to be examined another time. Tonight was meant to be a celebration, and he wasn't going to spoil that for any reason.

"I'm pretty sure you're safe from food poisoning," he said with a smile and held out her chair.

Once she was seated, he opened the sparkling wine and poured them each a glass. After taking his seat, he raised his crystal flute and held it toward Olivia.

"To new beginnings," he said.

She lifted her glass and quietly repeated the toast before clinking her flute against his. He watched her over the rim of his glass as they drank, taking in the shape of her brows, the feminine slant of her eyes and the neat straight line of her nose. Her features were exquisite, dainty, until you reached the ripe fullness of her mouth, which hinted strongly at her own appetites. Her lips glistened with a little moisture from her wine, and he ached to lean forward and taste them again. He reminded himself anew that the best things in life were to be savored, not rushed.

The meal proved he'd forgotten none of his prowess in the kitchen. After dinner they took the rest of the bottle of wine into the sitting room and watched a movie together, sipping slowly of the wine and of each other's lips. When Xander suggested they go upstairs, she didn't hesitate. As he rose from the sofa, where she'd been curled up against him, and held out his hand, she took it and allowed him to pull her upright.

He led her upstairs and into their bedroom. Filtered light from the street lamp outside drifted through the windows, limning the large iron bed frame and the furniture around the room and creating a surreal atmosphere. In some ways this *did* feel surreal. Knowing that they were going to make love again. To be what they'd promised one another they'd always be when they made their wedding vows.

Olivia's fingers went to the buttons on his shirt, and she made quick work of them before pushing the fabric aside and pressing her palms against his chest. Her palms felt cool to the touch; beneath them his skin burned in response, as his entire body now burned for more of her touch. Or, more simply, more of her.

A shudder went through him as her hands skimmed down over his ribs, across his belly and then lower, to the buckle of his belt. He shifted, taking her hands in his and lifting them to his mouth to kiss her fingertips.

"You first," he said, his voice rough with the strain of

forcing himself to take it slow. "I want to see you again. All of you."

Her delicious lips curved into a smile, and she inclined her head ever so slightly. It was enough to make his already aching flesh throb with need. She slowly unfastened each button of her shirt. When the last one was undone, she shrugged her shoulders back and allowed the garment to slide from her body. His eyes feasted on the sight of her. Her breasts were full and lush, pressing against the lace cups that bound them, swelling and falling with each breath she took. Olivia reached behind her, and he swallowed hard as, with the hooks undone, she slid down first one strap, then the other, before pulling the bra away.

He'd told himself he could wait, but he'd lied. He had to touch her again. Had to familiarize himself with the curves and hollows of her body. A body that had been imprinted on his mind and his soul over and over but that now seemed strangely different. He reached out to touch her—to cup her breasts in his hands and test the weight of them, to brush his thumb across the eager points of her nipples. And then, finally, to bend his head and take one of those taut tips with his mouth. She moaned as he swirled his tongue around her. First one side and then the other. Her fingers tangled in his hair and held him to her as if the very beat of her heart depended on it.

He made short work of the fastenings on her jeans and slid the zipper down before shoving the aged denim off her hips and down her legs. Xander slid one arm around her waist while the other dipped low, over her hips and to the waistband of her panties. Everything about Olivia felt familiar and yet different at the same time. There was a softness about her that he didn't remember. Her hips, once angular, were now more gently rounded, and her breasts seemed fuller and more sensitive than he remembered, too.

It was crazy, he thought. He knew her like he knew the back of his hand. She was still the same Olivia he'd fallen in love with and married and made a home with. She was the same Olivia who'd rushed to his bedside when he'd woken from his coma and the same woman who'd brought him home and cared for him this past month. And yet she was slightly altered, as well.

His fingers hooked under the elastic of her panties and tangled in the neat thatch of hair at the apex of her thighs. His long fingers stroked her, delving deeper with each touch until he groaned into the curve of her neck at the heat and moisture at his fingertips.

"You're so wet," he said against her skin, letting his teeth graze the tender skin of her throat.

"For you, Xander. Always for you," she murmured.

He felt a ripple run through her as he stroked a little deeper, the base of his palm pressing against her clitoris while he slid one finger inside her. The heat of her body threatened to consume him, to render him senseless with reciprocal need. He gently withdrew from her body and lifted her into his arms, ignoring her protest as he walked the few short steps to the bed and laid her down on the covers.

"You shouldn't have done that—you might have hurt yourself," she admonished in a husky voice that tried but failed to sound scolding.

"What? And miss doing this?" He wedged one knee between her legs and eased them apart, settling himself between them with the familiarity of the years of their love. He pressed his jean-clad groin against her and was rewarded with a moan from his wife.

"We're still wearing too many clothes," she pointed

out, her fingers drifting across his shoulders before tugging playfully at his hair.

"I'm getting to that," he answered, shifting lower on the bed and pressing a line of wet kisses down her torso as he did so. "One." Kiss. "Thing." Kiss. "At." Kiss. "A." Kiss. "Time."

With the last kiss he tugged her panties to one side and traced his tongue from her belly button to her center and slid his hands beneath her buttocks to tilt her toward him. As his mouth closed over her, his tongue flicking her sensitive bud, he heard her sigh. There was a wealth of longing in her voice when she spoke.

"I've missed this. I've missed you, so much."

And then she was incapable of speech or coherent thought, he judged from the sounds coming from her mouth. All she was capable of was feeling the pleasure he gave her. And he made sure, with every lick and nibble and touch, that it was worth every second.

She was still trembling with the force of her orgasm when he slid her panties off completely and shucked his clothes. He quickly reached into the bedside table drawer, grabbed a condom and sheathed himself. Settling back between Olivia's legs and into her welcoming embrace felt more like coming home than anything he'd felt before. The rhythm of their lovemaking had often been frenetic in the past, but, tonight at least, he wanted to take it slow. To truly live and love in each special moment. He positioned the blunt throbbing head of his penis at her entrance and slowly pressed forward, taking her gasp in his mouth in a kiss as he slid in all the way. Her inner muscles tightened around him, and he allowed himself to simply *feel*. Feel without pain. Feel without emptiness. Feel without frustration or loss.

Loss?

She squeezed again, and he stopped thinking and gave

himself over to the moment, to the beauty of making love with the woman he loved more than life itself. And moments after he'd slowly brought her to the brink of climax again, he pushed them over the edge and took them both on that wondrous journey together.

Later, as he drifted to sleep, his wife curled in his arms with her hair spread across his shoulder, he knew that everything had finally started to fall back into place in his world again. He might not remember everything, but he remembered this and he never wanted to let go of it—or of her.

Olivia woke before dawn with a sense that all was well with her world again. She'd slept better than she had in months, maybe even since before Parker had died. Xander slept deeply beside her, and she gazed at his profile in the slowly lightening room. She would never have believed it was possible to love a person as much as she loved him and she never wanted to lose him again.

That meant she had to talk to him. Had to tell him about Parker and his death; about their separation. But how on earth was she to start talking about something so horrible when they'd just reaffirmed everything about their love in the most perfect way possible? She didn't want the darkness of their loss and the cruel words they'd thrown at each other to taint the beautiful night they'd shared. Maybe they should take another day, or even a week.

It wasn't going to be easy telling him, whether he remembered eventually or not. But he deserved to know what had happened. Objectively and without emotion or harsh words clogging everything. It also meant facing up to the full truth about her contribution to the slow and steady breakdown of their marriage.

How did she explain why she'd taken decisions they

should have made together and made them herself? Decisions like getting Bozo—like stopping her birth control pills before they'd even really discussed when they'd have a family. They'd been in no way emotionally ready to be parents, but she'd forced the issue because she'd had an agenda and nothing and no one would sway her from it.

Looking back, she could understand why she'd behaved that way, but it didn't make it right. She'd had to become a mother at only twelve years old, caring for her three younger siblings—aged ten, eight and six—when their mother died. Waking them each morning, feeding them breakfast, packing their lunches and making sure they all got on the school bus on time. Then, at the end of each day, making sure everyone's homework was completed and a hearty meal was prepared and on the table when her father came in from the farm.

She'd hoped that taking care of everything would make him happy and proud of her. But it never seemed to work. She did everything she could to try and put some of the sparkle back in her father's dull blue eyes, but it seemed that no matter how hard she tried, no matter what she did, his grief over her mother's death locked his joy in life and his children in a frozen slab.

She became even more organized, more controlling of what happened around her, especially when it came to taking care of her family. And that didn't let up, not even when she went to university or began teaching. No, she continued to supervise and encourage her siblings' career aspirations, pushed them to apply for student loans and to enter university while working part-time jobs to help cover their living expenses just as she had. It was only after the youngest of them had graduated, and Olivia was teaching full-time at an Auckland high school, that she began to relax—and then she'd met Xander.

There'd been an aloofness, a self-sufficiency about

him that had appealed to her. While in some ways it
had reminded her of her father and how he kept himself
emotionally detached from his children, it also meant
Xander wouldn't need her as much as her siblings had
needed her. For the first time in years, she could focus
on herself. She could be independent, to a point, and do
what she'd always wanted to do. Paint and create her own
family on her own terms. And she had done all that—
but she'd forgotten the vital ingredient to a truly happy
marriage. Making those big decisions as a couple, not as
a pair of individuals.

She had a lot to make up to Xander for. Caring for
him once he'd been released from the hospital had been
a start. Repairing their marriage was next.

Xander's hand skimmed the curve of her buttocks even
as he slept, and she smiled and closed her eyes again.
She had plenty of time to work out when she would tell
him everything. For now, she'd just revel in the moment.

Ten

When Olivia woke again, the sun was streaming into their bedroom windows. The space beside her in the bed was empty, and she could hear the shower running. A smile of deep satisfaction spread across her face as she stretched and relished the sensation of her naked skin against the sheets. Everything was going to be okay; she just knew it.

A perturbing memory flickered on the periphery of her mind. The condom Xander had used last night—she'd completely forgotten about them being in his bedside drawers. After Parker's birth, Xander had taken control of that side of things. They hadn't discussed it, but she suspected it was mostly because he didn't want to be hijacked into parenthood again. She'd had no objections. But how old would those condoms have been? And was the fact he'd reached for one so automatically an indicator that windows on the past were subconsciously opening for him again?

She leaned over the bed, slid open the drawer and

squinted a little as she tried to make out the date printed on the box. As she read the numbers her stomach somersaulted. Expired. Well and truly. She quickly put the box back in the drawer and closed it, her nerves jangling. Surely they'd still be safe, but just in case, she'd buy some more and replace the expired box.

Olivia grabbed her robe and shrugged it on. *A big breakfast*, she thought. Maybe pancakes made from scratch with maple syrup and bacon. She did a mental inventory of the contents of the refrigerator and her pantry as she made her way downstairs. After using the downstairs bathroom to quickly freshen up, she went into the kitchen and began whipping up the pancake batter.

She'd just put bacon on the grill when Xander came into the kitchen. She looked up and drank in the sight of him.

"Well, you look better than you have in a while," she said with a smile before crossing the kitchen to plant a kiss on his chin.

"I think we both know the reason for that," he said, playfully tugging on the sash of her robe and sliding his hands inside to cup her breasts.

Instantly her body caught flame. How had she survived without him all this time? she thought as he bent his head and kissed her thoroughly. Her body mourned the loss of his touch when he pulled away and straightened her robe.

"You hungry?" she asked. "I'm making pancakes."

"I'm always hungry around you," he said. "Are we eating in here or outside?"

"It's a beautiful day—why don't we eat on the patio?"

"I'll set the table."

While Olivia ladled batter into the heavy skillet she had on the stove top, Xander gathered up place mats, cutlery and condiments, and took them outside. She was humming with what she knew was a ridiculous smile on her face when the phone rang. After checking quickly on the bacon, she reached for the handset and answered the phone.

"Mrs. Jackson? It's Peter Clement here."

Olivia's joyful mood bubble burst instantly. Her lawyer. The one representing her in the divorce proceedings Xander had brought against her.

"Could you hold the line a moment?" she asked. Muting the phone, she popped her head out the back door. "Xander, could you keep an eye on the bacon for me and finish making the pancakes? I just have a call I need to take."

"Sure," he said, moving with his still-careful gait toward the house.

As soon as he was in the kitchen, Olivia went upstairs to their bedroom and sat on the bed.

"Sorry to keep you waiting."

"No problem," the lawyer said smoothly. "I've had a call from your husband's lawyers following up on the dissolution order I forwarded to you for your signature the other week. Did you receive it okay?"

"Y-yes, yes, I did. But there's been a change in circumstances."

"A change?" the lawyer pressed.

"Xander is back home with me. We…uh…I think it's safe to say we're no longer separated."

There was a long silence at the end of the phone before Olivia heard a faint sigh, followed by, "I see."

"Can we halt the divorce proceedings?"

"Is this something your husband is agreeable to?"

"Yes, of course." She crossed her fingers tight and prayed it wasn't a lie. It couldn't be. Not now. Not after last night.

"And has he instructed his lawyers in that regard?"

"Um, not yet. You see, he's been in an accident and unable to communicate with them—up until now, that is," she amended quickly. "But I'm sure he'll be in touch soon."

"This is quite irregular, Mrs. Jackson. Your husband has already signed the forms—"

A sound from behind her made her turn around quickly. Xander stood in the doorway. How long had he been there? How much had he heard? Too much, judging by the look on his face.

"Mr. Clement, I have to go. I'll call you later and confirm everything."

Before he could reply, she disconnected the call and dropped the phone onto the tangled sheets of the bed in which they'd made such sweet love last night. Her stomach lurched uncomfortably under Xander's gaze, and she reached out a hand toward him.

"Xander?"

"You mind telling me what that was about?" His voice was cold, distant and too much like that of the man who had left her two years ago.

"It…it's complicated."

She stood up, tugging the edges of her robe closer together—her hands fisting in the silky fabric.

"Then find simple words to explain. I'm sure I'll grasp them eventually even with my brain injury."

Sarcasm dripped from his every word, and she was suddenly reminded of the piercing intelligence he'd always exhibited, which she'd ridiculously assumed was impaired with his amnesia.

"Don't be like that," she implored. "Please."

"Then tell me, how should I be? Are you telling me I didn't overhear you instructing your lawyer to halt divorce proceedings? I'm assuming those would be *our* divorce proceedings?"

She quivered under the force of his slate-gray glare. "Y-yes," she admitted reluctantly.

"Divorce proceedings that obviously started before my accident."

She nodded, her throat squeezing closed on all the words she should have said long before now. She'd been an idiot. She'd had ample opportunity to be honest with him, and she'd held back the truth at every turn. Putting her own needs and desires, her own wish for a second chance, first before everything else. Including the man she loved. A sob rose from deep inside. Had she ruined everything?

Xander pushed a hand through his hair and strode across to the window, looking out at the Auckland harbor and the city's high-rises. That was his world—the one he had chosen. Not the enclosed space of this house they'd bought and renovated together, not the confines of the land surrounding it. This was supposed to be his sanctuary, not his prison, and she'd made it that by withholding their separation from him.

"How long had we been apart?" he demanded harshly, not even looking at her.

"Just over two years."

He abruptly turned around to face her, but she couldn't make out his features as he stood silhouetted against the window.

"And you brought me back here as if nothing had ever happened."

"Xander, I love you. I've always loved you. Of course I brought you home."

"But it's not my home anymore, is it?" he asked, his face tightening into a sharp mask of distrust. "That's why you didn't have all my clothes, why I didn't recognize everything...I can't believe you thought you could pull something like that off. What *were* you thinking?"

"I was thinking we deserved a second chance at making our marriage work," she said with a betraying wobble in her voice. "We still love one another, Xander. This past month has proven that to me as much as to you, hasn't it? Haven't we been great together? Wasn't last night—?"

"Don't," he said, slicing the air in front of him with the flat of his hand. "Don't bring last night into this. Do you have any idea how I feel right now?"

She shook her head again, unable to speak.

"I'm lost. I feel about as adrift as I did when I woke up at the hospital and found myself surrounded by people I didn't know and too weak to move myself without assistance. Except it's worse somehow because I should have been able to trust you."

Olivia moaned softly as the pain of his words struck home. He was right. She'd owed him the truth from the start.

"Why were we separated?" he asked, coming to stand in front of her.

Olivia's legs trembled, and she struggled to form the words in her mind into a sentence.

"We had begun to grow apart. I guess the gloss of our first year of marriage wore off pretty quickly. A lot of that is my fault. I made decisions about us that I should have included you in. Getting the dog was one of them."

She took in a deep breath, preparing to tell him about Parker, but an icy-cold fist clutched her heart and she couldn't push the words from inside her. Not yet, anyway. "We both got caught up in our separate lives and forgot how to be a couple. You spent a lot of time at work—initially, before you made partner, you put the time in so you could show them how good you were at your job. After that, you were proving you were worthy of the honor.

"I…I was unreasonable about it. I resented the additional hours you spent there, even though I knew you were doing it for us. We wanted to finish the house off quickly, and it was a juggle for us both. I was still teaching during the day and painting at night. When you were home, you expected me to be with you, but I had my own work to do, as well. We allowed ourselves to be at cross-purposes for too long, and we forgot how to be a couple."

What she said wasn't a lie, but it wasn't the whole truth, either. Their marriage hadn't been perfect before Parker had been born, but she'd ignored the cracks that had begun to show—plastering them up with her own optimism that as long as she stuck to her plan, everything would be okay.

But it wasn't okay. Not then and not now. Their marriage hadn't truly ended until they'd lost Parker—but the problems that had been in place all along were the reason why they hadn't been able to pull together after the death of their son. They'd gotten too used to going on their separate paths to find their way back to each other even in their time of greatest need.

"You don't exactly paint me in a very good light," Xander said. "I don't like the sound of who I was."

She stepped closer to him and laid one hand on his arm, taking heart when he didn't immediately shake her off. "Xander, it went both ways. I wasn't the easiest person to live with, either. We both had a lot of learning to do. We met, fell in love and got married so fast. Maybe we never really learned to be a couple like we should have. But I still love you. I've always loved you. Can you blame me for wanting to give us another chance?"

Xander looked at her and felt as if she'd become a stranger. She'd withheld something as important as their separation from him. A separation that had been on the brink of becoming permanent, according to the conversation he'd overheard.

And worse than the doubt and suspicion were the questions that now filled his mind. Why had he left her? Was there more to it than the growing apart? Was she keeping something else from him?

One thing she said, though, pushed past his anger and confusion to resonate inside him. She loved him; and he knew he loved her. Maybe that's why her betrayal in keeping the truth from him made him so angry. Was this the reason behind the disconnect he'd been feeling all this time?

Her fingers tightened on his arm. "Xander? Please, say something."

"I need to think."

He pulled away and left the room. Thundered down the stairs and out the front door. He vaguely heard Olivia's voice crying out behind him, but he daren't stop. He needed space and he needed time to himself. He powered down the hill, anger giving him a strength, coordination and speed he'd been lacking the past few weeks. His footsteps grew faster, until he broke into a jog. It wasn't long before a light sweat built up on his body and his lungs and muscles were screaming, reminding him that he was horribly out of condition and that if he kept this up, he'd likely be on bed rest again before he knew it.

He forced himself to slow down, to measure his pace. Automatically he went toward the beach. Seagulls wheeled and screamed on the air currents that swirled above the sandy shoreline, and he looked up, envying them the simplicity of their lives. But how had his own life grown so complicated? At what point had the marriage he'd entered into with Olivia become the broken thing she'd described to him just now?

He shook his head and began to walk along the beach, unheedful of the small waves that rushed up on the sand, drenching his sneaker-clad feet and the bottom of his jeans. The sand sucked at his feet, making walking difficult, but still he pushed on.

Why the hell couldn't he remember anything? The man she'd described, the driven creature who worked long hours and then expected her attention when he got home—that wasn't him. That wasn't who he remembered being, anyway. When and why had things changed so dramatically?

He remembered meeting Olivia at a fundraiser at an inner-city art gallery. He'd been drawn first to her beauty—her long red hair, porcelain-perfect skin and wide sparkling blue eyes had made his physical receptors stand up and take immediate notice. But it had been talking to her that had begun to win his guarded heart. He'd known he wanted her in his life right from that very first conversation, and it had been readily apparent that she felt the same way.

They'd spent that entire first weekend together. When they'd made love it hadn't felt too soon—it had felt perfect in every way. Six months later they were married and home owners and beginning to renovate the house he'd just fled from. Six years later they were separated and on the point of divorce. What on earth had happened in between?

He stopped walking and raised both hands to his head—squeezing hard on both sides as he tried to force his brain to remember. Nothing. Another wave came and sloshed over his feet, further drenching his jeans. He let his hands drop to his sides. He continued to the end of the beach and dropped down into a park bench on the edge of the strand.

Runners jogged by. Walkers walked. Dogs chased seagulls and sticks. Life went on. *His* life went on, even if he didn't remember it. There had to be something. Some way to trigger the things he'd lost, to remember the person he'd been. After ten minutes of staring at the sea a thought occurred to him. If he hadn't been living here in Devonport, with Olivia, where had he been living? Surely he had another home. A place filled with more recent memories that would trigger something in his uncooperative brain perhaps?

Olivia had to know where it was. The clothes she'd haphazardly shoved into their shared wardrobe had been a mixture of casual wear that he'd worn years ago and new items as foreign to him as pretty much everything else had become since coming home from the hospital. That meant she had to have picked up some things from where he lived. Which meant she could take him there.

He levered himself upright, his legs feeling decidedly overworked and unsteady as he turned and headed back on the paved path at the top of the strand and toward home. *Home?* No, he couldn't call it that. Not now. Maybe not ever again. Until he knew exactly why they were apart, exactly what his life had been like, he wondered if he'd ever belong anywhere ever again.

Eleven

Olivia clutched the now-cold mug of coffee she'd poured before sitting at the kitchen table. The breakfast she'd been cooking before the phone call from the lawyer had dried up in the warming oven. Xander had obviously finished cooking it, as she'd asked, and plated up their meals before coming to tell her it was ready. Before overhearing the conversation she'd have done anything to avoid sharing with him today. She'd finally had to throw the breakfast away, but she'd attempted to salvage the coffee. She'd even tried to drink it, but her stomach had protested—tying in knots as she wondered where Xander was.

She'd been frozen here since he'd left the house, alternately staring at the mug and then the clock on the wall as she worried herself sick about him. He'd been gone well over an hour. Unshed tears burned in her eyes. Where was he?

Maybe she should have run after him, wearing nothing but her robe, instead of remaining rooted to the bedroom floor until the front door had slammed closed. But she hadn't. Instead she'd showered quickly and dressed, then debated getting in the car and driving around looking for him. In the end she'd decided that would be a futile exercise. She simply had to wait for him to come back. *If* he came back.

A sound at the front door made her shoot up from her chair, unheeding as it tipped over behind her and bounced on the tiled floor.

"Xander? Are you okay? I've been worried sick—"

"I'm going upstairs to get changed. Then you're going to take me to where I've been living," he said bluntly.

"To where—?" Her throat closed up tight again.

He meant to his apartment. She couldn't refuse him as much as she wanted to.

"To my house, apartment. Whatever. Where I've been living. You know where it is, don't you?"

She looked up and met the accusation in his stormy eyes. She nodded slowly. "Yes, I've been there once, before you came home."

"Let's not call it home," he said bitterly. "It obviously hasn't been my home for a while."

She swallowed back the plea that she wished she had the courage to make to him. It could be his home again— it *had* been these past weeks. Why couldn't he just let them start afresh? She knew why. Xander was the kind of man who did nothing without weighing all the options, without being 100 percent certain of whatever he did. He didn't like surprises, and this morning had definitely been a very unwelcome one.

"Okay, let me know when you're ready."

"I'll be right down," he said and left the room.

Olivia took her mug to the sink and tipped out the congealed contents. Even thinking about the dash of milk she'd stirred into her coffee made her stomach lurch in protest.

The prospect of taking him back to his apartment terrified her. What if he remembered everything? The anger, the lies…the grief?

She had to face the truth. He may not want to even see her again after today. In fact, if he remembered the rest of his lost memories, he very likely would get on the phone to his lawyer and tell them to continue with the proceedings she'd requested a halt to. There was nothing she could do about it, and the helplessness that invaded every cell in her body was all-consuming.

Olivia found her handbag and car keys and went to the entrance hall to wait for him. The keys to his apartment were in the bottom of her bag, exactly where she'd left them the day she'd brought him home from the hospital. It felt like a lifetime ago.

Xander was dressed in a smart pair of dress trousers and a business shirt when he came back down. He'd obviously had a quick shower, and his hair was slicked back from his face. He'd trimmed his beard to a designer stubble. Now he looked far more like the corporate Xander who'd walked out on her two years ago.

"Ready?" she said, needing to fill the strained air between them with something, even something as inane as the one word she'd used.

Of course he was ready. He was here, wasn't he? Impatience rolled off him in waves.

"Let's go," he grunted and held the door open for her.

Even in his fury he couldn't stop being the gentleman he intrinsically had always been. His courtesy, however, brought her little comfort.

The drive toward the harbor bridge and into the city seemed to take forever in the frigid atmosphere in her car. Once they hit Quay Street, Xander shifted in his seat.

"Where are we going?"

She could tell it frustrated him to have to ask. "Parnell. You have a place on the top floor of one the high-rises."

He nodded and looked straight ahead, as if he couldn't wait to get there.

By the time Olivia pulled into the underground parking garage and directed Xander to the bank of elevators nearby, her nerves were as taut as violin strings. She felt as if the slightest thing would see her snap and fray apart. The trip up to Xander's floor was all too swift, and suddenly they were at the front door.

She dug in her bag and drew out the keys, holding them up between them.

"Do you want to do the honors?" she asked.

Xander took them from her and looked at the key ring. "I don't know which one it is," he said, a deep frown pulling between his brows.

She pointed to the one that would lead them inside and held her breath as he turned it in the lock and pushed the door open. Olivia followed him as he stepped inside. The air was a little stale, and there was a fine layer of dust everywhere after a month with no cleaning service. She almost ran into Xander's back when he stopped abruptly and stared around the open-plan living area off the entrance hall.

"Do you…is it… Is anything familiar to you?" she tentatively asked.

Xander simply shook his head.

He hated the place. Sure, it was functional—beautiful, even, in its starkness—and heavily masculine. But it didn't feel like home. The lack of a feminine touch, with not even so much as a vase on display in the built-in shelving along one wall, confirmed that he lived here alone. Of course, if he'd had a new partner, she'd have been the one at his bedside after he woke up, not Olivia.

He walked around the spacious living area and clamped down on the growl that rose in his throat. This place should at least feel familiar in some way. These were his things. His recent life. Yet he didn't sense even the remotest connection to anything, not like he did to some of the things back at the house across the harbor.

The anger that had buoyed him along since he'd overheard Olivia on the phone left him in a rush, only a deep sense of defeat remained in its wake. He looked around one more time. Still nothing. A hallway beckoned, but he found he lacked the energy to even want to push himself down that corridor and see what lay beyond it. A bedroom, no doubt. It would almost certainly feel as foreign to him as the rest of the apartment already did.

Weariness pulled at him with unrelenting strength. He didn't belong here, either.

"Take me back," he said roughly. "Please. I've had enough."

Olivia came to stand at his side. Everything about her seemed to be offering refuge, from the expression on her face to the arms she gingerly curved around his waist.

"Maybe losing your memory wasn't the worst thing, Xander. Have you stopped to consider that? We've been good together. Happy. It's proof we can do better together—*be* better together. Can't we just take that and build something great with it now all over again?"

He wanted to say yes, but some unnamable thing held him back. They started toward the door, then stopped abruptly at the sound of the doorbell, swiftly followed by the sound of a key being inserted and the door being opened.

Olivia's eyes opened in shock as a petite young woman let herself into Xander's apartment. She recognized her instantly. The woman had been an intern at Xander's office shortly after their marriage. Olivia knew she'd worked her way up since then. But what was Rachelle doing here, and why did she have a key to Xander's apartment? Her shock at seeing the woman was nothing to what came next.

"Rachelle, how are you?" Xander asked with a smile on his face that had been missing for the better part of today.

Olivia couldn't help it. She felt an immediate pang of jealousy. There'd always been something about Rachelle that had grated on her—a familiarity with Xander even when their marriage was at its best that had made Olivia feel as if she was operating off her back foot around her all the time.

Rachelle came forward and gave Xander a welcoming hug and kiss on the cheek. Olivia wondered if her eyes were turning an unbecoming shade of green as a wave of possessiveness swept through her. It was all she could manage to stand and smile politely, especially when what she wanted most was to drag the other woman off her husband and push her out the door. She took in a steadying breath. That wasn't her. She'd never been the jealous type, but Rachelle brought out the feral in her, always had.

"Xander! It's so good to see you," Rachelle gushed, still hugging him. "We were all so shocked at your accident. I'd have come to see you at the hospital, but they restricted visitors to immediate family only. But I called the hospital regularly and stayed up-to-date with your progress. Until recently, that is."

Rachelle finally looked at Olivia, who bit her tongue to keep from replying. The obvious reproach was there in the younger woman's words. Olivia lifted her chin, accepting the challenge.

"I've been in touch with Ken to let him know Xander was recuperating at home," she said firmly.

"Of course you have," Rachelle said with a slight curve of her lips. She turned her attention back to Xander. "I just thought I'd call in to see how Xander was and to see if there was anything he needed. This is his home, after all, isn't it? I didn't realize he was staying at your house." She turned to face Xander. "So, are you returning soon?"

Olivia held her breath. Was he?

Xander shook his head. "I don't know. I don't think so. Not yet, anyway."

Olivia fought to hold herself upright. No easy feat when she wanted to sag in relief.

"In fact," Olivia said with a forced smile, "we were just leaving."

"Oh," Rachelle said, disappointment clear in her face. "That's a shame. I've been looking forward to catching up."

Before Xander could respond, Olivia spoke again. "Perhaps another time."

She maintained eye contact with Rachelle, neither woman backing down from the silent challenge that hovered between them. Rachelle was the first to break.

"Of course," she muttered.

Xander excused himself to use the bathroom, leaving the two women alone in the foyer. Rachelle waited until they heard the bathroom door close before wheeling to face Olivia.

"He doesn't know, does he?"

"Know?" Olivia remained deliberately evasive.

"About you two. About your divorce. About Park—"

"He knows that we're separated and we're working through that. The doctors have said not to try and force anything."

"Olivia…"

"No." Olivia put up a hand as if she could physically stop the younger woman from doing anything she wanted to. "If his memory comes back, it will do so in its own good time."

"But what about when he comes back to work? Everyone there knows about his past. People will talk to him."

"But he's not fit to return to work yet anyway, so that's a bridge Xander and I will cross when we get to it."

Rachelle looked at her in disbelief. "I can't believe you're lying to him like this."

"I'm not lying," Olivia replied emphatically. *But I know I'm not exactly telling him the truth, either.* "Look I think it would be best if you leave. I'll take care of the plants before we go. You can leave your key with me."

Rachelle shook her head. "No. Xander gave me this key and if I give it back to anyone, it'll be to him."

Olivia didn't say anything, not wanting to push the issue and definitely not wanting to explore the idea of why Xander would give one of his colleagues a key to his apartment.

"You're going to have to tell him sometime," Rachelle continued. "If you don't, I will. He deserves to know. You can't just reclaim him like a lost puppy. He left you, Olivia. He had his reasons."

A sound down the hallway made both women turn and look. Xander—something was wrong, Olivia thought and quickly headed in his direction.

Xander stood at the basin in the bathroom, his hands gripping the white porcelain edge in a white-knuckled grip. A headache assailed him in ever-increasing waves. He had to lie down, to sleep, but he couldn't do that here. This place was all wrong. As angry as he was with Olivia, he needed her right now—needed to go back to their home. He must have called out, made some noise or something, because she was suddenly at his side, concern pulling her brows into a straight line and clouding her eyes.

"Another headache? Here," she said, rummaging through her handbag. "I brought some of your painkillers, just in case."

She pressed two tablets into his palm and quickly filled the water glass on the vanity with water and handed it to him.

He knocked the pills back with a grimace. "Take me back to the house, please."

"You don't want to take a rest here?"

He shook his head and immediately regretted it as spears of pain pushed behind his eyes. "Just get me out of here."

She slid a slender arm around his waist and tucked herself under his shoulder to support him. Slowly they made their way out of the room and down the hall. Rachelle still stood in the living room. He caught a glimpse of the shock on her face.

"I have to take him home," Olivia said with a proprietary note in her voice that even he, in his incapacitated state, didn't miss. "Please make sure you lock up behind you."

"Do you need me to help?" the other woman asked, stepping to his other side.

"We can manage," Olivia replied firmly and guided him to the door.

"Xander, I hope you're better soon. We miss you at the office…I miss you," Rachelle called out as they left the apartment.

The door swung closed behind them, and Xander winced again as it slammed. They made it down to the car and Olivia adjusted his seat back a little so he could recline and close his eyes. Throughout the drive back to

Devonport his mind continued to whirl around the stabs of pain that continued to probe his skull.

He'd thought the apartment would bring him answers. Instead it had only brought him more questions. Nothing had felt familiar or right or as if it truly belonged to him. Not the furnishings, not the clothes in the wardrobe he'd gotten a glimpse of before heading into the bathroom— not even the cups and saucers he'd seen in the kitchen cupboards when he'd looked there.

And then there was Rachelle. She'd been so familiar with him, as if they were far more intimately acquainted than mere work colleagues. Had he moved on from his relationship with Olivia so quickly? It seemed almost impossible to believe. Yes, Rachelle was attractive—if you liked petite brunettes with perfect proportions. But he had a hankering for slender redheads, one in particular—even if she had been holding out on him about them living apart.

But Rachelle. He'd recognized her. She was a part of his past, although he couldn't remember all of it. She was deeply familiar to him, more so than could be accounted for with his memories from six years prior. Did that explain why, when she'd come into the apartment, she'd gone straightaway to hug him and kiss him? The fact that her kiss had landed on his cheek had been a result of him moving slightly at the last minute; otherwise he knew she'd have planted one right on his lips. Judging by Olivia's reaction to the other woman, he doubted very much that she'd have been pleased about that happening.

Still, it made him wonder what his relationship with Rachelle was. She was more than just a work acquaintance. He knew that much from her behavior, not to mention the fact she had a key to his apartment.

Had he gone from one failed whirlwind relationship into another? It didn't seem right, not likely somehow. If only he could remember!

Twelve

Olivia lifted Xander's feet up onto the sofa and drew the drapes in the sitting room to block out the afternoon sunlight. He hadn't even wanted to tackle the stairs when they'd arrived home. His headache must be bad, she thought, checking to see that his chest continued to rise and fall as he slipped deeper into sleep.

But she had him back here; that was the important thing. He could so easily have told her to leave him at the apartment. Maybe even leave him with Rachelle. The very thought painted a bitter taste on Olivia's tongue. She'd tried to like Rachelle on the occasions she'd met her at company functions, back before her marriage had ended. Had even attempted once or twice to be friendly. But the other woman had always carried herself with an air that implied she believed she was several notches above Olivia on the totem pole of life. How could she not be when Olivia had been, first, a schoolteacher, then, second, a stay-at-home mother while Rachelle was actively and successfully pursuing a high-flying career?

Rachelle had never made a secret of the fact she found Xander attractive, and Olivia had felt threatened by her confidence, not to mention the increasing number of hours in a week Rachelle spent with Olivia's husband. But Olivia had never once believed that Xander would embark on an affair. That simply had never been his style. But then, he'd changed so much after Parker's death. Maybe he *had* picked up with Rachelle after he'd moved out. Goodness only knew the woman hadn't been subtle about her attraction to him.

In the two years of their separation, Olivia had been working so hard just to keep herself from falling apart over the loss of both her son and her husband that she'd never stopped to consider that Xander might have gotten himself a girlfriend. Hadn't wanted to consider it, more like, she forced herself to admit. In fact, the idea hadn't even occurred to her when she'd brought him home from the hospital. Why should it, when the doctors had never mentioned Xander having any visitors other than his mother? Surely a girlfriend would have had some visiting rights?

She pushed the thought out of her head, preferring not to allow her mind to stray down that path. But she couldn't help it—she kept seeing Rachelle insert herself into Xander's arms and kiss him. And not only had Xander recognized Rachelle; he hadn't exactly pushed her away.

Olivia forced herself to do the math about just how far back in his memory Rachelle could be found. Rachelle had started at Xander's firm before Parker had been born. Did his memory loss stretch back that far or was he actually beginning to recall things and people from his missing years?

She checked on Xander one more time; then, satisfied he was deeply asleep, she went to the kitchen to make herself coffee. As she automatically started the machine and poured milk in a mug, her thoughts kept straying back to Rachelle and Xander—and how at home the woman had seemed in Xander's apartment. Just how large of a role did she play in Xander's life outside work, and how long had she been there? A year? Two years? Longer? Had she been hovering in the background even during Xander's marriage, just waiting to snatch him up as soon as he was free? And had Olivia herself furthered the woman's plans by not being the wife she should have been? Had her focus on her newborn son and then her developing little boy been so singular that it had driven her husband away from her and into the arms of another woman? It wouldn't be the first time in history that had happened.

But she hadn't been the only one wrapped up in Parker. While Xander hadn't initially been thrilled about the pregnancy, especially when he'd discovered it hadn't been a blessed accident but a decision she'd made without him, he'd been as besotted with their son on his birth as she'd been. Had they both gotten so caught up in being parents that they forgot to be partners? Was that something Rachelle had taught him how to be once more?

Fear and insecurity wended their way into Olivia's psyche like the persistent vines of a climbing weed. She couldn't lose him again—she simply couldn't. She hadn't fought when he'd left. And even though on the surface, at least, she'd looked as if she was coping, she'd still been too bruised, too grief-stricken, after Parker's death to have the energy. But she had energy now, and she knew she had to dig down deep and fight for her man. To consolidate her place in his life and in his heart so that they could work through everything together.

The second she'd seen him at the hospital, she'd known she'd do anything for him. She loved him as much now as she had when they'd first fallen headlong into love together.

Nothing, and no one, was going to get in the way of her repairing their broken marriage.

They deserved a new and better start together. She'd certainly learned from her past mistakes and accepted there had been many of them. She wasn't perfect by any standard, but, then again, neither was Xander. She loved him, imperfections and all. She'd grown as a person since he'd left. Deep in her heart Olivia knew that as long as Xander was willing, they could really make a go of things. They could build their marriage into the loving and lasting state of union she'd always wanted.

What if he wasn't willing? What if his recall, if it came, included every awful word she'd flung at him in grief and anger in the aftermath of Parker's death? What if he couldn't forgive her those things? She couldn't blame him if they were enough to make him leave. After all, they'd had that effect the first time around, hadn't they? She closed her eyes on the memory, and sucked in a deep breath. This time would be better. They had the cushion of time and distance now, and surely these past few weeks had shown him that they were far better together than apart?

So what could she do? There was only one thing that echoed in her mind. She had to give herself to him. Heart and soul, holding nothing back.

The afternoon passed in a blur. Xander locked himself in the office off her studio and told her quite emphatically he didn't want to be disturbed. She filled her afternoon packing her car with the paintings she needed to deliver to a gallery in the morning. With Christmas in only four weeks' time, she and her agent were hopeful for a high level of sales, especially now demand for her work was growing.

By the time she prepared their evening meal, Xander still hadn't come out of the office. Worried about him now, especially in light of the severity of the headache he'd suffered that morning, she risked knocking on the office door and popping her head in without waiting for him to respond.

"Xander? Are you hungry? Dinner's ready."

She'd gone to the bother of making one of his favorites—steak Diane with fresh spears of asparagus and baby potatoes. A pathetic peace offering given the day they'd had, but in lieu of being able to talk this out with him she'd felt she had to do something.

"I'm not hungry," he said without turning his head from the computer screen on his desk.

She ventured into the room, looking to see what held his attention so strongly. A ripple of unease went from head to toe as she recognized the staff profile page from Xander's firm. Up front and center was a photograph of Rachelle. Olivia's hands curled into impotent fists as she forced herself to breathe out the tension that gripped her. One by one, she uncurled her fingers.

"It's steak Diane. Would you like me to bring a tray out to you here?"

"Trying to butter me up?" he asked, finally turning to look up at her. A cynical smile twisted his lips.

"No. Well, not entirely. I'm not sure that any food could make up for the shock you had today. I'm sorry, Xander. I meant to tell you sooner. I just…couldn't."

Xander rubbed at his eyes wearily. "I guess it's not the kind of conversation you have on an everyday basis with a convalescent husband, is it?"

Olivia felt the tight set of her shoulders ease a fraction. It was an olive branch. One she'd grasp with both hands.

"Come, eat," she implored, gingerly putting a hand on his shoulder.

He lifted his hand and briefly laid it over hers. "I'll be through in a minute. Just let me shut everything down."

She wanted to stay and wait for him. To ask him if he'd discovered whatever it was he'd been looking for, but she knew she'd be pushing her luck. Slowly, she walked back to the kitchen and plated up their meal. All the while, the image of Rachelle's profile photo burned through her mind. Why was he looking at it? Was he remembering what they'd been to each other? Were his feelings for the other woman resurfacing? Thinking about losing Xander again just killed her inside.

The past weeks had taught her they belonged together, now more than ever. She loved him with every breath in her body, every movement, every thought. She just had to prove it.

Xander was surprised when Olivia went up to bed ahead of him. Then again, she hadn't slept half the afternoon away like he had. She'd been on tenterhooks all night, and he'd had the impression she'd been on the verge of saying or asking something several times, only to back down at the last minute.

Today had been a revelation for them both. He'd had the shock of learning about their separation, and Olivia had certainly looked stunned when Rachelle turned up at his apartment.

He thumbed the TV remote, coasting through the channels mindlessly as he turned over the things he'd discovered today. None of it made any sense to him, no matter how he approached it. He didn't feel as if he'd developed a romantic bond with Rachelle at all. Surely if they'd been a couple, he'd have experienced something when he'd seen her. He'd only felt mildly uncomfortable when she'd hugged and kissed him. Not like when he touched Olivia and certainly not at all like when they'd made love last night.

His fingers curled tight around the remote, making the plastic squeak. Even just thinking about his wife—and she was still his wife—was enough to awaken a hunger for her in him. How could things have gotten so bad between them that they'd separated? Why hadn't they been able to work things out?

With a harsh sigh, Xander switched off the TV and got up to turn off the light and head upstairs. He may as well lie awake in bed upstairs as sit here alone with the inanity of the TV clogging his brain.

He took the stairs confidently, but he hesitated when he reached the top. There was muted light coming from the bedroom, and a delicate scent wafted toward him. Vanilla maybe? His footfall was silent on the carpet runner that led down the hall toward their bedroom. He hesitated in the doorway, taking in the room and the setting Olivia had obviously gone to some lengths to create.

The drapes were drawn but billowed softly in the evening breeze. Dotted around the room—on top of the bureau, the bedside tables, the mantelpiece of the fireplace—were small groups of candles in glass jars. The scent in the room was stronger, and he felt his body respond to the seductive scene.

Olivia came through from the bathroom, wrapped only in a towel. His breath caught in his lungs as his eyes traveled hungrily over the smooth creamy set of her shoulders. His gaze lingered on the hollows of her collarbone before dropping lower to the shadowed valley of her breasts, exposed above the moss-green towel that was a perfect foil for her hair.

She'd clipped her hair up loosely, exposing the delicious curve of her neck, and silky strands tumbled to drift across her shoulders. He was struck with a sudden deep envy of those strands.

"Looks like you're trying to seduce me here," he said, his voice thick with desire.

"Is it working?" she said, her voice equally husky.

"I'm not sure. Maybe you need to keep going."

He watched as she slowly untucked the end of her towel. The material dropped away, revealing her beautiful body in one fell swoop. Xander's mouth dried. He swallowed, hard. Olivia reached a slender arm up and tugged a few pins loose, sending her hair cascading over her shoulders. Her nipples, normally a pale pink, had deepened in color and were tight buds on her full breasts— just begging for his touch, his lips, his tongue.

Xander's body felt taut and hot, his clothing restrictive as his erection hardened even more. She was so beautiful, and she was walking toward him. He forced himself to keep his hands by his sides as she stopped in front of him. Clearly she had an agenda—far be it from him to make any changes to whatever she had planned.

"How about now?" she asked.

She caressed one breast with her hand, stroking lightly across her nipple, and he watched, mesmerized, as her skin grew even tauter.

"Yeah," he answered, his voice gruff with the need that pulsed through him like a living thing. "It's working."

A tiny smile played around her lips. "Good," she whispered before going up on her toes and kissing his lips.

It was a tease, just the lightest of butterfly caresses, but it acted like a torch to volatile liquid. In that instant he was fully aflame—for her. She must have sensed it, because her fingers were at the buttons of his shirt, deftly plucking them open and pushing the garment off his shoulders to fall silently to the floor. Her hands spread like warm fans across his skin, rubbing and caressing him. He was hot for her, so very hot his blood all but boiled in his veins.

He reached up to touch her and pull her to him, but she grabbed his hands and held them at his sides.

"Let me," she whispered. "Let me love you."

She bent her head and kissed his chest, tracing tiny lines with her tongue and then kissing him again. And then her tongue was swirling in tight little circles around his nipple. He groaned out loud, couldn't help it, as a spear of need bolted through his entire body.

Olivia's hands were at his belt, undoing the buckle, and then at the button of his trousers, then—finally— at the zipper of his pants. She slid one hand inside the waistband of his briefs, her fingers like silk as they closed around his thickness. She stroked him slow and firm, and it was all he could do to remain a passive subject in this sensual onslaught on his body.

He felt her move before he fully understood her intentions, felt his trousers and his briefs disappear down the length of his legs, felt Olivia's hot breath against his thighs.

Felt her mouth close around his aching flesh.

"Livvy," he groaned, tangling his fingers in her hair as she used her tongue in wicked ways that fried his synapses.

And then he was beyond thought, locked only in sensation until even sensation became too much and he lost control, soaring on the wave of a climax that initially made his entire body rigid as pulse after pulse of pleasure rocketed through him then left him weak and shaking with its magnitude.

Xander pulled Olivia up and into his embrace, holding her close to him until his heart rate approximated that of a normal person's.

"Ready for round two?" Olivia asked softly.

"Round two?"

"Yeah. I have a lot of time and a lot of loving to make up."

"Don't we both," he agreed, pressing a kiss on to the top of her head.

He let her walk him backward toward the bed, where she pushed him onto the mattress and bent to remove his clothes from where they'd tangled at his feet. She rubbed her hands over his body, from the tips of his toes, up his legs and over his abdomen as she positioned herself on the bed over him.

"I've missed you, Xander," she said, her blue eyes staring straight into his—honestly burning there like an incandescent flame.

In the gilded light of the candles' glow she looked more beautiful than he'd ever seen her. Her hair was a tangle of gold-red waves that tumbled in glorious abandon over her shoulders to caress her skin. Her breasts were high and full, her nipples ripe for his touch—and touch them he did, taking them between thumb and forefinger and watching her face as he teased and tugged on them.

His body was quick to recover from his earlier climax, and he felt himself harden beneath the heat that poured from her. He slipped one hand between her legs, smiling as he discovered her readiness.

"Show me," he urged her. "Show me how much you missed me."

She reached for a condom she must have slipped under the pillow earlier and covered him, taking her time over it and turning the act into an art form of simultaneous seduction and torment. Then she positioned him at her entrance and slowly took him inside her body. Her thigh muscles trembled as she accepted him deep within.

"You feel so right inside me," she gasped with a strangled breath. "I never want to let you go."

Then she started to move, and all he could do was glory in the pleasure she gave him, holding on to her hips as she rocked and swayed and dragged them both toward a peak that arrived all too quickly and yet not fast enough at the same time. She melted onto his body, her curves fitting against him like a puzzle piece made only for him. He folded his arms around her and held her tight, lost in the perfection of the moment.

Much later, Olivia rose and disposed of the condom they'd used. He watched her through hooded lids as she extinguished one candle after another. The room softened into gray, then into darkness as she worked her way closer to the bed and climbed in next to him. He rolled her onto her side and curved his body around her back, marveling again at the perfection of how they fit together.

"Good night, Xander," she whispered in the darkness. "And...I'm sorry about today."

In response he squeezed her tight and pressed a kiss at her nape. He listened as she drifted into sleep.

As sorry as she truly seemed to be, he felt as though she still held something back. Something vital and just out of reach of his battered mind. Would he ever remember?

Thirteen

Olivia woke late the next morning feel both well used and well satisfied. She turned her head on the pillow and looked straight into Xander's clear gray eyes.

"I love you," she whispered. "So very much."

She pushed back his hair from his forehead and leaned over to kiss him before rolling over and getting out of bed. Xander caught her wrist, tugging her back down into his arms.

"Stay," he commanded, lifting her hair and nuzzling the back of her neck.

Goose bumps peppered her body. Oh, he knew all the right places, and he took his time exploring them over and over again. It was nearly eleven when they rose and Xander joined her in the shower.

"We should just spend the whole day naked," he said, slowly soaping up her body and sending her heart rate into overdrive all over again.

"I wish I could, but I have to take my work to the gallery. I'll be busy all afternoon and into the evening with the exhibition opening." She rinsed off, then pushed open the shower door. "I have to do this, Xander. It's my career now, my reputation as an artist."

"Then go do your thing. I'll find something to keep me occupied today."

"You could come, too," she offered, feeling a spark of hope light within her.

"Next time maybe, okay?"

Olivia bit back her disappointment. She knew it would probably be too much for Xander to be out most of the afternoon and evening, but she was reluctant to break the bubble of this new closeness they shared. She quickly dried herself then blow-dried her hair. Xander finished in the shower and then dried and dressed right next to her. Olivia tried to think back to the last time they'd been in the bathroom together like this. It was such a normal everyday part of life, and she'd missed it more than she realized as she teased him about hogging the mirror.

"You're taking your beard off?" she asked.

"Yeah," he said, lathering up with shaving foam. "I'm ready to be me again."

Olivia's brush tangled in her hair, making her wince. Ready to be him again? What exactly did he mean by that? She disentangled the bristles from her hair and put the brush and dryer on the bathroom vanity before sliding her arms around Xander's naked waist.

"I kind of like the person you are now," she said, pressing a kiss between his shoulders.

"You didn't like the old me?" he asked, halting midstroke with his razor, his eyes meeting hers in the mirror.

"I loved the old you, too, Xander. But we've both changed. I like the person I am now better, too. Maybe that was part of the problem before. I was always trying to be something or someone else. Maybe I need to take a leaf out of your book and just be me again."

She pulled away from him and finished her hair—the noise of the hair-dryer making further conversation difficult. The stress and worries of the day before still lingered too close to the surface for her. If she didn't have to be away from the house today, she most definitely wouldn't be. But she'd been telling the truth when she'd said that her career and her reputation rested on this show. The gallery was one of the most prestigious in Auckland, and she considered herself fortunate to receive an invitation to exhibit there. Of course the cut the gallery would get on any sale was substantial, she reflected, but the exposure her work would receive was worth more than money.

Later, after they'd had fluffy omelets with chopped fresh chives and bacon, hot coffee and toast, Xander helped her carry the last of her canvases out to her car.

"Thanks," Olivia said as she closed the back on her station wagon. "I'm not sure what time I'll be home, but I'll probably be late, after dinner anyway."

"I can look after myself."

"And you promise that if you get a headache, you'll take your pills and rest?"

"You don't need to babysit me, remember?"

"I know." She pressed her hand against his cheek. "But I worry about you."

"I'll take care, I promise," he said solemnly before turning his head to kiss the inside of her palm.

Across the street Olivia caught a glimpse of one of their neighbors putting Christmas lights up in the eaves of their house. It reminded her again that the holiday was less than four weeks away. It gave her an idea.

"Maybe when I get home—or if I'm too late, maybe tomorrow—we can put up the Christmas tree. I didn't bother when…" Her voice trailed off for a moment before she took a deep breath. She had to get over her reluctance to talk about the past. "When we were separated. It brought back too many memories of the fun we used to have. Anyway, I'll go up to the attic and get the stuff down for us when I get back, okay?"

"That sounds like a good idea," Xander agreed. "I'd like that. Now, you'd better get going. I thought you didn't want to be late?"

Olivia glanced at her wristwatch and exclaimed in shock. "Oh, is that the time already? You're such a distraction!"

He laughed and swooped in for another kiss, this time a lingering caress full of promise. "Hurry back—I'll be waiting."

Olivia drove away with a last glance in the rearview mirror. Xander stood in the driveway, hands resting on his hips, watching her go. He made it so hard to leave him behind, for more reasons than she cared to examine. The shadow of a passing cloud suddenly obscured the sun, darkening the road before her and making her push her sunglasses up onto her head. A shiver traveled down her spine. Olivia shook off the sensation, not wanting to examine the sudden sense of unease that gripped her.

It was just because she was leaving Xander for several hours on his own, she rationalized. Since he'd been home again, the longest she'd left him was a couple of hours while she ran errands or went shopping. It was natural to feel uneasy, but there was no cause for alarm. Nothing would go wrong.

Xander watched her car turn out the drive and the automatic gates swing shut behind it. The gate. There was something about the gate, some memory attached to it that was just out of reach. A sharp stab of pain made its presence felt behind his eye, and he closed his eyes and shook his head slightly to rid himself of the pain.

Take your pills. It was as if Olivia's voice were stuck in his head, he thought with a smile as he headed back into the house. Well, he'd promised her he'd look after himself. And, he had to admit, he had no desire for a repeat of the headache that had struck him yesterday. Inside, he found the painkillers and took the required dose, then retired to the hammock for a while until the nagging pain eased off. It didn't take long.

While he rested, he thought about what he should do to fill the hours until Olivia returned. The Christmas tree! Of course. He knew she'd mentioned putting it up together, but he also knew she'd love the surprise of seeing it decorated and lit in the large front bay window to welcome her home.

They'd always stored the tree in the attic, and, since she'd said she hadn't even put it up the past couple of years, he shouldn't have too much trouble finding it. Motivated by the idea of her pleasure in seeing the tree finished, he went inside and upstairs. The stairs to the attic were as narrow as he remembered them, and he fought back an odd sense of light-headedness as he placed his foot on the first tread.

At the top of the stairs, he pushed open the door into the attic, taking a bit of time to allow his eyes to adjust to the gloom. Light streamed in from the small diamond-paned windows at each end of the attic and dust motes danced on the beams. Xander sneezed and cursed under his breath.

Moving farther into the attic, he got his bearings and looked around at the boxes and shrouded pieces of furniture they'd stored there. He shifted a few cartons in an attempt to get to where he last remembered seeing the tree and decorations. If Olivia had told the truth, they'd be exactly where he himself had put them.

He straightened for a moment. *If* Olivia had told the

truth? Why would he think she'd lie about something like this? Why would she lie to him about anything? *Maybe because she lied to you about your separation*, a voice echoed in the back of his head. He pushed the thought down. She'd explained why she'd withheld that piece of information. Sure, he didn't agree with her choice, but if they were to move forward, he had to be willing to get past it. She'd accepted some of the blame for what had gone wrong between them. Considering what he knew of himself along with what she *had* told him, he could see how easily they could have drifted apart.

Born the youngest of two boys, he'd pretty much always been treated as an only child after his older brother died in a drowning accident when Xander was only about three years old. Looking back, he could see how his parents had each coped in their own ways. His mother by becoming a distant workaholic and his father, sadly, by retreating into himself and becoming unable to work at all.

Xander still remembered coming home from school and letting himself into their home, knowing his mother would still be at work and wondering if that particular day would be one where his father would be happy to come outside and kick a football with him or whether Xander would end up sitting on the floor outside his parents' bedroom, listening to his father sob quietly as he remained locked in grief for the son he'd never see grow up.

There was probably more of his mother's influence in him than his father's, Xander acknowledged. If nothing else, he'd always fought hard to live by his mother's example. Never letting life get him down, dealing with his grief privately and always striving hard for the future.

While he'd never seen his father as weak, because even as a child he'd understood what his father was going through had little to do with strength or weakness, he hadn't wanted to *feel* as overwhelmingly as his father had either. As a result, he'd always controlled his emotions strictly, keeping them on a tight rein. Xander hadn't dared to experience extreme highs or extreme lows in his personal life; he had, instead, poured himself into work and achievement. Now he wondered if that driven part of him had also been a part of what had put a wedge between him and Olivia? He couldn't remember, no matter how hard he tried.

What he did know was that he was prepared to give her the benefit of the doubt and to give their marriage another chance. Perhaps the accident and his amnesia were a good thing after all. He knew he could be stubborn and move on if he thought something wasn't working. Rather than work on their marriage, he would have rejected any overtures she'd made to work things out.

Even so, he couldn't deny the niggling feeling that there was more to their separation than the brief explanation she'd given him yesterday. And then there was the matter of Rachelle and the fact she had a key to his apartment. Something really didn't feel right about that, but he couldn't put his finger on it. He would, though. He felt so much better. Stronger both mentally and physically, except for these bloody headaches, he thought as he shifted a few more cartons, then squatted down to read the lettering on a box shoved to the back.

He recognized the writing—it was his own. The box was ignominiously labeled "Stuff." He tugged it toward him and opened the flaps. In it were framed certificates and some old photo albums. A surge of excitement filled him. Maybe the contents would cast some light over his lost years. He pulled out the first album and absently thumbed through it. It dated back to his years in university, before he'd met Olivia. No, there was nothing there that he didn't know well already.

He shoved the albums and certificates back in the box and pushed it back against the wall. With the digital age it was more than likely there were no physical albums of his more recent years. Maybe he needed to look harder at his computer files. See what was there that dated back from when he could last remember and up until now.

But before he could do that, he needed to find the Christmas decorations. Xander dug around a few more boxes but ended up with nothing more than a sneezing fit. He was just about to give up completely when he spotted two more boxes in a dark corner. Maybe this was what he'd been looking for.

He dragged the boxes under the remaining light. They weren't labeled like all the others were. Neither looked like the long narrow carton he knew had always stored the tree, but maybe one held the decorations. There was definitely something familiar about them.

A weird sensation swept through him, making him feel a little dizzy again as he rocked back on his heels. He shrugged it off, thinking that he probably just needed some fresh air. The tiny ventilation holes in the eaves near the windows weren't the most efficient. He'd been up there awhile already, and, with the sun beating down on the iron roof, it was getting pretty hot.

Xander tugged at the tape binding the first box with a grunt of determination. It came away with a satisfying sound. Once again that feeling of being off balance assailed him. Xander closed his eyes for a brief moment and waited for the sensation to pass. This one was worse than the last and left him sick to his stomach. He swallowed and forced his eyes open.

"Just this one," he said aloud as he lifted the flaps. "Then I'm heading back downstairs. What the—?"

His voice trailed off into silence as he pulled out the first of the items inside. A child's clothing, precisely folded in layers—a little boy's things, to be more precise. Xander put them to one side and reached in again. Toys this time. A teddy, a few die-cast trains and cars.

His stomach lurched, and Xander fought back the bile that crept up his throat. He *knew* these things. These pieces of another life, another time. The frustrating sense of limbo he'd been living in since waking up in the hospital began to peel away from him, layer after layer. The hairs on the back of his neck stood on full alert, and an icy shiver traced down his spine.

Without another thought he tore open the second box. Cold sweat drenched his body. More clothes, more toys and, near the bottom, photo albums. He lifted them from the box. Even in the muted light of the attic he could see the dates on the albums. He picked up the oldest of them and slowly opened the cover. There on the first page was a grainy sonogram picture. He traced the edges of the tiny blur on the picture with the tip of one finger as a powerful wave of déjà vu swept over him. And with it, a memory. A sense of excitement and fear and love, all in one massive bundle of emotion. And then loss. Aching, wrenching, tearing loss.

Xander turned the page of the album to a photo of Olivia, a younger and more carefree Olivia than the one he'd seen off today. There was a series of photos of her, first with a big smile and flat tummy, all the way through to a photo of her with her belly swollen with pregnancy and a finger pointing to a date circled on the calendar.

The next page saw him staring at himself, proudly holding a squalling newborn infant.

His son.

Fourteen

A sob tore from Xander's throat and his chest tightened, making every breath a struggle. *He remembered.* He remembered everything, all the way back to the day that Olivia told him she was pregnant—and the fight they'd had that night over her news.

He'd been furious with her for taking that step without his knowledge. It hadn't been an accident. It had been a calculated decision she'd made without him. He hadn't been ready. He could still recall the heady rush of their relationship, their haste to marry and build a life together. Hell, he'd barely come to terms with their closeness before she was telling him they had to make room for another person in their lives. A person who'd depend on them for everything.

Xander hadn't known if he had it in him to love even more than he already loved Olivia—at least not until he'd experienced the joy of Parker's birth. Tears ran unchecked down Xander's cheeks as he turned more pages, then reached for the next album and the next. Each one cataloguing their beautiful little boy's life, until there was no more. The last photos were of Parker's third birthday in the backyard. A pirate theme had been the order of the day, and even Xander had dressed in kind.

They'd been so happy. So complete. And then, with one stupid forgetful moment on his part, it had all ended.

The devastation of Parker's death, along with the certainty that he could have prevented it, had left Xander crushed by guilt. He wiped at his face, trying to stem the tears that wouldn't stop falling. This was what he'd forgotten. This was what he'd built walls around his heart and his mind for. To stem the searing, clawing pain that now threatened to tear him into tiny pieces.

Xander staggered to his feet, leaving the albums and the toys and clothes scattered around the cartons on the floor. He wobbled toward the doorway and stumbled down the stairs, as uncoordinated and clumsy as he'd been in those early days back in the hospital. At the bottom of the stairs he turned right and went straight to the bedroom next to his old home office.

Now he understood why his office had always been here. He'd hated every second he had to spend away from home when Parker had been alive. With this home office, he'd had the best of both worlds. Able to watch his son grow and learn every day, and meet the demands of his career and provide for his family at the same time.

His family. Their little unit of three. Xander could never have believed that the power of their triangle could ever have been torn apart. Hadn't understood that when you ripped away one edge of the triangle that the other two sides would collapse. Not together. No. But apart. In their grief, he and Olivia had inexorably turned away from each other.

He pushed open the bedroom door and looked around the bare walls and floor. The only thing that remained

was a bureau that had stored Parker's clothes. Olivia had
gotten rid of everything else. She'd wiped their son's existence from their home, in fact, from their very lives
with clinical precision—just like his mother had when
Xander's brother had died.

Xander dropped to his knees. Grief crashed over him
with the power of a tidal wave. It felt as raw and as painfully fresh as if it had been only yesterday that he'd been
forced to say goodbye to his son. The child of his body,
of his heart. He roared in frustration and anger and sorrow, the sounds coming from deep inside him. Sounds
he'd never allowed out, ever, but now it was as if he
couldn't stop them.

He had no idea what the time was when he pulled himself back to his feet and made his way to his bedroom.
No, not his bedroom anymore. Olivia's. He'd made his
home elsewhere, and now he knew why. He went into
the bathroom and showered again, all the while attempting to block out the memory of the last time, only hours
ago, that he'd shared this same space with Olivia, and
what they'd done.

The memory wouldn't be suppressed. His body, traitor
that it was, stirred to life at the images running through
his mind. He turned the mixer to cold, standing beneath
the spray until the pain of the icy water was almost equal
to the pain that pulsed in the region of his heart.

He leaned his forearms on the shower wall and let his
head drop between his shoulders, allowing the water to
pound on the back of his neck and down his back. Questions whirled in his mind. Why had she kept this from
him? What had she been thinking? Why hadn't she told
him everything when she'd had the chance to yesterday?

By the time he turned off the water and stepped out of
the shower to dry himself he was no closer to finding any
answers. She'd tricked him into coming here and she'd

tricked him into staying—just as she'd tricked him into parenthood. Why?

Xander studied his reflection in the mirror, hardly recognizing the man whose tortured gray eyes stared back at him. He couldn't stay here. He couldn't listen to another lie from Olivia's lips. The betrayal of what she'd done was as excruciatingly painful now as the words she'd flung at him after Parker had died had been.

They'd still been in the emergency room. Pushed to one side while the doctors and nurses had worked frantically to save Parker's life. Until they accepted that nothing they did made any difference. Until the frenetic busyness fell silent and Olivia had turned to him and said it was all his fault. He hadn't wanted Parker and now her precious child was gone. Oh, she'd apologized afterward, but once spoken, the words couldn't be unsaid. Their hurt had spread in him like a voracious disease. Eating away at him until he had nothing left to give.

She'd blamed him for their son's death, but no more than he'd blamed himself. It had driven a wedge between them, creating a void that might possibly have been repaired had he needed her less and she'd needed him more. And he had needed her. The depth of his grief terrified him, made him afraid he would sink into the abyss of misery that had claimed his father. So he'd made a tactical withdrawal from his emotions, and, along with that decision, Xander had pulled away from his wife. And she'd done nothing to pull him back again—not until she'd shown up at his hospital room with a smile and a lie.

Xander picked his clothes up from the floor and bundled them up into a ball. They stank of his fear for what he'd discovered upstairs in the attic and of his grief and anger. He never wanted to see them again. He grabbed clean clothes from the bureau and the wardrobe, then yanked everything else he owned off its hanger and from its drawer and piled it all onto the bed.

Rummaging in the hall cupboard unearthed a suitcase that looked both new and familiar. He remembered buying it before a trip to Japan last year. Olivia must have brought his things from his apartment in it. He squeezed his clothing into the case and zipped it closed. Then he picked it and the bundle of clothes he'd discarded up and carried them downstairs. The case he left just inside the sitting room. The other things he shoved in the trash bin outside the back door.

He should just go, he thought. Leave now before she came back. But some perverse masochistic impulse urged him to stay. To face Olivia and to ask her what the hell she'd been thinking. Masochistic? No, it wasn't masochism to want answers. He deserved the truth from her, at last. No more subterfuge, no more lies or half truths. Everything.

Olivia was on a high when she pulled her car into the drive. The exhibition had been an enormous success. The gallery owner had been thrilled not only with the commissions they'd earned but also with the requests for more of her work in the future. There was international interest in her work, too. Sure, she knew better than to think her success from this point out was guaranteed, but tonight the world was her oyster. She couldn't wait to share the news with Xander.

She looked up at the house as she rolled to a stop outside the garage. It hadn't been dark long, but no lights were on inside. At least not at the front of the house. Maybe he was around the back or even in his office in the cottage.

Grabbing her bag and the bottle of champagne the gallery owner had given her before she'd left the exhibition, she got out of the car, quickly walked up the front path and let herself inside.

"Xander?" she called, clicking on the hall light.

A sound in the sitting room made her halt in her tracks and change direction.

"Xander? Are you okay?" she asked, turning on the overhead light in the room as she entered it. "I hope you're up to celebrating. The exhibition was fab—"

Her voice broke off as she took in the appearance of the man sitting in one of the armchairs, dressed in what she thought of as his "new life" clothes and with an expression on his face that sent a spear of alarm straight to her heart.

His voice was cold. "How long did you plan to keep the truth about Parker from me?"

She sank into a chair behind her, her legs suddenly unable to hold her upright a second longer. "I…I didn't plan to keep it from you. I just couldn't talk about it. I didn't know where to begin, what to say…I still don't."

He cocked one eyebrow. "Seriously? Even now you can lie to me, Olivia? Yesterday didn't give you ample opportunity to fill me in? Hell, any time in the last nearly *two months* wasn't enough time for you?"

He stood, and she fought to find the words she should have said anytime before now. "Xander, please. Don't go."

"A little too late to be saying that, don't you think?" he replied, his voice as sharp as one of the chef's knives in her kitchen.

"I tried, Xander. Honestly, I wanted to tell you."

"But you didn't. You packed our son's entire life into boxes and shoved them in a dark corner. You already wiped Parker's existence from our home and our lives once before—why wouldn't you continue to do that given the opportunity? I don't know you anymore, Olivia. Maybe I never did."

She pushed herself to her feet. Even though her legs trembled beneath her, she sifted through the shock that near paralyzed her to find something to say.

"Didn't you do exactly the same thing? Wipe Parker from our lives when you walked out that door, when you walked away from me?"

"I left you because I couldn't pretend that the past had never happened, like you did. It happened. I know it did, and I've regretted that day every conscious moment of my life since. You seemed to find it so easy to just pick up and carry on. As if Parker had never been born," he accused.

"I couldn't hold on to the past." Olivia clutched at her blouse as if doing so could ease the tightness deep in her chest. "It was killing me, Xander. But you couldn't see that. Holding on to Parker's memories, seeing the reminders of his life every single day? It was killing me inside, destroying me. I had to move forward or die. I had to put everything away, or I knew I'd end up being buried with him."

"Even at the price of our marriage? At the expense of *us*?" Xander shook his head. "And you say I did the same thing as you? I didn't. I couldn't. I loved our son with every breath in my body."

"So did I!" she shouted at him. "And I loved you. I still love you. That's why I did what I did. I brought you home, and I hoped against hope that you wouldn't remember because then we could forget the past and the hurt and the awful things we said to each other back then. We could be together, like we're meant to be. The way we have been. But you, you're running away again, just like you did last time. Why stand and face our problems when you can just walk away, right?"

The bitterness in her words stained the air between them.

"You have the gall to accuse me of running away? You

didn't want me anymore. You made that patently clear when Parker died. Sometimes I wonder if you ever loved me or if I just conveniently fit into the plan you had for your future. You certainly didn't need *me*. It makes me wonder why you even bothered to lie to me all this time."

Her throat choked up—just like it had the last time he left her. Her words, her fears, all knotted into a tangled ball that lodged somewhere between her heart and her voice and made her too afraid to tell him how she really felt.

Her words, when they came, were nothing but a stifled whisper. "I did it for us. For our marriage. It, no, *we* deserved a second chance, but you wouldn't listen when I said the past didn't matter. That it was our future that was important."

"*I* wouldn't listen? You shut me out, Olivia. You shut me out from the truth. From our son's memory, from our past. No!" He waved his hand in a short cutting motion in front of him. "You don't get to do this again. You don't get to make my decisions for me."

"What about our decisions, Xander? The decisions we should be making for *us*?" she pleaded.

"Us? There is no us."

Outside, she heard a car pull up and the driver toot the horn. Xander bent and reached down for the bag she hadn't seen standing there before. She recognized the suitcase immediately—after all, it hadn't been that long ago she'd packed it herself.

"Goodbye, Olivia. You'll be hearing from my lawyer—and this time the divorce is going through."

He started to walk toward the door, and she followed him, her movements jerky as if she were some marionette being played by a demented puppet master.

"Xander, please, don't go. Don't leave me," she implored. "We've been happy together. Things have been good again since you've been home, and this is *our home*."

He kept walking. Olivia put on a burst of speed, passing him and getting to the door before him. She pressed her back to the solid wooden surface, barring him from dragging it open and walking away from her.

"Think about how well we worked together with your rehab and how close we've become again. This is our chance to rebuild our lives. We made mistakes before— I know that. But we can work past them. Please don't throw away this chance for us to make it all right again. To rebuild our marriage."

He put his hands on her shoulders and physically steered her away from the door. She lacked the strength to fight him and just watched as he turned the brass knob and opened the door wide.

"You're good at this, you know," she murmured, using the only weapon she had left. "Walking away. You blame me for lying, for withholding the truth from you, but you're equally to blame for the way things fell apart. You always walk away instead of accepting or asking for help. You're prepared to share your body, but you've never shared your deepest feelings or your thoughts with me. Ever.

"Please, Xander. I can be there for you. We can work through this. Let me help you come to terms with your grief. You say I put Parker's life away into boxes, but you did exactly the same with your feelings. You stopped working at home and you spent every hour you could at work. We never talked. We never admitted how much we needed each other. Help me, Xander. Let me help you."

Xander shook his head again, his face a taut mask devoid of expression, his eyes cold. "You are the last person I will ever ask for help."

He stepped through the open door and out onto the

porch. Past his shoulder, out on the street, Olivia saw Rachelle get out of the car and look toward the house. Xander raised a hand to Rachelle in acknowledgment and kept walking.

Olivia stayed there, frozen in the entrance hall of her home, as she watched her husband walk away from her for the second time in their marriage. His parting words echoed in her mind. As the sound of Rachelle's car driving away faded into the distance, Olivia slowly shut the door and rested her forehead against its surface.

Every part of her body hurt from the inside out. She'd thought it was bad the last time he'd left her, but she'd still been so numb with losing Parker that she hadn't had the capacity to think or to feel too much. But now—given all that had developed between them since he'd been back, given how much she still loved him—she hurt in ways she'd never dreamed possible.

Where did this leave them, exactly? Wherever it was, she knew she didn't like it. Hated it, in fact. Hated that once again she'd allowed the best thing that had ever happened to her to walk out that door.

And still she loved him.

Fifteen

Xander sat in the car as Rachelle drove away from the house, his eyes fixed forward. *Look to the future*, he told himself, *away from the past*. Away from the hurt, the anger, the betrayal. Anger still simmered beneath the surface. At Olivia, at himself.

"Did you want to stop somewhere for a meal or a drink?" Rachelle said as they entered the harbor bridge approach.

"No," he said abruptly. "Thanks," he added. "Just to my place would be fine."

She nodded, but he sensed her disappointment. He remembered now that before his accident they'd become closer than two people who simply worked together. Friends still, not lovers. But they'd been heading in a more romantic direction. Although, when he'd been honest with himself, he'd found it impossible to engage his emotions to the extent he needed to in order to embark on an intimate relationship with someone. He knew she was a lot more invested in developing their relationship than he'd been. At least she'd never hidden that from him, not the way Olivia had hidden so much.

His stomach tightened on an unexpectedly sharp pain. Why did it hurt so much to be leaving her again? He'd already done it once before—and now that he remembered why, he understood and agreed with the choice he'd made two years ago. This time shouldn't have been any different, and yet it felt as if he was leaving a vital part of himself behind.

Being a Friday night, traffic was quite heavy. The journey gave him far too much time to think and reflect. He was relieved when Rachelle pulled into the underground car park and drew to a halt in one of the parking spaces allocated to his apartment.

She turned off the engine and twisted in her seat to face him. The smile on her face didn't quite match the uncertainty he saw in her eyes.

"Xander? Are you okay? Do you want me to come up with you?"

"Look, thanks for the ride, but I'd prefer to be on my own right now."

Her smile faded. "You're not angry with me, are you? I wanted to say something to you when I saw you and Olivia at the apartment, but she wouldn't let me."

Xander sighed. He just bet Olivia didn't let Rachelle say anything. "Of course I'm not angry with you," he said and leaned forward to kiss her on the cheek. "I'll see you on Monday, okay? At the office."

"You've been cleared to come back to work? That's fabulous. We've missed you so much. *I've* missed you."

"Cleared or not, I'm coming back. Even if it's only for a few hours a day. I need to get back to normal." *Whatever normal is now*, he added silently. "Again, thanks for the ride. I appreciate you coming to get me at such short notice."

"Anytime, you just call me. I'm here for you. I could even get you some groceries now, if you like, and bring them back. It's pretty empty up there right now."

He shook his head emphatically. "No, that's fine. I'll get some things delivered in."

"On the weekend?"

"I'll deal with it," he said firmly and opened his door to get out of the car. "See you Monday."

She took the hint and nodded, but her disappointment was clear in her eyes. "Monday it is. Good night, Xander. I'm glad you're back to your old self."

After she'd driven off, he took the elevator to his floor and let himself into his apartment. The soullessness of the space was just what he needed right now. He didn't want memories or feelings or anything. Except maybe a shot of whisky. He walked over to the cabinet where he kept his liquor and grabbed a bottle of Scotland's finest before going to the kitchen, where he splashed two fingers of amber liquid in a crystal tumbler.

He walked over to the windows that looked out over the harbor and toward Devonport—toward Olivia—and took a sip of the spirit. It burned as it went down, not the deep satisfying burn he'd anticipated but something far less pleasant. Xander looked down at the glass in his hand and wondered what the hell he was doing seeking solace in alcohol. He'd never done it before, and he certainly shouldn't be starting now.

He strode to the kitchen and tipped out the contents of the tumbler into the sink. He needed a distraction, but whisky wasn't it. He stared at the large flat-screen TV mounted on the far wall of his sitting room. No, not even watching a movie or channel surfing appealed. Instead, Xander walked down the hallway toward his bedroom, stopping at the door to his office.

His hand was on the handle before he realized what he

was doing. Work had always been a panacea for him—why should that be any different now? He should still have some client notes here he could go over. He rued the fact his laptop had been destroyed in the crash. Not even its leather case had protected its harddrive from the impact. If he'd had the laptop, at least he could have looked forward to losing himself for a few hours by updating himself on his files and who had handled what in his absence.

The minute Xander stepped in his office he knew Olivia had been in there. The picture of Parker that he'd taken with him the first time he'd left her wasn't on his desk where he knew he'd left it. A roll of rage swelled inside him. Wiping their son's memory from their house had been one thing, but tampering with his apartment, as well? That was going too far.

He searched the office for the picture, his movements becoming more frantic the longer it took him to find it. The relief that coursed through his body when he found the frame, face down in a drawer, was enough to make him drop heavily into his chair. He looked at the beloved face of his only child. Felt anew the loss and grief that he usually kept locked inside. Relived the guilt.

Carefully he put the picture back on his desk where it belonged and stared at it for several minutes. Losing Parker was a reminder that he couldn't stray from the path he'd set himself. He didn't want to love again the way he'd loved Olivia and their little boy because when it all fell apart it hurt far too much.

He understood why his father had collapsed within himself the way he had. His grief and guilt over Xander's brother's death had been too much for him to handle, especially with the way Xander's mother had locked herself in a non-emotional cocoon and forged her way through the rest of her life. He hadn't had the support he needed. After losing his son and his marriage, Xander hadn't had any support to lean on, either. But he was tougher, more determined not to become a victim of his own dreadful mistake, and if that meant separating himself from emotion—the way his mother had—then that's what he would do.

It had been the longest two weeks of her life and Olivia felt decidedly ragged around the edges when she forced herself to get out of bed and embark on her new daily routine. Who was she kidding, she wondered as she padded downstairs in her dressing gown, her hair askew and her face unwashed. This tired, halfhearted attempt to continue on as though everything was normal was a step back into the past, hardly anything new.

The house felt empty without Xander there, and her heart echoed with loss. She'd spent the past fourteen days listlessly wandering around, feeling unmotivated and empty. Even a call from the gallery owner to say they'd just sold the last piece and had requests lining up for more of her work couldn't lift her spirits.

She'd screwed up. Again. So what now? She aimlessly went through the motions of making coffee and pouring it into a mug. As she lifted the brew to her lips to take a sip, the aroma filled her nostrils and turned her stomach. She'd been off and on different things for days now, and coffee was just another to add to the list. With a sigh she tipped the contents down the drain and turned instead to put the kettle on. Maybe a cup of peppermint tea would revive her flagging appetite.

As she pulled a teabag from the box in the pantry she forced herself to acknowledge that it would take more than a cup of herbal tea to make things better. There was only one thing—one man—who could make a difference in her life. The only one who had ever mattered. Xander.

She'd just finished brewing the tea when the phone rang. She recognized the number on the caller display with a sinking sensation that pulled at her stomach. Her lawyer wasted no time on pleasantries.

"Mrs. Jackson, we've been instructed by your husband's lawyers to expedite matters relating to your dissolution of marriage. Do you need us to forward new forms to you, or do you still have the ones we originally sent?"

So, he hasn't wasted time, Olivia thought as she acknowledged the lawyer's request. "No, I still have the originals."

"All you need to do is sign them, put them in the enclosed envelope and post them today. Or I could arrange a courier to collect them from you if you'd prefer. It seems Mr. Jackson is in somewhat of a hurry."

Olivia closed her eyes against the burn of tears. Her voice shook as she spoke. "I see. I'll get the papers back to you. There's no need to organize a courier."

There was a brief silence on the other end before she heard her lawyer clear his throat. "Thank you," he said. "And, Mrs. Jackson? I'm so very sorry things didn't work out for you."

"I am, too, Mr. Clement."

She hung up without saying goodbye, and the phone fell from her hands to the floor. She wrapped her arms around her waist and bent over as uncontrollable sobs racked her body. It was over and it was all her fault. If only she'd been up front with Xander from the beginning, he might have been receptive to starting again. But now, with the stupid decisions she'd made, with her inability to face the pain of the past, she'd ensured they had no future together at all.

Eventually she dragged herself back up the stairs and into her en suite. She pulled open the drawer where she'd stowed the papers and reached inside, her hand hesitating as it hovered over the sanitary products stored there. Something wasn't right. She reached into the drawer and grabbed the little pocket-size diary she kept a record of her cycle in and counted back the days. She was two days late. Nothing really to worry about. Unless you factored in the minor detail that her periods always came every twenty-eight days without fail.

Her hand trembled as she shoved the diary back in the drawer and slammed it shut—leaving the folded envelope exactly where she'd put it, forgotten now in light of what she was dealing with. She'd been under a lot of stress, hadn't been eating or sleeping properly. No wonder she was out of kilter, she tried to tell herself. But all the while she knew her excuses were a waste of time. She knew the signs as well as she knew her face in the mirror each morning. The lack of appetite, the need to nap at odd times of the day, not to mention her reaction to the coffee she'd made this morning. And then there was the metallic tang that had been in her mouth the past couple of days. A tang she remembered vividly from when she'd become pregnant with Parker. She'd been ignoring each and every sign. Choosing oblivion over reality—which was what had led her to this situation in the first place.

Pregnant. With Xander's child. What the hell was she going to do now?

Three days later Olivia had her confirmation. The nurse at her doctor's surgery had been filled with quiet excitement on her behalf. An excitement that Olivia was hard-pressed to feel. She had to tell Xander straightaway. This wasn't something she could, or would, withhold from him.

The minute she got home she called his cell phone. It rang only a couple of times before switching to his answering service. Olivia disconnected the call. He must have diverted her call the moment he'd seen her number on the caller display. The knowledge that he wasn't even willing to speak to her on the phone was a blow she hadn't expected. Not prepared to give up at the first hurdle, she dialed again. This time it went immediately to the service and she left him a message.

"Xander, I need to see you. It's urgent. Meet me tomorrow, please." She named a café in Devonport, a short ferry ride for him across the harbor, and stated what time she'd be there.

Now all she could do was wait.

Sixteen

Xander arrived before the time Olivia had indicated, but she had still gotten there ahead of him. She saw him the minute he came through the door, and he watched as her cheeks suffused with color and her eyes grew bright.

"I got your message," he said unnecessarily as he sat down opposite her at the table. "What do you want?"

"I'm glad you came. I didn't want to tell you this in a message."

"For two months you've held things back from me and *now* you want to tell me something? What is it?" he asked, not making any effort to keep the irritation out of his voice.

He wasn't prepared for what came next.

"I'm pregnant."

He stared at her in shock. *Pregnant?* Silence grew between them. A waitress came over to take their order, and he waved her away. Finally he found his tongue.

"What do you mean, pregnant?"

"What it usually means." Olivia gave him a smile, no

more than a twist of her lips really and certainly not the fulsome smile he was used to seeing on her face. It made him look at her more sharply and note the dark bruises of sleeplessness beneath her eyes and the pale cast of her skin. Concern for her swelled inside him, but he ruthlessly quashed it. It shouldn't matter to him if she slept or ate or looked after herself. Unless what she'd just told him was true.

"We're having a baby," she affirmed.

Every cell in his body rejected the words. *A baby. No. Not again. Never again.* They'd used protection. Even in his amnesiac state he'd followed the protocol he'd instigated after Parker's birth.

"But how—?"

"The condoms we used were expired," she said by way of explanation, her eyes not leaving his face for a second.

"Did you know that before we used them?"

"No! Of course I didn't. I'd forgotten all about them, to be honest. You must have bought them well before..." Her voice trailed off.

Before Parker died. And, yes, their purchase had been made well before then. There had been little intimacy between him and Olivia during Parker's last year. Their son had been plagued with virtually every cold and flu known to man after he began preschool and was exposed to germs from the other children. Olivia had said his immune system would strengthen eventually. However, it had meant she'd spent more nights curled up in bed with Parker, trying to soothe him back to sleep, than she had with Xander. Their lovemaking had become sporadic at best as she'd poured all her care into nursing Parker to health.

Now she was pregnant again. An icy shaft of trepidation sliced through him. What on earth did she expect from him? Was she trying to manipulate him again? She said she hadn't known the condoms were expired, but could he believe her? Maybe she'd planned to become pregnant all along, making the decision without him just like she had the first time. Binding him to her through an innocent baby when everything else she'd tried had failed, perhaps?

"You're telling me you didn't do this deliberately?"

"Of course I am. I swear I'm telling you the truth," she said, her voice raising slightly and making heads turn toward them. She continued, "If you'll remember, you were the one to initiate things the first time we—"

"I remember," he said, cutting across the words she'd been about to say.

Words that all too easily painted vivid memories in his mind of every single exquisite moment they'd spent together. The sounds she'd made when they made love. The scent of her body. The feel of her as she climaxed around him and as he spent himself inside her. The intense sense of belonging as they came back down to earth and fell asleep in each other's arms. He didn't want to remember. He couldn't risk allowing himself to feel.

"Is this why you haven't signed the papers yet?" he demanded.

"No! To be honest with you, I forgot all about them."

"Honest? That's a novelty for you these days, isn't it?" At Olivia's shocked expression he huffed out a sigh. "I'm sorry—that was uncalled for."

His mind scattered in a hundred different directions, but everything that passed through his thoughts settled back on one thing. Olivia was pregnant, and, if she was to be believed, they were equally responsible for this situation. The knowledge was a bitter pill to swallow. Either way he looked at it, another child of his would be on this earth, which meant he had responsibilities to that child. Responsibilities he had promised himself he'd never bear again.

Xander abruptly pushed his chair back from the table and stood. "Thank you for the information," he said and turned to go.

He was forced to halt in his steps when he felt Olivia's hand catch him on the arm.

"Xander, stay—please. We have to talk about this." Her voice rose again, attracting the same attention as before.

"Don't make a scene, Olivia. You asked me to come here and I did. You've given me your news and now I'm going. In the meantime, perhaps you could complete your part of the dissolution document and return it to your lawyer as requested?"

He stared at her hand until she let go. The second she did so he started for the door. But the short walk to the ferry building or the ride across the harbor back to the office passed in a blur. All he could remember were Olivia's words. *I'm pregnant.* They echoed in his mind, over and over again.

He couldn't do this again—didn't want to ever face being a father again—but circumstance now forced it on him. There were choices to make. Tough ones. Xander reached for the phone and hit the speed dial for his lawyer's office.

Olivia was working in her studio when she heard a van pull up outside her house. She walked over to the driveway to see who it was and was surprised to see a courier there. She wasn't expecting anything. The courier handed her an envelope, got her to sign for it and went on his way. Olivia felt dread pull at her with ghostly fingers as she identified the source of the envelope. Xander's lawyer.

Slowly she walked to the patio at the back of the house

and sat down at the table. She stared at the envelope, wondering what lay inside. She couldn't bring herself to open the packet; she didn't want to see in black-and-white whatever demand or dictate Xander had dreamed up in response to the news he was going to be a father again. She was still having a hard enough time coming to terms with the way he'd behaved when she'd told him the news yesterday. She didn't know what she'd expected him to do or say, exactly, but it hadn't been to simply get up and walk away from her—again.

A blackbird flew down onto the lawn and cocked its head, staring at her with one eye before pecking at the ground, pulling out a worm and flying away. She felt very like that worm must feel right now, she realized. At the mercy of something bigger, stronger and darker than she was. Helpless. It wasn't a feeling she was comfortable with, and it reminded her of all the things in her life she'd never been able to control. Control had become everything to her. It kept her world turning on its axis when everything else fell apart.

She picked up the envelope and turned it over and over in her hands. Had she really thought for a minute that Xander would be pleased with the news that she was expecting another baby? Maybe, in a sudden rash of idealistic foolishness, she had. The news had obviously shocked him—it had shocked her, too. She hadn't anticipated his utter indifference. So where did that leave them?

The obvious answer lay right there, in her hands, but still she couldn't bring herself to tear the envelope open. Instead, she placed it squarely on the table and went inside and brewed a pot of chamomile tea—taking her time over each step. Only after she'd carried her tea tray back outside to the table, poured her first cup and taken a sip did she pick up the envelope again.

She placed one hand on her belly. "Okay, little one, let's see what your daddy has to say."

With a swift tear it was open, and she pulled the contents out. She scanned the letter quickly, then read it more slowly on a second pass-through. Olivia went numb from head to foot. Xander's feelings couldn't have been spelled out more clearly. While he was prepared to offer generous financial support toward the child, he wanted no contact with the baby or with her whatsoever. There was a contract enclosed, setting out his terms and the sums he was prepared to pay, but she didn't even look at it.

Slow burning anger lit inside her. How dare he dismiss their baby like that? It was one thing to be angry with her—to not want anything to do with her—but to reject their child? It was so clinical and callous.

Olivia tossed the letter onto the table and propelled herself to her feet. She paced the patio a few times and came to a halt outside her studio. Through the open door she could see the canvas she was working on—a commission she'd earned as a result of her exhibition. Painting had always been her refuge in the past—through sorrow, through loss—but she knew that she needed to work this anger out of her system before she picked up a brush again.

With a growl of frustration she closed and locked the studio doors before she took the tea tray and Xander's wretched communication inside. Then, after grabbing her keys and sliding her feet into an old pair of sneakers, she went out the front door and down to the beach. She powered along the sand, oblivious to the sparkle of light on the rise and fall of the sea and the growing heat of the sun as it approached its zenith in the sky.

By the time she'd made it to the end of the beach and turned back again, she had worked the worst of her anger and, yes, her indignation, off. Olivia sat down on a park bench in the shade and waited for her breathing and heart rate to return to normal.

What had driven Xander to such a decision? she asked herself as she tried to rationalize his stance. This cold distance he insisted on maintaining was not something she recognized from the man she loved. She knew he could be distant and independent. He could also be stubborn and insanely detailed at times. But he wasn't the kind of man who could reject a child. Even as angry as he was about her pregnancy with Parker, he'd loved their son with an intensity that had often taken her breath away. Surely he couldn't *not* love another child of his?

She watched a lone gull as it circled on the thermals in the air before changing its direction and swooping down to the water. Was it that he wanted to be free like that gull there? Answerable only to himself? Had her lies and losing Parker the way they had made him incapable of loving ever again?

The answer that repeated in her mind was an emphatic no. In the weeks before he'd regained his memory she knew to the depths of her soul that he'd loved her. But if he was capable of love, why then would he withhold it from this baby?

Fear.

The word—so small, so simple and yet so powerful— came to her with blinding insight. He was afraid to love again—certainly afraid to love their baby but maybe even afraid to love her, too. After all, wasn't love based on trust? And hadn't she destroyed his trust in her not once but several times over?

Had she given him her shoulder to lean on in the wretched dark days after Parker died? No, she'd been filled with recriminations and pain and projecting her own guilt onto him. Had she tried to stop him leaving that first time? No, she'd been too numbed by grief to do anything.

She knew a little of his family's circumstances, even though Xander had never discussed it much and Olivia had never been close with her mother-in-law. Knew how his father had so grieved the loss of his firstborn son that he'd completely withdrawn from the family he'd had left. Understood that Xander's mother had worked hard every day she could to support her surviving son and her husband. His mum may not have shown her love with hugs and kisses, but she'd done the best she could to ensure their family was secure.

Was it any wonder then that Xander hadn't known how to express his grief? Why had she never thought about that before? He'd grown up with two complete extremes of how to cope with loss. Had anyone ever asked him how *he'd* felt about losing his brother, let alone his son?

She knew she certainly hadn't.

Where to now? How was she going to break through the armor Xander now protected himself and his emotions within? She'd already lost his trust, so was it even possible for him to forgive her and allow her back into his heart?

There were no secrets left between them now. She could only try. They'd made a child together out of love; that had to count for something. She owed it to Xander, to their baby and to herself to fight for what was right— to fight for their love and the chance to start again.

It was late when Xander listened to the latest message from Olivia. He'd been putting it off most of the day. Once he was home, he knew he couldn't put it off any longer. She'd been blunt and to the point. She'd acknowledged receipt of the offer through his lawyer, but she wanted to discuss it with him face-to-face first. She said that if he agreed to meet with her again, she wouldn't delay any further. Everything he wanted signed would be signed and returned at that meeting.

He knew he should call her back. Instead he dropped his phone on the coffee table in front of him and stretched out on the wide sofa that faced the view over the harbor. Lights sparkled in the inky darkness, like the stars of a distant galaxy. *Distant*, now there was a word. It described exactly how he felt when it came to just about everything in his life. Distant was safe; distant didn't flay a man's heart into a thousand shreds, nor did it betray a man.

He'd thought that distance was what he needed, what he wanted, and he'd tried to throw himself back into his work to gain emotional distance the way he always had when faced with personal upheaval. But in unguarded moments thoughts of Olivia kept creeping in. Her image when she came to the hospital, and he saw the love and concern so stark and clear on her face. Her determination to see him through the physical therapy he needed to do each day to regain muscle tone and strength after his coma. The sweet, soft sigh she made as he entered her body, as if, in that moment, everything in their world was perfect. And it had been.

And then there were the memories that went further back, to when Parker was alive, to the cute little family they'd been and how happy they were together. A visceral pain scored deep inside and reminded him anew that he'd never see Parker grow up. Pain laced with guilt that he'd been the one to leave their front gate open and that he'd been the one to throw the ball Bozo had chased out onto the road. Only two small things, each taken on their own, but put together they'd led to a tragedy of inestimable proportions.

The bitter irony that his little family had faced the

same awful loss as his parents had hadn't escaped him. But he wasn't his father. He wouldn't give in and buckle under the grief he felt. Instead he'd locked his feelings down. He would not be weak or needy. He would not, above all things, need Olivia more than she needed him. When it had become clear to him that she didn't need him at all, that she'd moved past their tragedy without him, Xander had left.

He groaned out loud. This was doing his head in. He needed a distraction, but what? Or who? He picked up his phone again and scrolled through his contact list. He wasn't in the mood for testosterone-driven company. His finger hovered over Rachelle's number. She'd made it more than clear these past few weeks that she was interested in picking up where they'd left off before his accident. In fact, she'd also made it clear she was willing to jump a few steps on that particular ladder.

Was that what would finally dislodge Olivia's presence from his mind? He could only hope so.

Rachelle arrived within thirty minutes of his call, and she glided into his arms as if she belonged there.

"I'm so glad you called," she said with a sultry purr as she lifted her face to his.

He kissed her and tried to feel something, anything but indifference, and failed miserably. Maybe he was just out of practice, he thought. *But what about Olivia? You didn't need any practice there*, came the insidious voice in the back of his mind. He pushed the thought away and led Rachelle into his sitting room.

"Would you like a drink?" he offered.

"Sure, a pinot noir if you have it," she replied, settling herself on the couch and crossing her legs.

He couldn't help but notice the way her skirt rode up on her shapely thighs. She might be petite, but there was nothing about her that wasn't perfectly formed—and she knew how to dress to highlight those assets, he acknowledged wryly. Again he anticipated the surge of interest, of desire, that should be starting a slow pulse in his veins. Again, nothing.

Xander snagged a bottle of wine from the wine rack and went to the kitchen to pour them each a glass. He returned to where she sat and passed her the wine. They clinked glasses.

"To new beginnings," Rachelle said with a glow of hope in her dark brown eyes, flicking her glossy black hair back over her shoulder. "And happy endings," she finished with a smile.

Xander nodded his head and took a sip of wine. Even that didn't taste right. In fact, nothing about this evening felt right at all. Rachelle began to talk about work—she'd recently received a promotion and was excited about bringing new ideas to the table. Xander enjoyed her lively conversation and approved many of her ideas, but when she turned the conversation to more personal matters and placed one dainty hand on his thigh as she moved a little closer on the sofa, he knew he had to bring the evening to a premature end.

"Rachelle, look, I'm sorry, but—" he started.

Regret spread across her face, but she mustered up an attempt at a smile. She lifted her hand from his leg and placed her fingers across his lips. "It's okay," she said. "I can feel you're trying, but it's not working, is it? And, really, you shouldn't have to *try*. The problem is—you're still too married to Olivia. Maybe not on paper and maybe not in your mind, but—" she placed a hand on his chest "—you most definitely are still married to her here, in your heart."

She leaned forward, put her wineglass on the table and rose from the sofa. "Don't get up," she said as he started to rise, as well. "I can see myself out. Oh, and I guess I'd better leave this with you, too."

Rachelle pulled a key out of a side pocket of her handbag and put it on the table next to her glass.

After she'd gone, Xander stared at the key on the table. He'd given it to her about a week before his accident. They'd been scheduled to attend a client function together, and he'd offered his place for her to get ready since she lived fairly far away. As she'd finished work ahead of him, he'd given her the key so she could let herself in and they'd then traveled to the venue together. He hadn't asked for the key back that night, or the next day, either, thinking that they would be developing their relationship further. He couldn't have been more wrong about that—accident or no accident.

He played her parting words over in his head. Was he really still in love with his wife? He got up and took the wineglasses to the kitchen. After pouring their contents down the drain and leaving the glasses on the counter top, he headed to his bedroom.

The room felt empty. Hell, *he* felt empty. It was past time to be honest with himself. He missed Olivia. And, more, he missed their life together and the new closeness they'd developed during his recovery. But could he forgive her? Could he let himself care for her—and for the baby on the way—when he knew they had the potential to hurt him so deeply?

No easy answers came to him through yet another sleepless night. They didn't come through a particularly arduous time at work the next day. He was tired and more than a little bit cranky when he arrived back at the apartment at eight o'clock that evening. The last person he wanted, or expected, to see was Olivia standing at his door, waiting for him.

Seventeen

Olivia straightened the second she saw him come out of the elevator and walk toward his apartment. Her face was pale and drawn, and he fought to quell the expression of concern that sprang to his lips.

"Olivia," he said in acknowledgment.

"I...I couldn't wait for you to return my call. I needed to see you."

"You'd better come inside."

He opened the door wide and ushered her into the apartment. His nostrils flared at the trace of scent she left in her wake, and instantly his body began to react. Why couldn't it have been like this last night? he asked himself. Why was it only Olivia who drew this reaction from him?

"Take a seat—you look worn-out," he commented as he put his briefcase down and shrugged out of his jacket. "Have you eaten?"

"Yes, thank you. I had dinner before I drove over."

"Were you waiting long?"

"Awhile," she answered vaguely.

He stood and watched as she took a seat.

"Xander, is it really too late for us?" she suddenly blurted, her hands fluttering nervously in her lap. "Can you truly not find it in your heart to forgive me and allow us to start over?"

He pushed a hand through his hair and breathed out a sigh. He'd asked himself the same question over and over last night and still he had no answers. Sure, his heart told him to give in and find a way to make their way forward in their lives again, but his head and his experience emphatically told him to walk away while he still could.

The thing was, he still felt so much for her. Even now every nerve, every cell in his body was attuned to Olivia—to every nuance and expression on her face, to the gentle lines of her body, to the fact she was carrying his baby. Reality slammed into him with the subtlety of an ice bucket challenge. Except this was no challenge. This was his life. The thing was, did he want it? Could he risk everything again and start a new life with Olivia and a baby?

"Xander? Please, say something."

Olivia's voice held a wealth of pain and uncertainty. A part of him wanted to reassure her, to say they could work things out. But the other, darker, side remembered all too well the child he'd been, the one who'd come home from school to a house filled with sorrow and devoid of emotional warmth—remembered the void left by his brother that was too big for Xander to fill on his own. A void like that left by Parker's death. One too painful to imagine even attempting to fill again. Love hurt, no matter which way you looked at it, and he was done with hurting.

He sat down next to Olivia, his elbows resting on his thighs and his hands loosely clasped. His head dropped between his shoulders.

"I don't think so," he finally said.

"At least that's more promising than a flat-out no," Olivia commented, although her voice held no humor.

He turned his head to look at her. Her features were so familiar to him. This was the woman whose gentle touch and quiet encouragement had helped him to recuperate and grow strong again. The woman he'd fallen even more deeply in love with as they'd lived together and made love. If he only let himself, he would be completely vulnerable to her again and to their unborn child. But he couldn't let go. He had to make the break and make it clean and fast.

"You'd better go. We have nothing to talk about anymore, Olivia," he said wearily.

"Not until you've heard me out," she insisted. "I have a right to tell you how I feel. I love you, Xander. Not just a little bit, not even a lot. I love you with every single thing I am. Every breath I take, every choice I've made since I met you. It's all about you. I know that some of those choices were the wrong ones, and I'm deeply sorry for those, but I'm learning as I go here. We both were—*are*," she corrected herself emphatically.

"I never asked for anything from you," he replied and started to rise. She grabbed his arm and tugged him back down.

"I know you didn't. I know you probably don't even want to admit that you want me, us, in your life at all. It's why you're pushing me away now. Why we probably lived such a parallel life before." She drew in a deep breath, then let it all go on her next words. "I've talked to your mother. I know what it was like for you when you were little."

"You what? Why? You had no right to talk to her."

Anger boiled thick and fast deep inside. Anger at Olivia for contacting his mother over something that was between the two of them only, and anger at his mother for talking to Olivia when she never spoke to him about the past.

"I needed to know, Xander. I had to find out if we had a chance. When Parker died, I did what I do. What I've always done for the past twenty years of my life. I picked up the pieces and I carried on."

"You didn't just pick them up. You boxed them up and put them away for good. You treated Parker's memory as if it was something to be forgotten, something to be swept away as if it had never happened."

Her voice was quiet when she replied. "It was all I knew how to do. I couldn't talk about it, Xander. We didn't talk about emotions in our house, and I suspect your house was very similar. Your mum told me about your dad, about how unwell he was. His grief went far deeper than mourning, and eventually it broke him completely.

"I don't want that for you, Xander. I want you to be whole. I want us to be whole, together. We can't do this on our own, apart. But maybe we can pull the pieces back together if we work together. Please, Xander, tell me you'll try. Tell me we're worth it." She took his hand and pressed it on her still-flat belly and begged him, "Tell me all three of us are worth it."

He looked down at his hand, then up to her face, where her eyes shone with unshed tears. His own eyes burned in kind.

"I can't tell you what you need to hear."

He could see this wasn't the answer she'd hoped for, but she rallied enough for one more try. "Think about it a little longer, Xander. Please. For all our sakes. Neither of us is perfect, but together we can make a good attempt at it. I know I pushed you away. I was as guilty as anyone of not sharing how I felt.

"It's not that I didn't care—I cared too much. If I let any of it out, how would I function? How would I manage to keep putting one foot in front of the other day after day? I couldn't let that grief float to the surface and still care for you at the same time. If I let it out, it would consume me. The only way I knew how to get through was to work. To put away all the reminders. To lose myself in being busy. I never meant to push you away."

"You didn't just push me away, Livvy. You pushed away every last physical memory we had of Parker, too. I felt like once he was gone, he didn't matter to you anymore. You never talked about him. You barely even mentioned his name."

"I never meant for you to believe that I didn't think Parker's life mattered. He mattered. You matter. *We* matter, don't we?"

She got up and began to pace the floor.

"After Parker died and you left, I threw myself into my painting. The time I spent working was the only time I didn't feel the pain of losing you both. All I could do was work, day in, day out. I couldn't sleep, couldn't eat, but I could paint, so I did. I produced my most emotive work ever. I even scored an agent from the paintings I did at the time, and they became the platform for my current success. But you know what?" She stopped pacing and faced him, her face a mask of pain and remorse. "I can't take pride in that even now. I feel like I cashed in on Parker's death. I painted out my grief, my frustration, my anger—my guilt."

"Guilt? What do you mean?" Xander stood up, his body rigid with tension, his hands curled into tight fists of frustration. "It wasn't you that left the gate open, nor were you the one who threw the ball for Bozo toward the road. That was all my fault."

A single tear slipped down Olivia's cheek. He ached to wipe it away, but he daren't touch her.

"I know I said it was your fault, Xander. It was far easier for me to point the blame at you than to admit my own accountability for what happened. Parker had been happily playing in my studio that morning—don't you remember? But the sounds he was making with his train set got on my nerves, and I couldn't concentrate on my work.

"I told him to go outside. If I hadn't done that—" Her voice broke off on a gasp of pain, and she hugged her arms around herself tight.

When he said nothing more, she went over to the sofa and grabbed her handbag. "I'm sorry, Xander. More than you'll ever know. I'd hoped, that if we talked—properly this time—that maybe we could work things out. But I guess the river runs too deep between us now for that to happen."

Before he could stop her or form a coherent sentence, she was gone. Feeling more horribly alone than he'd ever felt in his life, Xander sank back down onto the sofa and stared out the window. The last rays of the evening sun caressed the peninsula across the harbor. The peninsula where his home lay and, if he was to be totally honest, where his heart lived, as well.

He replayed Olivia's words over and over, thinking hard about what she'd said and in particular about her admission of fault in what happened that awful day when their world stopped turning. Why had she never said anything about that before?

I did what I do. What I've always done for the past twenty years of my life. I picked up the pieces and I carried on.

Of course she did. It was the example her father had set her and it was what he'd clearly expected of her after her mother died. In so many ways it was a mirror to what Xander had gone through as a child. Keep putting each foot forward straight after the other—no time for regret, no time for emotion. Do what needs to be done at all times. And whatever you do, don't talk about it.

Could he have made more effort to salvage their marriage after Parker died? Of course he could have. But he'd been turned in too much on himself. Focused too hard on protecting that facade that he'd spent most of his lifetime building, as his mother had built hers. He'd never seen his mother show weakness, never seen her so much as shed a tear. When the going got tough, as it had so often as she struggled to keep everything together, she just worked harder. And wasn't that exactly what he'd done, too?

When Olivia had told him they were expecting a baby, he'd thrown himself into work. He'd distanced himself from her and from the impending birth by doing whatever he could to ensure their financial security. He'd earned a promotion along the way. Successes like that he could measure, he could take pride in. What the hell did he know about being a father? Heaven knew he hadn't had a good example of one to call upon. He hadn't had any time to research it, to even get his head into the idea—they'd had no discussion, nothing, before she'd sprung it on him. And then to his amazement, when Parker had been born, the bond and the love had been instant. Equally rewarding and terrifying in its own right.

Fatherhood had become an unexpected delight. He'd been amazed at how effortlessly Livvy had transitioned from high school teacher to homemaker and mother. She did everything with an air of efficiency and capability that was daunting. Did she never question her ability to be a good parent? Did she never question his? If she had, he'd never seen any sign of it.

Part of his original attraction to her had always been to her self-sufficiency, but that very thing was what had slowly driven a wedge between them. It shifted the balance. But what he realized now, weighing her words and the feelings she'd finally opened up to him about this evening, was that in trying not to become a victim of his past, in trying not to be like his father, he'd fallen in the trap of behaving like his mother.

Why hadn't he been able to see that he didn't need to be a part of a dysfunctional relationship? When had he lost sight of all that was good and right about life? He thought back to the joy and excitement of meeting Olivia, of falling in love with her. He'd met a lot of women over time—beautiful, strong and successful women—and none of them had touched his heart the way she did. Why should it be wrong to be vulnerable to the one person he wanted to be close to?

Had he, with his own determined aloofness, contributed to the demise of their marriage? Of course he had. He had to accept that he couldn't be all things to all people. Surely his own mother's example had shown him that. Then why had he followed her path in life instead of his own?

He'd been a fool. A complete and utter idiot. He'd pushed away the one person in the world who loved him unconditionally. A woman who was flawed in her own ways but who needed him as much as he needed her. Of course he wanted, no, *needed* to be close to her. And that was okay. It didn't weaken him; it didn't diminish him as a man. It made him stronger because he loved her.

He got up and walked over to the window, one hand resting on the glass as he looked toward the dark bump on the distant landscape—the hill on which their home stood. So she'd made some stupid choices—hadn't he made some equally dumb ones? More importantly, could he forgive her for manipulating him when he'd come out of hospital?

The last vestiges of anger that had filled and driven him these past weeks faded away. Of course he could. They both needed to work on this. And now there was another life to consider, as well. How on earth had he even imagined that he could cut that child from his life? Not be there to see him or her be born and grow and learn and develop. It hurt to even think about it, and instinctively he began to shut down that part of him that felt that pain. But then he stopped. Pain was okay. *Feeling* was okay.

He closed his eyes and turned away from the window. Was he man enough, strong enough, to do this? To take a leap of faith and let love rule him and his decisions rather than depending on distance and control? He had some big decisions to make, and he had to be certain he was making the right ones. More importantly, he had to be making them for the right reasons.

Eighteen

It was Christmas Eve. Just under a week since Olivia had last seen or heard from Xander. She'd decided to make some effort with the decorations that morning and had gone up to the attic to find them. But the decorations had been forgotten when she'd stumbled across Parker's things that Xander had left scattered on the attic floor. She'd tucked away the clothes and toys, then picked up the albums. She was about to put them back in the box and seal it up again, but she changed her mind and took them downstairs instead.

Putting them back on the bookcase in the living room felt right. So did putting the framed photos of Parker back where they belonged. She got the toys out of the attic and loaded them into a carton in the room that had been Parker's. The room that would now become this baby's. After she'd done all that, she realized that the house felt different. Lighter somehow. Right. All of these things had been missing and, with them, a giant piece of her heart and soul.

She would never stop missing her firstborn, but at least now she could remember him with less of the sorrow that she'd been trying to hide from these past two years. And she could begin to forgive herself for her choices that day, too.

It was time for a new beginning. If only that beginning could be with Xander by her side. She'd lost count of the times she'd checked the answering machine at the house or the display on her cell phone to see if he'd called. It was time to face the awful truth. There would be no future together.

The dissolution order and Xander's offer of financial maintenance for the baby sat on the kitchen table in front of her. She had a pen clutched in her hand.

"Just sign the damn things and get it over with," she said out loud. Her hand fluttered to her belly. "We'll manage, you and me."

Before she could put pen to paper, the front doorbell rang. With a sigh of exasperation, she dropped the pen to the table and got up to see who it was. She felt a physical shock of awareness when she saw Xander standing there with one arm leaning up on the doorjamb, wearing his old uni sweatshirt and a disreputable pair of Levi's. Her heart picked up double time as her eyes raked his face, taking in the gleam in his slate-gray eyes and the stubble growing back stubbornly on his chin.

"Are you here about the papers?" she said, rubbing her hands down the legs of her jeans.

"Not exactly," Xander replied. "I have something for you, for Christmas. For you and the baby, actually."

Olivia felt confused. "For…?"

"Come and see."

Xander spun on a sneaker-clad foot and went down the path to the front gate. Beyond him, Olivia could see a family-friendly SUV. Clearly he'd been cleared to drive again, but she knew he'd never be seen dead in something like this. She was the one who'd always had the practical station wagon while he'd had the sporty little two-door foreign import. Maybe he'd borrowed the vehicle from someone else? Maybe his present was bigger than would fit in his car?

"Are you coming?" he called from the gate.

"Sure," she said, slipping through the doorway and down the stairs to the path. "Is this yours?" she asked, gesturing to the SUV when she got nearer.

"Yeah, I decided it was time to leave the racing cars to the experts and grow up a little. Grow up a lot, actually."

The back of the SUV was open. Through the tinted glass on the side Olivia could see an animal crate. She came to a halt behind the car and gasped when she saw the beagle puppy inside. Xander opened the crate and lifted the puppy out, depositing it squirming in Olivia's arms.

"Merry Christmas, Livvy."

The puppy lifted her head and enthusiastically licked Olivia on the chin, making her laugh out loud.

"But why?"

"Every kid needs a dog, right?" He grabbed a bag filled with puppy toys and food, tugged the blanket from inside the crate, then went to the front of the car and grabbed a pet bed from off the seat. "You mind if I bring these inside for you?"

"Oh, sure," she said, completely flustered. "Come in—have a coffee. Does it have a name?"

"She, actually. And, no, she doesn't have a name yet. I thought you'd like to choose one."

As they walked into the house Olivia saw Xander notice the photos of Parker that had gone back up on the hallway wall.

"You've put them back?" he asked, pausing by one

of the three of them—their faces alight with happiness and fun.

She swallowed past the lump in her throat. "They belong there. I...I should never have hidden them away. It wasn't right or fair—to him or to us."

Xander said nothing, but she saw him nod slightly. Tension gripped her shoulders, and she wished she could ask him what he thought, hoping that he'd at least tell her she'd done the right thing, but he remained silent. In the kitchen he spied the papers Olivia had been agonizing over signing.

"You were going to sign them, today?" he asked.

"I still can't bring myself to do it," Olivia admitted with a rueful shake of her head. "But I guess, now you're here. You may as well take them with you."

His face looked grim. "We need to talk."

Olivia felt her stomach sink. The puppy squirmed and whined in her arms. "Shall we take her outside first?"

"It's as good a place to talk as any."

Xander deposited the puppy's things on the floor and then he followed Olivia out to the patio where the puppy gamboled about, oblivious to the tension that settled like a solid wall between the two adults, all her attention on sniffing the plants and trees before she squatted happily on the grass.

"She's gorgeous, Xander. But why did you buy her?" Olivia asked, barely able to take her eyes from the sweet animal and hardly daring to look at the man standing so close by her side.

"I never had any pets growing up. My mother said she always had enough on her plate, no matter how much I begged and pleaded and promised to look after one. I guess I forgot how much I'd always wanted one and reverted to acting like my mother when you brought Bozo home that day."

Olivia couldn't help herself; she rested one hand on his forearm and reached up to kiss Xander on the cheek. He turned his head at the last minute, his lips touching hers and sending a flame of need to lick along her veins. Startled, she pulled back.

"Thank you—I love her already. She's beautiful."

"No, *you're* the one who's beautiful. Inside and out. I just never really appreciated how beautiful before. Livvy, I've been doing a lot of thinking. I've come to understand that I only allowed myself to see the outside, the surface. I convinced myself that was enough, that we could make a life together based on the physical attraction and chemistry between us. As long as it was just the two of us, I didn't have to delve any deeper into how I felt. I knew I loved you—but I don't think I ever really understood how much, and I hadn't really counted on sharing you with anyone else, whether it be dog or child."

He lifted a hand, gently tucked back her hair and cupped her face.

"Livvy, I'm sorry. I was a fool. I don't think I ever really knew what love was, or what lengths it could lead a person to, until I met you. I didn't deserve you, or Parker, or any of what we shared. If I'd been a better husband, a better father, maybe none of what happened that day would have occurred."

Olivia bit back a sob. There was so much pain and regret in his words, and she knew that he had little to apologize for.

"Xander, no. You were a great dad, and Parker loved you so very much. Don't sell yourself short. You weren't the one to make important life decisions without including me. You weren't the one to cast blame without seeing where blame truly lay. Those faults were all mine."

Xander shook his head. "I was his father. I should

have been able to keep him safe. It was my duty to him and to you, and I failed."

Her heart wrenched when she saw the tears that shimmered in his eyes. "The only person to blame that day was the guy driving the car that hit Parker and Bozo. If he'd been paying attention instead of texting, if he'd been driving to the speed limit instead of racing along a suburban road—then he'd have seen them run into the street and been able to stop in time. But we can't keep plaguing ourselves with 'what if,' and we can't keep blaming ourselves or one another for what happened. It happened. We can't turn back time, as much as we wish we could.

"I would have done everything differently that day too, if I could have, but nothing I do now will change that. And it's the same for you. Surely you see that? Xander, you *have* to see that and accept it to move past it."

Xander swallowed and turned away to watch the dog as she continued to explore the garden. "It doesn't make it any easier, though, does it?"

"And it's no easier handling it alone, either."

"No, you're right there. I watched my mother handle everything on her own while I grew up. She became so adept at it, so automatic about it all, that she wouldn't even accept help from me once I was able to give it. She told you that my father suffered a complete breakdown after my brother died, didn't she?"

Olivia moved to stand beside Xander, slipping her hand inside his. "Yes, she did. Until then I never understood how tough it must have been for either you growing up or for your mother—or even your dad, for that matter."

"I didn't really know any different at home. Sure, I knew what other families had and I knew our household was odd by comparison and that I couldn't bring friends home, but it wasn't until Parker died that I fully understood what my father must have gone through. I didn't want to fall down into that dark hole. In fact, I did everything I could to prevent that from happening. I never let out any of it—not my fears, my sorrow." He shook his head. "I tried so hard not to be like him. He couldn't even function without my mother there he depended on her so much. She had to go to work each day because if she didn't, we'd have nothing to eat, no roof over our heads. But from the second she left the house each morning to go to work, he'd weep. I'd let myself out the door to go to school, with the sound of his sobbing echoing in my ears. Some days, he'd find the strength to pull himself together, but as I got older, more and more often when I got home, he would still be crying.

"You know, when he died, I felt relief rather than sadness or loss because for the first time in years I knew he finally had peace. He couldn't forgive himself for my brother's death, couldn't talk about it, nothing. Most days he could barely get out of bed. He needed my mother for everything. I couldn't let myself be like him—not even the slightest bit."

Olivia squeezed his hand, hard. "Your whole family should have had more help."

Xander nodded. "Mum is not the kind of person who accepts help. She soldiers on. Does what needs doing and keeps looking forward. She was strong and capable and solid as a rock through all of it, and I really thought that was something to aspire to. In fact, I saw a lot of that in you, too. I don't think I ever saw her shed a tear or admit she couldn't handle anything.

"After Parker died, you coped with everything that had to happen afterward with the funeral—even giving our victim impact statement at the sentencing for the driver who killed him. Your composure scared me. Made me look at myself and question why I couldn't do those things. Was I my father's son?"

Olivia hastened to reassure him. "No, you weren't. You were grieving, too. Everyone copes in their own way, Xander. You couldn't be anyone other than yourself or feel anything other than what you were feeling at the time. Me, I pushed all my feelings aside, the way I learned how to do when I was a kid. Life goes on and all that," she said bitterly. "It got to the point where everyone in my family turned to me when it came to making choices about their life, even my dad. It became second nature to me, and it made me who I am.

"I never thought twice about involving you in the big decisions I made because I was just so used to following my own plan. And when I met you and we fell in love and got married, I thought I'd be able to craft the plan for both of us—for our life together. It's no wonder we fell apart through the very happening that should have driven us closer together."

Xander sighed. "It wasn't all your fault. Through our marriage I let you take control of everything because it was so much easier that way. It left me free to do what I saw as my role, the role my father never had in my memory. I needed to compensate for all the things he didn't do, but it wasn't without its own cost, was it? Do you think we can make it work? Give ourselves another chance at this thing called love?" he asked, still staring out at the garden.

"Yes, I *know* we can. Not because I want to or because you want to, but because we owe it to ourselves, and to Parker's memory and to the life of this new child we created, to do so—to be happy." She reached up to stroke his face and smiled when he turned into the touch and planted a kiss on her fingers. "I've never stopped loving you, Xander. I never will. I just needed to learn that to make a marriage work it needed to be a joint proposition—from start to finish—and I'm totally not ready for us to be finished yet."

Xander nodded. "Nor am I. I guess neither of us had the ideal example growing up, did we? And yet, somehow we managed to find one another—love one another." He looped his arms around her waist and stared deep into her eyes. "Will you help me, Livvy? Will you help me to grieve for our son properly? Will you let me help you, too? Will you let me love you for the rest of your life and raise this new baby, and maybe even others, with you?"

"Oh, Xander, I would love nothing else. I love you so much. I don't want a life without you. I want to be there for you, always. I want us to be the family we both deserve."

"As do I with you. Together, I promise. We're going to do this together, and we'll get it right this time, in good times and in bad."

He bent his head to hers and sealed his vow with the tender caress of his lips against hers. His touch had never felt more right or more special. Olivia knew, as her heart rate increased and as warmth began to unfurl through her body, that her heart beat for this man with a passion and a love that was equally reciprocated and that, together, they could do anything.

Xander looked across the lawn at the puppy who was now sitting down, staring at them both. "So, what are you going to name her?"

Olivia looked up at her husband, the man of her heart and the key to her happiness. "I think the question should be, what are *we* going to call her, don't you?"

As Xander's laughter filled the air around them and he squeezed her tight, Olivia knew without a doubt that this time they'd make it. This time was forever.

* * * * *

COMING SOON!

We really hope you enjoyed reading this book. If you're looking for more romance, be sure to head to the shops when new books are available on

Thursday 2nd May

To see which titles are coming soon, please visit

millsandboon.co.uk/nextmonth

LET'S TALK
Romance

For exclusive extracts, competitions
and special offers, find us online: